THE SUITCASE

THE SUITCASE

AND ALL THAT THAT CONTAINED

Michael Pitt

Matador
9 Priory Business Park
Kibworth Beauchamp
Leicestershire LE8 0RX, UK
Tel: (+44) 116 279 2299
Fax: (+44) 116 279 2277
Email: books@troubador.co.uk
Web: www.troubador.co.uk/matador

ISBN 978-1783063-444

British Library Cataloguing in Publication Data.
A catalogue record for this book is available from the British Library.

Typeset in Aldine by Troubador Publishing Ltd
Printed and bound in the UK by TJ International, Padstow, Cornwall

Matador is an imprint of Troubador Publishing Ltd

To Flora

CHAPTER ONE

30th July 1986

"More toast?"

Edgar Mason was opening the post but he looked up. "More toast?" was Helena's way of attracting his attention. He never had more toast. She had something to say. His hands continued to deal with the envelopes but he was listening to his wife.

"Can you drive me into town this morning?" 'Town' was York, some fifteen minutes drive away.

Edgar was not yet thirty. He was clean shaven with an unruly mop of dark brown hair. Full-faced but just short of being fleshy, his looks were redeemed by the clean lines of a determined jaw and by the intelligence in his eyes. He was well-built and had only recently stopped playing rugby football. He had played a physical game. His six feet of bone and muscle made him a formidable wing-forward. When he stopped playing, he started to put on weight – which was why he never had more toast. He tried to stay in condition if only to stay attractive to his wife.

By profession he was a photographer and he ran a shop where he did some of his work. Some of it he did at their home. To do so he had a dark room, a studio and a junk room. This arrangement allowed him flexibility in his working hours except when, for example, he had contracted to shoot a wedding. Then he was completely committed.

Helena, two years younger than him, had no difficulty in keeping her figure. Slim and fine-boned, she moved with effortless grace. Her hair was naturally blonde, needing no treatment to enhance its shine and her soft blue eyes added to the impression of extreme youthfulness. Edgar claimed that she had sold her soul to the devil in exchange for perpetual youth.

Yes, he would enjoy driving her. He had planned to frame some of his photographs but the exhibition that they were intended for was several days away. The framing could wait.

"No problem. Are you going to spend some money?"

"As a matter of fact, I am. I need to buy a hat."

"A hat? You need a hat? Is it for you? You don't wear hats."

"Just one hat. Marilyn and Bill have finally fixed a day for their wedding!"

"About time too!" Edgar was distracted by the contents of one of his envelopes but Helena knew his views on the matter of Marilyn Greene and Bill Thomas. Marilyn was Helena's oldest friend. They had been at school together and if either wanted someone to celebrate with, or a shoulder to cry on, the other was always first choice. Marilyn and Bill had been living together as 'partners' as they called themselves since before Edgar and Helena had got married – a very different arrangement.

Edgar, from early on in his relationship with Helena, had wanted them to get married but was cautious about suggesting it because he felt that she enjoyed her freedom. Helena, on the other hand, in response to their developing intimacy, had suggested that they give living together a try to see if it worked before committing themselves. She had been brought up short by his response.

"It's got to work!" was his reply delivered in almost a grunt.

Helena had no complaint about Edgar's approach to romance. He bought her red roses on special occasions and other flowers for no reason at all. He was likely to return from a morning walk, a daily constitutional as part of his slimming program, with a bloom or two from the hedgerow. He sought out books and exhibitions for her entertainment and delight. He took her out to meals at restaurants which he could not afford, to the theatre and to films. He bought her chocolates even if he did eat most of them himself but, of all his gestures, she cherished most that fierce statement of intent.

They were married within days. On those occasions when it seemed that things were not going well or that there might be conflict, she, to herself, would mutter under her breath, "It's got to work!"

This went through her mind now. It, the marriage, had worked but then so had the relationship between Marilyn and Bill and she wondered if going through a ceremony would put any strain upon the way her friends lived.

Bill was a writer. He earned his money as an investigative journalist with a special interest in international politics. He was good at what he did and, apart from his independent work, he was often employed by the BBC and by the heavyweight weekly magazines to cover stories in his area of expertise. He was, as all such writers were, engaged in writing his first book. The difference between him and the majority of his fellow would-be authors was that his master-piece was about to be published. His work did mean that he was often travelling overseas, leaving Marilyn to hold the fort.

Edgar asked for the date of the wedding and Helena said it was on the twenty-first of August, a Thursday.

"No rush for the hat, then?"

"It takes a long time to buy a hat." Anything else that she was about to say however would have been lost. Her husband had a big grin on his face and he pushed the contents of the last envelope across the table.

"Your Dream Come True!" it shouted and there was a premium-bond cheque for a thousand pounds.

"I'll put that in the joint account." he said and he added, smiling, "I think this is going to be one posh hat. If you don't spend it all, we'll make a day of it."

In the normal course of events, Helena would have bought the hat from her own account. She had studied History at university and emerged with a First-class degree. Her tutors thought that she might take up an academic career but by then she had met Edgar. She used the skills taught her to become a free-lance archivist and her income, though erratic, allowed her to pay for her personal expenses and then some. Their car belonged to Helena. This was because Edgar ran a small van as part of his business. He was always grateful on a shoot that he had gear in the van if he needed it. All this was part of their financially pragmatic relationship and a compromise with Edgar's rather old-fashioned feelings that he did not want his wife to go out to work. All thoughts of working in his studio that morning were chased away.

"I'll change and drop you off in town. We'll take the van and I'll do a little window-shopping of my own and we'll meet for lunch."

The van had a comfortable passenger seat and he did not allow it to be used for any other purpose. No gear would be dumped on it; not even a shopping bag. He had an assistant who sometimes went on a shoot with him but if he was to sit in that seat, he was warned about leaving a mess. Edgar liked to act as Helena's chauffer and she was entitled to a proper seat even if this was a working van.

When Edgar spoke of window-shopping, he mostly meant second-hand book-shops and the charity shops. The books were for his own consumption but he was also on the look-out for anything that he thought he could use in his photographs. The bread-and-butter of his work was studio portraits and wedding photography but he had an increasing market for his art work and one such successful theme was what he called 'recovered objects'. Apart from the charity shops, he would also, when it was convenient, take a look round the auction rooms. There, if he saw something that he could use, he would ask what they estimated it would fetch in the sale. Often the object had a market value which meant he was not interested. It was the undesired clutter that he wanted, the pieces that had aesthetic value only to him, that he could exploit with his photography. Recently, one of the auction rooms had commissioned him to illustrate their catalogue. Another source of income.

Window-shopping by Edgar was all right with Helena. If he was busy, it would give her more time for her own shopping. She had a suggestion about lunch.

"At 'The Jolly Fisherman'?"

"Great idea, we can eat outside.

★★★ ★★★ ★★★

Edgar stopped the car as close as he could to Helena's first choice of shops. He could only do so long enough for her to get out. It was always difficult to park in York's shopping centre. The shop she had chosen was the closest that the city had to a big department store. The couple joked about her extravagant spending but both knew that Helena Burroughs, as she was then, had been taught thrift from an early age. She would need to be satisfied that the hat would be right but she would see if there was something off the peg before she visited the more expensive specialist milliners. Edgar handed her a ten-pound note before she got out of car.

"Get a cab." he said "One-thirty at the pub? I'm looking forward to it."

This was more than a broad hint. 'The Jolly Fisherman' was out of town and he knew that she would probably spend all the morning on her choice. Taking a cab would mean that she would gain at least half an hour for her shopping but taxis she viewed as a luxury and, left to herself, she would take a bus and perhaps be late.

She was late, but only by a few minutes. Edgar was seated at a table on the staging that overlooked the river and it was one of those days when the water came into its own. The river was calm and flowing sluggishly. The sun sparkled on the wavelets created by the stately movements of an occasional canal long-boat converted for pleasure-cruising and the wavelets, in their turn, lapped gently against the staging. Nor were there the shouts of the coxes and coaches. There were no crews on this stretch of the river.

'The Jolly Fisherman' was a river-side pub of some antiquity and the owner, who was also the landlord, attempted to retain a comfortable and traditional ambience. The pub sign, however, had been replaced recently and showed an angler dozing in his folding seat while sundry fish were poking their heads out of the water and laughing at him. The sign now read "The Jolly Fish(erman)".

Edgar was already sipping at his champagne-flute whilst looking at the menu. He poured Helena's wine into her glass as she approached. Characteristically, he rose to his feet and pulled out a chair for her to sit in, bending to kiss her cheek as she sat down.

"Bubbly." she said. "That's nice."

"Well, it's only Cava but it does have bubbles."

"A whole bottle? – and you're driving."

"I'll stick to one glass and we can take the rest home."

Helena was carrying a hat-box. Edgar had never seen an actual hat-box before and this one looked expensive all on its own. His wife was looking just a little bit defensive and ignored his pointed glance at her purchase.

"I don't know why you are looking at the menu." she said. "We always eat the same thing here." and, as she spoke, a waitress delivered what Edgar had ordered: a tray laden with smoked-salmon sandwiches and crab salad.

"Something to read while I was waiting." he countered but she did not rise to the challenge. She had seen, on the ground beside him, a large leather suitcase.

"And what is that?" she asked, pointing at it; happy to have some ammunition of her own. Edgar had made a purchase, as he was wont to do; sometimes with a purpose, often on a whim. It was true that he kept most of this accumulated paraphernalia in his studio or his junk room but sometimes an object would end up in the house, even to become a bone of contention. Helena was getting her blow in first.

He cleared a space on the table in front of him and lifted the suitcase into the space with the handle towards himself. From the way he hefted it, it was not too heavy but it certainly had some content. It was a suitcase from the past and of a rigid structure. It was certainly too big for hand-luggage in an aeroplane and probably weighed as much as three modern cases. It was solidly made of light tan leather and much battered. The corners were strengthened with a thicker leather in dark brown. It was studded with little brass domes in those places where it might need protection. Some of these were missing and the once robust leather handle was held together with string. The lid was secured with two locks.

Helena was at a loss. "We need a suitcase? This one of your objects?" she said.

"Well it has a nice tonal quality." he said. "I'll stick some labels on it to 'romantic places' – a sort of wish-fulfilment picture. Another possibility is a railway poster campaign. Any rate, that's what I thought when I first saw it."

Helena asked the obvious question. "Where did you get it?"

"A garage-sale, would you believe. At least I thought it was a garage-sale. I was on my way here – nothing worthwhile in town – and I saw this stuff laid out on a drive-way. I had time, so I stopped the car and had a shufty. It turned out to be a house-clearance and they were just finishing up. I heard the boss cry out that anything else was to go in the skip. At that moment one of his men came through the front-door carrying our case. He said he'd found it in the loft. His boss wasn't pleased but I was already thinking of ways that I could use it. It could be a prop in a wedding shoot; with some confetti to give it a splash of colour."

"So you did your usual bargaining and got it cheap."

"It was odd that. The man in charge was in a hurry to get to another job and it was clear that whatever he got for it would go in his pocket and not to the firm. I asked him if he would like to empty it and sell me the case. I offered him twenty pounds. He said there were no keys and breaking the case open would destroy any value. When I suggested that there might be something of value in it, he laughed. How did he put it? 'That's what I used to think when I started in this business. After the first thirty or so bags full of rubbish, I stopped looking'. It's yours, mate, with contents, for thirty.'"

Edgar now did his dramatic bit. "By then," he said, "I'd seen this." He swung the case around so that the front with its two locks faced her. Stencilled in deep and abiding black capitals was the name of the erstwhile owner, 'E. MARSH'.

"It is a common name." said Helena flatly. Marsh was the maiden name of her paternal grandmother but it would be silly to get excited.

"Yes. I know it would be a hell of a coincidence if it belonged to any of your lot but it would be worth the money to find out. I think it is too big for a schoolgirl."

9

Edgar had remembered that Esme Marsh was a name to conjure with from his wife's family traditions. She was the younger sister of Helena's grandmother. The two girls were the children of an important diplomat and Esme, the story went, had been recruited as a secret agent. This was a story full of mystery and this in itself was held by some to be evidence that she had been a spy. What was known for certain was that her parents were seldom in the country, that her mother had died young and she had been sent to a boarding school. This last explained Edgar's reference to a schoolgirl. He had assumed that the stencilled name would be normal procedure for someone in such a school to identify their belongings. He had thought that it was unlikely that this was Esme's case but perhaps, just perhaps, they had been given a chance to steal a look at one of Helena's antecedents.

Helena's grandmother had died just over a year ago and the talk at her funeral had included some highly coloured suggestions about the sister's role as a spy. Far too highly coloured, Helena had thought. Most of it came from the next generation. Her young nephews and nieces had lively imaginations.

By now, however, Helena had shaken off her caution. She was hooked and hopeful. She dismissed Edgar's remark out of hand.

"Don't you believe it." she said. "She would have a list of garments as long as your arm – including seven pairs of 'knickers, dark blue, elasticated'. I understand they had pockets in them. Then there would be Gym Kit and at least two hats, one for summer and one for winter. All this and her school uniform."

By now, Edgar was looking at his empty glass; he offered Helena the last sandwich and, on her refusal, ate it himself.

"Time to go home." he said. "We'll look at it there. There must be a key to fit it in the collection. Will you carry the bubbly!"

Edgar's first action as they entered the house was to put the bottle into an ice-bucket and add ice from the fridge. Only then did he take the suitcase and put it on the work-top in his studio. He returned into the house proper to see his wife carrying the hat-box up the stairs. She leaned over the banisters and, without emphasis, said, "Give me five minutes and bring the bottle!"

Edgar spun the bottle in the ice and took from the drinks cupboard two old-fashioned champagne glasses – much nicer to drink from than the flutes – even if it was only Cava. Once more he blessed the people who had made the drink fashionable. Before he climbed the stairs he poured some of it for himself and drank it. He was, after all, a glass behind.

Helena had used her five minutes well. From somewhere she had found some potpourri, thrown back the bedclothes and scattered the fragrant petals broadcast. Now she was spraying some perfume into the air. She was completely naked.

Edgar passed her a glass of wine, enjoying the movement of her body as she took it from his hand and sipped from the rim of the glass. Her eyes were alight with mischief as she looked at him over the drink.

"I thought you were going to model the hat." he said.

"Would that help?" she asked.

Edgar moved towards her and took her empty glass.

11

"You don't need a hat." he said. "And I don't need five minutes."

She had fallen asleep in his arms, her head with its scarcely disarranged fair hair, nestling into his shoulder. Edgar was comfortable. He knew that in a few minutes he would want to move but for now he felt content. He did stretch out his free hand to touch the wood of the bed-frame; he had no wish for hubris. Let the gods stay on his side – their side!

Before the position became irksome from lack of movement, Helena stirred. She turned her face to his and kissed his cheek and then she whispered in his ear. He was not completely disappointed, being a little bit worried that it was bit soon for a replay, when he understood what she was saying.

"The suitcase!" she said sleepily, and then, "You sort out the keys, I'll make a pot of tea." Edgar was just awake enough to see his wife, clad now in a dressing gown, heading for the bedroom door.

Edgar shrugged himself into his own dressing gown, donned a pair of slippers and headed for his studio. He was never sure what clutter there might be on the floor of the work-space. Edgar's studio was a space, a multifunctional space. There was, of course, half a room organised for taking portraits and then there was a sort of work-shop kitted out for all sorts of repairs and craft-work as well as for the day-to-day production of his photographs in their final form. His dark-room was separate. The studio had a large work bench and excellent lighting. One of the drawers in the bench he referred to as his 'useful drawer' and it held what he had called 'the collection'. This included a massive accumulation of keys that had arrived over the years by devious means. There were some very large iron door-keys which had probably outlived the locks they belonged to. Sometime, he was going to photograph these. Most of the keys were small: drawer keys and padlock keys and, accrued, almost without noticing, a large number of suitcase keys.

It was the fifth one that he tried that fitted. He sprang one of the locks and, with great restraint, stopped. Fortunately, Helena entered at that moment with a tea-tray. She had raided their dining room and dug out from the sideboard the remains of the family tea-set. It was only the remains, just two cups and saucers and a chipped milk jug. No matching tea-pot; that would have been of silver or, at least, of silver plate, so, on the tray, incongruously, sat the fat blue china pot used half a dozen times a day.

She was reminding him that the cups had belonged to her grandmother, the closest she could get to Esme, when she saw that he was waiting to open the second lock.

"What discipline!" she said and, then, "Go on!"

So he did and made room, as he lifted the lid, for both of them to get the same view of the contents.

It was not very revealing. The case itself was lined with a sort of check material and whoever had filled it had stuffed what appeared to be a woman's dress in a light cotton material over the rest of the contents as packing.

"Not a case filled carefully – I could do better than this. I don't think this is Esme's." said Edgar, who, by now, had been expecting a school-girl's suitcase filled with numerous garments. He reached forward to lift the dress off.

"Hold it. Disturb nothing!"

Edgar turned to her for her tone had been incisive. It worried him a little.

"Do you think we have a Pandora's box?" he asked.

"No, no! Nothing like that" and she took his hand and indicated what she had spotted. It was the corner of what, at first sight, seemed to be a book. Helena's professional instinct told her that this was no book but some sort of bound album or diary. "Someone in a hurry has just shoved stuff into here and then added the frock for padding. It's a bit like paper archaeology." she said. "A coin found together with a piece of pottery may help date it; add a human skull and you might be able to tell a story of the person's life. Each, on its own could tell us something, but nothing like as much as the three together. Some of these documents, and I'm sure that underneath that pretty frock are documents, will be dated. Others will not. The way the documents are packed may give us clues that will disappear if we move them carelessly."

Suddenly, this was something more than a long-ago school-girl's bits and pieces. It had the potential for discoveries about the past. Helena stopped speaking and Edgar, feeling her intensity, stepped back from the case and fetched, from his useful drawer, a hand-held tape-recorder. He earned a smile of thanks as Helena took it from him. He then selected a camera and took a photograph of the open case. This project was going to be fully illustrated.

Helena switched on the tape-recorder and tested it. Edgar knew it worked but said nothing. This was a professional at work. With precision and great economy, Helena described the suitcase and how it had come into their possession and then how they had opened it and what they could see.

Then she stopped recording. "Esme was always away at school, she went to a sort of boarding prep school to start with. Even when the girl was a small child, her father – he was called Reginald; later, Sir Reginald – travelled all over the world and his wife went with him. She died young, as you know, but what a passionate marriage that must have been. To choose your husband before your child, you must love him beyond reason."

Edgar didn't say anything and then Helena realised what she had said. Her hand went to her mouth. The two of them were looking forward to the parental phase of their marriage. They had even established two funds; the first they had called 'Wedding Breakfast' and the second, more seriously, "Further Education" They had just not decided when to have children or, even, how many.

"I've just put my foot in it, haven't I? You know I couldn't do that and… "

He cut her off. "Two points since you raise the matter." he said and he had already defused the situation by pulling her towards him. "First, I would like reason to always have a place in our relationship and, second, I wouldn't let you!" and although he spoke lightly, there was an edge to his voice that echoed his original statement of intent, 'It's got to work!' and Helena was wise enough not to challenge the idea of his control of her actions – nor, at that moment, did she wish to. This was a moment to be treasured.

CHAPTER 2

September 1937

St. Ermengild's School for Girls' was situated in the southwest highlands of Scotland. It was confident enough in its reputation not to qualify what sort of girls it catered for. Let other establishments claim that their girls were the daughters of gentlemen. If they needed to do so, then it did not speak well for their provision. St. Ermengild's reputation was that it provided individual education for the disparate and outstanding talents of all its pupils. It advertised in a monthly magazine for 'Ladies' and published a brochure. Both delivered, in succinct prose, the facts. The brochure was illustrated with informative and well-composed photographs. The school's treatment of its pupils as individuals it did not need to advertise. It had a reputation acknowledged by all. If any fond parents detected something special about one of their daughters and enquired of anybody who knew of such matters, the advice would be to try St. Ermengild's. They would be told that it was expensive but there were many scholarships endowed by former pupils.

The main building, an erstwhile manor, was built from the granite on which it stood. There was something symbolic about that. St. Ermengild's was the epitome of stability and strength. The building was graced with large windows and crow-stepped gables and was approached by a sweeping gravelled driveway that encircled and was bordered with lush lawns. Around three sides of the building were formal gardens which extended into shaded shrubberies and young woodlands and beyond them the legacy of the original owners; the great trees of an arboretum; Douglas Fir and Monkey Puzzle Trees and some flourishing Pine trees. Looming above all, there were two specimens of the Giant Redwood.

Against this background, the chauffeur-driven Rolls-Royce was entirely appropriate and made a gentle noise as it rolled over the gravel and came to a halt.

Esme Marsh, a 'new-girl', helped her grandmother, Phoebe Marsh, out of the car. This was not a difficult task; it was a big car with a substantial foot-board and wide-swinging doors and Phoebe Marsh was a very sprightly grandmother. Silver haired, slim and elegant, she took the few steps needed to get across the gravel to the terrace and stood waiting before the school doors. Helping her out of the car was just a gesture by Esme since she had been brought up to be polite. Actually, it was more than that. After all, her grandmother's chauffer would have done a much better job – it was something for Esme to do. It cloaked her nervousness but her nervousness was still there.

"Watch your wee feet!" she had said sillily and in what she thought was a Scottish accent and then went pink. The long journey with her grandmother had emboldened her but this was not good behaviour. She could feel her cheeks redden with embarrassment but her Grandmother squeezed her hand and thanked her. From that moment she forgot to be nervous.

Fair haired and fair skinned, Esme was a girl who viewed the world warily. She was of a slight build and, because of her shyness, seemed frail. This was not the case; either physically or mentally. Her slenderness concealed her athleticism and her apparent timidity an inner strength that her childhood had reinforced. Her face, even at fourteen, had a charm that was difficult to resist. Her eyes were the clear blue of a winter's sky and they often sparkled with humour. Her smile was enchanting.

She had faced this situation before. This was not her first boarding school. She had spent three years at the previous one called 'Godstone's' before this unplanned-for move. This time she was old enough to realise that she needed something to cover the sadness and apprehension. She had to present, if not a brave face, an indifferent one to her new environment.

At the beginning of each of the terms she had spent at 'Godstone's', she had a feeling of abandonment. She had had longer than usual to prepare herself for this arrival to her new school. The drive from her Grandmother's house in Somerset had been too long to attempt in one day and they had stopped overnight in a hotel. There had been a number of advantages arising from this.

Her grandmother, who was always kind but somewhat distant, had put herself out to entertain her. That she had charge of her son's daughters was something that she could have done without. Now she had to take Esme to a new school, hundreds of miles away even from her own house – the old lady recognised that the girl would not see it as 'home' – and must be feeling anxious. Esme, shyly at first, had warmed to this attention. The two of them had actually swapped anecdotes about the short-comings of the hotel.

The overnight stop allowed Esme to wear her normal clothes on the first leg of the journey and she only changed into the school uniform in the hotel. This meant a day's extra freedom and also that the uniform was not creased when they arrived.

This new uniform felt somewhat restraining but she knew she was appropriately dressed and had confidence in her appearance. Her grandmother was particularly careful about such things. Esme, herself, was quite pleased with her blazer. It had an attractive badge representing a flaming torch on the breast pocket. She was even more pleased with it when her grandmother said that it suited her. Phoebe Marsh had also commented on her hair and Esme cherished the comment.

"The haircut has to stay, I'm afraid. All these schools seem to insist on it but it is still your crowning glory." This was a remark that any independent observer would have endorsed. The girl's hair was a soft blonde that no chemical treatment could have achieved. Esme was fond of her grandmother but these sympathetic remarks made her see, for the first time, that she was a friend and not a keeper. She realised that this lively old lady was just as much a victim of her father's profession as she was. She acted as ward to Esme's sister, Stella, as well as herself but Stella was old enough, most times, to travel with their father. Why should an old lady have to put up with teen-age schoolgirls? She must have other things that she would prefer to do.

The chauffer was dealing with the cases; one small, but holding Esme's precious things, and one large and new in tanned leather. This one had been dressed with saddle soap for protection and shone with a soft glow. Esme was already fond of this suitcase. It was a present from her father who had had it delivered from Harrods. Separately there had been a letter with exotic stamps from Russia. The letter was mainly well-wishes and instructions on how to treat the case but it was signed 'Love, Daddy'. Sometimes, on post-cards especially, he just put his initials.

Her arrival at this school was different to the previous one which she had joined when she was eleven. There, she was the same age as all the rest of the new girls. Here, most of the pupils of her age had been attending for three years already. There had been a crisis at her old school and, in consultation with the head-teacher, her father had moved her. They had used her curriculum as a reason and it was one of the reasons. They had played down the incident that had made a move necessary.

Suddenly, her arrival was very different from any previous experience. Two girls of her own age had burst through the front door of the building, jumped down the steps of the terrace and were running across the gravel towards her. One, a girl with a very freckled face and with flaming red hair, almost bounced up to her.

"You're Esme Marsh." she cried without ceremony. "I'm Deborah Wilson and they call me 'Rah'. This is Rachel Castle and we call her 'Rachel'. We daren't do anything else." The other girl, slim and elegant with dark hair, smiled affectionately at her companion and also, with warmth, at Esme. For just an instance and with a flash of envy, Esme lost the self-confidence she had been building up so carefully. If the blazer suited her, it had been made with Rachel in mind.

How could a girl move with such ease and elegance in clothes which to her and to Deborah, who patently did not care about her appearance, were just a uniform? Esme noted that Rachel had also been subjected to the same hair cut. On her, it looked almost fashionable.

Deborah was still in action. "Are these all the cases?" she asked the chauffer and told him that they would look after them. A large man who needed no instructions about his duties, he was amused. "That's all right, miss." he said. "I'll do it."

"This is St. Ermengild's. We are taught to be independent." said Deborah and awarded him a smile. "And we don't let men into the dorm!" The chauffer was not sure what his employer would say but he surrendered the bags with a big grin.

It was Rachel who spoke next and directly to Esme. "We are here to look after you." she said and she spoke in an almost grown-up voice but there was nothing patronising in what she said. "We'll take you up to the dorm as soon as possible but I have a message to deliver."

Esme saw her move across to her grandmother with great self-confidence and she spoke to her with respect and clarity. Esme heard every word she said. "The headmistress apologises for being late. She will be with you shortly. Deborah and I are here to settle Esme into the domestic aspects of the school. We are looking forward to making friends with her. If it's all right with you, we'll take her to our dorm now." Esme's grandmother was somewhat taken aback by this prim speech from such a young girl but she responded in kind, as one adult to another. "I'll need to see her before I go." she insisted. Rachel joined Deborah in her struggle with the cases.

"I hope there's tuck in here." was Deborah's comment on the luggage.

"The tuck is in the small one." was Esme's response. Rachel was hushing her friend but without much effect. Some of Esme's anxiety about joining the school was diverted by these two girls. How could they, so different in appearance and behaviour, be such close friends? She crossed her fingers behind her back, hoping that she too could join in that friendship. Her grandmother had anticipated the demand for tuck and had given instructions to her cook-housekeeper to provide for a growing girl's appetite. The small case held, together with Esme's most precious possessions, a sundry collection of cakes and bottles of pop – even some apples from her grandmother's orchard – and, best of all, chocolate.

Esme blessed her grandmother and the cook-housekeeper silently. Now she had something to offer to Deborah and Rachel. She could hear her grandmother pronouncing, 'the gift-bearer doubles her welcome!'. She was given to pithy sayings. More practically, she had warned that the sandwiches and the pork-pies would need to be eaten shortly but the potted meats would keep for a week or so. She said nothing about the cakes. They would be eaten long before they were stale.

As the three girls headed for Esme's new home, Deborah was still chatting. "You're in our dorm." she said. "We've organised it so your bed is between ours. Not for protection from the others. They're all nice in their own ways but

Rachel and I can both talk to you. You are in for a grilling – and you can learn about us."

By the time they had reached the dormitory, all Esme's apprehension had vanished. She felt as though she belonged.

CHAPTER 3

30th July 1996

Helena poured them both another cup of tea. She was enjoying this and there was no rush. She drank her own, taking pleasure from the delicate thinness of the china, and replaced the cup in the saucer and placed them on the tray.

She turned back to the suitcase and took the dress out. In doing so she revealed the files, note-books, envelopes and albums that lay beneath it. Sticking to her method, she described the garment first; it was a young girl's party-dress with short sleeves but a high neck-line. Before she put it aside, she held it up in front of her.

"Would it fit?" Edgar was interested. Esme Marsh was Helena's distant relative. Helena was slim with fine bones; could it be that they had the same build?

"Possibly. Too young for me, I'm afraid."

There was a small pocket in the left-hand sleeve. Edgar reached across and took from it a square of cambric. It was a handkerchief 'for show and not for blow' and it had 'Friday' embroidered in one corner.

The first thing she could get at under the dress, and sitting on top of the rest, was the album that had alerted her to what might be in the case. It was a stamp album, labelled as such. Without disturbing it, she was able to open the cover. There was a book-plate with the owner's name in neat, schoolgirl writing. 'Esme Marsh' removing any doubts about the ownership of the case. Helena, controlling her triumph, described this and the date that went with it into the tape-recorder. The album itself was a substantial, good quality product, bound in red cloth and with marbled end-papers. There was a proud claim that it was an album for the 'Postage Stamps of the Whole World' and a list of the album's 'distinctive features'.

One distinctive feature that was not listed was a neatly ruled table on a blank page at the front of the album headed in pencil

'RECORD OF THE NUMBER OF STAMPS I HAVE COLLECTED'

Esme had recorded, on what seemed random dates, just a number. The pencil had faded somewhat and Helena asked for a lens. She turned back to the book-plate.

"Two minutes only." she said and headed for the door. "Don't touch anything!"

It was less than two minutes before Helena returned and Edgar, not daring to move, used the time to drink his tea. Helena had brought with her a file and she was opening it as she re-entered. She had been to her own study. The file was colour-coded green which meant it was concerned with her family. Edgar, before she could find the reference, said, "Esme was born on the eighteenth of November."

Helena had just found that date. "How did you know?"

"It was what you were hoping for." he replied, "It makes sense that what she wrote in the album she did so when she received it. It was a birthday present. Tell us what year she was born and we can work out how old she was when she got it."

"Esme was born in 1923. The date in the album is 1937, so on her fourteenth birthday she is given it as a present. She's already shown it will be not be wasted. Some of her data is missing but in the previous months she has added more than five hundred stamps to her collection. Then there is sudden surge and, by the time she was given the album, she had more than a thousand. Some of them would probably be part of the present."

"Is that a lot?" Edgar was seeking information. "It was not a hobby of mine but I do know that you could buy transparent envelopes full of foreign stamps for the equivalent of ten pence."

Helena was turning the pages of the album but she did answer him.

"Yes, I think it would be a lot for a schoolgirl. She would certainly have bought such packages but many of these in the album don't come from such a source. Remember that her father – my great-grandfather – worked for the Foreign Office and travelled a great deal. One assumes that some of these exotic ones came from his letters. Some are franked and some are unused. So it may be that he bought the stamps and sent them inside the letters. In any case, by the end of the summer term of 1938, she recorded a thousand plus more. I think she stopped counting after a couple of years. Some commemorative stamps post-date her record keeping."

"I'm warming a little to this 'Foreign Office Father'." said Edgar, "The only letters I ever got from mine were when he was 'travelling'" This was a family joke. Edgar's father had been a travelling salesman. "Postmarked from Brighton or Portsmouth and always a second-class stamp. Give him his due, each one held a postal-order and always the same message. 'Here's your pocket money, make it last!'"

He was peering over his wife's shoulder. "Some of these places don't exist any more." he said. "Do you think we could trace her father's career from the stamps?"

"No! I'm afraid not, there's no evidence which ones, if any, came from him and there are no dates of when she acquired them. But the hobby must have occupied a fair amount of her time."

Helena had gone back to the beginning of the album and was following ideas as she flicked from country to country. Every now and then, she spoke into the tape-recorder.

"There is evidence that some of these stamps came from an older person's collection – probably her father's since they all come from countries once part of the British Empire. Some of them come from the reign of Victoria. Esme might have bought old stamps for her collection but they would be much commoner when Reginald, if it was he, was collecting."

She broke off because she was interrupted by Edgar. "Do you think they are worth anything?"

"Unlikely but it would be easy enough to find out. It is still a big industry – bigger than before possibly because countries publish stamps especially for the collectors."

She turned back to her recorder. "I'm interested in the stuff from Germany. There is evidence of the collapse of their currency. Some with values of four thousand marks. Others are labelled '800 Tausend' and one with the number, two hundred million. There are some with Hitler's portrait and a handful from the 'Zone Francaise'. How did she get these?"

She paused and turned over a few more pages. "There are lots and lots of Polish stamps. Did she have a pen-friend?"

She turned the recorder off and spoke instead to Edgar. "I didn't realise how informative the stamps themselves can be about the countries that they come from. I shall have to do something about that. Nor did I realise that that they could be a powerful tool to investigate individuals. It may be only implied but this album shows something about Esme's relationship with her father."

"When we've sorted Esme, I'll go on a course."

CHAPTER 4

September 1937

The dormitory was a model of practicality. There were eight beds, four on each side of the room – each of them neatly made up with the covers folded down. On one side of each bed was a wooden locker and, on the other, a small chest of drawers with a lamp upon it. Some of the girls had put framed photographs on this chest; one or two had small vases of flowers. At the foot of each bed there was a bench to hold a suitcase, with space underneath to store another one; at the head there was a large pin-board. One or two of the girls had used their pin-board for pin-ups of film stars, others for photographs of one sort or another. One girl had a painting, a watercolour landscape, pinned to hers.

At one end of the room there was a small book-case filled with books. Most of these were battered from much reading. Esme suspected that they were the legacies of pupils past. There was a magazine rack with ancient copies of publications devoted to the world of film.

Esme approved. The dorm in her previous school had been much larger, with more beds but less space between the beds and no provision for a display of originality. It had certainly no suggestion of frivolity.

The two girls put the big suitcase on the bench provided for it and turned to Esme. What did she think of it?

Esme was relaxing rapidly and she thought she would try out what was to her, a new expression.

"The cat's pyjamas!" she said and was pleased to see that the other two were impressed. It was Rachel, of course, who reminded them that they had to get back to Esme's grandmother and, indeed, to take Esme, herself, to the headmistress.

Those two ladies had, meanwhile, established rapport.

The headmistress had come out almost as soon as the girls had gone and made herself known.

"I've handed your grand-daughter to two of my brightest pupils. Rachel Castle and Deborah Wilson." she said. "The two of them, oddly, have established a bond that could easily include Esme."

"An excellent move." Mrs Marsh replied. "This is not why her father decided to change schools as you know but, although she is a friendly child, I think she needs friends more than most people."

They spoke together about the girl and, indeed, about her father. The school had already been briefed about his position and the special precautions that might be necessary. Esme's grandmother confirmed these.

She looked around. It was time for her to leave but she must say 'goodbye' to Esme.

The headmistress re-assured her. "Rachel will bring her here." she said. "She is a remarkable child." She excused herself, said good-bye and re-entered the building. As she left, the three girls came running across the gravel. The other two held back when Esme hurried across to her grandmother. She was about to shake hands formally in farewell but changed her mind and reached up to kiss her on the cheek. Mrs. Marsh was touched. Only duty to family ties persuaded her to act as a parental substitute. She was not good with young people and she realised that Esme had every reason to resent her authority.

"You have my phone number." she said. "The school will let you use the phone if you think it is necessary – and the decision is yours. I know that you are not a fussy girl but you are aware that strange things can happen. If they do, let me know. If you need me, even just for advice, do not hesitate. You know the procedure if the matter is not domestic."

Perhaps this was the closest she had ever been to her Grandmother and Esme nodded in confirmation of what she had said. There was one more thing to do and she walked across to Treadwell, the chauffer, and offered him her hand. It was swallowed in his great fist.

"We'll miss you, Miss Marsh, but you'll be coming home for Christmas." He reached into the car and brought out a small, neatly wrapped package. "Mrs Treadwell asked me to give you these." he said gruffly. "They are only handkerchiefs but she embroidered them herself. There's one for each day of the week so that you will remember us every day." Esme had been staunch and self-contained until that moment but his little speech brought her almost to tears.

She had often wondered why her grandmother, who seldom used the car, had needed a chauffeur. Sometimes she thought they might be involved with what her father called security – but security for whom? She would miss them – or would she?

By standing on tip-toe, she was able to reach up and kiss the now embarrassed chauffer on the cheek.

"You can give that to Mrs Treadwell from me." she said.

The car drove away and was out of sight before Rachel allowed Deborah to remind Esme that the headmistress was waiting for her.

★★★ ★★★ ★★★

"You address her as Headmistress." Rachel was talking to settle the new girl down as well as to give her instructions. "Her name is Miss Salway. We call her 'Salty' but she is actually rather sweet."

Her study was at the end of a corridor. There were two doors. The first was labelled 'Office' and the second 'Headmistress'. Both had the instruction 'Knock and wait!'. There were three straight-back chairs lined up on the wall between the doors.

"If you are asked to see the headmistress, you knock on her door. Any other time you try the office first." Rachel was still doing her job in briefing Esme. She was doing it well because she only offered simple instructions and not many of them. Esme, in turn, was grateful. The long walk down that corridor was almost frightening. The colours of the walls were dull; there was a dark green dado above the skirting board and, above that, the cream walls were the same colour as the ceiling.

It was Deborah who knocked on the second door. It was opened by the headmistress, who pulled it wide and ushered Esme into the room. She turned to the other two. "You can disappear if you want to but be back in ten minutes."

Then she crossed to her desk, and Esme stood in front of it. Still young enough to be seen more as a child than a teenager, she was presenting a four-square front to Miss Salway as she did to the world. The headmistress was sorting through some papers and this gave the girl time to glance around the room. Behind the teacher's desk was a large ornate window. One wall had boards listing the academic achievements of former pupils. These boards flanked a large glass cabinet from within which shone innumerable trophies: cups and salvers and shields. There was a wall lined with photographs; mostly groups of staffs and pupils. The fourth wall was reserved for about a dozen photograph portraits. Esme guessed, correctly, that these would be famous old-girls.

In a flight of fancy, Esme saw the room as a shrine to the spirit of the school and Miss Salway as the high priestess. This feeling passed quickly. There was little that was spiritual about the proven record of this establishment and nothing distant or aloof about Miss Salway.

The papers that the headmistress was looking at concerned Esme and they were even more surprising than she had thought. She put them down and gave the girl her full attention.

"Sit down, Esme, please!" she said. "You only stand on that spot when I think you have done something wrong. Esme took the chair that was clearly intended for her and put it on the spot where she had been standing. The headmistress continued in her friendly address. It was only reasonable that her new pupil would be nervous and no purpose would be served if she remained so.

"Those are portraits of former pupils that we are proud of." she said. "I think every one of them stood on that carpet at one time or another. I have called you Esme. My name is Miss Salway but you address me as Headmistress. It contributes to the paternalistic society of the school; though perhaps that is a misnomer."

Simply with the lifting her voice on the last word, she was asking Esme a question. Almost without thinking, Esme responded.

"Paternalistic means pertaining to the father but it infers a certain degree of authoritarianism. All your staff are ladies but 'maternalistic', on the other hand, if it is a word, would mean something different; something softer."

Miss Salway had difficulty in controlling her face. It would appear that even the reports she had just read did not do this girl justice.

"Your father asked that we would take you into the fourth year as a special favour. There is a general agreement that you are in some ways special but…"

Esme interrupted her. "My father says that everybody is special." she blurted out. "That I must be careful with the gifts that have been given me."

"Exactly." The headmistress agreed smiling. "Certainly we treat all our girls as individuals. I would have said only that you mustn't show off."

"Bearing that in mind, don't try and hide your abilities. If you are worried that others may mock you as being a 'swot' as they call it, then you should not be in this school. Especially do not pretend with Rachel and Deborah. Deborah might seem to be a bit of a chatter-box but she is just as bright as her friend and together they make a formidable pair."

Once more, Esme crossed her fingers behind her back – 'Make that a trio!' she thought.

"They will take you now to your House-Mistress. All the girls in the same year are in the same House and stay there whilst they remain here at the school. Your House-Mistress is Miss Jackson and her House is therefore called 'Jackson House'. "

She escorted Esme out of her room as she said this and, sitting in the chairs outside, were Rachel and Deborah. They sprang to their feet, both of them eager to know how the meeting had gone but knowing that they could not ask yet.

The headmistress was giving nothing away. "Take Esme to Miss Jackson and ask her to come and see me when she has finished settling her in. I am relying on you two to look after Esme. Make her feel part of the school!"

The girls had passed down the corridor before the questions could be asked.

"Well?" said Deborah. "What do you think."

"She's certainly not salty. I thought she was very kind. I was still a little nervous and may have said some wrong things but she asked me to sit down and even made a joke of it."

In some things, Esme could be most secretive but this was not one of them.

"She said nice things about you two and she warned me not to pretend – I think that's the best way of putting it – with you."

It was Rachel who surprised her. So far Esme had seen her as an undemonstrative girl. Now she put her arm around her shoulders and said, without emphasis, "I don't think 'pretending' is something that you would normally do."

Esme tried not to show how much she was moved by this response. The good opinion of these two girls, even after this short acquaintance, was something that she wanted very much.

Deborah's agreement was almost overwhelming. "We need a name." she said, "Not 'the three musketeers'; that's too corny. 'We three' might do but I suppose that is a quote from the Scottish Play."

It was 'a trio'. Esme felt suddenly happy. Mostly it was the warmth with which these two had welcomed her but some of it was because they assumed that she understood what they were saying. 'The Scottish Play'; Shakespeare's 'Macbeth' and the superstition that it was unlucky to quote from it was part of her upbringing. She wondered how many more of the books she had read were known to her two new friends. In her mind, she dared to call them 'friends'.

"Tell me about the House Mistress idea!" she said. Miss Salway had said that she should not pretend to be ignorant. By the same token, she was not going to pretend knowledge when she had none.

Rachel answered the question without more ado. "The House Mistress is, apart from Salty, the most important person in your school life. She controls what you do every day and, sometimes, if it is necessary, every night. If you had a nanny at home it will give you some idea of the House Mistress. She will see that you clean your teeth, wash behind your ears and wear clean clothes – and she will give you advice about growing up. With Matron, she'll care for you if you are ill. She stays with you throughout your time in the school. Probably all the House Mistresses are splendid but we are especially pleased with ours. We call her 'Jack'. I think she knows but she doesn't let on. Remember she may be Miss Jackson but she has dealt with hundreds of growing girls. You really can rely on her. Here she comes. I've got a message for her."

CHAPTER 5

30th July 1986

Helena closed the stamp album and put it to one side. She had recorded a general description of the album with some outstanding points and now she said, still to the tape, "We'll come back to this later. I want something earlier than 1937."

The next layer of the case yielded a very much worn quarto manila envelope. She peered into it and then emptied it carefully on to the bench top.

"Photographs, Edgar." she said and he moved to claim them. Just as Helena had treated the album with such care, so he did now with these old photographs.

Edgar retained the dark-room facilities in his shop but he had also set up the workshop-cum-studio at home. When he had first done so, Helena had pinned to his notice-board an impressive poster. It was presented as an antique public announcement, complete with a red sealing-wax medallion hanging from a silk ribbon. In a flowing and illuminated font, it was headed 'The Photographic Archivist's Ten Commandments'. It was a nice thought but most of the time Edgar was dealing with today's images, not those early and extremely fragile photographs to which it referred and it was not usually applicable. He did dislike and avoided any finger prints on any of his material. With the suitcase's contents, he was going to be extra careful.

The first of the commandments was 'Wear lintless cotton gloves when handling photographs.' and Edgar took his out of his drawer and pulled them on. It was almost as though he were a forensic scientist examining a crime scene. Using a pair of forceps designed for that purpose, he laid out the collection. The photographs were all black-and-white and were mostly holiday snaps.

He sorted them rapidly by subject, and muttered darkly if they were creased or damaged in any way. He selected those that featured a young girl shown at different ages. Sometimes she was shown with another girl who looked like her elder sister.

"That's Esme." Helena spoke with certainty and she was referring to the younger girl. "We had that one at home. The other girl is Stella, my grandmother."

"Here is, perhaps, the earliest one of your great-aunt." said Edgar and laid it top left of his display. It showed the girl, aged about three with an elderly lady walking along the promenade of some sea-side resort. The girl carried a small and bedraggled teddy bear in her right hand and was reaching up with the other to the elderly lady. She wore a light summer frock with a broad collar, sandals and white socks. The expression on her chubby face was one of complete trust.

"She looks as though she was really a charmer, even at that age." said Helena. "But did they have to cut her hair like that?"

"It was called a 'pudding-basin'. I'm not sure whether they actually used one."

Edgar was looking closely at the photographs. He gave

special attention to one that showed the girl a couple of year's older. She was standing on a beach, backed by sea and rocks. She stood square to the camera; the wind was blowing the folds of her skirt sideways.

"A good quality photo, this." he said. "This is a special outing for this tubby little girl. The photographer has not only got the lighting right, he has got both her nervousness and her enjoyment of the occasion. Was this the girl who was going to be a spy?"

"Stop right there, Edgar Mason." Helena broke into what he was saying. She looked fondly at the girl in the photograph. "First of all, this could be a photo of me. I was a 'tubby little girl' myself."

"Whoops!" was her husband's reply and he pretended to cringe.

"And secondly, we are not dealing with gossip. The spy story may have been just that, a story. Here, we are making no assumptions."

Edgar took a moment to look seriously at his wife. "You are going to reconstruct the life of Esme Marsh, aren't you? That's a big ask."

"Yes, as far as possible, we are." Edgar noticed, in passing, the 'we'. He was to be involved in the project, regardless. He had no excuse to avoid it. After all, it was he who had discovered the suitcase. In any case, working with Helena was fun.

"There will be gaps." he said. They both knew this was inevitable; he was really asking for policy in such a situation.

"We leave them as gaps." Helena was very firm. "We don't accept the unfounded dramatic stories about lost lovers and the Secret Service and we don't speculate."

"And if we find that the stories have foundations?"

Helena paused and looked at him. She knew he had to ask the question. The story was that her great aunt had, as an agent of the Secret Service, made love to a Russian spy in order to get evidence against him and his network. It seemed highly unlikely but she would hate it if this were true. If they were going to quit this was the moment to do so.

"We'll cross that bridge when we come to it."

"Are we allowed comment?" he asked and he laid out more snaps. "As I say, this girl is a charmer and I suspect she knows it. Look at the way she glances sideways at the camera with just a slight smile. You do that. It's bewitching."

"Bewitching is it? I cast spells as well, you know." – and she ignored his response. "I know damn well you do!" and went on, "and brew potions! Did your tea taste all right to you?" but as he started to stand up, she backed away. "It's not supposed to work until tonight."

Edgar sat back down. "A time-delay switch on a love potion. What would happen if, say, we were in a restaurant, or, indeed, if I was with somebody else?"

"Don't you dare think about it. In any case, who said it was a love potion?"

"Enough! I know that you are a witch and you know that I'm completely in your power, with or without potions. Let's get back to Esme. Here's a snap where she's no longer a little girl but she's still a bit tubby, and another one where she is clearly a teenager. Her legs have started to grow. Where were they taken?"

"Her paternal grandmother looked after Esme whilst her father was overseas. She also looked after Stella, my grandmother; some of the time Stella was judged old enough to travel with her father on some postings. Esme and, sometimes, Stella lived with their grandmother in the school holidays but boarded in term time – at least, Esme did. Grandmother Marsh had a big house in Somerset, called 'Bridge House'. That is, it was the family house and she ran it. The family had plenty of money and, I suppose, you would call them 'County'. One of those strange words particular to that era. It meant that they were socially acceptable but not actually aristocracy. What a stratified society it was. Ours isn't quite as bad, I hope. Esme's father had a decent salary as well and most of his own outgoings would be paid for by the government. Perhaps they even paid Esme's school fees."

"Esme's grandmother had a staff of servants. I suspect that they were only too pleased to have the girls about the house. Most of these photographs were taken in the grounds, which would have been extensive, probably including a small-holding. I would like to think that my grandmother – and Esme – got to milk the cow."

She glanced up from the increasingly ordered display.

"You look shocked!"

"Not that she might milk the cow. It's just that is a different world. Every time that I read or hear about the war, it is the stories about people that affect me most. You can read the list of names on the memorials, knowing that every name has such a story. Once a year, the nation stops to consider those who gave their lives and to sympathise with those who survived and who parade in wheel-chairs or march bravely with the help of their white sticks. This is right and proper but where are the war memorials to the children who were physically unscathed, but whose lives were ruined by the war. Those who lost their parents or were just separated. What happened to their education or to their growth of love. Here we've got just one variety of such trauma. The parents, I suppose, had no choice. The children would have had a worse life if they had to follow their father to all his postings."

"And a dangerous one if he were posted to a war-zone and there were an increasing number of those."

Edgar worked for few minutes more while Helena recorded the number and characteristics of the photographs that he had laid out.

"O.K." he said, "Let's have a look at what we have got. Esme Marsh, born in 1923, is looked after by her grandmother whenever her parents travel overseas though they are more likely to take her elder sister with them. Her father is in the Foreign Office working in the country's interest. We think he's a big cheese but how big we don't know. Then her mother becomes ill and, when Esme is very young, dies.

Esme changes her secondary school in 1937. Her new school caters especially for those children whose parents served overseas. Are the pupils only chosen because of that? Not much else yet from this lot. You want our results to be factual. I'm tempted to draw conclusions but you won't let me but this upbringing does not bode well for the girls, especially Esme. Is there anything certain about her early life from your family?"

"Indeed there is. Esme Marsh was an all round bright girl. With languages, she was phenomenal. I think that is what you mean when you ask about how the pupils are chosen. The school catered for gifted children. They discovered Esme's astonishing gift when she went to her first secondary school. She would learn a new language based on Latin in a little over a term. Slightly longer for Anglo-Saxon languages. She exhausted the facilities of her first senior school within three years and was transferred to the one of the 'stamp-album'. It was called St. Ermengild's. Her father was particularly anxious that she master Russian and they employed a special part-time teacher for just such a purpose. In this case, they employed a Pole who had served in the RAF. As it turned out, he was a Jew. His was a tragic story."

"Then later, after university and working in the Foreign Office, she is supposed to have married a man called James Bygrave – just before she disappeared."

"So, no 'happily ever after' then. Is that what we are doing this for?"

"In part. The family story doesn't say any more than that – and what little it offers it does so with caveats. There were those in the family who did not approve. They called Bygrave a book-keeper, even an office-boy. If she did marry him, we can find out. We have both names and we have Somerset House where all weddings are supposed to be recorded."

"James Bygrave! Well it sounds a dignified enough name. Do you realise what time it is? We haven't even eaten. I suggest that we have a bacon sandwich and come back to this tomorrow."

CHAPTER 6

September 1937

Esme had started to think of her two new friends as providing security. Here was another example of that word. It wasn't exactly the word she was looking for. When her father used the term it usually seemed to imply the threat of some external physical danger. He never elaborated. She dimly remembered, that even with her mother, its use finished any conversation, answered every question. She was too young to understand what he meant and, even now, she was not quite sure. Esme had what she thought was a very odd idea. She saw the Treadwells as 'security' in her father's sense. This gentle giant of a man and his affectionate wife were 'security'.

The 'security' offered by Rachel and Deborah, was different. The settled atmosphere of the school and its structural organisation, the sense of continuity, the benevolent authority of the headmistress and, above all, her acceptance by the two girls, made her feel secure, protected, even sheltered. Most other girls would have settled for 'at home'; Esme had never really had the advantage of that concept.

She now had to concentrate on her House Mistress. Miss Jackson, at first sight, a benign, motherly figure, became impressive; not just because of her genuine welcome but also because of the shrewd way in which she eyed her new charge.

Esme remembered the advice Rachel had given her. This woman had dealt with hundreds of girls like her. Moreover, she would have prior knowledge from Godstone's. She would know, for example, about the fight she had there. She would have reports from her previous teachers. Madame Longley, her French teacher, would have given her a good one, she was sure. How would she herself stand up to Jack's (Esme tried out Miss Jackson's nick-name in her own thoughts) assessment?

"Esme," she had said, "Deborah and Rachel will have told you who I am. You are to come to me, just you, at four o'clock so that we can get to know each other. The girls will show you around the school now and bring you to my study."

She paused and looked at the other two girls. "Don't let her eat too much tuck." she said, "I'll be giving her tea."

Esme was thankful for the breathing space. She would be able to learn more about Miss Jackson from the two other girls.

To start with, they did show Esme round. They did a quick tour of the assembly hall, the teaching rooms, the sanatorium, the gymnasium and the playing fields but it was not long before they went to the dormitory to raid Esme's case. "Cake and lemonade, I think." was Deborah's decision as she viewed the provisions. Then they made their way to a spot behind the pavilion that was hidden from view from elsewhere.

"Not much cake for you. Jackson's teas are renowned." was Deborah's verdict.

Esme rejoiced in this. It was astonishing how she was able to relax with these two girls. Deborah was a girl with a hearty appetite but she showed no sign of the flabbiness that one might expect from this. Moreover, although she clearly enjoyed eating, it was without greed. Admonished by 'Jack' and by Deborah, Esme only ate enough to keep the others company. After they had started to enjoy the food, there was a sort of pause.

"Great cake, this." said Deborah but for once this was just something to say. Deborah seemed lost for any further conversation. Rachel came to her rescue.

"Deborah is bursting to ask you a question." she said. "She doesn't want to be rude but is always driven by the need to find things out. I'll fill you in with what she wants to say."

She was speaking seriously and Esme, who knew what she was going to ask, listened patiently. She thought that the two girls had shown great restraint in not asking already.

"It isn't often we get someone joining the school in the fourth year." said Rachel. "Everybody is curious about this and rumours have circulated since we learned you were coming. A Rolls-Royce and a chauffeur didn't help. Some of the rumours are just catty but many of them suggest that you were expelled from your previous school – and some of the reasons offered can only be described as colourful."

Esme heard her out. She was getting used to the way in which Rachel spoke. The rounded sentences seemed a bit stilted but they made her sense completely clear. She was prepared for this and had experimented with ways to answer the question. In the end, she was plain spoken.

"You needn't worry about the rumours." she said. "One or two of the colourful ones may be true but they aren't relevant. Everybody will know what it is all about very shortly. It is one of the reasons why Salty warned me not to pretend."

She was pleased that she could actually use the headmistress's nick-name. It was part of belonging – but she pressed on.

"There was an argument with a couple of the girls who wouldn't let me alone but I won't go into that." she said and then more seriously, "The real reason is the languages. I've got a funny sort of a brain and I learn languages very fast. The French Mistress, Mademoiselle Longley, at my last school, was French and she spotted it first. I kept putting my hand up in her lessons. I thought everybody would know the answers. She explained afterwards that she made the questions more difficult and I still put my hand up. She gave me a couple of extra lessons and then took me to the headmistress, who wrote to Daddy and my grandmother."

Esme almost stopped in mid-sentence. She always called him 'my father' when she spoke of him except to her grandmother and her sister. Rachel and Deborah were now part of her own inner circle.

"Daddy asked various people he knew. Apparently, it works best in your early teens. Then he asked other people. Daddy knows lots of people. They suggested St. Ermengild's because of its reputation. – and here I am."

"How fast?" Deborah was curious.

"Ten weeks for what Mademoiselle called Parisian French, another three to speak French like a native."

"Has it got a name?" Deborah pressed on with her questioning.

"I don't think so!"

"And your father?" but, at this, Rachel protested and then turned to Esme.

"If I'm right, there are questions which we shouldn't ask." Esme couldn't quite get used to Rachel's self-confidence. It was as though she were a grown up. The way she phrased this was exactly right and Esme nodded her thanks.

"Or if you ask them, I cannot answer." she said.

"I didn't mean that." Deborah was quite indignant. "I'm not daft, I'm talking about the money. St. Ermengild's is dashed expensive and if they are going to employ extra language teachers that will make it more expensive. Sometimes, my father complains that the rest of the family is going hungry to send me here. He's joking, of course and mum says he should think of the starving Chinese."

"There are scholarships." Rachel said quietly. "I have one! Now you have put up with our questioning without fuss or complaint and, since you have admitted to being a freak, you might as well know that we are freaks too. Rah has a phenomenal memory. They call it 'total recall' but it isn't quite that. I can do sums."

"There was a shout of laughter at this from Deborah. "Sums! This girl does sums that have baffled mathematicians for years. They are thinking of naming an equation 'the Castle Equation' but some of them don't believe she could have produced it herself. Oh, and it's time for your tea with 'Jack'. I can remember that."

Esme leaped to her feet but was told to relax and that she had plenty of time. The two girls gathered up the remains of the impromptu picnic and took her back to the dormitory.

Esme felt that she had enough for one day but she brushed herself down and, combed the bits of grass out of her hair. The three girls headed for Miss Jackson's office. Then Rachel and Deborah left her, making re-assuring noises.

There was the expected sign on the door 'Knock and Wait!' and she did so but did not have to wait long. Miss Jackson opened the door and ushered her into the room. Part of the room, it was true, was an office but the space in front of the fireplace was organised differently.

There were two arm chairs, one on each side of the hearth, although the fire was not lit. Between them was a low table, set for tea. Esme was glad that she had eaten only one piece of cake with the girls for there was a three tier cake-stand on the little table. On the bottom layer were finely cut sandwiches, with brown and white bread. The middle tier held fruit scones already spread with cream and piled with jam. Tiny tartlets and iced cakes graced the top layer.

"Please sit down – and relax…" said Miss Jackson. "St Ermengild's is not a finishing school." and the implication was clear that such institutions were of an inferior kind. "We do recognise, however, that our girls will need to behave properly at social gatherings. Hence the tea!"

She passed Esme a plate of fine bone china, offered her the cake stand and asked her to help herself. Then she picked up on what she had said before.

"That mustn't stop you enjoying it. I hope the girls did warn you."

"They not only warned me but Deborah ate half my slice of cake." was Esme's response. She had, to her own surprise, followed Miss Jackson's instruction to relax.

Miss Jackson was pouring tea, ascertaining that Esme preferred milk to lemon and did not take sugar. She passed Esme her cup-and-saucer and the girl noted that they did not match and were of a different pattern to the plate. The House Mistress, watching her charge carefully, saw that she had made this observation but was not showing it. Perhaps she was thinking that the school was short of money? This was a good start. Her new pupil was not only observant but had the discipline to keep her observations to herself.

"The china is part of the learning process." she said. "Unless we give you variety, you cannot decide what is preferable. If you turn the plates over you'll see who made them and, usually, what the pattern is called. Some time in the distant future, you will be buying your own china."

"But we'll leave that for another time. Today, we are here to decide about one spot on your daily time-table. You already know that there are games on Wednesday and Saturday afternoons. I understand that you don't like games. That's unfortunate but I'm afraid you still have to do them. There is, however, an hour before the evening meal on the other days which is designated 'Choice'. It is a controlled 'choice', of course. You can't choose to spend it smoking behind the pavilion and it has to be a group activity. You will need two of these spots for your extra language lessons. Your father would like you to include Polish and Russian and we are bringing in a part-time teacher for that purpose."

"There is one 'choice' which everybody chooses and that is dancing. This session is the one done by year groups. Your year group takes dancing on Thursdays. In your year there will be some conventional ball-room dancing but the teachers are aware that styles change. There will still be some country dancing; the girls seem to enjoy that. It is a disadvantage that you have to start learning ballroom dancing with only girls as partners. We wait until your next year before we invite some of the senior pupils from 'Burley's'. That's the local boys' school. They come along once a fortnight. All part of the process of learning about the outside world."

The 'choices' seemed to be rapidly vanishing but Esme said nothing. Dancing was all right. It was, according to Jane Austen, a pleasurable form of socialising. They had done some country dancing at the Godstone's and she looked forward to doing so at St. Ermengild's. What she had done so far had been fun.

"Apart from 'Dancing' the 'Choices' are based on the whole school, not on houses, so you get the opportunity to meet girls of different ages. We have a 'Watercolour Class' and a Choir. The Choir are quite good and sing a wide range of different sorts of songs. Then, on Tuesdays and Fridays, the Stamp Collectors Club meets at that time. That would seem appropriate. Miss James runs that, you'll like her. What do you think?"

Esme had no idea of what a Stamp Collectors Club did but the activity became 'appropriate' when Miss Jackson followed up by saying that, "Deborah and Rachel are members."

CHAPTER 7

31st July 1986

Edgar started well the following day but, after a while, was beginning to flag. He had got to the tedious part with the photographs. He had given each one a number and its own data sheet and on each of these he had written a full description of what the photograph was about. Helena was a meticulous worker and Edgar tried to complete as much as he could. This took time but it did mean that they had all of the pictures referenced. Now he was filling in on these data sheets an extensive form that asked specific questions about the photograph. Some questions he could answer. Many he had to leave unanswered. Only when he was certain did he write in, for example, where the photograph was taken. Sometimes he used a pencil when he was almost sure about the answers.

Helena allowed them to break for lunch and Edgar had an early afternoon appointment for a portrait session. The local Amateur Dramatic Society were proud of their performances and advertised them with photographs of the players in costume. They also illustrated their programs with them in the same way. They used Edgar every time for these. He had a knack of enhancing the characters portrayed. It only took a couple of hours and he dutifully returned to Esme's photographs.

'This looks like a wedding' he wrote on one and then stopped.

"What have we done about the wedding?" he asked.

Helena was filling in some of the blanks, also in pencil because she was not sure. If she was going to follow them all up, they promised that there would be a great deal of work.

"*We* have done nothing about the wedding." she said. "*I* have arranged for Bill and Marilyn to come for a meal this evening and we'll sort things out."

"This evening! Do you want me to get something in?"

"Relax. There's a wild-mushroom risotto in the bottom of the Aga. Marilyn will bring the pud – knowing Marilyn, that means puds – plural. You can do the wine. A bottle of decent champagne, do you think?"

"Sounds great. Perhaps two bottles. I'm not risking any inferior Cava. You know what happened last time"

Helena said something about a potion but Edgar, on his way to the cellar to get the wine, realised what his wife had said earlier and was distracted.

"When did you make a risotto?" he asked.

"When you were moaning on about forms and I was getting lunch. It only takes a minute or two; but you are right, its time to get a move on. I'll set the table. Leave the gear here, they'll be interested."

They were, of course, more interested in the arrangements for their long-delayed nuptials and, for a while, the conversation was about the future and not the past. The champagne, as it was intended to, broke down their initial embarrassment about their plans. Edgar offered them snippets of raw vegetables and salad; particularly radishes, which he called 'burpers'. This and the provision of drinks, was his contribution to the feast. He felt that the risotto and Marilyn's puddings would provide enough solid food.

The meals that the two couples shared were always casual affairs. This did not stop them from eating well. Often they tried out recipes on each other and, sometimes, they drank too much. They lived within walking distance of each other so they did not have to drive home. The two men took these meals as opportunities to dress down and totally relax. Marilyn and Helena tried out new ideas on how they dressed their hair or some different jewellery. They did this with just a touch of rivalry. Everybody looked out for this and enjoyed it as part of the evening's entertainment. Marilyn was as dark as Helena was fair so between the two them they produced a show that was varied and, sometimes, complex.

That evening Marilyn had a new hair style which did not satisfy her. Both men knew how useless it would be to try and reassure her. It was Edgar who, checking first with Helena that Marilyn's hair now showed her ears which her previous hair-do had not, said how nice the new pendant ear rings looked. He had never realised how perfect the lobes of her ears were before. This was so far over the top that even Marilyn laughed. Actually, there was some truth in the joke. The smooth skin of her face, the curve of her cheek bones and her soft delicate ears set off the boldness of her eyebrows and her dark brown eyes in a startlingly beautiful way.

People who met Marilyn and Bill for the first time wondered how she had been attracted to him. There was nothing outstanding in his appearance. He was of average height, he had brownish hair and brownish eyes and always seemed not to have shaved that day. Helena, when her friend had introduced him at a party was, at first, puzzled – but not for long. His hand-shake was firm but gentle and so distinctive that she glanced down at his hand. It was slim, elegant and powerful and when she looked again at his face, she could see a depth of understanding in his eyes. She said to Edgar afterwards that he was like an ice-berg. Very little of Bill Thomas showed above the surface. Edgar agreed. "I think its a professional device that he hides his intellect from the people he interviews so that they tell him more than they think they have. Marilyn knows of course and I wouldn't be surprised if she told him off for using it. I don't think he realises that it has become part of him."

He was right; certainly about Marilyn telling Bill off. He actually called the following day with a bunch of flowers for Helena and said how sorry he was that he had not been more open. He had not appreciated the depth of friendship between them and Marilyn.

"That's a keeper!" was Edgar's comment when he had gone – and indeed it was. The two of them had been together ever since.

This time when the two of them arrived, they brought a wedding-present list that they offered with some diffidence. Helena brushed aside their apologies. The truth was that they had presented an unconventional front for so long that they were worried that they appeared hypocritical.

It was going to be a full scale job and, it transpired, Marilyn's father was going to pay for everything. She said that he had been fretting for years about their cohabiting. His mantra had been – 'If you have a child and Bill dies, you'll then be just another single parent. Go through a ceremony and, in that situation, you'll be a poor widow-woman.' She said he was like a dog with two tails.

"So are we." said Helena. "Except, I suppose, with four tails. The 'wedding list' is an idea that solves so many problems. Fancy us coming round for a meal in ten years time and, once more, the fruit bowl, which we chose, is brought out of the cupboard which it has cluttered up for the rest of the time."

They offered the list to Edgar but he waved it aside.

"Helena can deal with that." he said. "From me you get the special Wedding Album – or albums if you want copies for your parents. Since you are going in for it in style, I'll do it with Bells and Whistles."

"Great!" said Marilyn. "Dad's paying!"

"He's not paying me. This is my wedding present. If you like, I'll tell him how much I would charge and he can buy you something special."

Bill had brought a bottle of white wine that went well with the risotto. There was a bottle of Monbazillac to go with the puds and, somehow, all this fitted into what was a momentous day. Then, Helena remembered the hat.

"I won't be long." she said and rushed up the stairs.

"Helena has bought a hat and you haven't seen it?" Bill was incredulous.

"Wait until you have been married as long as I have." said Edgar with a straight face. "You'll think differently."

When Helena came down again she was wearing the dress from the suitcase. It was old-fashioned and somewhat crumpled and, indeed, too young for her but the fine material clung to her slim figure as though it had been made for her. The hat was a stunner. Straw and trimmed with lace it had an understated elegance that emphasised the gold in Helena's disciplined curls and gave sparkle to the soft blue of her eyes. Edgar was, once more, astonished by the woman he had lived with for so long. Marilyn said just one word, "Where?" but Bill whistled and he only just stopped it from being a wolf whistle.

The hat and, especially, the dress and its story led them, inevitably, to the suitcase. Edgar had worked the incident into a free-flowing anecdote and Bill asked some shrewd questions and they finished the dessert-wine and moved on to coffee. They relaxed completely as they drank this; taking on board the series of events that led to Edgar's purchase when Bill asked. "Did you say the name was 'Marsh'?"

"Yes, we know now that the suitcase belonged to Esme Marsh, my great-aunt."

"The name rings a bell, somehow." he took another sip of coffee and then raised his head. "I've got it." he said triumphantly. "A whole bunch of documents, previously classified as 'Secret' have just been released. Their secrecy is no longer thought to be in the 'National Interest' – a lovely phrase that."

"And?" It was Helena who prodded him to continue.

"There was a trial early on in the war – World War Two that is – of some communist spies. They were British citizens but they were Russian agents. The press suggested that British Communist Party was mixed up in the affair but this proved to be just the right-wing newspapers trying to make capital out of it. The defendants were accused of sending plans of aeroplane sites to their masters. They were all found guilty and did time but the prosecution evidence was given *in camera* – 'in the National Interest' again. This evidence was part of the mass of literature we had to wade through. The prosecution was brought by one Reginald Marsh."

Helena's reaction was all that he could have asked for. She gave a little gasp and her hand went to her mouth. "That's my great grandfather." she said, turning worriedly to Edgar who knew that she was thinking of the story about Esme that she had dismissed earlier that day as tittle-tattle.

Neither of them said anything else and Marilyn, who had seen the expression on Helena's face and suspected that something was wrong, drew attention to the time and gathered up Bill to call it a night. Helena went with Marilyn to fetch the short jacket she had worn and Edgar used this opportunity to speak quietly to Bill. He asked him to find out as much as he could about Marsh and the trial. He also asked him if he could find out anything about Esme Marsh's school. It was called 'St. Ermengild's' and was somewhere in Scotland. He invited both of them to come back so that they could learn more about the suitcase.

He and Helena took their guests to the door and watched them set out on their short walk home. Helena stood close up against her husband and he held her gently.

"Why would Reginald want to keep it secret?" she asked.

"A dozen reasons and none of them anything to do with Esme."

"Name one."

"We are talking about the Secret Service here. This was at a time they wouldn't even admit that there was a Secret

Service. It was a cloak-and-dagger culture and they did try to protect their agents. If there was a net-work of spies they might have a double agent in place, someone who provided the evidence to prosecute."

"That doesn't exclude Esme. If the gossip was true, she was a sort of double agent."

"Esme was the daughter of a high up official in the Foreign Office. She could never be a secret agent. Where did the gossip come from?"

Edgar held her more firmly and brought her back into the house. "Do you want to stop?"

Helena knew he was talking about the suitcase but her response was almost immediate. "No. We are in now. I don't want to find out that my great-aunt was a honey-trap. Is that what they call them? If she was, she did it for England. Her father was an old-fashioned patriot. He died before I was born but I remember my grandmother asking me if I wanted any of his books. They were mostly for boys and included Rider-Haggard; John Buchan, Jack London and, of course, Anthony Hope's 'The Prisoner of Zenda.' From a later date there were even some of the Hornblower series; so he didn't change much as he grew older. Would he have used a young woman to trap the enemy by seduction? Would he use his daughter in that way?"

"The answer is, obviously, 'no'. So why are you worrying about it."

"I suppose because gossip is insidious and it was the sort of thing that some of my relatives would enjoy. Horrid things!"

They pottered around, making sure that any leftovers were

put away in the fridge. Sometimes Helena said this was just so they could throw them away tomorrow but Edgar was always firm on this point and he said the same thing every time.

"Waste not, Want not!" A phrase that he had inherited.

This time, he elaborated. He wanted to take Helena's mind off her great-aunt. "We had our own family rider to that: 'Wilful Waste Makes Woeful Want' and I found a picture of that piece of propaganda in a book of photographs illustrating the war and its aftermath." he said. "A cracking photograph. It was just a water-tap; an old-fashioned one with four knobs on the handle and in gleaming chrome. There was a drop of water falling from it. It was one of those big posters that they used to put on the hoardings that hid the bomb-damage. They were no longer 'digging for victory' and 'walls' no longer 'had ears' but food was still rationed. Some genius created that poster. He's telling me to put the trifle in the fridge forty years on."

On this occasion, he had Helena's full approval. Marilyn had brought three puddings; chocolate cake, her own version of 'very sherry trifle' and for, as she put it, 'the healthy eaters', a fruit salad. Not surprisingly the 'healthy eaters' sampled the other alternatives as well. There was plenty left and they found room in the refrigerator. "Leave the rest." he said. "I'll do it first thing. We've done enough today."

He was licking the trifle spoon and paused to say, "That hat was really something. It shook Marilyn. She said that she wished she'd asked you to be a bridesmaid. Her two sisters will do that job but you could have been Matron of Honour. What's a 'Matron of Honour'? Then you would have had to wear what she told you."

61

It passed through his mind to mention 'the potion' but just at that moment he felt more affection than lust and, somehow, he thought that she felt the same.

*** *** ***

He awoke betimes the following morning as usual; leaving his wife to sleep on. First of all, he made himself a pot of tea and sat down to drink the first cup. Then, he did, indeed, clear up; stacking the dish-washer and giving it his daily blessing. He did not run it because of the plumbing noises. By the time he had taken his own shower and, in response to the signs of stirrings from Helena, taken her a freshly-made cup of tea, the kitchen was spotless and all the gear was put away.

"Thank you!" said his wife. "This is above and beyond the call of duty."

He grinned. "I didn't dare do anything with the suitcase so I cleared the ground for the expert. I did wake up with a memory however; the 'old girls' of St. Ermengild's include several prominent academics including one very famous philosopher. She was tipped for a Nobel Prize three years ago. The newspaper reports at the time called it a 'hot-house' of learning. It's wonderful what a night's sleep will do to the memory.

That morning also, the post proved significant. Helen passed across one of her letters, clearly concerned with business. It was from a client. He had employed Helena to trace his ancestry so that he could make a claim on a relative's estate. He was pleased with the research that she had done and was asking that she write a report on it. He needed it to give to his solicitor.

"He's got a good case." she said. "He is a relative. The deceased died intestate and he should get a share of the inheritance. People who don't write wills create work for the legal profession and, sometimes, for me. I should write his report first thing. It shouldn't take more than a couple of hours but we'll have to leave the suitcase."

Edgar was disappointed. He knew his wife was worried that the rumour that Esme was a secret service 'agent' would be confirmed by further research. This would not stop her carrying it out and she would continue to fret about her relative's history until they had finally laid her ghost to rest. They were a long way from doing that but the sooner they had done so, the better.

"I'll do that framing." he said. After all, that also needed to be done but he had plenty of time to fulfil that order. It was an unusual one, a Christening – few parents employed a professional photographer to record such an occasion. He was pleased with what he had done. He had encouraged not just shots of a largely shrouded baby but family groups as well. Proud parents and grandparents would, he thought, enjoy his work and in years to come it would bring pleasure to the descendants of this little girl.

The report took less than two hours. Helena sent it by the messenger service they both used. Edgar had done his work, the pictures he had framed just needed packing. The two of them were able to approach the suitcase again. Edgar had the strange feeling that it was waiting for them, eager to answer their questions but he kept that idea to himself.

Helena changed the tape in her machine, carefully labelling the one she had used the day before.

Before they could start there was a knock on the front door. It was a messenger from Bill. The envelop he handed in held a hand-written note.

Edgar read it aloud.

"'St. Ermengild, said by some to be a virgin, was certainly a nun, even an Abbess but she had two children, one of them a king. With a name like that, the school should have had the best of both worlds. Unfortunately, late in the war, a German bomber dropped a stick of incendiaries on it and it was burnt to the ground. The accepted official view was that the plane was unable to get to the Clyde ship-yards and was just dumping its payload No casualties and a commendation from Downing Street for the way they had organised their air-raid warnings and fire-drill.'"

Helena and Edgar read these missives together.

"An incendiary bomb." Helena was horrified. "Did they mean it?"

"Unlikely. Though there was, late in the war, an incident in South London where an attack upon a school was almost certainly deliberate. That really was a tragedy. A number of kids were killed and some teachers. It was supposed to be a propaganda raid delivered in daylight to panic the population. The official view about St. Ermengild's was probably correct. This lot was something to do with the Clyde."

"That Miss Salway must have run a tight ship."

"You've just rung another bell. They made her a Dame. She was interviewed by the press. I've seen her photograph in a special exhibition at the National Portrait Gallery of 'War

Heroes from the Home Front'. If I've got the right image in my mind, I remember thinking that the photographer had found the kindness beneath the efficiency. And there was a quote – something about the courage of her girls, standing in disciplined ranks possessing only what they stood up in."

Helena looked closely at her husband, whose voice was steadier than it should have been, and she stretched out her hand to his.

"This is bad for us," he said, shaking off the sentiment, "Bill underlined the bit about the school being burnt to the ground. There go all those records we were hoping for."

Also in the envelop was a photocopy of an advertisement from a 'Magazine for Ladies', as it called itself.

St. Ermengild's, they learned, offered exclusive education for talented girls. It also offered full-board in term-time and, in special cases, throughout the year. It had extensive playing fields and its own grounds with secure boundaries. It even had a small loch. The staff included a qualified nurse as a matron and teachers qualified to provide an extensive curriculum and extra-curriculum activities. The headmistress was a Miss Salway with a string of letters after her name.

He had scrawled a postscript at the bottom: "More to come on the other matter."

Shrugging off the feeling of sadness, they returned to the suitcase. Amongst the paraphernalia and easily accessible, was a sort of file; two thin textured boards hinged by cloth and tied shut with a ribbon. It was a professionally produced folder and it was entitled 'Camera Portraits' with the name, address and telephone number of the photographer in an embossed cartouche. Apart from its dull beige colour, Edgar was quite impressed. He could do something like that.

Helena was reaching in to take the file from the case and stopped.

"What other matter?" she asked.

Edgar, under his breath, cursed Bill for adding the postscript but he knew better than to try and avoid the issue. He answered without emphasis.

"I asked him to chase up the spy-trial." he said. "But we might as well wait for what he says. That is if there is anything worth saying. The suitcase is demanding attention."

Fortunately, it was and in a way that distracted Helena's attention. Underneath the folder there were two books. She spoke into her microphone: "There are several books in the case but they have been put in higgledy piggledy. Two of them are sitting more or less on the top. The first is 'Cranford' by Mrs Gaskell – nice copy, hard-back with green covers, gold lettering on the covers and gold on the edge of the pages, published 1898 and illustrated; edges of the cover and spine slightly scuffed but in fine condition. Inscribed 'From Grandmother. You will enjoy this.'"

There was no date on the inscription and Helena reluctantly put the book to one side. Edgar could see that she would enjoy it also.

She went on to the second one in the same way. "Then there is 'The Wind in the Willows' by Kenneth Grahame. Hard-back with dark blue covers, front cover embossed with the picture of Pan and the spine decorated in gold with Toad in his motoring get-up. – the fifteenth edition published in 1923 and inscribed 'R. Marsh' – no book plate, spine and edges of cover scuffed, pages rough cut and binding under stress."

She stopped. "Esme was born in 1923. Surely he didn't buy it to read to her?"

Edgar made a noise. "One, she had an elder sister. Two, even Reginald Marsh was entitled to buy second-hand books and three, he might have bought it for himself. I thought you said we weren't supposed to speculate. Shall we look at the books later, these and the others may form a group. They are two super books. I can claim to have read both of them. They would be on my short list for a desert island."

Helena, somewhat reluctantly, congratulated him on his understanding of the mechanics of unpacking the suitcase. Edgar simply muttered.

They returned to the card folder, pulling the bow of the ribbon and opening it on the bench. At first, it appeared not to hold any photographs; instead there were some loose sheets of card and paper.

This was treasure trove indeed. The first item was a short, type-written letter on the official note-paper of 'Godstone School for Girls' and it was dated, 1st July, 1937. Helena wanted all the girl's life and this was the earliest that they had discovered. They read it together.

Dear Mrs. Marsh,

Thank you for your letter. I am in full agreement concerning the transfer of your granddaughter. I like the girl and, as I am actually teaching her, come across her a great deal.

We spoke on the phone earlier about the

contretemps with some of the senior girls but we have dealt with that. I can assure you that the incident was not initiated by Esme.

We lack the staff, however, to develop properly her remarkable talent.

You asked me about St. Ermengild's and, yes, within the profession, they have an outstanding reputation.

Please give my best wishes to Esme.
Yours sincerely.

There was an unreadable signature.

"Contretemps?" Edgar asked. "What does that mean?"

Helena had picked a reference book off the shelves and, before she replied, she consulted it.

"It means that something went drastically wrong with the first choice for Esme's school. They sent her to Godstone's. It was a girls' boarding school which was specifically for the children of British Officers and Civil Servants serving overseas. Similar to St. Ermengild's in many ways but providing only normal education for normal children. Esme would have been very different from the other girls there because of her facility with languages."

"You're going to speculate!"

"You asked me to."

"Go ahead. The more we know about this girl, the more likely the speculations are to be correct."

"All right. In such a place it can happen that someone different becomes a victim. It just needs one bully to make most of the rest form a front against such a person and difficult for others to take her side. Esme, with her upbringing, would suffer from such treatment."

"O.K. You've created the atmosphere. What about the 'incident'?"

"This is code for, at least, an argument; possibly a physical one. Esme is being bullied. I would like to think that our Esme would not take bullying lying down."

CHAPTER 8

Summer term 1937

Esme Marsh was sitting alone in the quadrangle of Godstone's Boarding School for Girls. She was thinking that she did a lot of sitting alone and she had found a corner that nobody else used. Here she read a great deal. Mostly, she realised, the books she read were pretty mushy. One sort were books that featured schoolgirls who, with their friends, had exciting adventures; the second sort had strong, silent heroes who, having rescued their tremulous heroines from diverse fates, were forever passionately sweeping them into their arms. She was a bit worried that she absorbed, 'like a sponge', so many of these. But, nudged in that direction by her English teacher, she had discovered the joys of reading Jane Austen. Jane Austen's heroes might not have done much physical sweeping up of heroines into their arms but they were still heroes and they rescued their heroines from social rather than physical disasters. Her heroes and heroines were, beneath the conventions, just as passionate.

After Austen, she moved on to the darker world of the Brontes. Their heroes and heroines also did what heroes and heroines were supposed to do but the authors ensured that they fulfilled their roles with superior style.

On this occasion, she was metaphorically hugging a present from her Grandmother; an illustrated edition of

'Cranford' by Mrs Gaskell. From the opening sentence: 'In the first place Cranford, is in possession of the Amazons;', she had known that this book would give her hours of delight and she could not help chuckling at some of the illustrations.

"There's that swot, Esme Marsh, reading again." was the harsh interruption of her escape from Godstone's into her own world. It was the two girls who had identified her as a special target. Somehow they picked those incomers who would suffer most from their bullying and homed in on them like hunting dogs. Esme they saw as a choice victim. They were a couple of years older than her and much bigger. They weren't consistent in their bullying, they just did it when she was at hand and they had nothing else to do. Nonetheless, Esme, who tried to avoid them and suffered the harassment without protest, had had just about enough.

One of the girls tried to snatch her book away, taunting her, and said that she was hiding photographs of boys in the book and demanded that she give it to them.

This was not what Esme wanted but she heard herself saying.

"Touch the book and you will regret it."

This sent them into shouts of laughter. One of them cried, "Get her!" and the two of them rushed at her.

It was a mistake.

★★★ ★★★ ★★★

In the summer of 1934. That is, in the holidays before Esme went to Godstone's, one Company Sergeant Major Peter

Williamson was told to report to his Colonel. He was not best pleased because he was getting ready to go on leave.

Williamson was a professional soldier. Recruited as a teenager he still had the characteristic marching step of the 'boy-soldier' with the little flick of the hands on each stride. He had all the attributes expected of a Sergeant Major especially one engaged in the teaching of unarmed combat. He stood at just under six feet and was in the peak of physical condition. Those he trained feared him from day one, especially the edge of his tongue. By the time their course was finished, they not only held him in great respect but saw him as a friend.

He had one other rather odd job. If it was judged that a civilian should be taught unarmed combat, it was C.S.M. Williamson who did so. His pupils were usually those who had to operate as agents behind the enemy lines. His avuncular personality was especially suitable in the teaching of young people.

He marched into the Colonel's office, came to attention and threw an impeccable salute.

"At ease, Sergeant Major. I'm afraid you are not going to like this. First of all, sign here. It's the Official Secrets Act."

"I've signed that before, sir."

"Well you don't need to read it then; but sign it in any case; I've got to witness your signature."

He watched Williamson sign, added his own signature and blotted it and then took it to the safe.

"Everything from now on is included under that act. You say nothing to anybody about it. You are going on special ops for three weeks."

"Sir, I'm just off on leave. What about my wife?"

"You can tell your wife that is special ops." he consulted a piece of paper, "You can tell her that there is no danger involved – that's all."

Company Sergeant Major Williamson, not surprisingly wanted to know what was going on. He waited for some sort of information.

"Don't look at me like that. I know very little about it. I was asked to provide my best instructor in self-defence especially someone who was successful in teaching young women and that it would help if he had 'clearance'. 'Clearance', what's that all about? You, apparently have 'clearance'. I don't. You certainly fit the bill otherwise."

"You are my best instructor and you are good with the ladies, so you can blame yourself for being selected. You are to pack for three weeks. No uniform and no evidence of your rank. You will leave your pay-book with me. You will travel by train to Frome. Here are the tickets. You will notice that it is not a warrant and that it is First Class. You will be met at your destination by a civilian who will say one word, 'Williamson'. You will reply, 'Company Sergeant Major Williamson and you will then obey his orders."

The Colonel delivered his instructions and then paused.

"Not only am I not allowed to tell you what this is all about, I can't do so because I don't know myself. All I can think of is that it must be something to do with the fact that this war is getting closer."

"The best of luck, Sergeant Major. We'll sort you out some leave when you get back." and then as Williamson saluted. "Somebody up there amongst our faceless bosses has a bit of a conscience. I'm to send your wife a dozen roses – as from you. Red?"

"If they are from me, certainly they should be red. You'll need to send them from 'Pet'; not Peter, but 'Pet'. Otherwise they are not from me. That information, sir, comes under the Official Secrets Act!" and Company Sergeant Major Williamson left on his special mission.

The meeting with his contact took place as planned and the man, bigger even than the Sergeant Major, took him through the public door of the railway buffet and, after a brief pause, through the kitchens to the street. There he ushered him into Grandmother Marsh's Rolls.

Reginald Marsh had decided that his daughters should be taught to protect themselves. He was always concerned with their safety and he had advanced this scheme to give them some intensive training in self-defence. His mother did not approve and only agreed to be party to the scheme because Reginald had appealed to her on the grounds that he had promised his wife that he would do everything he could for Stella and Esme.

"If there is something of Elizabeth left in this world apart from the girls, it is in my brain. I said I would do everything I could. Well, I can't do much, but this I can do." he had said and his mother, still disapproving, both accepted his motives and gave the project her full support.

Company Sergeant Major Peter Williamson was, at first, another person that disapproved. That he had been ordered to sacrifice his leave to instruct two young girls in self-defence did not go down well. He told himself that it must be important for reasons he did not understand and he determined to do a good job. It did not take long for the three of them to work together.

Stella Marsh, the elder of the two sisters, was enthusiastic from the start and quickly earned Williamson's approval. Esme took a little time to become committed to the idea of physical violence. She was far too hesitant, not to say gentle, in her attacks. This was until the instructor, frustrated by her timidity, exploded with the sort of reprimand he might have made on the barrack square; "You're supposed to be breaking my arm not breaking my heart." he cried. He had wanted to say something stronger but stopped himself in time. It was, however, enough to raise a laugh from Esme. She relaxed and accepted that she might, in some circumstances, actually need to fight. Once she had overcome the idea that ladies did not indulge in violence, she was as violent as her sister.

★★★ ★★★ ★★★

As the two girls rushed her, Esme apologised in her mind to Peter Williamson. This was not why he had taught her how to defend herself and he would have seen the opposition as laughable. Nonetheless, he had insisted that if you did fight, you had to mean it. Hesitate or try to let your opponent down lightly and you would be the one let down.

She stepped inside the outstretched arms of the first girl and head-butted her in the face. She had time then to treat the other one more gently with a blow to the solar-plexus.

The first girl's screams and loud cries claiming that Esme had broken her nose brought the prefects and then the teachers.

"She attacked us!" claimed the second girl, gasping for breath. "We just asked to look at her book and she came at us like a wild-cat. She should be locked up."

The prefects took one look at these two hulking girls and then at the younger, almost delicate, Esme Marsh and made their own interpretation of what had happened. They were not called upon to offer their opinions by the teachers who arrived after them and they wondered later what had happened to the three girls involved.

The headmistress agreed with the parents of the two older girls that they had been in school long enough and, more positively, with Esme's grandmother about a change of school.

Esme read and re-read 'Cranford' for years afterwards.

CHAPTER 9

1st August 1986

"So 1937 was a big year for Esme March. Her astonishing ability with languages is recognised, she changes schools partially because of this and partially because of a 'contretemps' with some 'senior' girls. At her new school, she meets a whole host of different people and she starts collecting stamps." Edgar summarised the facts that had emerged from their previous session with the suitcase.

"Congratulations!" Helena glanced impishly at him as she said this. "Everything founded on written evidence and not an assumption in sight. On that basis we can move forward. What do you think of this?"

'This' was the one photograph she had found in the ribboned file. It was included within a bunch of papers but seemed not to belong there. Perhaps it was a left-over from the file's original function. It was a posed group-portrait of an elderly lady and a middle-aged man both seated and flanking two girls The girls were also seated but on lower stools. Helena had seen something like it before so there was no difficulty in identifying the group. They were Esme's Grandmother Marsh, Stella, aged about seventeen, and Esme, about three years younger, and the much travelled father, Reginald. The photographer had chosen to have a light source of an un-curtained window in the right corner of the scene, just behind the lady. It was not in a studio and, balancing the composition, there was a small Christmas tree. Both the adults were completely composed and Stella was attempting to be the same. Esme was sparkling with pleasure.

Reginald exuded authority. Barrel-chested and broad shouldered, he sat with his legs crossed at the ankles. He had a heavy moustache but his hair had receded far enough to allow a description of him as bald. His dark jacket and pin-stripe trousers and the watch-chain across his waistcoat were entirely fitting garb for a diplomat. The starched cuff of the left sleeve of his shirt showed as a point of light on the photograph and mirrored the white lace at the neck of his mother's blouse.

Edgar gave the image a number and fetched another form. Helena started to fill it in, being able to identify the people and the place. Edgar, as he had been asked, commented on the photograph itself.

"He nearly got it right." he said. "Great composition and a sharp print. This fellow had a cracking camera but I'm afraid Esme let him down. I don't suppose our Esme was capable of looking solemn for any length of time and she's always more ready to smile at the camera than not. When she doesn't, she's usually putting on her charm."

"Not often that Reginald was photographed. I suppose even he couldn't refuse a Christmas group." said Helena. "They didn't have many photographs taken together. This must have been a rare family occasion. Would you like to guess the year?"

"Well you'll be better at that than me but your grandmother is now almost a young lady. Her legs have grown. Esme is still young enough to be her father's little girl; though not for much longer. 1936 or 1937. Not 1938; Reginald would be too busy that close to the war to be home for Christmas."

"Well done!" said Helena and turned the photograph over. On the back was the notation. 'Xmas 1937'. "So it was a big year – she spends Christmas at home."

"We haven't got many shots of Phoebe either." she went on.

"Phoebe?"

"Reginald's mother, she would be my great, great grandmother. She was supposed to have acted as a sort of secretary as well as looking after the girls in the vacations. She must have been privy to some of his secrets."

"Perhaps that's why there aren't many photos."

Helena took another look at the photograph. "Pretty girl, my grandmother." she said.

"Yes." her husband agreed, looking over her shoulder. Stella Marsh, sitting up straight with her shoulders back, presented the only image of either of the girls they had seen so far without the pudding-basin hairstyle. Esme's was once again in that unattractive cut. Stella's dark hair was frizzed out. She had been dressed, drilled and had even had her hair done. She was, as her grand-daughter had said, even in those artificial conditions, an attractive girl.

"Both Stella and Esme had star quality but each was different. Curious things, genes. You look more like Esme than Stella. You have Esme's fair hair and her enchanting eyes. Re-assortment of their parent's DNA through Stella and then your father produced Helena Burroughs and has given me all that is best of all your ancestry" and he ruffled the top of her head.

Helena said nothing about having 'enchanting eyes'. She would save that up for a future occasion.

CHAPTER 10

Christmas 1937

Esme did spend Christmas of her first year as a pupil at St Ermengild's at her Grandmother's home. Her sister was there as well and the family was, for the two days over the New Year, made complete when their father came. He was in transit from one posting to another and, of course, they were unable to discuss where he was going to or even where he had come from. That did mean, however, that they had time to talk about Esme's school. She was able to share the pleasure she got from it, especially, from her two friends. Her pleasure had its effect on her father, who was surprised and delighted that she had settled so well and, for a brief interlude, this was a happy family.

One topic that Esme spoke of with her father was the Stamp Collectors' Club, telling him how pleased she had been with her birthday present and how many stamps she had collected. He had collected stamps himself as a boy and said he would send her the small collection that had survived and this common interest was one of the things that Esme was able to take with her on the bleak journey back to school.

It made the Stamp Club even more appropriate. Those girls who belonged to the club collected stamps with varying degrees of enthusiasm. They all had albums that had pages for different countries. Esme, when she joined and until her birthday, had only an exercise book. This did not trouble her. Miss Jackson had said that they were allowed to change their 'Choice' session if they wanted to and she had been brought up to try things out first on a small scale.

The stamps came from different sources and there was a certain amount of swapping that went on as one girl might want to complete a set of perhaps the Silver Jubilee. Most of the time was spent in mounting their acquisitions on tiny adhesive hinges – and talking. About once a fortnight one of the girls would give a short account of a particular aspect of her own collection. Esme was a natural collector and enjoyed the variety of approaches that the other members took. Deborah went in for bulk and did a great deal of classification, by country, by colour, by the subject on the stamp, the stamp's shape and, somewhat obscurely, the perforations. Rachel, oddly, collected those that had pictures of birds.

After a short while in the club, it was clear that this was a very good 'choice' for Esme and she asked to look at the albums that the other girls had. Some of them had page heading for the different countries and Esme began to note those countries that her father had visited, and, of course, he sent her letters from many different places with some very fine stamps. Esme convinced herself that he looked for flamboyant stamps especially to send them to her. He did include unused stamps inside his envelopes.

These letters came with the morning post. The morning post was distributed by placing it on the board in the dining room where the criss-cross webbing held it in place for the girls to collect as they went to breakfast. Miss Jackson even relaxed the rule about not reading at table for those girls who had been lucky enough to have a letter. Esme's father wrote regularly and his short notes were welcome but rather stiff. He never said what he was doing; she did not expect him to, or where he was – letters were actually forwarded from his London base. Since she had joined the stamp club, he would send some stamps and write about them. Sometimes, there was a letter from her grandmother. Such letters included a contribution from her older sister, Stella.

Any post she had, she would carry to her place at table. She would sort out her breakfast first and then, before she buttered her knife, use it to slit open the envelope. One morning she was just about to do this when she saw that something was wrong. The flap of the envelope was slightly crinkled and was misaligned.

Esme laid the letter to one side and calmly ate her breakfast. She could ignore this and do nothing about it. It might just be someone thinking the bulky envelope held money. If she chose to ignore it, the normal procedure then would have been to get ready for the morning's lessons and then attend assembly. Instead, Esme went straight to Miss Jackson's office. The House Mistress opened the door and showed her in. This bore out her two friends' opinion that Miss Jackson was always available to help.

Miss Jackson waited for Esme to speak and the girl came straight to the point. "Please, Miss Jackson, I would like to phone my grandmother."

"That sounds serious, is it a domestic matter?" The use of the word 'domestic' told Esme that Miss Jackson was party to at least some of the odd world that she lived in.

"Not domestic." she confirmed.

The House Mistress picked up the phone and dialled a number.

"That's an outside line." she said handing the phone to the girl. "I'll wait in my secretary's office. Take all the time you need."

Esme dialled her grandmother's number and heard her familiar economical response. "Hello!" Mrs Marsh gave very little away.

"Hello, Grandma. It's Esme."

"Hello to you, Esme. Is anything wrong? Is it domestic?"

"No. It is not domestic. I am in Miss Jackson's office. There is no-one else here and I have an outside line."

"Good girl. What's wrong?"

"One of Daddy's letters has been steamed open. I can't tell when."

"You are absolutely sure it has been tampered with? Have you opened it?"

"Yes to the first question." she said and she described the condition of the envelope. "No to the second, but I have it with me."

"Open it now and tell me what's in it."

Esme laid out the contents on the desk. "Note from Daddy and some stamps – Russian ones."

"Read what your father has written; see if they mention any other enclosures."

Esme did so and reported that there was no such mention.

"You've told nobody else?"

"No. Miss Jackson asked no questions but I would not have answered them."

There was a moment's silence on the line and then Esme's grandmother, with almost a hesitation in her voice, said. "Well done, Esme! It must be tough there on your own but I'm sure we've chosen what is best for you."

Esme was touched and hastened to say that she was enjoying the school and especially that she was making friends. At the thought of that, she said, "One of them was much struck by Mrs Treadwell's chocolate cake. Perhaps you could say so and give them my regards."

There was a chuckle from the other end of the line and Mrs Marsh said. "I'll let Mrs Treadwell deal with the cake. I'll deal with the letter – or rather, your father will." and then, most uncharacteristically, "You know we all miss you." She finished with a request that Esme leave the line open and ask Miss Jackson to come to the phone.

*** *** ***

Two days later, at the Stamp Collectors Club, two girls arrived late, bubbling and full of news. "Have you seen the new gardener? He's the bee's knees!"

Miss James brought them to order. "You are late!" she said, "Apologise, please" and, when the girls had done so, "This is the 'Stamp Collectors' Club'." she said. "Not the 'Discuss the Staff Club'. 'The bee's knees' may have the merit of being a neat rhyme but it is slang and young ladies avoid slang whenever possible and he is not a gardener but a groundsman."

They did return to the business of stamps. Esme, herself, was enjoying the fact that she was in demand in the Club because they had just discovered that she was able to tell them something, though not a great deal, about the writing on those stamps that did not use the Western alphabet. With the Greek stamps, she was able to provide a full translation and she was particularly good with the Russian ones. With the Arabic, Japanese and Chinese, she was able to say what the value of them was and something about the pictures.

In spite of Miss James' ticking off, the advent of a new male member of staff, especially a young one, was a matter of interest to most of the older girls and there was not much chat about stamps that day.

They called the new man, 'George'; not because that was his name and it was unlikely that any of them would have any cause to address him by name but just so they could refer to him easily. 'George had taken his coat off and rolled up his sleeves', 'George has been checking the fence behind the school buildings'. He had an attractive face and was clearly very fit. When addressed he was more likely to look down than make eye contact but his dark brown eyes held an intelligence that was at odds with his slowness of his speech. His face was tanned from working outside in all weathers, as were his hands. Like most horticultural workers, he wore the same garments at all times, whatever the weather, including a tweed jacket with bulging pockets. He did take his cap off when he was spoken to and this showed that he had a mop of dark hair and that the top of his head had escaped the sun. He was a topic of conversation and his activities were watched closely by the girls. One of the older girls expressed a wish that he would take his shirt off. This, in spite of the cool weather. He had a powerful build and his muscular and workmanlike hands wielded his tools almost as though they were weapons. Fulfilling his job seemed to involve moving around the grounds a great deal and in an apparently haphazard manner. Whatever his methods, there had been an improvement in the tidiness of the grounds even in the short period he had been working at the school. Some overgrown bushes on the edges of the paths and drives had been severely pruned.

Esme said nothing about him and she noticed that neither Rachel nor Deborah had yet to make any comment.

The older girls were still talking about him a week later. 'That George is a real swoony.' said one and, finally, there was a comment from down-to-earth Deborah.

"I wouldn't call him 'swoony'" she said. "Rugged perhaps but just an ordinary specimen of a young male. We don't get many of those."

Esme had seen him several times and he did look like a groundsman. He was certainly skilled in driving a mower. There were reports, however, that he spent a lot of time on the fences. Others were suspicious that he took every opportunity to watch the girls play hockey

CHAPTER 11

1st. August 1986

The next item in the ribboned file was a card headed, 'Lieutenant Castle's Tea Party' the word 'Lieutenant' was underlined. Written neatly below was a menu, listing cakes and scones and sandwiches. There were lots of cakes and several types of scones but only one variety of sandwiches – **SARDINE** – in proud capital letters. At the bottom of the menu was added, in a different hand, 'This time for four'.

Helena, speaking into the tape, was pleased that they had a name. She could find things out with names, especially if they were army names and with, in this instance, a rank. She was disappointed that it was also from the St. Ermengild's school and not earlier. Edgar pointed out that they were not really interested in Esme's childhood but his wife said she wanted it all.

"Who were the four do you think?"

"Well Lieutenant Castle for a start – and Esme. I suppose the other two have to count as a gap."

Helena spoke into the tape. She did speculate that 'tea' at a girls' boarding school would be a special treat, and it would be worth keeping the menu as a souvenir. She left open the question as to who Lieutenant Castle was and why he should be treating Esme and others to tea. Edgar suggested that since there were no tomato or cucumber sandwiches, the tea was probably not in the summer term. She set the menu to one side.

With a little cry of joy, she brought out the next object from the folder. It was an autograph-book; an unpretentious little booklet about six inches by four with a hard cover, papered to imitate leather. The pages were in various pastel colours and Esme had written her name inside the cover in neat capitals, ESME MARSH. On the next page there was a book-plate, this time with an owl, in black and white, standing on a book. There, she had given her full name, 'Esme Eleanor Marsh'.

Many of the entries were illustrated with little pictures or a line or two of verse. Some of these were childish; as were some of the written sentiments. A number of them showed talent. All had a measure of sincerity in their good wishes to 'Esme' – some to 'Esme Marsh'. Because some of the signatures had dates they were able to work out that Esme had collected the autographs over a period of several years; another sign of her tenacity.

There were a couple of entries from adults, the most striking was a picture of a girl in a traditional Polish dress – elaborate and detailed – not something that was dashed off in passing but a work of dedication. The artist had carefully coloured in the dress and given the girl a basket of flowers. He had written below it 'to my brightest pupil and, I hope, my friend. I would like to see you in my country wearing such a folk dress." It was signed Mosze Friedman. They could just decipher the signature.

Then there was a Latin tag from another of Esme's schoolteachers.

Some pages had multiple signatures. One such was headed 'St. Ermengild's School'. Another page had been divided, as it were, into bricks on what was labelled a WALL OF FRIENDSHIP.

Helena was delighted by the plethora of names, some of them carrying the writer's date of birth. Before she had finished rejoicing, she had to change the tape and label the full one. Her frustration with those contributors who wrote only their Christian names formed part of her recording. These would include the girls who were Esme's closest friends and it was not easy to find out something about somebody from fifty years ago with only their Christian name to go on.

Then, she had a break. She turned a page of the book to find a whole page devoted entirely to a clover leaf drawn large upon it. Each of the three leaflets held a signature. The first was Esme's own, Esme Eleanor Marsh. The two others were Rachel Castle and Deborah Wilson. Deborah's had 'Rah' written in brackets.

Underneath the drawing was written, in what they now recognised as Esme's hand, "The Trio".

She drew Edgar's attention to the entry.

"I think that's one gap filled." she said.

Edgar spoke carefully. "If you are happy that there are no assumptions there, we can speculate further. Esme, we know joined the school three years later than the others. Lieutenant Castle has taken the other two girls out to tea before and we now have an explanation for 'This time for four'. I reckon I'm good at this. It must be all those detective stories I read as a teenager. There is only jam on the scones, not strawberries. There are no cucumber or tomato sandwiches. We can date it either late in 1937 or early in 1938. Lieutenant Castle has just been promoted – hence the underlining of his rank – or perhaps has just joined – and is taking his sister and her friends out to tea. I don't think he is Rachel's father. Most Lieutenants would be promoted by the time they were old enough to have a teenage daughter. So he is probably Rachel's brother."

"And the colour of his eyes?" Helena stopped him in full flight. "Let's not get carried away and you still read detective stories."

Edgar, who had turned back to the autograph album, held his hand up in agreement.

"O.K.!" he said and, then. "Isn't 'Eleanor' a form of 'Helen'?"

"Well spotted. Eleanor was a family name but fashions change and Mum wanted something more up-to-date."

"I should think so too. I'd hate to call you Nora or Elie. 'Helena', my 'bright one', trips nicely over the tongue."

"You'll be giving me that line about 'the face that launched a thousand ships next'. I'm not fond of Helen of Troy – a self-centred piece of work."

CHAPTER 12

February 1938

"It's your brother that's 'swoony'" Deborah said. "When do we see him again?"

Rachel laughed. Her brother, an army officer, visited her occasionally at the school. When he came, he put on his best uniform at her request. She said it cheered up the other girls. Moreover, when he came he took Deborah and her out to tea at the village tea-shop. He was visiting shortly and Rachel now let the other two girls know.

"Hands off." she said, "He's more than spoken for. You only think he's 'swoony' – what an awful expression – because he buys you scones. As a matter of fact, he's coming this week-end. Salty says the three of us can miss games."

By now, Esme expected to be included in whatever Rachel and Deborah were doing but this was different. She had heard the two girls talking about Rachel's brother and she had kept very quiet but 'Salty says the three of us can miss games' removed the tiny worry that this was a treat that did not include her. Rachel saw that she wanted to ask questions and started to answer them before they were asked.

"Gerald, my brother, is eight years older than me. He is an army officer, a professional soldier as many of my family have been. That's where my scholarship comes from: 'for the education of the children of army officers'. He has just been promoted from second to first lieutenant. He occasionally uses some of his leave to come here on a visit – just half a day but we make the most of it. You know Mrs Whinstanley at the shop and her normal teas. Gerald has her eating out of his hand and lets her know that he's coming in advance. She puts on a special tea for him and us. I've told him that you will be with us, so they'll have to set an extra place. When he first arrives, he and I will find somewhere to be together and alone. We'll do the brother-sister thing; talking about the family, making sure everything is all right. Because he's older, he thinks he's responsible for me and warns me about boyfriends. I'm afraid that I'm a little naughty and pretend to be shocked. With that out of the way, we'll join you for tea."

"Spoken for?" Esme was not sure what Rachel had meant.

"Gerald is married. He has a young son, a darling three-year-old called Charlie. Betty, his wife is lovely and sends us boxes of chocolates when he comes. I think that that is to re-assure us that she also thinks that he should come here sometimes – but, obviously, he can't spend too long with me. Very occasionally, she brings Charlie."

When Gerald arrived, Deborah and Esme made their way to the village tea-shop on their own. They were welcomed by Mrs. Whinstanley herself. Her establishment was more than just a tea-shop. It sold groceries and sweets. It even sold little packets of stamps. Indeed, it sold anything that might tempt the girls at the school to part with their pocket money. The girls called it 'the Saturday Shop'.

The three friends were favourites of Mrs Whinstanley in

any case but doubly welcome because Gerald Castle was coming. She showed Esme and Deborah to a table that was set for four in the window and was laden with scones and cakes.

"I'll put the kettle on and get some sandwiches." she said and went into the kitchen. Esme was impressed by Deborah's discipline; she had made no move to start on the scones before the others appeared. She was not asked to restrain herself for long. Before the kettle had boiled, Rachel and her brother came through the door.

Gerald Castle may not have been 'swoony' but he was a well set up young man and his uniform enhanced his good looks. He had the same dark colouring as Rachel and some of her style. His movements were emphatic rather than graceful like his sister's. He was clearly very fond of her and wanted to meet her latest friend. He showed a maturity befitting a family man and something of the authority of an army officer. Esme, sensitive to such things, thought she saw that he was deeply worried about something. She saw also that he was determined that his concerns would not interfere with this treat. She assumed that they were to do with the threat of war.

"Are your family well?" she asked, hoping that he had no problems there.

He smiled warmly at her and said they were fine. He smiled even more warmly at Deborah as she sat with her hands firmly in her lap. This was clearly a ritual and part of his visit. His first action was to take from a small bag that he was carrying, three boxes of chocolate – one each for the girls. "Betty hopes you like chocolates too." he said to Esme. "She knows that if you don't Deborah will help you eat them." This earned him the approval of both girls and he returned to the ritual.

"Will you pour the tea, please Miss Wilson." he asked and the two of them play-acted a formal tea-party. Esme, who had wondered if she was really welcome, was addressed as Miss Marsh and there was a great deal made of the passing of the tea-cups and the offering of cake. The formality only descended into mirth when Deborah grabbed her first scone. Esme, diffident at first, was quickly caught up in the mutual enjoyment. Gerald, in the midst of the racket, spoke quietly to her and said how pleased he was that Rachel had found another nice friend. If she had felt part of the trio before, this confirmed her belief that she belonged – belonged also to the Castle family. She knew she was lucky to have Stella as an older sister but how nice it would be to have an older brother as well.

They had eaten almost all the scones and Deborah and Rachel headed for the kitchen. They said they were taking the empty plates and refilling the hot water jug but the move left Esme alone with Rachel's brother.

"They're not very subtle, are they?" Gerald's immediate understanding enhanced Esme's thoughts about having an elder brother.

"If it were a scene from Jane Austen, that ploy would have been a mother making sure a suitor was alone with her daughter. But they want you to give me the once over. I'm not sure why."

Gerald was happy to answer. "You're just as Rachel described. The reason is that they are proud of you and they want me to see why they are."

Esme, from the moment they had met, had wanted the esteem of the two girls but somehow that had become less important than their friendship. That Rachel's brother said they were proud of her was a bonus but it was the friendship that was most important. The two were not allowed much time for their tête-à-tête. Gerald had to get back to camp but he repeated how pleased he was that his sister had made friends with her. Once more she felt as though she belonged.

She watched Rachel walk with her brother back to the school and would have felt even more accepted if she could have heard their conversation.

"Do you like her?"

"Yes, I do. I said I was pleased and I meant it. She is a delight."

"But?"

"But me no buts! What do you mean?"

"You have other thoughts about her. Tell me!"

"I may be wrong but I think she's vulnerable. She needs to be liked, even to be loved. You say her mother died when she was very young and her father is often away. I think your friendship and Rah's have just come in time."

CHAPTER 13

2nd. August 1986

Helena and Edgar were more eager than ever the next day to return to the suitcase and Helena's great-aunt. They seemed to be getting places and Bill had phoned to say he had some information for them.

"What else have you got from the autograph album?" Helena had done some work on her own without getting very far. She was hoping for something from Edgar.

"Well, she's numbered the pages but I'm afraid the chronology isn't helpful. The book spans more than five years from when she was about ten to about when she was sixteen or more. But the dates are mostly scattered randomly. It may help if I make a list the names and, where they are given, the dates. I'll do that on the computer and then we can access them readily. This is not a celebrity autograph album. Those who have written in it seem to be mostly friends from school." Edgar was following orders. Speculation had to be kept to the minimum.

"But one or two adults have contributed."

"I noticed that. A couple of school teachers; one with a line in Latin. Bill has come up with a curious point. The Polish teacher, remember we had his name, Mosze Friedman, died in a concentration camp just before the end of the war. He was a Jew and returned to his country to try and rescue his wife. The group of resistance fighters who helped him was betrayed to the Germans and he was captured. Bill says we were lucky to get this information but one of his compatriots, who was with him in the concentration camp, had written an account of life in the camp. This man had survived the experience and the account was published. In the book he described how Friedman had tried to escape and had been shot. He wrote that Friedman had only one leg and had to use a crutch. We have a remarkable man here. It was when he was in the RAF, flying reconnaissance, that he lost his leg."

Edgar hesitated but he thought that he had better confess.

"I'd got the impression from the entry in the autograph album that Mosze Friedman was a little more than a youth. His reference to Esme as 'my friend' sounded almost as though he was attracted to her. Clearly I got that wrong. I'm glad of that. We don't want any disreputable relationships between a pupil and a teacher."

"That comes of making assumptions. Such misdemeanours were not likely at St. Ermengild's. They would see any male working there as a threat and they would require impeccable references. Mosze Friedman would have been cleared by the Board of Governors. In this case, he would also have been cleared by Esme's father's Department. You can also be sure that the House Mistress kept an eye on him."

At that moment, they were interrupted by the door bell. It was a messenger with a thick envelope from Bill. They assumed this was the information he had promised and they opened the package eagerly.

It held a wad of papers, photocopies of the transcript of a court proceedings. Fortunately, it had a covering letter from Bill.

"Dear Researchers, Helena's great grandfather, Sir Reginald Marsh, as he became, was one powerful operator and he employed some pretty smart lawyers. I have read the whole transcript of the trial which will be a classic in espionage literature. You can read it yourself, of course, but here is the gist.

Two spies were accused of sending plans of an aeroplane factory to the Russians. I think this was the easiest thing to prove with as little fuss as possible. As I think I said earlier, they were found guilty and served a term in prison.

What you are interested in is that one of the spies was actually employed by Marsh's department as a researcher and may have done some of the work on getting Esme cleared for security. His lawyers kept trying to bring some reference to her into open court. You will not be able to see that because Sir Reginald's lawyers kept insisting that the actual questions they asked had nothing to do with the trial and that they should be 'struck from the record'. I talked to an old friend who reported the case as best he could. That was with difficulty because, if you remember, the prosecution was 'held in camera'. He said that the 'strike that from the record.' entries were usually about Esme.

Finally, the judge got shirty and threatened that

he would hold the defence lawyers in contempt of court if they continued.

Nice to see a dad defending his daughter. I hope that helps.

Bill

Helena read the letter first and then handed it to Edgar who was skipping through the transcript. He put the court proceedings down with relief and accepted Bill's summary with mental thanks.

"Does it help?" he asked when he had finished

"Yes, I think it does. I never believed the gossip. It was never likely that this school-girl would be capable of fooling an enemy agent to the extent that he would tell her his secrets. This makes it less likely still. No Russian spy is going to be seduced by somebody they are actually investigating.

CHAPTER 14

February 1939

Esme's extra language lessons meant that for part of the week she was separated from her friends but they had studies of their own to pursue. Rachel and, especially, Deborah did ask her about the new teacher.

St. Ermengild's, as their brochure promised, employed extra staff for their especially talented pupils. For Esme they had been asked, in addition to the languages that she was nearly fluent in, for a teacher of Russian and Polish.

Mosze Friedman, the man they appointed had a history of his own. Some this history Esme knew but some he did not want to talk about. Esme was the last person to press him to do so. Mosze was Polish and his English was correct if a little formal. He was, however, completely fluent in Russian. Eight years ago he had come to England to train as a schoolteacher. When he was asked why, he pointed out that English was the most useful of languages to learn. If he trained in Britain he could teach virtually anywhere. He did not add that, as a Jew, he felt the growing anti-Semitism not only in Germany but also in his own country.

He took his qualifications back to Poland. There was a good reason for this move for there was a girl, Sophia. His first action on returning to his own country was to ask her to marry him and, yes she would. This did not work out as well as he had hoped. Within weeks, her mother had died and Sophia had to take on the role of full-time carer for her father. This was why he had left his wife in Poland and sought for work in England. She could not go out to work and his salary as a school teacher was not enough to support the three of them. Especially they found difficulty in affording the drugs her father needed. He was dying of cancer but clung to a life of pain.

The young couple had sat through many an hour of discussion about their problems in their small apartment and even then they left the door open to his room, in case he needed help.

Finally, they had decided that Mosze should return to Britain. He could earn more money there, live cheaply and send most of his salary home.

Events had over-taken him. He had been in Britain when the war broke out and his wife was still in Poland. He had volunteered, together with many of his compatriots, for the armed forces.

As a youth, he had spent much time at the local air-field and, recognising his enthusiasm, they had taught him to fly. The Recruiting Office seized upon this detail and sent him to the RAF. They gave him a short course and before he knew what he had let himself in for, they had sent him up in a reconnaissance aircraft. Friedman was a good pilot and survived more than one encounter with enemy fighters. His skill did not allow him to escape when he was attacked from a superior altitude and his plane crashed. Fortunately this was in allied-held territory. He was able to bail out but his right leg was smashed just below the knee.

His appointment as Esme's teacher at St. Ermengild's was greeted by some of the girls with awe. Not only was he handsome but he was also a war-hero. He had the added glamour that he had been so badly wounded that he had to use a crutch. More than one of them attempted to strike up an acquaintance with him but he only came into the school three sessions every week. Esme was his only pupil.

He had been there for a few weeks when he appeared one day with an artificial leg. He retained his crutch and struggled desperately to hobble about.

He had come in to give Esme her lesson but it was clear that the new leg was giving him some pain. After ten minutes, Esme took charge and insisted that they cut the lesson short. After a token protest, he agreed.

So Esme was early to the spot where the three friends met behind the pavilion. Deborah, who was on a diet, had brought some cake. Her method of dieting was to allow the others larger than usual chunks of it.

"This new leg, tell us about it." she asked. Deborah always wanted to know things and, since Rachel was also interested, Esme answered.

"He tried to tell me about in Polish." she said. "He really is a dedicated teacher. I couldn't concentrate because I was so worried about it. He switched to English. It's a sort of scaffold. There is a padding that cushions the knee, light-weight steel rods down to a shoe that is made so that it matches the other one but adapted to take the steel rods. His trousers are made especially to fit easily over the frame-work. He pulled his trouser leg up to show me. That was most peculiar, you could see straight through what would have been his leg. A bit like 'The Invisible Man'."

"You are fond of him, aren't you?" Rachel asked the question without emphasis. She could hear her brother's advice that Esme was vulnerable and needed to be looked after. She didn't entirely agree. She thought that her friend had integrity and proper feelings. Esme was not wayward, her feet were firmly on the ground. On the other hand, Gerald was a man and he may see things that she did not. It would do no harm to ask a few questions.

"Of course I am." said Esme, as though it were a silly question. "Who could not be? He teaches me the Polish and Russian nursery rhymes and fairy stories because the words are simple but he enjoys them himself, chortling over the Polish equivalent of Jack and the Beanstalk but he leaves out the frightening bits. He tells Jewish jokes in Polish and expects me to laugh."

Now, Rachel was worried. She broke into Esme's exposition and driven by her brother's advice faced what she thought was the problem head on.

"Have you got a crush on him?"

Esme stopped and took a good look at her friend. This was an absurd suggestion but it came from Rachel, who was not absurd. So instead of dismissing it out of hand, she attempted a reasoned reply.

"I'm not sure what a crush is." she said. "I admire him greatly, not only because of his bravery and the way he tries to ignore his injury but also because he is a fine teacher. He makes me laugh and sometimes, when he is sad, I grieve for him. But I have no sexual feelings for him. If I did there would be no danger. He's like a knight of the round table; concerned only with chivalry. He tells me the stories of his people and chooses the ones where the strong are protecting the weak. All the time he is thinking of his wife and he does so with great fear."

"So much for my brother." thought Rachel.

To Esme, she said, "Sorry. Some of that was because I heard two girls being smutty about you and him. Some was because of Gerald. He said he thought you were vulnerable and I was to take care of you." She said nothing about how he thought that she needed love.

Esme positively grinned. "Men!" she said. "What do they know?" but once more she felt part of Rachel's family.

It was only a few weeks after this that master and pupil agreed that teaching of the two languages could provide no further progress; that Esme needed only to practice.

Nonetheless, Friedman arrived at the next scheduled lesson to tell the school and Esme that his father-in-law had died. He was determined to travel to Poland, he did not say how and Esme, whose life was entangled in secrets, did not ask. He did congratulate her on the progress in her work on the two languages and said once more that there was nothing else he could teach her. All she had to do now was to read widely in both. "Try Tolstoy." he said, "You could start with 'Tales for Children' before tackling 'War and Peace'"

She asked him about his leg and he said he thought it would be up to it. It had been much better since they had modified the padding on the knee. Then there was an emotional good-bye with Friedman kissing her on both cheeks and saying that that was how his people did it

CHAPTER 15

3rd August 1986.

Helena and Edgar, with the anxiety about Esme removed, had both had an untroubled night. They woke on that Sunday together but Helena rolled over and went back to sleep. Edgar took the opportunity to catch up on work that he had neglected in the pursuit of Esme Marsh. He also put together the makings of a full English breakfast and then he went for a walk.

The last few days had left little time for such exercise and it was a clear quiet day. His thoughts were not of Helena's distant relative but of Helena herself. Her university friends had wondered why she had taken up with him when she could have chosen from a dozen of her high-flying fellow students. He had never fully understood why himself. It was when he was just setting out on his career as a photographer and working long hours to build up his business. He needed better equipment and it was expensive so he had to plough back into his shop and studio any money that he could spare. His social life was non-existent.

They had met when he was photographing an end-of-term ball. Those attending it; the ladies in their evening gowns and the men in dinner jackets wanted a record of how they looked that night. Many of them had hired their evening dress and often they did not fit all that well. Edgar worked hard to angle the shots that showed them to best advantage. Sometimes this required tact, especially with those of the men who had already had too much to drink. It was not a job he liked but it was both lucrative and good advertising. When they saw the results, the revellers would be pleased. Edgar was cynical enough to realise that they would think that they looked like that naturally and would give the photographer no credit but if they were asked who took the photographs, his name was stamped on the back of them.

One of the girls, a slight blonde in the simplest of black dresses, was so naturally photogenic that he took several shots, asking her to pose in slightly different ways. She gave him a smile that was the high point of the whole session.

Edgar left the ball as soon as the dance started to deteriorate. Nobody wanted a photograph of themselves drunk or misbehaving He went back to his shop and started the work on the photographs. The sooner he produced them, the more prints he would sell. Most of the students would not realise that developing and printing took time and Edgar was not one to lose trade through tardiness.

The following morning he was back in his work-shop hanging some prints up to dry – several of them of the girl in the black dress. He heard the shop bell ring and called out "I'll be with you!" and stood back to look at his work. "That was a very attractive girl." was the thought in his mind when he heard an amused cough from the doorway. There she was, the very same girl. He buried his head in his hands. All he could manage at first was, "How embarrassing!"

When she said nothing, he had time to recover.

"All your fault." he said, "You smiled at me."

She continued to do so now and took a look around the room.

"You're good at this aren't you?" she said.

"First she smiles at me and then she flatters me." Edgar was no longer embarrassed. It seemed the most natural thing in the world to talk to this girl.

"Are you busy at the moment?" he asked. "I just need five minutes to sort this job out. We could go for coffee!"

"Can't you make it here?"

"This is one fast worker. First she smiles and then she pitches a line and, before you know where you are, she's inviting you in for coffee. There are the makings in the kitchen. Would you like to put the kettle on?"

They had then exchanged names in a formal fashion; Edgar Mason, which she knew because his name was everywhere, met Helena Burroughs and they were sitting down and drinking their coffee before Edgar remembered that she had come into the shop as a customer.

"I should be asking you what I can do to help. Presumably you are here for a reason."

Helena knew that what she was doing was absurd but she had decided on this course of action and she would stick to it. She responded, speaking quickly and saying, she knew, too much.

"You said it yourself. I'm a fast worker. Well, in this instance, I am. I asked where I could order the photographs and they said you worked and lived here. I have nearly finished my university career. There's just the ordeal of a *viva* and it is all over. I went last night not only because it is the done thing but because I was looking for a man who would interest me. For the last three years I've been disappointed. I've met some lovely people, some of them have become great friends but I wanted something different. Last night I reached a state of despair. Of all the men there, you were the only one I found interesting. This came to me when I woke up this morning. Edgar you are my last chance."

"Interesting? All I was doing was taking photographs. You're not talking 'love at first sight' are you?"

"I'm afraid not! Though that would be convenient. No! Not even infatuation just a real contact with a man. I've made such contact with lots of women – no, that came out wrong but I don't know how to put it. I'm friends with lots of my fellow students. I'm interested in some of the women but none of the men. You were not just taking photographs; you were manipulating those people, even the arrogant ones and the drunks and they did not know it. You did it with consummate skill and with apparent consideration for them. One of the things that interested me was whether that was genuine consideration."

Edgar glanced at his watch.

"Look at this photograph." he said in what seemed a complete non-sequiter. He was pointing to one of Helena. "It needs a spot of bright colour there just below the collar bone." He turned to her. "Didn't he give you an orchid or something? I thought that was what you were supposed to; but what do I know? I haven't taken a girl out in donkey's years."

He then returned to her question. The diversion, Helena realised was one of the things that made him interesting. When he had been taking the photographs, he had kept up a patter that included instructions to his subjects. "Look up!" he would say and then. "There are low flying pigs!" "I want you to think of your girl friend, not your teddy bear. Sorry did I put my foot in it?"

"Much of the manipulation you are talking about stems from professional expertise." he said. "But I think my consideration generally is genuine. I take much better photographs of people if I can understand something of their personality. That's what got me involved. You can't take a honest photograph of someone unless you see them as an individual. For you, consideration is the wrong word. When you came into the shop I was looking at the photographs I took of you and asking why I took so many. I thought at first that it was just because you were a pretty girl. Then I realised there was more to it than that and wondered why I had not done anything about it, especially in view of the smile. I would like to do something about it now but you must give me a couple of hours to get this work done."

"Can I stay and help?"

"Well, you can't help. I'll work much faster on my own but I'd love you to stay if you could keep out of the way. We can talk some of the time and that seems to me to be a good idea. This is a situation in which I have no expertise and there are times when I need to concentrate. Perhaps you can tell me about yourself. I need to know. When I've done, I'll do the same for you and you can decide if I'm interesting enough for us to meet again."

Helena said nothing. This was the sort of response that she had hoped for. Edgar Mason's behaviour, she decided, would never lack in courtesy but always be unexpected. On the other hand, it was exactly what was needed. She was already sure that he was interesting enough for them to meet again. There was no additional spark as yet. That, she thought, was just as well given the circumstances. She had thrown herself at his head. She could not blame him if he took advantage of that. She would be disappointed if he did but would she let him? How did she know that he would not?

She sat down in a corner and told him that her degree was in History, that she had specialised in research techniques and, in response to one of his few questions, that she expected to get a good degree. He showed more interest when she said that she had done some work-experience in a firm of solicitors and they were now employing her on a piece-work basis for doing their research. She made some more coffee and, after investigating the mug he had used but not washed up, poured him a cup. He was so deep in what he was doing that she was surprised when, tasting the result, he raised his hand in thanks.

He buried himself back in his work and she investigated his tiny kitchen. There were eggs there and they looked to be quality ones and there were field mushrooms – had he gathered them himself? There was fresh salad and olive oil and white wine vinegar. Was there any bread? She could not find any and there was only a pathetic crust of cheese.

"I'll be about twenty minutes." she said as she left through the shop and, on her return, there followed the first of a thousand impromptu meals supporting one or the other, sometimes both of them as they worked. Over this lunch, he told her something of himself; a brief outline of his life. How he had left school at sixteen in spite of being moderately successful in his exams and tried a number of unsatisfactory jobs. The photography he explained, in response to a question, had been started at school and then was mostly about the chemical reactions. It really took off in a dentist's waiting room where there was, amongst the magazines, a thin book illustrating the black-and-white work of a number of photographers. The local library was his next stop where he discovered Man Ray and, above all, Cartier Bresson. This man's work gave him a new insight into the character of other people. He had never looked back. Since then he had been turning his inspiration into a business. He wanted to be independent so he had set out on a plan that involved hard work for long hours.

Then, with another of his asides, he said "I'm glad you found me interesting. At the moment I don't know how I feel about you. You confuse me."

As she said much later, "You could have sex with a man who was not interesting but you could only live with someone who was.

All that he remembered of his part in this meetings went through his mind, not for the first time, as he strode along the river bank, greeting the usual dog-walkers with mutual congratulations about the weather – as though each of them was personally responsible for it. He gathered a bunch of flowers, a single stem of each of the common ones: Toadflax, Hawk's-beard, Vetch, Clover and White Campion. They probably sent all the wrong messages in the language of love. He was only concerned that they brought something of his walk into the house. Something for Helena to enjoy.

By the time he returned, she was already grilling the

sausages. Rarely did they indulge in such a breakfast and Edgar insisted that they take their time over it to get the full enjoyment.

"What's a nosegay?" he asked, presenting her with his collection of flowers.

"Off hand, it is a bunch of flowers, like this."

"So what does the word mean?" He reached for a dictionary. "Gay." he read. "'something pretty – Middle English for the nose' synonym 'Bouquet'. That would be derived from the French, I suppose. I'll call them 'nosegays' in future."

Helena was plating the breakfasts. They looked delicious.

"Am I still 'interesting'?" he asked.

"You've been thinking again." she replied. "I've told you about that before. As for still being interesting; when you stop interesting me, I'll let you know."

Neither the breakfast nor the nostalgia prevented them returning to the autograph album with their coffee.

"What about the sketch of the girl in the swimming costume. Is that Esme?"

The sketch he referred to was of a young girl. She was drawn in pen and ink. The artist had stood behind her. She was at the end of a diving board which stood not over a swimming bath but over a wide stretch of water with mountains rising the other side of it. It was drawn with skill and economy. The girl, her hair cut in the ubiquitous pudding-basin style, wore a one-piece costume. She faced the water as a challenge to overcome and be enjoyed and the stance was very like that of the girl in the photograph they had discussed earlier. Neither Helena nor Edgar had any

113

doubt that this was the same person. Helena had asked the question only for form's sake.

She was, however, no longer a little girl but on the threshold of puberty. The sketch was signed only with almost illegible initials. Perhaps the first letter was 'R'. Some friend had used her artistic skills to create an enduring tribute.

"That's Esme all right." Edgar defied caution. "That girl faced the world with courage and optimism even if it was from an insecure base and the artist has said just that." He paused and looked at the sketch again. "And it wasn't drawn by a boy. Esme is about to blossom. If this artist had been a boy, he would have shown that in sensual terms."

"Edgar, stop it. You're getting carried away again."

"O.K. but it was certainly drawn by someone who knew her well. Could those initials not be 'R something' but simply 'Rah'

Helena, uncharacteristically, turned back to the ribboned file. "She could certainly swim." she said. "Here are her certificates."

Helena had got something before 1937 – if only two years before. The certificates, to her relief, were dated. The first one was issued by 'Godstone's School for Girls' – and asserted that Miss Esme Marsh had swum One Width (10 yds.) and was dated the 10th September 1934.

Edgar listened with admiration as Helena read the details of the others into her tape. Next, young Esme had swum a Length (30 yds.) and by the twenty fifth of the month she had swum 'Ten Lengths'. All signed by the 'Mistress in Charge of Swimming'.

There was a break until the following May. Helena

recorded this and surmised that the swimming bath was open air and not heated. In May, Esme went on increasing her range and one of the certificates recorded the time rather than the distance.

"This slip of a girl swam for an hour?" Edgar queried what Helena had read.

"Indeed, she did and now listen to this!" and she went on to the Life-Saving Certificates. These were issued not by the school but by an institution and, by July, Esme was awarded a 'gold' medal. It was a sort of badge in a yellow metal and encased in a yellow box.

Helena and Edgar grinned at each other. Their reconstruction of the life of Helena's great-aunt was providing some heart-warming facts.

It was with this feeling that Helena had moved on. Immediately she found a sketch that was almost certainly drawn by the person who had done the one in the autograph album. This was on a larger sheet of paper and was of a pool of water surrounded by steep crags but with a path leading down to it. At the water's edge was a tablecloth spread with cakes and other schoolgirl delights.

"Those girls had great fun." she said.

She was looking now at the papers that had been together with the certificates. More evidence that the suitcase had been packed in haste. There were what looked to be some letters.

She spoke, once more, into the microphone. "A bunch of letter writing paper of different sorts, one of them a blue air-mail letter. I'll start with two sheets of a cream inlaid writing paper folded once as though to have fitted into an envelope."

She unfolded one and just a glance was enough. She gave a little crow of delight.

In passing, Edgar noted that the tape-recorder was still on. Later he would rescue that recording. It was a moment of great charm.

"It's a letter from my Grandmother." she said. "Listen" and Edgar hoped that the recording would be good enough to show the delight in her voice.

Dear Esme,

Daddy may have told you already. I have become engaged.

There, I've written it down in black and white. You are the first person, apart from Daddy, that I've told. The words on the paper are magic enough but nothing to the feelings inside me.

My husband-to-be is called Edward Burroughs. 'Ted' to you, and to me in public. One day I might tell you what I call him in private.

You know how we used to talk about our future husbands as knights in shining armour. Edward, to the outside world, is no such knight. To me, he does all that we wondered not with a sword but with his understanding of what I need. He's not handsome, indeed he looks very ordinary, nor is he dashing, except to me.

I could go on like this for pages but you'll want the prosaic details. He is older than me and he works for Daddy. Which means he will not need to be investigated. He makes me feel special and protected.

Daddy approves of him in an odd way. I think he saw me being carried away by somebody more romantic. His comment when I told him was a sort of rumble. "Sound man, Burroughs!" he said. I think I can endorse that description.

No, he is not a secret agent or anything like that. He's an academic, an adviser on European History, especially the Soviets. He wanted to speak to Daddy first before proposing and he is old-fashioned like that. He said he should have got my father's permission to address me but he couldn't wait any longer before asking me.

Why am I in love with him? I don't think there is a why question about this. He makes me laugh. He makes me feel special – I've written that already but it is worth repeating. On each of the several times we met, apparently by chance but I think he must have contrived some of them, we talked as though we had known each other for ever.

Daddy says the sooner the better for the wedding. I think this is because of the situation in Europe. Ted agrees with him. He goes very quiet when the subject comes up. Somehow, his learning and his emotions come together to give him a measure of inflexible resolution. I know, for certain that he will want to be involved in the conflict that is almost upon us. It frightens me a little but this is the man I love.

I trust that sometime in the future, you too will meet such a man.

Love, Stella.

There were tears in Helena's eyes as she put the letter down and she attempted the commonplace when she spoke again.

"The family photographs and the impression I had of my grandfather were of a nondescript man. He had enough hair to escape being called bald and he was rather stout. He was a very gentle man and kept a biscuit barrel especially for me."

Her attempt to avoid the dramatic did not last long.

"Nothing about him suggested the 'inflexible resolution' that my grandmother writes of here." she said. "But he served in the war in the red berets. He parachuted into the Netherlands in 1940, fought in Egypt and was amongst the first to land behind the enemy lines on D-day. He was also at Arnhem, where he lost an arm."

She held her hand out to her husband and he passed her the handkerchief she was asking for. She touched her eyes with it and then blew her nose in an unladylike fashion.

"I remember that he would cuddle me with only one arm. Nothing could have been more comfortable."

Edgar wondered how Helena would describe her feelings for him in such a letter. While he was still wondering she brought his handkerchief across to him and pretended that she was going to give it back. He pulled a face and she reached her other hand to the back of his neck and pulled his head down to her so that she could kiss him.

"I'm with Stella." she said. "I have found my man and he has survived the first rapture – and more so as the years go by."

"And you've lost your cool." he said, enjoying the embrace. "You haven't recorded any date or address."

118

"It's from Stella's London flat. No date on the letter but since we know he was in the Netherlands in 1940, it will be just before the war.

CHAPTER 16

April 1939

Not everything at St. Ermengild's suited the newcomer. There was one thing in particular that made her miserable but she was prepared to put up with it throughout the Michaelmas and indeed into the, curiously named, Spring Term. At this school, as at Godstone's, they insisted she play games every Wednesday and Saturday afternoon. Sometimes, they played tennis on the hard courts but mostly it was hockey or lacrosse. Some girls who were averse to these activities attempted to be excused, usually through pretended injuries or illnesses. They seldom succeeded in outwitting the school matron. Esme would not make such an attempt. In a sense, she thought it unfair that, enjoying so much of the school as she did, that she should reject something that was part of it.

Esme was no good at games. She lacked eye-and-hand co-ordination. She disliked running. Much of any game that she was playing, she stood about and froze. Deborah claimed that Esme, when asked what she was doing standing about, replied that she was redesigning the goal-posts.

Worst of all were the chilblains. Her hands and, especially, her feet were a constant source of irritation and of pain. After one particularly painful episode, she resolved to act. She shared her resolution with Rachel and Deborah; with

Deborah she was almost apologetic. Deborah was good at all games and enjoyed them thoroughly. Rachel, almost without effort, was competent but uninterested.

It was on one Thursday morning, after a particularly unpleasant afternoon on the previous day, that she announced to them, with some hesitation, "I'm going to ask Miss Jackson if I can do something else instead of hockey." She had scarcely managed to get to sleep the night before and she looked it.

"Such as?" Rachel's interest was aroused.

"Well, swimming, for a start, we have a perfectly respectable loch we could use." and as she spoke about her idea, she became bolder. "Then rambling. That's a popular outdoor activity and there are lots of places we could walk."

The other two girls listened with interest. They had been brought up to regard sport as 'games' and as team games at that. They were supposed to provide valuable exercise at the same time as encouraging the team spirit – part of their education. There was a pause and Esme, thinking that perhaps she had offended them, asked diffidently, "What do you think?"

It was Deborah who responded.

"Worth a try. We can't have you miserable twice a week into the foreseeable future. I'll do it. I think I've got an argument that Jack might listen to."

"We'll do it together." Rachel said quietly and then, "Tell us about the swimming. I detected enthusiasm there."

Esme nodded. Not much got past her two friends and she knew that they would not see her as boasting if she told them about her certificates. She took them from her suitcase and showed them to the others.

"These life-saving qualifications give you what you might call 'authority'." said Deborah. "I doubt if even Miss Cassel has reached that level." Miss Cassel was their formidable P.E. teacher, whose office was hung with team photographs and certificates of her prowess in all sorts of sports

So the three girls presented themselves to their House Mistress. They had planned their campaign and metaphorically, as well as actually, smartened themselves up. They knocked on her door at the time set aside for private study; a time when Miss Jackson made herself available to her charges.

She let the girls into her room and retreated behind her desk. Any of these three was capable of adding extra interest to her life. The three of them together, especially, as now, on their best behaviour, boded something out of the ordinary. She did note that Esme was not looking her usual sparkling self and wondered what was wrong. She could see that they were nervous; which was not normally the case. She made them sit down, not only to make them feel more relaxed but also so that they did not loom over her. The chairs in her room were deep and it was difficult to be other than peaceable when sitting in them.

"Go ahead." she said. "Who is going to speak for you?"

"Esme has an idea!" said Deborah. "But we decided that, from her, it would be special pleading. I think its a good idea, so I'm going to present it for her."

"And Rachel; just offering moral support?"

"Not entirely!" Rachel answered for herself and did so with her usual composure and precision. "Something has to be done about Esme. This idea may serve the purpose. I am indifferent to whether you accept it or not but it does seem to have great merits."

"And the idea?"

"That you extend the range of activities on games afternoons." Deborah had practised this phraseology.

"That's a broad brush. What sort of activities?"

"We've got swimming and rambling so far but there are other tentative possibilities."

The House Mistress directed the next question at Esme.

"The idea comes from you; why do you think it is necessary?"

The girl gathered herself together. She had rehearsed this before-hand and it was important to her not only to achieve the change but not to be seen as a whinger.

"I know I am not very good at, for example, hockey, but I'm not getting any better. I let the others down and sometimes I'm miserable. At the moment, however, all I can think about are the chilblains."

Somehow, she knew that this perhaps banal aspect had scorned a point. Was Jack a fellow sufferer? Had her schooldays been made miserable in the same way?

Miss Jackson turned to Deborah.

"You are one of our best athletes." she said. "I expect that you have got something to say for this notion that has nothing to do with supporting Esme. Let us hear it."

Deborah had rehearsed her little speech. She even had some notes to help her.

"First of all there is the variety. You have taught us that we cannot meaningfully choose unless we have a range of things to choose from."

She looked up, Miss Jackson raised her eyebrows. Perhaps she had taught these girls too well.

"Go on!"

"Then there is something I have noticed myself. Esme is not alone in disliking 'games' and there is resentment, not only from those that feel that way at being made to take part but, in turn, the rest of us resent that we have to play with them. It can't be good for the school to have pupils resenting one of the school's activities and each other. Finally, but I've only just thought of this, one of the reasons we play games is to develop 'a healthy mind in a healthy body'. I don't think Esme's chilblains are very healthy."

The two other girls were looking at their friend with respect. This was not their everyday Deborah. Perhaps for the first time, she had used her analytical talents to their potential.

Miss Jackson was also impressed. She asked. "Why swimming?" She was looking at Esme but, again, Deborah cut in. "Esme is very good at swimming. I know that one should work at the things one is bad at but she is wasting a valuable talent."

"Very good? How good?"

Rachel had anticipated this question and, without letting Esme know, she had gathered up her certificates. Now, without saying anything, she handed them to the House Mistress. A brief glance was enough for Miss Jackson and she handed them back.

The girls waited to see if their House Mistress was cross.

"I will have to think about this." she said. "I'll need to speak to the headmistress." Then she turned to Esme. "Take those chilblains to Matron. I think she may have something that will help. You are excused games until they heal."

Much relieved with this outcome, the girls left.

Esme, still nervous, broke the silence as they walked down the corridor.

"That was a great quotation you found; 'a healthy mind in a healthy body'. The original was written over two thousand years ago. The Latin is *Mens sana in corpore sano*. 'Healthy' is a sloppy translation. More correct would have been 'sound'. I suppose you couldn't refer to my chilblains as 'unsound'"

"Swot!" said Deborah.

The school accepted the arguments put forward by the three girls. Miss Salway greeted it with enthusiasm. Her constant worry was that she was teaching her pupils, who were the future, within a system that was perpetuated by those who had succeeded in yesterday's education. Her staff were all fine scholars but they had a vested interest in the way they had been taught. Here was an opportunity to modify their curriculum. The school would not lose very much by not insisting on team games for everybody. There would always be those, like Deborah who would enjoy them. It might gain a great deal by widening its outlook.

Swimming was one activity that would be popular and, perhaps, other water sports like canoeing. She was pleased that the girls had suggested rambling which she herself enjoyed. She went further and introduced an idea that she had kept to herself previously as being too experimental. She allowed the senior girls, on one afternoon every month freedom to walk in the hills. Their route had to be approved and they had to have a party of at least three. "One to stay with the body and one to go for help" was what she told her pupils who were much impressed.

CHAPTER 17

4th August 1986

Helena and Edgar were almost resentful of the time that they had to spend on things other than the suitcase. They did have their own businesses to run and their own lives to live. Some time before, Edgar has bought two tickets for a performance of Shakespeare's 'As You Like It' and they had been looking forward to an evening out together.

On such occasions, they pretended that they were a courting couple. A harmless piece of fun, it allowed for either of them to introduce a new element into the evening's entertainment. Each of them would dress smartly for the occasion to impress the other and they would do so separately from each other. This usually lent itself to a certain amount of mirth but sometimes to something more important. They would arrange to meet, usually at places that they had met before. Sometimes Edgar would buy her a small box of expensive chocolates but when they were going to see a show, he bought her an orchid which he would present to her when they dined together before hand.

It was late afternoon. Helena, half wanted to get on with the research since she was thinking of the air-mail letter and half wanted to prepare for their date. Even as she was asking herself what to do and, if they went, whether to wear a dress or a trouser suit, Edgar took her hands in his and said, "As you like it!". He was not referring to the choice of garment.

That was enough. Helena laughed, "You've booked a table somewhere and told them that we need to get to our seats in time. I bet I can guess where. Having done so, you don't want to mess them about. There isn't much chance that the theatre can use the tickets and I'm fond of Ganymede. Let's go. We can come back to Esme with our Horlicks."

For about the first year of their married life, they had drunk Horlicks before bed – even when it was not their initial intention to go to sleep. After a while, Helena noticed that her husband was acquiring what she called a 'spare tyre'. The Horlicks was discontinued and, indeed seldom substituted for. If it was, it was with something stronger. From then on, however they filled it, that last relaxing part of the day before they went to bed or even when they had done so, was called 'our Horlicks'.

"Six o'clock, then on the Minster steps." said Edgar.

So they carried out their original intention, promising the suitcase, as though it were pet dog, that they would return and with Edgar muttering "'fond of Ganymede', indeed!"

Part of the custom they had instituted was that Helena should arrive late, though not by more than five minutes. Edgar maintained that she had always been late for their dates and this was tradition. This was not entirely true but the arrangement meant that Helena was never standing on her own in a public place. Edgar would go through the charade of looking at his watch when she appeared but he would also pull her to him to kiss her before presenting her with the orchid or the box of chocolates.

"'The Fifth of November'" she said and kissed him again when he nodded. It was but a short step to that oddly named restaurant – one they had actually dined in before they were married. The manager of 'The Fifth of November' greeted them as valued customers and not just in the financial sense. He had been employed there as a waiter when they had first used it and counted that actual occasion as one of the favourite moments of his career. Helena and Edgar had been interested only in each other and, as soon as he saw them together with that special glow, he had directed them to the best table in the room and took pleasure in their enjoyment of each other. When they were spending too long over their coffee, it was he who had had reminded them of the starting time of the Mystery Plays that was their theatrical destination that night.

Since then he had observed their courtship and marriage with interest and affection. Edgar had booked in advance and, when he spotted this, he changed the duty roster so he could look after them. When he had finished that night, he would report back to his wife, who also had become interested in the couple. She would ask him what play they were going to see, what Helena was wearing and even the colour of the orchid.

The restaurant was well-sited both for their meeting place but also the theatre and, that evening, they walked there. As usual, Edgar had secured good seats, central and some six rows back from the stage. They were in good time to study the program. They knew who the leading actors were but they spotted a couple of their favourites playing minor roles. Edgar, complaining as usual about the price of the programme, fulminated over the notes that were written up about the play. "I can't help feeling that they should let Shakespeare tell us what it is all about." he said.

"Shush!" said Helena who had heard it all before.

It was a good performance, lightly produced and the Forest of Arden was an enchanting piece of staging. Rosalind/Ganymede was played by a young but very talented actress with colouring and a figure similar to Helena's and, as Edgar handed Helena into their cab, he said, soft-voiced, "and I think I could be fond of Rosalind."

In the cab, he claimed the best line in the play was the instruction to one of women to get *'down on your knees, And thank heaven, fasting, for a good man's love.'* Helena replied that even in that play there were a number of bad men.

On return to their house, Edgar made not Horlicks or even tea but coffee to help them stay awake. Helena did, as she had said, return to the suitcase but she set aside the air-mail and the other letters and turned to the ribboned file and the next item brought an exclamation of joy.

"Edgar! You'll not believe this." and she handed him what was clearly a play-bill. It was headed:-

BY KIND PERMISSION OF THE GOVERNORS OF
ST. ERMENGILD'S SCHOOL FOR GIRLS

and laid out neatly below this:-

Michaelmas Term 1939
'JACKSON HOUSE presents:-
As You Like It – by William Shakespeare

Adapted by Rachel Castle.
Produced by Deborah Wilson
A private production for members of the School and their guests.'

There was a short program note:-

Rosalind, daughter of the true Duke, is banished by the Duke's usurping brother to the Forest of Arden. There she disguises herself as a boy, 'Ganymede'. Before that she has seen Orlando, a well-born young man, win a wrestling match and has fallen in love with him. He, in turn falls in love with her. Believing Ganymede to be a boy, he asks advice on how to woo Rosalind. Ganymede suggests that she should play the role of Rosalind and, as a game, he should pretend to woo her.

Prepare to enjoy the fun!

Edgar had crossed to her side to read it. "Now that's a proper program note!" he said. More importantly he asked the question both wanted an answer to. "The cast?" and Helena knew, that like her, he was hoping for a mention of Esme.

She turned the slip of paper over, it was no more than that, and they were rewarded. The editors of this well laid out play-bill had stuck to the idiom and the list of actors was headed:-

'THE PLAYERS'

Rachel's 'adaptation' of this great play had obviously been done most importantly to shorten the playing time. She had reduced the *Dramatis Personae* to about ten characters. Helena and Edgar, having just seen the play entire could understand how this school-girl had chosen shrewdly who to leave out.

She had obviously disposed of at least one sub-plot and, they suspected, much of the word-play. They were, however, only concerned with one role:

'ROSALIND, *daughter to Duke Senior,* played by Esme Marsh.'

The two researchers took one second to absorb this before Edgar gave his wife a hug that threatened her rib-cage.

"You know this is all down to the hat." he said.

Helena, almost breathless, managed to say.

"And do I need a hat?"

They did not do much more work that night.

CHAPTER 18

Michaelmas Term 1939

The world outside the school gates had become a very nasty place. The German dictator had roused the nationalistic pride of his country's people, still smarting from their defeat earlier in the century, to make claims on the territories of other nations. Hitler's armies had swept across Europe enforcing those claims with military might. Britain and the other Western powers had attempted to negotiate peacefully and had failed. St. Ermengild's had returned from their summer holidays just as Britain declared war on Hitler and the forces of fascism.

Miss Salway responded pragmatically. She prepared for the unlikely event of an air-raid so that the girls in her charge would understand that the nation was in a state of total war. She herself was an historian and she pointed out that this was very different from the frequent but distant conflicts which they learned about in their history lessons. The war they were now engaged in was something immediate and all pervading.

So the windows were adorned, criss-cross, with adhesive tape to reduce the chance of shards of glass raining on her pupils. She had a number of shelters dug in the kitchen garden and devised a signal to warn the girls and her staff when to use them. She ensured that they practised this response. The ground staff were set the task of filling sandbags and she doubled the number of fire buckets and fire extinguishers. All the pupils were taught which fire extinguishers to use on which sort of fire. She called fire drills every day for a week asking and getting feed-back on how to improve them and reduce the time that they took. It was Deborah Wilson who looked for the ways that the drills could go wrong and how changes in the procedures could allow for such complications.

What she could do, Miss Salway did. Otherwise, the school continued normally. There would be no change in the lessons, in the games or the 'choice' sessions; nor yet in the social activities. It was the Michaelmas Term and there would be a play performed at the end of it and, early in the term, they would invite the pupils of the local boys' school to the usual dance.

This, in one way, would not be a usual dance. Many of their guests, those who were now schoolboys in the upper sixth would, very shortly, be called up into compulsory military service. All the more reason, thought Miss Salway, to have the dance. Those boys would have a chance to enjoy themselves in civilised circumstances. It would be an example of what they would be fighting for. At the same time, she made a mental note to ensure that the dance was properly supervised. Every time there was such an occasion, some young man would try to extract one of her girls from the security of the dance hall. The risk, she thought, would be greater if they saw themselves as protective males defending the weaker sex.

They used the assembly hall as the 'dance hall' and all the domestic and the ground staff were employed in arranging the furniture and cleaning generally. Esme caught sight of George engaged in carrying out some of the unwanted chairs and waved cheerfully. By now she was pretty sure that he was 'security'. He worked well on the grounds and there was some improvement in their appearance because of this but he did seem to interest himself in any visitors and he was reported as prowling around the grounds at night. Esme thought that he should know that she appreciated his presence. As usual, he glanced round to make sure nobody could see him before he waved back.

The hall was transformed. They had brought in additional lighting and the musicians of a small band were seated on the platform normally occupied by the teaching staff in assemblies. There were even a few balloons decorating some otherwise dignified portraits.

There was one of these dances arranged each term. The one in the Michaelmas term was formal with the boys wearing dinner-jackets and the girls their party frocks. They were heavily staffed and the boys' school sent over some of their own teachers to add authority. Not that Miss Salway's staff needed any support. This did not stop the visitors dancing with them

Some of the boys came to the 'dance choice' once a fortnight so they had met most, if not all of the girls. Nonetheless, these affairs always started slowly with the boys too shy to make a move and the girls, although they were officially hostesses, reluctant to put themselves forward. Once there were enough people assembled, one of the younger teachers would take the microphone and announce a country dance, instructing everybody to take the floor. A lively set of such dances meant that, when the band next struck up a quick-step, most of the boys were ready to ask the girls to dance.

The three friends, Rachel, Deborah and Esme, sitting together, attracted a host of such applicants. The convention was laid down. A girl would accept the first request regardless of her feelings. This was on the grounds that she should have no reason not to.

Esme was asked by one of the older boys; his name was Philip Brotherton. She knew him already because he took part in the 'choice' dance lessons. He was conventionally handsome and a good dancer. He dressed very well. Rachel said that he must have his school uniform made to measure. His dinner-jacket fitted him to perfection and his shirt, gleaming white, was fastened with studs rather than buttons. He and Esme made a striking couple. Rachel, who did not like him, called him 'posh'.

In the dance lessons, he made a point of partnering Esme to the extent that some of the other girls suggested that he was her boyfriend; telling her what a 'good catch' he was because he was so rich. His parents were both dead and the capital of his inheritance was held in trust but he had a substantial income from it. Esme knew this because he had told her. She disliked the fact that he made a point of telling her about it but had sympathy for him as an orphan.

The business about having a boyfriend was something that most of the girls made a great deal of. According to the accepted fashion, it gave one a desirable status. Esme was not so sure but was not entirely unaffected.

At this dance, when he asked her, with conventional

politeness, she stood up and he led her on to the floor. Perhaps she was a little put out because he reached her just before another boy who had a cheerful look which appealed to her. He danced, however, with his usual skill and she began to enjoy the movement of the dance. This evening, somehow, he seemed even more artificial than usual but Esme expected boys to be so at the beginning of a dance.

Subsequently, she stood up for most of the dances with a number of partners; one of them with the boy with the cheerful look who was a very poor dancer indeed and, what is more, not cheerful at all.

Later in the evening, Philip Brotherton asked her to dance with him again. She was not too enthusiastic but did not allow him to see that, standing up immediately to agree. He always talked a lot about himself and this occasion was no exception. She told herself that it was only for the short time of the dance that she had to listen to him. He spoke at length of his position in his school's Officer Training Corp and built on that to tell her about how the war was going to be fought. Esme was as concerned as the next person about the coming war, more so perhaps because of her father. Philip Brotherton talked as though he knew all about it and he did so as though he was the only person who did. Esme thought that perhaps he was trying to talk away his fears of the coming conflict and listened. Not that she had an alternative; he spoke about nothing else.

That particular set ended at the interval. Brotherton took her to a chair and said he would get her a glass of something and she opted for iced coffee – a great treat.

He brought it, balancing it and his own glass on a tray.

"It is a bit warm in here. Shall we take it outside?" Esme, without thinking, agreed about the temperature and they went and sat on one of the benches on the covered way outside the hall.

Then he said he needed a smoke so they would have to walk away from the building so nobody would see him. They walked towards the trees, he put his arm around her shoulder. Esme was not sure that she wanted it there but did not want to seem unpleasant.

"It's tomorrow." said Brotherton in grave tones. "I have to report to the basic training barracks. I won't see you for at least six weeks." Not only was the young man talking about himself again but there was a certain assumption in the phraseology of what he said. Had she given him the impression that she was anxious to see him again? What he said next suggested that this was the case.

"After that, they may post me overseas. They will need officers in the front line. Perhaps a Jerry bullet will mean that we never meet again."

Esme was silent. This was far-fetched but he seemed to imagine himself as a tragic hero. He went on, "I understand the troops call it 'comforts'"

"Call what 'comforts'?"

"Well, you know. The girl provides comfort so that the soldier has something to fight, even die for."

She found that they were standing together in a group of trees on some turf that she knew had what was left of the foliage of some spring flowers. He had backed her up against a tree and she let him kiss her. When she had been kissed before she had always enjoyed it but this was not quite the same. Apart from anything else, she could smell alcohol on his breath and the taste of stale tobacco. He was also aggressive. The boys who had kissed her before had been tender. She was also worried that she was giving him the wrong signals. She was uneasy when he went on about facing the enemy and dying for his country.

He put his hand on her breast and she could feel his fingers through the thin cloth of her dress. At the same time he was repeating that he may be dead within weeks and was making suggestions about what they could do with the rest of the evening. She did not want this but he became more insistent.

"No!" She said. "Stop it"

"You are a bit of a tease, Esme Marsh. There's no good protesting now when for weeks you've been leading me on at the dance lessons. You wanted me to dance with you."

Esme was appalled. Maybe she had been encouraging him.

"That was dancing. You are a good dancer."

"You might find I'm good enough at this to satisfy you." he said and he pressed her against the tree and slid his hand down to her crotch pulling at her frock. She told him to stop but he persisted. She wondered whether she should summon the help of Company Sergeant Major Peter Williamson. To get into a fight at this school as well as at Godstone's would not be a good idea. Or she could cry out. She was deciding which of the two alternatives would be preferable when she was saved from this embarrassment by a familiar voice. Well, it was a familiar voice but it had acquired a broad Scottish accent.

"You'll not be treading on the flowers, sir."

It seemed to be the silliest possible thing to say but it stopped Philip Brotherton in his tracks. George, the groundsman, known to walk through the gardens around the school at night, sounded only concerned about his plants but his very presence served to put an end to Philip's ambitions.

George continued in his local yokel role, "The young lady will catch her death!" he said, "Perhaps she'd best be indoors. It's nastier than it seems out here. I'll take her, sir. You've got your shoes muddy. You'll need to clean them."

Philip started to bluster but George, for reasons best known to himself, was carrying a spade. He shifted this from one hand to the other and that was all that was needed. Esme got the impression that the schoolboy looked down on the servants as he would call them. An altercation with the hired help was not something he wanted and he walked off. Esme noticed that he did not say anything; certainly not that he was sorry. Somehow, she felt sorry for him.

"Thank you, George." said Esme. "I know your name isn't George but perhaps it would be better to leave it that way.

"Strange fellow that, miss. He wasn't giving you any bother was he?"

George was continuing the masquerade for her benefit. She, in spite of her disturbed state, thought that he deserved credit.

"Well I thought you were very clever. Shall I tell my father?"

George shook his head. "Tell your father, miss? Why would he be interested in the plants?"

His blank look went well with the slow way in which he asked the question and Esme almost believed that he was what he pretended to be.

"Come off it, George. I know you're not here to protect my virtue but he would be pleased to hear that you had."

"Best not, miss!" said her rescuer, giving in. "The boss has enough on his plate to worry about at the moment without having to be the protective father. In any case, your protection from the likes of that young man has arrived."

He was referring to Rachel and Deborah who came running up at that moment.

"There she is." cried Deborah and – "she stopped and, puzzled, said "It's George. What are you doing here? Silly question, sorry! Forget I asked it. Hang on, you have to be able to give a reason!"

George slipped back into his gardener role but without the Scottish accent "It's the moths, miss. I'm checking the traps. It is part of a national survey. You'll have seen the traps in the trees. I have to check them every night."

Esme, still recovering from her narrow escape, giggled nervously. What a splendid cover story. The two girls looked at her and realised that they were not to ask any more questions.

"George has been very useful." she said. "I think we should leave him to his own business. You can thank him nicely for looking after me."

She was grateful he had saved not only herself but also Brotherton from embarrassment. Neither St Ermengild's nor the boys' school would welcome a scandal. George had arranged that there should not be one.

Esme resolved to trust her instincts with boys in future. Certainly the ones where there was a suggestion that something was not right. George certainly deserved a thank-you for his quick thinking but it was difficult to acknowledge that. She would mention it next time she phoned her grandmother. How would she phrase it? This thought made her chuckle to herself and cheered her up no end. She would tell her to keep the matter from her father. She had noticed that George had spoken of her father with concern, almost with affection. It was pleasing to think that Daddy was well regarded by his staff. The fact that he would be busy was self-evident.

Rachel and Deborah enveloped her in their concern. Nonetheless, although Brotherton had destroyed any regard she may have had for him, she still had concern for that young man. There was something wrong about the way he saw his immediate future. Esme thought that he was frightened by it. She was troubled for several days about him.

★★★ ★★★ ★★★

The 'welcoming dance' was not the only extra-curricular activity in the Michaelmas term. Each year, one of the houses presented a play towards the end of the term. Sometimes a Shakespeare play and when this was the case, someone had to simplify the action to shorten it for they were only allowed an hour on stage. One way was to remove minor characters. This was just as well because often they did not have enough girls to fill all the roles. This year the House to present such a play was Jackson House. They chose 'As You Like It' and they chose Rachel Castle to adapt it. This was not a good choice. Rachel grieved for every character, indeed for every line that she cut. The result, however, was a well-worked version that concentrated on Orlando and his relationship with Rosalind/Ganymede' and the product was a reflection of the meticulous way in which she tackled any task set her.

"This is never going to work." It was Esme, cast as Rosalind, struggling with her lines. "I've got to play a girl pretending to be a boy when the original role was actually played by a boy."

Deborah, as producer, was dismissive, "That makes it easier." she said "Rosalind, in the play, never mind who plays her, is a girl. You are a girl. Some of the play, you have to pretend to be a boy."

Esme looked unconvinced but turned to Rachel. There's an awful lot of lines to learn." she said. "Can't you cut some of them out?"

"I've cut your role to the bone. Any more and Orlando will have no one left to love."

"And do I have to kiss him, I mean her? It wasn't in the text."

It was Deborah who intervened.

"If you've got problems, just think of Orlando. Rosalind makes him woo someone who he thinks is a boy but who is not only a girl but is actually his girl. You've got it easy. Apart from anything else, you and Rosalind have a great deal in common."

"I'm not so sure about that. I don't see myself going overboard about someone just because he's good at wrestling."

"No! No! It isn't because Orlando has won the wrestling match but because he defies the odds to do so, even to take part in it. Let me take you through the role again." Deborah was somewhat shocked that Esme didn't understand her role until she saw the mischief in her smile.

"Esme Marsh. You will stop messing me about. I love this play and have seen it done more than once by professionals. There can be nobody better suited to play Rosalind than you. I wouldn't mind betting that Shakespeare knew a previous incarnation of Esme Marsh, loved her to distraction and wrote the part to make her immortal. You will learn your lines and you will learn what they mean. We've got a week to go. Then, not only the school but also dozens of guests – and they will be paying good money to see one of Shakespeare's most heart-warming plays – will be watching you. I promise you, you will warm their hearts."

Which indeed, she did. There was magic in her desire for Orlando and cheerful humour in the trick she plays upon him. She was splendidly supported, even if she was worried about being kissed by her, by the girl who played Orlando and by the rest of the cast. The school choir, brought in particularly for 'Blow, blow thou winter wind' and for a 'Lover and His Lass' were a great success.

The cast took three curtains and asked for applause for the back-stage support. They also dragged both Rachel and Deborah onto the stage for their own plaudits.

Miss Jackson's contribution was one enormous 'tea'. Which they had on the stage. She had brought in Mrs Whinstanley to do the catering and provided sherry herself for the audience.

Esme's grandmother had come, supported by her chauffer, Treadwell. Gerald Castle had brought his wife but they had to go soon after the play was finished. His wife came across to the three girls and passed a carrier bag to Deborah.

"For tomorrow." she said. "When the excitement has died down. Gerald has to report back to camp, I am afraid. I've got to rescue Charlie from his baby-sitter. For me, I enjoyed a brilliant performance and a lovely evening."

The next time they met, the circumstances would be very different.

CHAPTER 19

5th August 1986

Helena and Edgar both woke late the following day and both had other commitments. Moreover, the other names on the playbill of the school's performance of '*As You Like It.*' might yield information if they followed them up. The last thing Helena had done the night before was to add their names to those already in her note book.

Rachel and Deborah had been very much still there at the end of 1939. What had happened to them afterwards? Perhaps it was about time to chase them up too.

Edgar was still thinking, as they ate their usual weekday sketchy breakfast, about the play itself. "The date of that performance is almost incredible. The country had been at war since September." he said. "It is as though they had declared their own war against war itself. They not only work on the production but they invite guests. They are shaking their fists at Hitler."

Since they had indulged themselves the previous evening in going to the theatre this meant that both of them had to put in a full day's work. They had yet another take-away for their supper and they returned to the suitcase.

The next thing that Edgar lifted from the case was a school badge, probably off a blazer pocket. He showed it to Helena. It depicted a flaming torch. Not perhaps an original idea for a school badge but an idea that had driven home the concept of the continuity of knowledge to thousands and thousands of school-children.

"St. Ermengild's." said Helena who had seen it on the play bill. Then Edgar lifted a second badge. This depicted the letter 'A' as a capital, swathed in flames. The badge was a striking image in orange and scarlet. This one was far too aggressive to be from an educational institution and, in any case, the emblem was set against material that was clearly army khaki.

"Not a cap-badge!" said Edgar. "Too big. It is about the same size as a sergeant-major's badge – worn on the arm but I don't think it's that. Should be easy enough to find out. This one has been much worn, as has the school badge."

Helena recorded these remarks and then switched the recorder off and put it down.

"That was symbolic." she said. "I'm not recording this. What I've got to say now may move us forward but since I've told you not to speculate. I'm ready to accept that it is nonsense."

She paused for breath before committing herself. "I think Esme Marsh has stored in this suitcase all those small things that were precious to her. Most of them, so far, concern her life at school and will have carried her memories of the school and her friends. This badge is not about her school, cannot have even been hers but it too carried a precious memory. She was close to and wanted to have a 'foolish thing' to remind her of someone in the army. Maybe one of her school friends joined the army but I think this badge enriched the arm of one of her knights."

"I am with you there." said Edgar "But you haven't thought it through. Soldiers lose their insignia only when they are court-marshalled or they are dead. If you are going to speculate, you will need a scenario that allows you to remove the badge from the sleeve in happy circumstances. I refuse to research a tragedy."

"Serves me right for not following my own rules." said Helena ruefully. "You have now got to rescue me. How did the badge get there?"

Edgar grinned. "Our unknown soldier has finished his service and is demobilised. Which means that he and Esme will have been together after the war and may even only have met then. It is likely that the suitcase is closed late in 1945 or early in 1946. It might be earlier than that but there is nothing in it, so far, that we can date after Christmas of 1945. Our soldier is demobbed at the end of the hostilities. There were complaints about the slowness of the demobilisation. Our soldier's badge is well-worn. It must have been on his arm for several years so he'll probably amongst those first released. Esme need only have known him for some of that time. VE Day was the eighth of May – VJ Day was the fifteenth of August. Between May and Christmas of that year, our soldier becomes so attached to Esme Marsh that he gives her this badge as a token of his affection and it means so much to her that she squirrels it away for her future."

His grin got broader and broader as he advanced his argument and Helena smiled with him.

"Thank you." she said. "I did ask for it and you are very good at it. But, as you say, they may have known each other for some time before." Then she looked smug and said,

"Apart from the drastic extremes of his death or Court Marshal, he may have simply been wounded and invalided out – or simply had the sleeve of his tunic cut off so that the nurse could get at the wound. Perhaps Esme was helping in a nursing station. Is there any blood on it?"

Edgar was prevented from capping this as the two of them started to laugh. When they stopped, he said, "More facts!" and Helena went for one of her reference books.

Returning shortly and summarising the text of the book, she said. "The Flaming 'A' was the insignia worn by Ammunition Examiners – X-Class tradesmen of the Royal Army Ordnance Corps. Their remit was to inspect ammunition and ensure that it was safe for use. If it was not, then they had to prepare it so that it could be safely disposed of and, in emergency, to dispose of it themselves. All such Ammunition Examiners were non-commissioned officers and carried the rank of corporal or above."

"Well done!" said Edgar. "Now we are moving onto solid ground. Esme's soldier is an Ammunition Examiner in the Ordnance Corp at the end of the war. Go for it! What was James Bygrave doing at that time?"

CHAPTER 20

June 1940

Miss Salway knew that it was her duty to make her pupils aware that the whole nation was fighting this war but she would have preferred fewer reminders from the war itself. Each assembly offered prayers for combatants at the battle fronts. It also, perforce, reported on individual casualties. Most of the names she read out were those of former members of the local boys' school; killed or wounded or reported missing.

Rachel and Deborah were standing either side of Esme when Philip Brotherton's name was added to that growing list of those 'killed in action'. It was as well they were for Esme's reaction was a near faint and it took both of them to support her. Rachel knew that Brotherton was serving in her brother's unit and was concerned that he too might be a casualty but his name was not reported.

The two girls continued to support their friend through the short silence that followed the announcement and, after the assembly, took her back to their dormitory. They knew that something had passed between Brotherton and her on the night of the school dance but not how serious it was. All she had told them was that he had kissed her and she had not liked it. There seemed no reason for this reaction.

Esme avoided any questions they asked and sought places where she could be alone. She was a different girl and so much so that she barely spoke to them. When they insisted, she asked if Rachel could find out how Brotherton had died but would say nothing else. This withdrawal lasted a couple of days until her friends decided to do something about it.

It was Rachel who asked the headmistress if she could phone Esme's grandmother and was given the use of her office to do so. Esme had spoken frequently to her grandmother of her two friends so Mrs Marsh expected a sensible reason for the call. Rachel tried to be unemotional but Mrs Marsh remembered how collected the girl was that she had met and was immediately concerned about her granddaughter. She said that it was unlikely that would be able to get in touch with Gerald Castle but they could try. Rachel should write to her brother but through an address that Mrs Marsh gave her. She herself would try to reach Esme's father. Rachel should wait by the phone.

Rachel considered where she was and consulted Miss Salway. The headmistress said she could wait outside the office. She was not there for more than half an hour before she was called back in and the headmistress, once more, headed for her secretary's office.

It was Esme's father, himself, who called back. Esme had told him about her two friends. With his normal thoroughness, he had found out everything he could about them. He was, therefore, prepared to give due consideration to anything that Rachel had to say. He assured her that she could speak freely, so she did.

As she spoke, he could hear once more the short and final words that he had exchanged with his wife:-

"Look after the girls, Reginald! You will be all that they have."

"Hush now. I promise I'll do everything I can – everything!"

He knew that sometimes his job prevented from doing things that would have helped them. He was especially aware that he could spend so little time with them. Other things demanded a higher priority but he had, he thought, done everything he could.

Esme had been open and enthusiastic about Rachel and Deborah to her father but she had told them very little about him. She had told the story about CSM Williamson and the un-armed combat and she had said shyly that her father would do anything for her. Rachel thought about the relationship she had with her own parents whose support was their constant presence, not dramatic exhibitions of power but she realised that such power was what was needed now.

She explained the situation with great clarity and force and without interruptions from Reginald Marsh. When she had finished, he asked a couple of questions about Gerald's whereabouts. There was an edge of urgency in his voice. He then thanked her for letting him know and said he would do what he could. Rachel, at that point, realised that he could do nothing about her brother if anything had happened to him. Reginald said that he had to make some phone calls, thanked her again and rang off.

★★★ ★★★ ★★★

Escaping from the blood-soaked beaches of Dunkirk, most of Major Gerald Castle's platoon had managed to climb aboard one small fishing boat and now, bone-weary and suffering from a bullet wound in his fore-arm, he marshalled the survivors on the quayside at Dover. He turned to thank the skipper of the boat that had rescued them only to find him preparing to set off once more and all he could do was wave with his uninjured arm.

"Sergeant." he said. "Write down the name of that boat for me." Thinking that not many orders of that kind had been issued over the last few days. His sergeant was himself amused but the officer only had the use of one arm. He may have been able to fire his revolver but he could not manage, without a surface, to do any writing.

Gerald's own men were in good order and he was pretty sure that all the survivors were with him. Help had been organised. The NAAFI, supported by all sorts of organisations and even by individual housewives, was delivering tea, most importantly, and food. The tea was by far the most important. His men were dehydrated as well as exhausted and he doubted if any of them had any water left in their canteens. He had briefly checked and noted with pride that every man still carried his rifle and his packs though he knew that this was due to his Sergeant Major, not himself.

A number of couriers presented themselves to him with instructions and information and requests for a report on his command. He dealt with these before bedding his men down. Then he sought for treatment for his own wound. The doctor gave him enough pain-killers to send him into a deep sleep and when he woke it was late in the morning.

There were more messages and amongst them, oddly, a request from his sister. How such a message could get to him he could not understand. It asked that he phone her, if possible. She needed to know about one of his men who had been killed earlier as they retreated to the beaches.

For the moment, he could do nothing about it but when he presented himself to his Commanding Officer, he was congratulated on his handling of the unit in the retreat and the embarkation and told that he had to take some sick leave. "That's all right by me. It will be a while before we are in action again and you won't be much use dealing with recruits. Oh! There's a gong in it for you!" he said."

He then consulted a document that he had been reading and went on. "I understand that, not only have you got to take sick leave but that you have to report to somewhere in Scotland. St. Ermengild's! What's that?" The C.O. permitted himself a question even though it was obvious to him that Gerald was not supposed to answer.

"I've got a car for you and I've allocated a driver. You'll be happy with Corporal Bygrave, I assume. He gets a gong, as well, by the way. When you've dealt with whatever this is about, just tell us where we can get hold of you!"

Gerald was baffled. There was only one thing that he was clear about. Corporal Bygrave was, at that moment, one person he would be happy with in any scenario. The two of them had been caught up in one almost fatal situation in the final day of the retreat to Dunkirk and it was only Bygrave's driving skills and quickness of thought that meant they were still alive. Gerald was glad to hear that he had got off the beach unscathed. The last time he had seen him, he had been driving back towards the enemy. He had said something about a booby trap. The corporal was a tall, slim young man.

He was a specialist tradesman in ammunition and he came with a reputation as a skilled driver. He had joined Gerald's unit about a couple of days before they reached the beaches with a brief to help him delay the enemy's advance. He drove his own Jeep; a Jeep loaded with mysterious gear. All of which looked dangerous. The young corporal, who seemed in complete control of what was needed of him, had explained that this was not his usual job but he would do his best. His best had been spectacular.

He had set up trip-wires to explosives that would bring down trees and telegraph poles. He set up trip wires without any devices attached to them at all. "They won't know the difference." he said in explanation. "They have to treat them all the same. Perhaps they'll get careless." He had some anti-tank mines and as he put these in place, he admitted that he didn't actually know how they worked. "Perhaps Jerry will find out for us." All the while the enemy were getting closer. At one point he judged it was worth while firing some white-phosphorus mortar bombs to lay down smoke. He had prepared a time-device that would detonate a series of cartridges as though the position was still held and, to add to the confusion he fired flares above the smoke. It was as though he was a one-man fireworks display.

Gerald co-ordinated with him to cover his unit's retreat. He sent his men to the rear and moved forward with the corporal to assess the enemy's advance.

It was Gerald, who was on foot, who first saw the tank looming up as it mounted a ridge between them. He shouted a warning. Corporal Bygrave leaped into his Jeep and drove straight under the rearing vehicle. The tank-driver tried desperately to depress its gun. He was too late. Corporal Bygrave grabbed a weapon, and fired it into the least armoured part of the tank. It was a shaped charge and it drilled through the armour to explode inside. This was the first time Gerald had witnessed such a device in action. The army called it 'a boil up'. The turret of the tank was thrown open but none of the crew emerged. The Major had that dehumanised moment when all he could think was "Serve the bastards right" but was checked when he heard the corporal say "Us or them, Sir!" in flat emotionless tone.

The tank was supported by infantry but Bygrave had no sooner fired the bazooka than he had picked up Gerald and was spinning the Jeep and heading off at speed.

"Yes!" Gerald replied to his C.O.. He was still bemused but he agreed. "I'll be happy with Corporal Bygrave as my driver."

It sounded as though he was expected to go somewhere immediately. Surely he was not being told to drive to St. Ermengild's. Just in case, he asked one question.

"Petrol?"

"Corporal Bygrave has the paper-work and coupons. The Quartermaster has put some gear together for you. Your family is here. Would you like them to travel with you? I got you a big car."

This was even more bewildering. Someone had pulled strings. "No!" thought Gerald. "Not strings; ropes, ship's cables even." He was delighted that he would see his wife and child so soon but whether Betty would want such a long journey was doubtful.

However, when he got to the car, which was parked

outside the married quarters, he found he had been pre-empted. Betty had already made herself known to Corporal Bygrave and they had stowed her luggage in the boot. The Corporal seemed as fresh as a daisy and was already 'Jim' to both Betty and Charlie. He saw the major approaching and instead of greeting him, walked into the building. Gerald appreciated his tact and swept his wife into his arms, lifting the boy to share the embrace and saying the things to her especially that he would not want anybody else to hear.

Jim re-emerged from the building. "Just checking, Sir!" he said.

Gerald regarded his diplomatic driver with appreciation. "Thank you!" he said and both of them knew that it was not for 'checking' that he had left the scene. "I can't have my wife and child calling you 'Jim' and go on calling you 'Corporal'. For the purpose of this journey and for whenever it will not be contrary to good order, I am 'Gerald'.

"Betty, you should know that this man saved my life" and almost before he had finished speaking she was giving Jim a kiss. She saw that he had a plaster on one cheeks, touched it gently and kissed it even more gently. "Thank you!" she said and did not elaborate. At this point, their son, who had been grinning hugely and had only just let go of his father said, "Do we have to call him 'Jim'? I wanted to say, 'Home, James! and don't spare the horses!" A pronouncement that had them all smiling.

"Not home! I assume, Jim" Gerald wanted confirmation of where they were going. 'Corporal Bygrave has the paper-work' was all the C.O. had said.

"No!" Jim Bygrave replied avoiding familiarity on this

official business. "We are heading for a place in Scotland. We'll do most of the journey today. I've fixed a billet in a camp just south of Glasgow for tonight. We should get to St Ermengild's School tomorrow afternoon. The C.O. has let them know."

So this trip was related to Rachel's letter asking for help. Somebody had great influence at the War Office. He thought he knew who but, for the moment, there was no gain in asking who or, even, why.

Charlie was sent to visit the lavatory and the rest of them did the same. This was going to be a long drive with as few stops as possible. The family sat in the back of the car. At the start they did so in a family hug and Jim drove. He had shown how he could handle a Jeep in France, now he nursed the big staff-car to great speed with a smoothness that had his passengers dozing off in the back. There were checkpoints on some of the roads but Gerald's uniform was usually enough to remove any real delays. When it wasn't, Jim produced some of his 'paper-work' that smoothed away any objections.

So, a few days after he survived the shells and bullets that killed so many others; after he had witnessed the agonies of men dying from ghastly wounds, heard the screams of those aware of the destruction of their own bodies, Major Gerald Castle, neatly dressed in a fresh uniform, with the jacket loose over his wounded arm in its gleaming white sling, and together with his wife and child, was driven north on a privileged journey and was deposited on the gravel drive of St Ermengild's. He glanced at the school's carefully tended green lawns before making his way to the school's terrace.

There, waiting for him, was the headmistress. He presented himself to her.

"Could I see my sister, please?"

Of course he could. He would get the full V.I.P. treatment. Always a favourite, he was now doubly so. Miss Salway called one of the prefects across and spoke to her. "I've sent also for Esme Marsh," she said. "I think, somehow, your visit concerns her. It will be best if you wait for them, perhaps on the terrace. Your wife is with you? Perhaps she would like to come in for a cup of tea. What about your driver? I have a couple of girls eager to entertain your son"

Gerald Castle had known that Esme Marsh was in some way different even from the other girls in this school. There had been occasions when his sister would check what she was saying and change the subject. Indeed, there were subjects which they did not even discuss. The only glimmer he had got in the past to explain this was that her father was someone important.

There were three girls waiting on the terrace. Esme and Deborah did not move but Rachel walked across to her brother.

She seemed a little hesitant but she reached up to give him a kiss on his cheek.

"You're wounded." she said "They told us it was only a flesh wound but it must be painful. All the more reason to thank you for coming. I know you really should be concentrating on Betty and Charlie." she said. "But I hope you can help here."

Her brother smiled. He looked across to the car and could see that Miss Salway's invitation had been delivered.

He was then surprised to see Corporal Bygrave get out of the car itself, open Betty's door and hand her out. He then lifted Charlie and walked, carrying the boy, with Betty across to the school. Why would he do that? Charlie was more than big enough to walk. Bygrave would not intrude on the ladies and their tea. Gerald was also surprised that Charlie submitted to being carried. He 'was a big boy now' but he had established a relationship with the driver. Some of the journey, Jim had let him sit in the seat beside him and told him about the instruments even let him work the wind-screen wipers. Jim could do no wrong in Charlie's eyes.

"They are being looked after." he said. "There is a lot of 'looking after' going on: private letters in the official post, the fastest grant of sick leave ever seen, a lavish allocation of petrol, my family delivered to the door, courtesy of the army. Then a car and paper-work to smooth a journey the length of the country and a war-hero as a driver." As he said this, he wondered what had happened to that driver. A glance was enough to see that he was at the school entrance. "I gather that this is about Esme Marsh."

"Yes and no! Esme had nothing to do with all that. I asked the headmistress if I could phone Esme's grandmother and I suppose everything followed from that call."

"You haven't said anything relevant yet, Rachel. This is not like you. What has Esme Marsh got to do with me?"

.Out of the corner of his eye, he saw that his driver had put Charlie down at the school entrance. He stood there looking around for a minute and then walked back to the car. Perhaps he was only stretching his legs.

"I just wanted you to know that Esme herself would not

have asked for help. To cut a long story short, she needs to know about Brotherton. I knew he was serving in your unit."

At the mention of the name, Gerald's face hardened. Fortunately Rachel was not actually looking at him at that moment and he recovered his composure.

"Go on."

"At assemblies they now report the deaths in action of the men who used to go to the local boys' school. When they announced his, Esme went white. Her shoulders went back and her hand went to her mouth. If it wasn't in the assembly, I would have sat her down and treated her for shock. Brotherton used to come to the dance lessons. The boys' school was only too willing to provide boys. Girls dancing with girls never really works. He also came to the Michaelmas term formal, and she danced with him then. They went outside. Deborah and I didn't trust him so we followed her out but she'd already been rescued by the groundsman, George. Esme spoke about Brotherton in an off-hand fashion afterwards. Since the announcement of his death she has said nothing about him and now refuses to answer our questions. She did ask if you could find out how he died. Esme Marsh, who was really happy here, perhaps for the first time in her life, is now a different person. She will not speak to us. The only thing I could think of was asking you for help. I know she sees you as a sort of elder brother and she did say that she would ask you how he died."

Gerald noted that his sister had referred to the young man as 'Brotherton' not 'Philip'. Rachel was a good judge of character but he did not need this to confirm that Philip Brotherton was not someone she would like. He had died at the beginning of the retreat to Dunkirk. Gerald would, in the normal course of events, have written to his nearest relatives. Brotherton was an orphan and his guardian, an uncle, had just died. There was no one else to write to. What had Esme to do with him? Had the two become close? Had they even been lovers? Gerald hoped not. He thought Esme was a charming girl but as he had said to his sister, he thought she was vulnerable. Perhaps she had become embroiled with Brotherton.

Gerald himself had matured rapidly over the last few months. Responsible for the well-being of a group of young men who shared only the war they had to fight, he had dealt more or less successfully with many of their problems. This was very different.

He turned to his sister and said soberly. "You must have asked yourself one question."

"Of course. 'Is she pregnant?' I knew it was a silly question. There was little chance that she had seen him since the Michaelmas term and Esme told us that he had kissed her and that she didn't like it. Esme Marsh does not dissimulate – in any case, there were no signs." Gerald did not comment. This was not the sort of conversation that he normally had with his sister but the situation was not normal.

Rachel went to join Deborah and the two of them had retreated so that he and Esme could have a private conversation.

"You want to ask me some questions" he said. "If I can answer them I will."

Esme herself was very calm. "Perhaps we could walk together" she said. "If it does not trouble your arm."

"Not at all." said Gerald. "It was only a flesh wound."

"I've always thought that a frightening expression." said Esme as they walked away from the two other girls. They passed the parked staff-car. The driver was reading a map. Gerald just held up a hand in passing and, oddly, Corporal Bygrave got out of the car as though he had been summoned and came towards them. Gerald shook his head and his driver returned to the car and his map. Esme glanced in that direction. Then, all in rush as though she was determined to get it over with, "Philip and I knew each other. Some of the girls said he was my boyfriend and I think he thought the same. That was not the case, I was just being polite but he got the wrong impression. At the school dance, he said that he was joining up the following day. He said there was great danger for soldiers and that he might be killed and never come back. He made other suggestions. Said I should give him what he called comforts."

Gerald cut in here. This was a story that he had heard before. "And he put it to you that he should be treated in some way special because of this —." and then he stopped, Esme needed to develop the theme. She surprised him by changing the subject slightly.

"You said to your sister, when you treated us to tea, that I need to be looked after because I was vulnerable?"

"Yes I did, and that is what I thought."

"You meant I would be vulnerable to that sort of appeal?"

"Yes, I did. Rachel didn't agree. Was I wrong?"

Esme paused for a little. This was embarrassing but very important, so she went on "I think so. Philip had been drinking which I found off-putting. What I found difficult was that I thought, underneath the bravado; the 'I am offering my life for my country', that he was actually afraid. What an awful thing! I thought he was to be pitied. Perhaps giving in to him would bolster his courage. But there was always something wrong about him and when I let him kiss me that made it worse. Aren't you supposed to enjoy being kissed? He tried to go further but I wouldn't let him."

The girl paused, this was the crux of the matter.

"Now I feel guilty. If I'd given in perhaps he would not have been killed. It may be irrational and Deborah said that what he wanted from me, he could have got from a brothel – but, it doesn't help. Tell me how he died!"

Gerald looked at this fine-boned school-girl and re-assessed his idea that she was vulnerable. This was one very remarkable teenager. He came straight to the point.

"You were right. He was afraid. Most of us were. Brotherton died because he was frightened to show that he was frightened. He demonstrated this bravado, as you called it, at the wrong point. This was more than a week before we were driven onto the beaches. We were faced by an overwhelming force and were heavily out-gunned. My unit's job was to help delay the enemy's advance so that the army could escape. What we had to do was present some opposition while we retreated. It was a retreat; not a route and ninety of every hundred men involved kept their heads down. We did our job with the minimum of casualties and every minute we gained gave more chance for the survival of what was left of the British army."

Gerald Castle paused. He had written his report of the action but that was formulaic. Now he was reliving the horror.

"I put a squad into a defensive position to cover the retreat of the rest. I did not select Brotherton as part of that squad. I knew him to be a risk. He disobeyed orders and joined them. They were to choose their moment to abandon the position and follow the rest of us. Just before they could do so, he broke cover and charged at the enemy. He was the only commissioned officer with the group and two of the men followed him. They were mowed down. Fortunately, the sergeant kept control of the others. They gave covering fire and the sergeant, who should have known better, went forward to try and rescue the casualties. All three were dead. Brotherton, officially, died in action in his country's cause. He is, rightfully, one of our heroes and his name will be honoured whilst the country survives. Nonetheless, he was flawed – as you put it 'there was something wrong about him' and he cost the lives of two brave men."

By now the two of them, who were walking slowly and stopping frequently, had got about half way round the playing fields. It was a while before they said anything more. The girl seemed to have gained in self-assurance and Gerald felt he should go on. This was much more difficult than the reports he had to make to the relatives of the men he had lost and they were difficult enough.

"Deborah was right." he said. "What that young man wanted from you he could get from a brothel. Perhaps it would help you to know that he did so."

In response to the girl's questioning look, he went on. "He was not the only one in the platoon who was at risk of going to his grave without having carnal knowledge of a woman." Gerald knew that the way he put this was stilted but he could think of no other appropriate phraseology. "We had time before embarkation for some of the men to have a twenty-four hour pass. I gave passes to those that I judged needed them most. Some to the married men who had time to get to their wives and others to Brotherton and those like him." He was rewarded with a shy smile and also with what was clearly a lifting of the girl's spirits.

"As well a coward, he was a braggart; boasting to the men of his conquests. Not something he should have done in any circumstances. What made his behaviour dangerous was that the men held him in contempt. It was not acceptable to speak of those left behind in that way. In any case, they would know that he was unlikely to have had the conquests he claimed. I suppose, in a sense, I gave him his pass because I hoped, as you put it, that it might bolster his courage."

He thought she could do with time to take all this in and they started on another circuit of the field. They had nearly finished doing so when Esme said thoughtfully.

"He had been drinking. That seemed to me to be totally wrong." and then, in a different tone. "If it had been somebody else, I might have said 'yes'." and she glanced up into Gerald's face as if to see how he would take this. His response was one of relief.

"Esme Marsh, you are flirting with me!"

"Yes. Apparently I need the practice and with you it is safe."

"Safe because of the arm?"

"Safe, because it is you. Your role is buying scones. A girl must be safe with a man who buys scones."

They had reached the broad sweep of the gravel and at

that point, they were joined by Rachel, who took in the wide smiles on both their faces.

"What is going on here?" she asked.

"Your young friend is suggesting that I am so much of an old fuddy-duddy that she can flirt with me with impunity."

For a brief moment, Rachel was concerned. Gerald was a happily married man with a young son. Was what she was seeing here some sort of sexual magnetism between her brother and her friend? Esme was a very attractive girl. The suggestion of vulnerability would add to that attraction. Then she realised how light-hearted their smiles were.

"You've dealt with Philip Brotherton then?" she said.

"Your brother has done just that."

The worried look had left Esme's face and Gerald, putting his free arm around her shoulders, said, "I suppose I'd better fulfil my proper role and buy some scones. I'll get Mary and the boy."

So it was scones all round but Gerald did not have to buy them. This time they were provided by Miss Salway. Not as lavish as the last time they had indulged but a welcome interlude. It wasn't quite 'all round' and it was Rachel who asked about the 'war-hero'. Why wasn't he with them? Gerald said that Jim was being tactful and claimed that he was the most diplomatic young man he had ever come across. There was a rush of offers to take a tea-tray to the car. Rachel said that she had asked first and piled a tray high with scones and cakes. She even found a small tea-pot and made some fresh tea.

When she came back, she had an odd look on her face. "He asked about you, Esme." she said. "No, not about that.

Just asked who you were and what you did. It was as though he had seen you before and was trying to place you. He asked with an intensity that was almost disturbing. Why has he got a plaster under his eye? Why is he a war-hero?"

"Just a joke on my part." said Gerald. "and not a very good one. He saved my life!"

He did not expand but he was thoughtful for a minute. "I've only known him for a short period of time but he is clearly a man of many parts. I think he will go far. He did his job with the explosives in France with brilliant effect though he said it should have been an Engineer who did it. He demonstrated not only rapid reflexes but rapid thinking. The plaster covers the graze from a bullet. There can't be many men even in this war that have been closer to death. What does he do? He sticks a plaster on it."

CHAPTER 21

5th August 1986

Helena set out to itemise and catalogue the contents of the suitcase. She did so without reference to their importance, their date or even the order in which they had uncovered them. This list was sorted by the nature of the materials: 'books', for example was easy, as was 'clothing' but 'letters' was not easy. There were brief notes and both personal and formal letters. Did she classify them under one heading? With her usual control of the organization, she would list the same artefact under more than one heading. Even then she ended up with the catch-all category, 'Miscellaneous'.

Some of the items they had examined in detail and tried to fit into the overall history of Esme Marsh. She listed those that had not had such treatment, and put them to one side. She checked through the lists that she had made.

"There seems to be something missing from this suitcase." she said.

"Missing? I've touched nothing!" said Edgar, wondering if he had.

"No, something that should have been there but isn't. There is no 'parchment'!"

"Parchment? Why should a young woman have ancient documents amongst her mementoes?"

"Sorry. 'Parchment' as in the certificates of her

examination passes. Esme would have passed a stack of exams at school. I think they were called 'School Certificates' then. We also know she got a degree at Oxford. We have her swimming certificates but where are her academic ones?"

Edgar was dismissive. Those bits of paper are important to us, especially to me since I have so few, but to Esme, they didn't mean anything – certainly not in comparison with the other stuff in here."

"Did you save yours?" Helena looked across over the neat piles of Esme's possessions. The question examined largely unexplored territory and in asking it Helena was reviewing one curious aspect of their relationship; the way her husband's largely self-taught knowledge meshed with her understanding of her own subject. Edgar had not been a good student at school and passed his fair share of exams but he did not enjoy formal study. He was accepted because of his prowess at rugby. One of his teachers, himself a rugby player of some note, had failed to get Edgar interested in his own subject, Chemistry. He did persuade him to join in some extra-curricular work with others who were interested in photography. The teacher's motive was to improve the boy's understanding of chemistry, perhaps even to arouse his curiosity in the reactions involved in the development of the film.

In this he succeeded. It was more important that he found that Edgar had a natural talent for photography itself. Edgar got so much pleasure from this out-of-school activity that he felt duty bound to work hard at chemistry. He was more successful in this subject than the others.

Helena knew, in general terms, about his school career,

especially his prowess on the rugby field. He even had a 'First Fifteen' team photograph hanging in his workshop. He claimed it was to demonstrate how not to take a team photograph but he did not fool anybody. He was two years younger than the rest of the side and his boyish face in the photograph said so. She also knew that, in spite of having the qualifications, he had decided not to go on to the sixth form.

Her own friends, including Marilyn at first, all of them graduates, had asked her what he did. He was 'big and strong' certainly. He was presentable if not handsome, dressed well and had perfect if rather old-fashioned, manners. What, they asked, did he do? They expected her answer to at least imply a university background.

"He's a photographer." seemed to throw them. What was the high flyer, Helena Burroughs doing with a 'photographer'? It did not take them long to be won over by his natural courtesy. They were surprised by the width of his reading, sometimes startled by his insight into their own disciplines and he was the one they turned to when they wanted the answer to a day-to-day question. It was his art work however, that won the hearts of each and every one of them. Helena did not entirely approve of his generosity for he presented a copy of the first of the photographs that they admired to each of them and refused to take any payment.

"From me, in thanks for looking after Helena." he would say. When she protested that he was robbing the family fund, he just laughed. "Most, if not all of your friends will get married." he said. "Who is going to take their wedding photographs? All of your friends throw dinner parties. Where will they hang a photograph your husband has given them?

Finally, how much does it cost for me to produce another print? Apart from being the light of my life, you are also a financial asset."

Helena acknowledged the truth of what he had said. She also knew that was not the main reason why he made such presents. He did so because he was Edgar Mason and she was his girl.

"Did I save my certificates?" Edgar gave it some thought. "Yes I did but I couldn't tell you where they are now. They would not feature on any short list about what I would rescue if the house was burning down and Esme's suitcase works a bit like that."

"I'm about the same." said Helena. "They were important for job applications but none of my clients are interested in what exams I passed at school. You are probably right. She just wasn't interested."

CHAPTER 22

Summer Term 1941

St. Ermengild's restricted the number of examinations that their pupils could enter. In many cases, the girls outstripped the standard of the examinations in their understanding of the subjects. They did, however, need evidence to present when they applied for entrance to universities so the school ensured that they entered the correct papers. The girls themselves ensured that they reached a high grade in every subject entered.

Some universities asked candidates to attend for interviews. Esme, Rachel and Deborah determined that they would, all three of them, go to Oxford. Miss Salway, when she learned of this, made several phone calls to the Oxford women's colleges and persuaded them to arrange for the interviews for the three girls be on the same day. They did not take much persuading, some of them had been pupils at St. Ermengild's themselves and most of them had taught other pupils from the school. If Miss Salway suggested it was worth interviewing one of her pupils, they would make arrangements to do so.

Esme's grandmother, when she heard of this excursion, offered to send Treadwell and the Rolls. This offer was refused. The three girls enjoyed the idea of driving up to what they hoped was their future college and being escorted by the burly figure of Treadwell. They imagined him frowning at any potential advances by the young men and being completely correct with the lecturers. If any place sported classic cars then Oxford would. Treadwell's gleaming monster would attract attention anywhere. Nonetheless they decided against it. Perhaps they wanted to be away from caring adults.

They said all the right things, even writing little cards to Esme's grandmother explaining that they wanted the experience of the journey.

This, they thoroughly enjoyed. They travelled by bus to the railway station and third class on the train but not knowing the lay out, they took cabs to their colleges. They arranged to meet once they had settled in. In each instance, it was an overnight stay in the college that they were applying for, breakfast in Hall and a morning interview.

They were bubbling when they met in a pub the evening they arrived. Esme had picked up the local terminology. She spoke of the High, and the Broad without any 'street' attached. She pronounced 'Magdalen' as 'Maudlin' and warned them to spell it without an 'e' at the end. She distinguished between the Cherwell and the Isis.

Deborah told them why the pub they were in was called 'The East Gate', was erudite about the 'Martyrs' Memorial' and 'Dead Man's Walk'. Rachel had found the Bodleian and charmed her way into the librarians' friendliness and been given a conducted tour. Three schoolgirls had a glimpse of their future and were enthralled.

They were a little more subdued when they met in the waiting room of the station after their interviews. Each had been told that they would be informed whether their application was successful or not by post. It was explained that there were other candidates who had yet to be interviewed. It should have been obvious to them that they were in competition with others but in the formal statements from the colleges, it was a sobering thought.

Deborah, as part of her application, had to write an essay and was worried that she had said the wrong things at the interview. They had asked her what sort of things she read and since she had devoured a couple of Agatha Christie's on the train, she had replied "detective stories'. When one of the interviewers had said, almost scornfully as Deborah thought, "Oh! Whodunits!", she replied that you could tell who the murderer was according to the author and the crux of the puzzle was 'why' it was done and even 'how'. She wondered now if she had blown it by her aggression. Her friends pooh-poohed the idea.

Rachel said that her interview panel had been augmented by mathematicians. She got the feeling that they really did not believe that what her teachers had said about her. She said they were not able to credit a schoolgirl with such understanding.

It was Esme who had the most interesting story. At breakfast, one of the college lecturers, trailing her gown 'a bit like the White Queen' had sat herself down next to her almost as though she didn't know where she was. Esme and her fellow interviewees were in the main body of the dining hall and what staff there were that had come in to breakfast had sat at the High Table. This lady had buttered a piece of toast and turned to Esme and said, "You do know about

Chaucer, don't you?" and then made off with the slice of toast to her proper place.

She was surprised to see her on the interview panel. They had quizzed her rigorously about why she was doing English and not Modern Languages since she was so good at them. Esme, unwilling to say anything about translating for her father, was beginning to waffle when the lecturer who she called the White Queen broke in to say in somewhat distant tones.

"Tell us about Chaucer!" She had pressed the right button. Esme had only read the Prologue and a couple of the Canterbury Tales but delighted in the resonance of older version of the text as opposed to the translations and said so. She hoped Rachel and Deborah approved.

What she did not say was that she had quoted from the original using the pronunciation that she had been taught at St. Ermengild's and that her eyes had lit up with the pleasure the words gave her. More than one member of the panel was reminded of her own first delight in the language and the 'White Queen' just smiled.

The girls went to bed anxious but tiredness sent them quickly to sleep. The next morning, even before breakfast, they were asked to the Head's rooms. There they found both the Head and Miss Jackson sitting down to a breakfast of croissants and coffee: two things that produced a delightful combined aroma which was enough to lift the spirits of the three girls who were not sure why they had been summoned.

There were three other places set and on each place was an envelope. Each envelope was addressed to one of the girls. When invited, each one sat at the place clearly intended for them. The two teachers were clearly enjoying themselves and, as soon as the girls were seated, Miss Salway said, "You could have your breakfast first if you wish but you might want to open them now."

They did not need to be asked twice and each of them found a letter accepting their application. The 'Trio' would be together at Oxford the following year.

It was Esme who looked up from her letter and said, "You knew didn't you?"

"Yes, Esme. You know I would not have raised your hopes like this otherwise nor did we expect any other result. I had a busy time on the telephone yesterday. I enjoyed speaking to old friends and former pupils and I was much amused at their accounts of your interviews. I would have loved to have been a fly on the wall when Esme quoted from Chaucer in what the professor said was 'clear and ringing tones and the music of early England' All three of you were fine ambassadors for the school. I'm proud of you."

Miss Jackson, smiling happily to herself, said "Whodunits, indeed!"

CHAPTER 23

6th August 1986

Helena and Edgar were able to catch up on the following day. They started the session by opening one of the books that Esme had hurriedly packed, higgledy-piggledy, into the case. It was a slim brown volume called 'The Silent Traveller in Oxford' written and illustrated by one Chiang Yee. It was a present from Deborah who had written on the title page. "The illustrations are a delight. They certainly take me back. Take a look at the 'FEMALE PUNTERS' on page 38. Do you think he was watching us? The poem on page 147 brought tears to my eyes." and it was signed 'Rah'. There was a postscript. "Peter and I are looking at a flat in New York. You must come and visit us."

Helena followed Rah's instruction to find a sketch of three young women wearing swimming costumes and holding punt poles. Edgar, looking over her shoulder, pointed to one of them; pretty and in control and said "My choice for Esme" Helena agreed. It was possible in that simple sketch to see the girl, slim but curvaceous and with a head of tight fair curls.

Then she had her own turn. One of the trio was rather stout, and with the school-girl's consumption of scones in mind, Helena pointed to her and said. "Deborah" and then stopped. She turned the book back to the title page where

Deborah had signed her name. Then she reached for the autograph book and turned to the drawing of the young girl on the loch-side. "I thought so, the artist was Deborah, just compare the signatures."

That was a nice point but apart from showing that Deborah had artistic skills it did not take them any further forward. From what Deborah had written, they could tell that, at some time, the three girls had been in Oxford. Now they had to ask themselves how long they had been there. They had reached a way of thinking that was designed to prevent assumptions. This book and Deborah's note could have meant that the two girls had spent a day or a short holiday there. Some of their questions were answered when they read the letter used as a bookmark.

It made clear that Esme had gone up to Oxford as a student to read English. Helena and Edgar shared the thought that this was a waste of her talents as a linguist. The letter explained the reason behind her choice of subject. It was written before she went up and was from her future professor rejoicing in the fact there would be someone who would enjoy Anglo-Saxon and Early English. Most of her students, she wrote, were concerned about Jane Austen's sub-conscious or the sociology of the Russian authors, not about the beauty of the English language.

Edgar was glancing through the slim brown book. Deborah was right, the illustrations were a delight. He turned to the poem on page 147 as instructed by 'Rah'. The author had composed it and written it both in English and Chinese. He read to Helena:

'How sympathetic and kind the Oxford moon must be,

Shining idly on companions walking together
As she has done through the ages.'

She pretended not to notice his voice breaking on the last two lines and allowed him to recover.

"A couple of points." he said. "This wasn't published until 1944. They had probably gone down before Deborah bought it. Had they gone their different ways by the time she sent it? They certainly were what they called 'a trio'. Several years at boarding school, perhaps three at Oxford. Deborah, we can only assume has probably got married. In those days you didn't 'look for a flat in New York' with your 'partner'. They may have only been engaged at the time I suppose. You'll say that not everybody who gets engaged gets married." He ended on a flat note. He only knew of Deborah from their research and had never come across Peter before but he wished them happy even at the distance of time and place.

Helena rejoiced in his romanticism. "What happened to Rachel Castle?" she asked.

More important to Helena and Edgar than the stories of her friends, this discovery meant that they now had a handle on the next three years of Esme's life. For Helena there would be a rich source of evidence to put together. It made sense that Deborah and, probably Rachel, would also have gone up. The class lists of the university were in the public domain which would confirm that the girls had spent three years there. Edgar remarked that, at last, this delightful girl could now meet some worth-while men.

He was not allowed to get away with it. Helena stopped him.

"You are falling in love with a mental construct." she said.

"We don't know that Esme was delightful and, what is more, you are making unwarranted deductions. There would not have been many worth-while men at Oxford when they were up, they would have all been in the forces."

"Oops!" Edgar acknowledged his error but he did ask, "Mental construct? Isn't that what we are up to? However much evidence we obtain, Esme is coming out of our minds, not out of the suitcase. Out of my mind is coming something very similar to one Helena Burroughs – now Mason – and I'm entitled to fall in love with her. There's a precedent."

"Oh, hush! I'm trying to work out if you would have been classified as 'worth-while'" was Helena's response but, as she got up, she brushed her hand through his hair. "I'll be back for lunch!" and she left the house without offering an explanation of where she was going.

Edgar assumed that she was chasing up Esme's university career reference and, not daring to touch the suitcase, turned to the work he was doing. He had been attracted to the quality of the shine on Bakelite surfaces and was experimenting with some such artefacts that he had accumulated over the years. He spent a considerable time arranging the tones of a black telephone and a rich brown wireless-receiver. The lighting had to be powerful enough to produce the sheens he wanted without flooding the picture. When he next looked at his watch, he realised it was almost lunch time and, expecting Helena to be in the house, he rinsed his hands and headed for the kitchen.

She was not there but he had scarcely started sorting out something for the two of them to eat when she opened the front door. She did not come further in and Edgar could hear her making noises in the hall; sort of distressed mutterings. He went to investigate. Helena was wearing an anorak with the hood up. He had a suspicion she had put it up when she heard his approach.

She turned towards him and there was enough anguish in her face for him to move quickly forward to hold her. She tried to wriggle free but, by now, he was concerned enough not to let her. He reached to put back her hood but she clung to it tenaciously. Only when he held her face firmly in both hands and placed his lips on hers did she relax into his embrace and allow him to fold it back.

"It's a hair-cut." he said, laughing. "You are not supposed to behave like this. You're supposed to wait until I say, 'You've had your hair done. That looks nice!' That's what husbands are for."

"It's not funny." was all she could manage between the sobs. "It's all gone!"

Indeed it had. Her head of controlled fair curls was no more. Her hair had been cut short like a boy's, with a parting on one side and what was left combed away both sides from the parting. It was like a boy's except for her high forehead and the arches of her eyebrows. What it did do was enhance her always soft blue eyes and emphasise her delicate cheek-bones.

Edgar took a moment to study it. His response could be important but he was unable to stop himself.

"It may not be funny but it is certainly sexy."

This got a tremulous smile but a still tearful denial. "You're just saying that!"

By now, he had removed the anorak itself and was holding her comfortably to his chest.

"Well I could demonstrate that I mean what I say but I guess that wouldn't help – at least not just yet. Tell me what's wrong."

"How can you say that? I'm nearly bald. You have so many times waxed lyrical about my hair. Now you've got a bald wife."

"Because your curls were enchanting, that doesn't stop this hair-style being adorable – and I choose my words carefully. Your hair-dresser is a genius, he – I'll give odds that it is a man – has emphasised another facet of your attraction. It was there before but now it is clearer and if I did not adore you before, I adore you now. In case you haven't understood what I've been saying: with that hair-style, you would not be plausible as Ganymede"

Still not convinced, she reached up and kissed his cheek. "And I 'thank heaven, fasting.'" she said, as though to prove that he was not the only one who could produce the appropriate quotation. "I'll wash my face if you'll put the kettle on."

"I'll have to stop taking you to these high-brow shows." he said to her disappearing back. "And I haven't seen you 'on yours knees' yet."

Helena returned and with her eyes dried and a restorative cup of tea in her hand. She was calm again but, as though wishing her hair was back, she kept passing her hand across her head.

"So why the hair-cut?"

"Us ladies call it a 'hair-do'. Most times the cutting is kept to a minimum. Not today. I was thinking about the wedding. A new style might have been nice."

"The wedding's weeks away."

"Which would have given time for the style to have grown out if I didn't like it."

"What foresight." said Edgar and offered her another cup of tea. "I think perhaps I'd better have my suit cleaned."

"You won't be wearing your suit. Marilyn has decided it will be full morning-dress. You'll have to hire one."

CHAPTER 24

Michaelmas Term 1944

Esme looked around the room that she would study and sleep in for the next year – no not the next year, only about eight months, from now until May of the following year. It was adequate but drab – just the place to concentrate on her degree. Two years living in college with all the social distractions was all very well but she wanted to get a First. This, especially since she was continuing with her foreign language work including translations for her father, would be a great achievement. Her English professor, now also her tutor, was confident.

Esme was not so sure. She had enjoyed the intellectual challenge but had lost the measure of application that she had shown in school. This was because she had been enjoying the people. Rachel and Deborah had not helped. The three of the them formed a magnet to all the intelligent young men in the university. Some of them had been invalided out of the services and their jaundiced view of the world they lived in was brightened by the trio of friends. The three young women were, perhaps because they had the support of each other, even more attractive than they would have been separately.

They had a small car, a pre-war banger that they shared between them and they made excursions into the surrounding countryside. All this left less time available for study.

Esme remembered her remark to Gerald Castle that she needed practice in flirting and that he was safe to flirt with. She had plenty of practice here but, after a while, she realised that this flirting was also, in that sense, safe. She would accept an invitation to go and see a play or to eat at a new restaurant but always insisted on paying her own share of the evening. She enjoyed the intellectual challenge of the men who were reading the same subject as her. Experimentally, she allowed an occasional would-be boyfriend to kiss her if she liked him but such kisses showed that there was nothing more than the liking. She wondered if her experience with Philip Brotherton had put her off men but deep within her there was the knowledge that this was not so.

There was one, an American, called Christopher Reynolds who she had liked. The three girls called him 'The American.' rather than 'The Yank' because it gave him more dignity. He was at Oxford on a rowing scholarship and was reading English in the same year as Esme. He was older than most of the other students, had served in the American Navy in the debacle at Pearl Harbour and been invalided out because of his eyesight. So there was a romantic side to him and physical prowess. He was also very bright. There was even, since he was reading English, a mutual interest in Shakespeare; or there should have been. Somehow his was not the same. He was informed and erudite about the works but he did not rejoice in the poetry as Esme did. For a short while she thought that their relationship might go somewhere. Then, at the most romantic of moments, it came to nothing. They had been walking in the Botanical Gardens and had missed the bell calling closing time. When they got to the gate, it was locked. Christopher, lifted her over the gate with ease and, whilst she was in his arms, had kissed her.

"That was nice!" she said as he put her down outside the gate. Then he climbed over himself. He did not say anything until he was on his feet on the pavement. Then he said, and there was disappointment, almost sadness, in his voice.

"But not nice enough?"

It was true. There was nothing more there than physical contact.

"You don't want to try again?" she asked. He shook his head and she knew he was right. She also was disappointed. Esme had the idea that somewhere there was a man who was meant for her. She blamed this on her early reading of so many romances. It was reinforced by something that was not really more tangible than a feeling that came to her at night. She would feel, in her sleep, that she was secure and happy and that this feeling was because she was held in the arms of a man. There had just been the glimmer of a hope that Christopher was he but no such feeling came from the kiss. She realised that the older she got, the more desperate seemed her need for that man.

He looked solemnly down at her. "Esme Marsh, you know there is no point." he said and he tucked her hand in his arm as the two walked back to her College. "You and I are two of a kind. Somewhere in this world there is the partner that each of us is looking for. I hoped that you were mine but deep down I knew that you were not. I had to make sure. You always knew that I was not yours."

Yes, it had been only a hope. Surely, the presence in her dreams must be somewhere and somehow she was sure that she would know. With Christopher there had never been that feeling. Strangely, it was his declaration that he too was looking for his ideal partner that encouraged her. She was not the only person in the world who had such dreams.

Christopher had remained a good friend but just a friend. He offered reliability and they both knew that the other was looking for somebody else. Both of them continued their search and sometimes Esme would see him with another girl. Tactfully, she would pretend that she had not seen him. Most often, he would wave to her and, with an abrupt shake of his head, let her know that he had failed yet again.

She stopped flirting and, encouraged by Christopher, looked to make friends with the men students as she did with the women. This was not always easy. More than one undergraduate imagined himself in love with this very attractive young lady. Some of them would not believe that she was not interested and she was careful not to give them any impression that she was. She learned how to deal with those who thought she might be. She found that, in her responses to such would-be suitors, she had acquired a reputation of being frigid. This worried her because she knew herself to be otherwise. She just was not attracted in that way to the men she met.

Rachel, Deborah and herself would meet after a party or a dance or some other social event and compare notes. The other two seemed to treat the subject much more lightly than she did. She remembered one such post-mortem – as they called them – when they had been sympathetic about

Christopher. They too had hopes that he and Esme would hit it off. She did not say anything about the two of them having the same dream.

It was towards the end of their second year that once more they were seated in the deep but battered arm chairs in the Junior Common Room of Rachel's college. Rachel and Deborah were scoring the 'candidates' of the night before. Their terminology expressed their casual approach to the matter. "I thought your young man was rather handsome – could we call him 'swoony'?"

This was Deborah asking Esme and they smiled at the schoolgirl term. Deborah was really asking if Esme had thought this particular aspirant to her affections met with her approval. She and Rachel were worried that their friend never seemed to advance at all with any of the boys she met.

Esme was aware of this and found these sessions helpful. She could always rationalise to her friends why the latest possibility had not met her exacting standards.

"No joy there, I'm afraid!" she reported on this occasion. "He only talked about himself and that in a rather grandiose manner. I did think perhaps he deserved a kiss but the thought occurred to me that he would talk about that in future – claiming that he was a great lover. I know. I know. You think I'm oversensitive. Some of them I think are very nice but they are just not for me. The most attractive man I've ever met is your brother Gerald. I think that's because he cares. I want somebody to care for me, just me. Is that too much to ask?"

The other two were silent. Esme was, they thought, asking for the moon. All the boys they had met were mostly interested in themselves but both of them could see why Gerald Castle would score so highly. Rachel remembered how Esme had responded to his sage counselling.

"You've never really fancied him." she said, remembering her feeling of relief when she first realised this.

There was a pause in their conversation. Neither of her friends wanted to ask the question that was troubling them. Esme looked from one to the other and her mischievous smile removed some of their concern.

"No, not Gerald, not that way but 'Yes, I do'! I do have sexual feelings. Which is what you wanted to ask. Not with any real person yet but sometimes I wake in the night and…" she hesitated because it seemed so silly; but she wanted them to understand so she went on in a rush, "and he's there. I don't see him, certainly can't describe him but I do know that it is always the same man. He blocks out everything else. It is almost as though he is part of me. It isn't actually a dream just an impression and I try and hang on to it, to ask questions about it but the waking me rejects the irrationality. And 'yes', there is a sexual feeling but that is only one element of it."

This confession had shaken Rachel and Deborah. They had long thought that their friend was like something out of a fairy story; it was clear that she needed a Prince Charming. Now, they rallied to her support.

"This must be a projection of your subconscious. Perhaps it is someone you've met." was Rachel's response. She was seeking some sort of reality.

"What makes him unique?" was Deborah's question.

"He cares! More than that, he wraps me in a protective shell. I'm not talking about a physical protection. It is more profound than that. In his presence, sometimes in his arms, I am safe, secure against 'the whips and scorns of time', certainly against 'the pangs of dispriz'd love'. Yes, there is lot of Shakespeare about him."

She looked at her two friends and saw the expressions on their faces.

"Am I really that odd? It only happens on occasion and it is only for an instant. I think it is because I read too many romantic novels when I was younger."

"It certainly explains why the cream of Oxford's young men don't get very far with you." Deborah brought the conversation back to where it was before. "The competition is too good."

Esme felt a little better for sharing her dreams with her friends but she added her constant wish. "One day, I'll get a fraction of that feeling from one of them. Just a fraction will do!"

Now Deborah and Rachel had gone to America on exchanges. Both of them would be away for the rest of the academic year. Esme was on her own, as were the other two, being in universities at different ends of their new country. Esme wondered if they felt the same emptiness as she did but resolved to shake it off.

Whether their absence was the cause or not, that term she had hit the ground running. She had never had any difficulty with the origins of English, astonishing her tutors with the ease in which she mastered them. She even branched out to do minor work on regional accents and idioms. She did, however, find dull some of the modern novelists – though perhaps 'modern' was the wrong word to use – and she was pretty scathing about some of the translations of the Russians.

Her professor had taken her under her own wing and was very patient with these problems. Esme responded to the faith she had in her and worked to overcome her difficulties.

She shared her accommodation with Barbara, another student. Each had their own room but shared the bathroom and kitchen facilities. Barbara was reading History and was also working hard. She was an ideal flat mate. She never made a mess and always stuck to the routine that they had worked out between them. She had a boyfriend but never brought him home. Occasionally, if she needed a translation of a document or a snippet of Latin, she would ask Esme, knowing that her version would make more sense than her own. Very occasionally, Esme would ask something about historical dates and the movement of peoples and Barbara would oblige by finding the appropriate text.

There were always disadvantages in sharing a flat and Esme was already aware of one of them. Barbara seemed to have a multiplicity of knickers festooning the bathroom – a bit like the bunting decorating a dance hall. Esme was amused that she had used the word 'knickers' to herself. This was the rudest word she had known as a child. 'Undies' was an acceptable synonym if they had to be mentioned. Was her use of 'knickers' a sign that she was now grown up?

There was one morning that having another person in the flat proved convenient. When Esme came home from a lecture, anxious to pursue a couple of points, she found on the kitchen table a package addressed to her. There was a note from Barbara saying that the postman wanted a signature for its delivery.

Esme recognised the handwriting. It was from Deborah.

The three young women exchanged letters but this was more than a letter. Esme, intrigued, unwrapped it to find a book about Oxford. Quite a charming one written by a Chinaman. Deborah had written inside it and what she had written made her laugh and, almost, cry at the same time.

Her father visited her rarely. His Department had been sending her low level translation work, magazine articles and papers from scientific journals. This was in part to judge her product and in part to get her used to the Department's routine. Reginald was deep in some continuing project of great import but they did get out on one occasion in a punt. Deborah had taken great care to teach Esme how to punt and she was pleased to show off to her father. She was much impressed when he took the pole from her and, for a short distance, had demonstrated his own remembered skill. It was only for a short distance.

"That's enough boasting. You are taking me for a boat trip, not the other way round." he said as they swapped places again. Esme accepted what he said without questioning but she thought that perhaps he was overtiring himself. She had never seen her father as an old man but as he sat down in the punt, he gave that impression.

Later he seemed fully recovered. He took her out for a meal and then to an open air performance of A *Midsummer Night's Dream* in the Magdalen College Deer Park. He survived the uncomfortable seats with equanimity. It was a fine performance in spite of the limited resources. It was timed to use the magic of the fading light and the 'Rude Mechanicals' milked it for every laugh.

Several of her fellow undergraduates greeted her but

judging that her father did not wish to meet them, she simply returned their greetings.

"What is wrong with the young men of today?" he asked. "I expected to have to beat off your suitors with a stick."

Esme, always honest, had to say that it was not the young men, it was her and she had already beaten them off.

"Is this that fellow Brotherton?" he asked. "I thought young Castle had sorted that out."

"For a while I thought it was." she replied. "I thought about it a lot. After a while I realised it wasn't that. None of them – modesty forbids me to say how many – seemed to be what I was waiting for. I suppose I'm still waiting."

Esme gave her father her sideways, mischievous smile and he felt re-assured.

CHAPTER 25

7th August 1986

The next thing that Helena took from the suitcase was a bundle of papers tied neatly with an elaborate but rather crumpled bow.

"At last!" said Edgar. "The love-letters."

"Stop that! I've told you before! In any case, schoolgirls in those days didn't get love-letters."

"That bundle wasn't tied by a school-girl." countered Edgar. "and it may be speculation but I think this girl deserved someone to love her. You've compared her to yourself in colouring and in physique. My mental construct, as you put it, has someone like you. If I had known her in 'those days', I'd have been sending her love-letters."

"You mean like the ones you've been sending me for the last five years?"

He turned from the ribbon-wrapped bundle to face his wife.

"You've kept them, haven't you?" he asked and there was joy in the question.

"You bet." was her response. "But not where you can get at them. I shall need them for the divorce settlement!"

Edgar had a ready reply. "Oh, no you won't. I meant every word of them. 'All that I am, I give to you.'"

Helena's head went up.

"You disarm me, sir." she said in formal tones. Sometimes Edgar was impossible. "And this is a menu – not a love-letter." she had slipped the bundle from the ribbon, retaining the bow in doing so and taken out one of the papers.

Edgar took it from her hand.

"It's not even that." he said and there was a trace of disappointment in his voice. "It's an announcement of an office-party and some idea of the entertainment offered. A sort of light-hearted invitation. Why would she keep this?"

Helena pointed to the bottom of the page where there was an addition; not printed but written boldly by hand.

"That." she said, explaining the curious grouping of letters and numbers, "Was a telephone number. On the same lines as 'Pennsylvania 65000." and the professional edge entered her voice. "And I might be able to find out whose it was."

Edgar, with a nod from Helena, lifted the next item from the bundle – a plain official brown envelope with the simple designation 'Miss Marsh' on the front. It held a card that was also plain; a white postcard with the line 'You <u>did</u> teach the torches to burn bright. Please phone me!' written in the same firm hand as the phone number on the invitation.

"Bit corny, that. Even pretentious. 'Look I'm quoting from Romeo and Juliet. What a sophisticated chap I am!'" said Edgar. "But Esme kept it; so I suppose she approved."

"What do you mean, 'corny'? You used the very same line to me."

"Not the same. I remember distinctly. I didn't write an office memo to you telling you what a pretty girl you were." said Edgar. "I delivered the full quotation with a slight alteration:

'*Whose* lady's that, which doth enrich the hand
of yonder knight?

O, she doth teach the torches to burn bright!'
and I made sure the 'knight', I forget his name – he played
fly-half – heard the question aright. He was drooling all over
you. He took the hint."

"So it was nothing more than a cock crow? What other
rivals did you frighten off?"

"He was no rival. It would have been a waste of time for
both of you. He – I remember now – his name was Fred
something – had a steady girl-friend who wasn't there for
some reason. He was hoping that you would fill the gap. You
would have held him in gentle contempt."

"So a full challenge was needed?"

"Well, I had drink taken but I did think that was the
moment that I knew I had to say something. Shakespeare said
it for me."

"And had you just come from mooning over some
Rosaline?"

"No, I'd come from a rugby match, as you well know
since you actually came to watch me play. By then there were
no Rosalines."

Helena, who had enjoyed that moment which she had
called 'nothing more than a cock-crow' more than she was
prepared to admit, brought the conversation down to earth.
"I never had much time for Romeo. He goes to a dance to
pursue Rosaline, his latest bit of fluff, sees a girl the other
side of the room and falls in love with her just because of her
looks. He knows nothing about her. He hasn't even heard
her speak. No wonder it was a tragedy."

"You may be right; but think of the words. They change everything. Magic takes control of the scene because of those words."

"And this works for Esme?"

"I'd like to think so and on second thoughts, I withdraw the 'corny'. This is indeed a love-letter, distilled to its essence. The 'Please' in the request that she phone him is a confession of humble yet hopeful aspiration. If she could resist such an appeal, they would have no future together in any case. I would like this romantic young man to be Jim Bygrave, the man you say Esme married. Why otherwise would she keep this briefest of notes?"

"He might be but he may just be another of her conquests. If, as you say, she was so attractive, there would be more than one young man in her life. We need something to tie him to the note; something more than wishful thinking."

"Such as?"

"An example of his handwriting would do. He was an administrator in the army and there just may be some surviving documents."

"That, my darling wife, should keep you occupied while I'm away on this shoot. I need to earn a crust."

"I've got work to do as well, you know. You're not the only bread-winner in this house."

Edgar had a wedding in Orkney. Some quixotic bride had insisted that she get married where she had met her husband-to-be. Bride and groom also had the ulterior motive that they wanted it to be a quiet ceremony. Nonetheless, they wanted Edgar not just for the wedding photographs but also a record of the scenery.

A travel firm had expressed interest in that part of the project.

What Helena had said was only too true. They had hoped to go to the Scottish Isle together but she had been called to attend a court case as an expert witness.

"Some other time!" he said. "I promise."

CHAPTER 26

16th December 1945

Esme got her 'First'. She took time off to visit Rachel and Deborah in the States and she did a bit of touring on her own. She stayed with the girls and cadged lifts which eked out her cash-allowance and returned to England when she had run out of it. She took up the translating job that she had learned while still a student. She was employed in the Department itself and full-time.

It took her new colleagues a little while to get used to the idea of the boss's daughter working with them but they were soon impressed by her abilities. Just before Christmas, she was at a party in the Department. A long-term employee was retiring. This woman had rolled up her Christmas and New Year breaks and what holidays she was due so that she could finish before the festivities. It was the tradition to throw an office party when a senior member of staff left.

It was the first time that Esme had been to one of these leaving parties and she was a bit lost. Many of her fellow workers were intent on consuming as much as they could of the buffet. Food and drink were provided by the Foreign Office. Some of her colleagues were taking the opportunity to get a drink at their employer's expense. The Department had gone to town on this occasion not only because the retiring member of staff was so popular but because it was easier now than during the war to get the wherewithal for a decent party. Since August, the nation had no longer been at war. It would soon be the first of the peace-time Christmases. It was time to relax.

The Department had commandeered the Conference Room and moved most of the furniture. The annexe was given over to a generous buffet, whence many of the staff had headed. There was a small band playing jazz in one corner of the main room but in a gentle fashion. Few of those present were concerned with dancing. Esme was not hungry and most of her work-mates were in groups of friends. She didn't want to be a wet blanket but this was not really her party. After all, she had only spoken to the woman who was retiring a couple of times. She wondered how long she needed to stay before she could excuse herself.

She did not see the slim young man until he took her hand in his. He seemed to have appeared from nowhere. It seemed perfectly natural that he should approach her in this way. She looked up at him, curious to see why this was so. There was a slight scar just under his right eye, an area of white skin, which, if anything, enhanced the smooth contours of an interesting face. A bit, Esme thought, like a 'beauty spot' of a Georgian lady. It drew attention to his eyes. They were more green than hazel and, at that moment, were fixed on her own face. She took in the way that he was looking at her and, for an instant, was very still.

The stranger wore an army uniform which set him apart from the office workers. It carried the insignia of a Major and he looked very young to have such a rank. His shoulder tabs read R.A.O.C. which meant nothing to her and his sleeve carried an even more enigmatic badge. It was a large letter 'A' resting in what looked like a burning torch. Where had she seen something like that before? He had the ribbons of three medals on his chest but Esme did not know what they were for. He seemed very relaxed about the fact that they were total strangers.

"You may 'teach the torches to burn bright'." he said and paused. His accent was just detectable as a South London one. "But that is no excuse for not dancing." he continued and he led her onto the small space left clear for that purpose. She did not object, did not want to object. The band was playing a subdued number designed for intimate dancing but he held her in the conventional ball-room hold. She could feel the thumb of his right hand in the small of her back, and, when necessary, his extended palm checking her or directing her into a turn.

She had so welcomed his intervention into her comparative isolation that she saw him as rescuing her and made no resistance at all. Now she was glad that she had not. This, she thought, almost as an aside, was why they taught the girls at St. Ermengild's to dance; so that they could respond with a degree of skill to such a dancer. There was something more here than the togetherness of the dance and Esme could not fully believe what it was.

She remembered herself saying when she had discussed with Rachel and Deborah how she woke at nights with an after image of a sort of guardian, a figure who threw a protective shield around her. She had said that 'there was a lot of Shakespeare about him'. She remembered that the discussion had arisen from her worries about her not being attracted to men. She told the other two that she was attracted to this fantasy guardian definitely as a man. She had spent hours thinking about this amorphous waking dream and finally agreed with her friends that she was asking too much. Fantasy lovers only came in fairy stories. This was just wishful thinking. The dream did not come back.

Now she was attracted to this man and she had been in his arms for minutes only. This stranger announced himself with a quote from Romeo and Juliet. Perhaps she should have said misquote but Romeo's line 'she doth teach the torches to burn bright' was not addressed directly to Juliet. He was allowed, surely, to modify it.

He said nothing after this first, rather colourful, introduction and she did not need him to do so. Ten minutes ago, she had felt out of place, now she was somehow comfortable but, more important, intrigued and, oddly, secure. That was it; she felt secure. She had said that she would settle for a fraction of the feeling she experienced in her dream. At the moment, there was an explosion of that feeling and it threatened to engulf her. Why should she be so sure that he cared for her?

When they stopped dancing there would be time enough to find out more about him. For the moment, she was both enjoying herself and telling herself to stay calm. Above all, there was a potential for excitement.

The music came to an end and he stood back politely to applaud the musicians. Before she could ask him who he was, one of the security staff spoke to her.

"Excuse me, Miss Marsh. Could you tell me who this young man is?"

So he had gate-crashed and she should say so but she was not going to do so.

"He's just a courier." she said. "He has brought a message from my father. This lot here seemed more interested in food than dancing, so I asked him if he would."

The soldier raised an eyebrow and with that simple gesture made her smile. He accepted and played his role as a courier. Somewhere he had found a piece of paper and was writing on it as though recording Esme's reply to his supposed message. The mention of her father was enough to quell any further suspicions that the security guard might have had and, with an apology, he returned to his post.

"That was kind, Miss Marsh." he said. "I'll go now. Couriers aren't supposed to hang about. You should know that I'm here because I boasted that the security was poor and, foolishly, took a bet that I could get in – even wearing my uniform."

"It is *your* uniform, then." said Esme and he responded in kind.

"I signed for it!" He took her hand. "I'll tell you what I've won if you call me." Then he left before she could ask how she could call him when she did not even know his name.

CHAPTER 27

13th August 1986

Edgar put his key cautiously into the front door of his house. It was half past seven in the morning and Helena might still be asleep this early in the day. He should have got back the night before but the van had developed a fault. Fortunately, he had been able to phone so that she would not worry about why he had not returned when expected. As it was, he had sat around in a cafe for several hours while the repair men dealt with the van. There was a part that they had to get, they said. Then he had driven through the night. He had plenty of time and, in any case did not want to arrive too early so he stopped a couple of times to top up his caffeine count.

Helena was up and came into the hall to greet him with a welcoming hug. She took one look at him and said. "Bed for you, my wanderer! I'll wake you for lunch." and she led him into the bedroom. She helped him out of his jacket, sat him down and removed his shoes. "Take your trousers off!" she commanded.

"Don't tempt me!" he said. It was good to be home. He did so then slumped out on the bed and fell asleep.

Helena did indeed wake him for lunch. She gave him ten minutes to shower and make himself presentable and then served them both with the lightest of mushroom omelettes with a grating of cheese to add that difference. This, harking back to when they first met, was one of the couple's 'come-home' meals and very welcome it was.

They exchanged accounts of what they had done over the last few days, happy to be together again. It was Edgar who pointed out that this was the longest period they had been apart since they were married.

Physically and mentally restored, they returned to the suitcase.

"There's an air-mail letter hidden here." Edgar had spotted a corner of the tell-tale blue paper but left it there for Helena to extract. She did so with care.

It was folded as it would have been for posting with the address of the writer on one side and that of the addressee on the other. It was addressed to Esme at her London flat and the sender was Rachel Castle and this information was greeted with a little cheer by Helena.

"About time we heard from her." she said. "I can just make out the date. 1945, I think. Things were getting back to normal." Then, more formally since she was recording. "The letter is hand written, as are the addresses. Rachel writes in a clear, rounded style which she would have learned at primary school but to which she has added some appropriate and rather elegant scrolling. That doyen of the spoken word, my Lord and Master will now read it for the tape?"

"You are quite excited by this, aren't you?" was Edgar's response but then did as he was told. He did, indeed, have a fine reading voice and was quick enough in his understanding of the text to add meaning to it.

Dear Esme,

I suggest you sit down before you read on.

You will remember Christopher Reynolds – 'the American', we called him. A week ago his university and ours had a boat race. A bit like the Oxford and Cambridge one except they row on their own rivers. This one was here. Chris was in the visiting crew.

I was walking across the campus to the library from a lecture and heard my name called out. He came across and made sure it was me. If you remember, he doesn't see all that well.

We went for coffee – and then for lunch. He had to row in the afternoon and I skipped a lecture to watch him. His crew went back to their own university but he stayed behind. He said that the term was nearly over, which it was, so I didn't protest. Somehow, things accelerated and yesterday, he proposed.

I did not hesitate. We were both puzzled that this had not happened at Oxford.

At first, before he proposed – there I've written it again – I didn't dare mention you but I sensed he wanted to clear the ground and, to tell the truth, so did I so I took the risk.

"What about Esme?" I asked. There wasn't any other way of putting it.

"Esme who?" he said with a big grin. Although I knew he didn't need to, he did clear the ground. I didn't tell him that I already knew the story. There is nothing wrong with a little forgetfulness and as he stumbled through his account – I'm glad it matched yours exactly – I knew, not so much from what he said but from the way he said it, that he was my Prince Charming, not yours.

We are not going to hang about for too long before the ceremony. Apart from anything else, when I finish the course, I run out of visa time. The others are calling me 'just another G.I.' but I don't care. I'll send you an invitation.

Rah is astonished about this. She is held in high esteem over here. I suspect she may get an academic job.

Have you found that 'fraction' of that feeling yet? My most profound hopes that you have.

Love, Rachel

The two researchers were, once more enjoying the history of their subject. Helena had insisted that not only would they make no assumptions about Esme but also that the research should stand up to her rigorous professional standards. This made the process long-drawn-out and exhausting. This meant that even something as startling as this had to be treated formally.

This did not stop Edgar from asking, "'Fraction of feeling'. What's all that about?"

"Well it is not about whether she's discovered the joys of smoking, that much is sure. Just as a matter of interest, did any of these girls smoke?"

Helena had her own ideas about what Rachel meant in her well-wishes to Esme, but she did not offer them as an answer.

"That's our second romance, not including Esme herself." she said. "Have you noticed all these references to fairy stories? My grandmother, we know, was 'happy ever after'. What about these two?"

Edgar said nothing but he had dragged out from under his desk, the box for recycled paper. He delved into it and emerged, triumphant, with an old copy of 'Time' magazine. He flipped through the pages.

"Well it was 'happy' until a few weeks ago." he said. He had turned to the 'Milestones' page of obituaries and handed it to Helena. The gist of the article answered her question. Christopher Reynolds, Olympic Oarsman, had died shortly after being admitted to hospital. He left a widow, the English Mathematician, born, Rachel Castle and their two daughters. Rachel had named her ground-breaking mathematical work, in honour of her husband, the 'Reynolds Equation'.

"I was thinking of trying to make contact with Rachel. In view of this, I think we will have to leave her for a while. They had been married for forty years. Knocking on her door and asking about someone she knew that long ago is not going to help." said Helena regretfully. Edgar was not so sure but he offered no comment. He thought it might benefit a recent widow to be reminded of the life past. He said nothing because he thought that it would not help Helena or take them any further with their research.

He did say, "It would be nice to hear about the third girl, Deborah Wilson."

In return for complying with Helena's rules, Edgar was adamant that they be allowed to eat meals at regular times and that, whilst they were eating, they be allowed to talk about things other than her distant relative. After the revelations from the magazine, Edgar had popped out for fish and chips and, on his return, he had decided to share something with his wife.

The previous day, they had been discussing Marilyn and Bill's wedding and the total commitment of the marriage ceremony; that

These two are firmly bound
By law and bands of gold.

Something that the couple had not previously found necessary. They had dealt with the historical significance of the vows in even the simplest of ceremonies – how the Romans had asked only for a public statement that each of them accepted the other as the spouse. Then they had moved on to the customs that had grown up around those vows. Even the Roman groom carried the bride across the thresh-hold to avoid her stumbling on it and bringing bad luck.

He brought in today's fish and chips and he broached the subject again. This time, as he said, introducing those customs current in the modern affluent society.

"They are determined that they don't miss out on anything related to their wedding. Do you know that Marilyn insists on Bill having a stag-night? His last night of freedom, his last chance to shed – is that what you do with them? – his wild oats. What codswallop. If he'd done any wild-oating over the last three years, he wouldn't have the wherewithal to produce any more."

"Boys will be boys." said Helena, and she did so without emphasis.

Edgar detected something in the way she had said that but pressed on. "It's worse than that. In my official position as 'Best Man', I've got to arrange it. Something I'm not looking forward to – neither the arranging nor the night itself. What's more, neither is he. He's only going through with it to please Marilyn. You're not to tell her that, by the way."

Helena transferred the paper-wrapped fish and chips on to heated plates, shifting some of her chips on to Edgar's. Once more, they had made Esme Marsh an excuse to indulge in one of Edgar's favourite meals.

"You had a stag-night, as I remember." she said. "Didn't you enjoy it? Your last night of freedom?"

"Well. I told you I was out with the lads but I had a job to do, a lucrative one and one I'd contracted for."

Helena clasped one hand to her brow and held the other out as though to repulse him. "So you've been lying to me for years. What other evil doings have you concealed from your deceived wife?"

Edgar ignored the histrionics. "It was the whitest of lies." he said. "And it gave us the best of both worlds. You had the moral high ground – 'these boys having to get drunk before they can give up their freedom'. You also got a groom who was not suffering from a hangover and the job paid for that hotel in Northumberland. I was a bit short of money at the time."

211

This had been their honeymoon hotel. She had noticed, but not remarked at the time, that it was an up-market establishment.

"For that hotel, I forgive you – such opulence. That enormous room with its incredible four-poster bed with its velvet curtains. One of those slept in by Good Queen Bess I shouldn't wonder; and there were those deep arm-chairs. There was even a log fire and a little library of books. I remember that the weather stopped us from walking. That library was useful. We needed something to do."

"I noticed you did a lot of reading. I remember the painting of the tasteful nude on the far wall. At a distance, she was offering encouragement until you drew the bed curtains."

"I thought you'd remember the nude." she said.

"Close up, the way the artist had applied the oils meant she looked as though she had a rather unpleasant skin disease."

"Close up! Have you no shame?"

"Well I was comparing particulars. As I remember, she had… "

"Don't you dare, Edgar Mason!"

"I was going to say, 'longer finger-nails than you'.

"And I didn't draw the curtains to exclude your nude. I did so to keep out the draught. After all, you may have needed some encouragement."

"Not then. Not now." he said, rising from his seat

"No! Not now! Sit down, you monster. The chips will get cold if you carry on like that but, in any case, I've got a question. When is Bill's stag-night to take place?"

"The nineteenth of August. That's two nights before the wedding instead of the night before. I introduced a note of caution, suggesting that Marilyn would not be happy if he appeared on the great day looking like something the cat had dragged in. He didn't take much persuading."

A slow smile spread across his wife's face.

"That is the same night as Marilyn wants me to arrange a hen-party. And, what do you think? She hates the idea and is only doing it to please Bill."

Edgar said nothing. He had seen the mischief in Helena's eyes. He knew that she was already scheming some escapade to take advantage of the coincidence of the couple's plans. He ate some of his chips, used a few of them to make a chip butty, put some vinegar on his fish before attacking it and waited.

"How about a hot-air balloon?"

"Go on!" said Edgar resignedly. What mad scheme was she proposing? All of a sudden, arranging a stag-party seemed to be an easy option.

"Simple. You book a hot-air balloon flight for Bill. I do the same for Marilyn. Just the sort of thing that they would expect except they are both on the same balloon."

Edgar breathed a sigh of relief. Helena had held her imagination in check. It sounded not only a good idea but also fun. He felt it incumbent of him to look for flaws.

"What if they compare notes?"

"Neither of them will know in what form the 'party' is going to take place. We won't tell them."

"These flights are often cancelled because of the weather."

"Good point. We'll have to have a back-up plan."

"Are either of them frightened of heights?"

"No. We know that. Remember when we went up in that ski-lift. You had a moment there yourself but they didn't even notice how far down the next bit of ground was."

It was Helena's turn to ask a question. "Do we invite their friends?"

Edgar stopped to consider that one but his answer went beyond a simple yes or no.

"This is their balloon flight." he said. "They have to have a pilot, I know, but, otherwise, they are on their own."

"You get more and more romantic as you get older." she said and brushed his head with her lips as she went to put the kettle on. He followed her into the kitchen and leant upon the door jamb.

"What do they do afterwards?" he asked.

"Go on! You not really asking, you're telling."

"It is only on their wedding day that the groom is not supposed to see the bride before the ceremony. Since they are having their 'stag' and 'hen' – what's the female of stag? – party on the same day, since they are going up in a balloon together, why don't we arrange they shed their wild oats together?"

"In a hotel?"

"Marilyn's dad has insisted on paying me and in advance for the albums. I said I would use the money somehow. We can book a posh hotel. A sort of pre-nuptial agreement."

"Even more romance!"

"Well, it is a wedding".

CHAPTER 28

17th December 1945

There was much chat in the office the following day. One of the girls had been proposed to at the party by her long-time boyfriend and was displaying her engagement ring. It was she who asked Esme the question that the others wanted to.

"So, who was the handsome soldier?"

Esme was at a complete loss. "I don't know." she said and as she did so she felt a touch of despair. "He was a gate-crasher. He said it was for a bet that he could get past our security."

"And when do you see him again?" At least two of the girls asked the question at the same time. Perhaps because of Janet's engagement, they were even more than usually concerned with boyfriends.

"How can I?" she said. "He said to phone him but he didn't give me his name, let alone a phone number. I can't help feeling he was just having a bit of fun."

They were in their break but the supervisor obviously thought they were taking too long about it when she came in carrying an envelope. It was an official issue envelope and was addressed to Miss Marsh. The address was typed.

"Miss Marsh." she said sternly. "I hope this letter is not a personal one. It was left by hand at reception."

Inside was a plain post-card. On it was written: 'You <u>did</u>

teach the torches to burn bright' and below that; 'Please phone me.'

Esme tried to conceal the card from the others but then she cried out in frustration.

"How can I phone him without a number or a name?" and dropped the card on her desk.

"Buck up, Esme!" Her friend Jane Clayton spoke reassuringly. Most of the translators were young and all of them were women. Jane was one of the older ones and she had taken Esme under her wing when she had first arrived. She was dark haired and cheerful. Her dark brown eyes were friendly. She offered a depth of welcome that reminded Esme of Rachel and Deborah. She was, as was only to be expected, less flamboyant than the two schoolgirls but just as sincere. Esme liked her very much and had, increasingly, come to rely on her.

Jane went on to say, "If that young man we saw last night has asked you to phone him, you have his phone number. I'd bet money on it."

"No!" she protested. "I've told you —" and then she stopped. He had written something down, pretending to take a message, but where? The only paper there had been the invitations. She had kept hers. She thanked heaven as she pulled it from her handbag. At the bottom of the page was a telephone number – nothing else. Esme didn't need anything else; how clever of him to return the paper to her bag!

She was tempted to pick up a phone straight away but she waited for her lunch break and sallied forth for a public phone with the well-wishes of her work-mates and a shower of small change.

She placed money in the slot – more than she could possibly need – dialled the number and waited. She did not wait long and was greeted with the voice she had hoped for.

"Please let that be Esme." he said, and although she had thought perhaps she might not, she pressed the button that took her money and opened her line to him.

"That's not fair." she said. "You now have my full name and I don't have a clue what yours is."

"Sorry. That was silly of me. Jim Bygrave is my name and I will try to stop messing about. I'm not normally like this. I've been cursing myself all night and most of the day. That was a daft trick with the telephone number. What would I do if you had thrown the invitation away? How would I know whether you had done so or not? Suppose you had the number and weren't interested in phoning me – and now I'm babbling like an idiot. I'll start again."

Esme was happy with the babbling. With her own sense of relief, this was just what she wanted from him. It was unexpected and completely charming. This was not the self-possessed stranger who had guided her so gently yesterday onto the dance floor but someone becoming increasingly familiar. Indeed, his very name seemed familiar. Esme put more money into the box, even though it did not need any, but did not let him start again.

"Hello, Jim Bygrave." she said. "You promised that, if I phoned you, you would tell me what you had won in the bet."

"So I did. Two tickets to 'the Windmill' on New Year's Eve. Can you make that? I mean, would you like to come?"

He stopped speaking and it was as though he had taken a

deep breath to start again. When he spoke it was in a much more measured tone.

"This is ridiculous! Esme Marsh, we have to meet."

"And before New Year's Eve!" she agreed and could not prevent her enthusiasm showing in her voice. Why should she? She was enthusiastic. "What about tonight?" Esme had a feeling that she already had something on that night but she did not care. She had to find out more about this man and the sooner the better.

"Marvellous. What time do you finish work?"

"Five."

"I'll be waiting outside your office."

"Sometimes we have to work late. We get busy in the afternoons."

"I shall walk up and down impatiently and believe that I've been stood up."

"Do you good!" replied Esme and put the phone down smiling.

She was, however, her father's daughter and before she left the booth, she made another call. She was fortunate and her call was answered promptly.

"Hello, Castle here."

"Gerald. This is Esme Marsh. How lucky to catch you."

There was a warm welcome in Gerald's voice as he asked how an old fuddy-duddy could help her. He stopped to write down what she was asking for, read the details back to her and waited for her to confirm before he spoke again.

Esme realised why he was so particular when she heard what he had to say.

"This is extraordinary. I knew a Corporal James Bygrave

in the army. He was the driver who took me to St. Ermengild's. You remember, we called him the 'war-hero' and were thankful for his tact. Didn't he carry Charlie across the gravel for Betty? I couldn't understand why at the time and then he went back and sat in the car. It must be the same man. I'll get back to you. Your first question is easy. R.A.O.C. stands for the Royal Army Ordnance Corps. Like the Medical Corps they are part of the service wing of the army. 'Ordnance' can be translated as guns and ammunition. My Corporal James Bygrave was certainly in the Corps but he is unlikely to be a major. You sound as though this is urgent. I'll get back to you as soon as possible. Am I allowed to ask why I'm enquiring?"

Esme realised why the name had seemed familiar and remembered Gerald explaining why he had called him a war-hero but she could not remember the man himself. What she could remember of the occasion was that Gerald had rescued her from a mood of total misery. Now, she was asking him, once again, to tell her something about a man. In complete contrast, her mood now was of total elation.

"Yes, you are." she said. "It is for something you've done for me before. Jim Bygrave is a man I met last night. He will be waiting for me outside the office when I finish work. All the details you can, please. I can't remember much about your driver but if this is the same man he has some questions to answer. I pray you come up with a positive report this time. I've an odd feeling that this is more important than seems possible."

"As soon as I can." Gerald still had concerns that Esme was a vulnerable person but she had survived so far. He allowed none of his doubts to show.

By the time she had got back to her office, she was smiling again. Even if this was the same Jim Bygrave; so what? He surely had not been stalking her for five years. She was smiling when she had a snatched lunch in the canteen and smiling when she returned to her desk and she positively beamed at the questions from the other girls but refused to give them details even though they demanded them.

Then the call from Gerald Castle came through. Esme got a frown from her supervisor but since he had given his rank – he was now a full colonel – Esme claimed that she was just checking a reference.

Gerald's voice was light-hearted, even cheerful. He wasted no time.

"Yes, it's the same Bygrave. He's the man who saved my life. You've found a bright lad there. I always thought he'd go a long way." he said. "Major James Bygrave runs a department at the Corps' Headquarters. They are writing procedures on how to deal with all the ammunition that has been issued and not used and is now scattered about the country. There is too much risk that will end up in the wrong hands. They think so much of him that I'm surprised that they let him out."

Esme thanked him. She had had no doubt that Jim Bygrave was one of the good guys but it was nice to hear how good he was. She tried to think back to when Gerald, with his arm in a sling, had come to her rescue at St. Ermengild's. Rachel had noticed that Gerald's driver had been left out in his car whilst they had enjoyed their tea party. She had put together a tray of goodies and taken it to him. Now Esme remembered, Rachel had said he had asked questions about her. She could not remember anything else about him. She would be interested to hear him explaining why he had not mentioned the St. Ermengild's affair. Would he say he didn't remember? Rachel had said that he had asked about her specifically.

Esme finished the phone call asking Gerald about Betty and Charlie and they made a vague arrangement for Esme to visit them. Gerald wished her luck with her date. He remembered her anguish about a man that had meant nothing to her and was thankful that he could make a positive report about Major Bygrave. That was a remarkable promotion! He had not even been an officer!

"Can I tell Rachel?" he asked.

"Oh, yes, and she can tell Rah. Tell her that there is a lot of Shakespeare about him. She'll understand." She wanted to share her hopes with her friends even if it was second-hand and even if all this was wishful thinking. "I'll phone them both tomorrow."

Just before he rang off, Gerald said, "He's not allowed to wear that 'flaming A' on his arm. It's against regulations but he doesn't care and his superiors turn a blind eye to it."

This did trigger a memory. Jim Bygrave, then just a corporal, was sitting in the front passenger seat of the staff car and he was reading a map but the window was wound down and his arm was resting on the door. She had walked past with Gerald and glanced at him. She remembered that above his two gleaming white corporal stripes, there was a red and gold badge; the letter 'A' set into a burning torch: the 'flaming A'.

The smooth young man, quoting Shakespeare last night

and again on official note-paper today, had some explaining to do. Esme debated whether to ask him to do so when they met or to leave that until she was more certain about her feelings.

CHAPTER 29

14th August 1986

Helena and Edgar were working out what they had to do to arrange the hot-air balloon flight when Bill phoned. When he said who he was, Edgar, who had answered the phone, gave a guilty start but there was no way that Bill could have learned of their plans; they had not done anything yet.

Bill was, as usual, business-like. "I've got a name and address for you." he said "I don't think it will get you anywhere but it is a concrete lead and you'll be able to talk to someone."

"I'm listening."

"The house you bought the suitcase from was owned by a Mrs. Martin. Mrs. Martin, before she was married, was Miss Jane Clayton. Miss Jane Clayton worked in the translation department of the F.O. at the same time as Esme. Recently, she sold her house and her children moved her to what I think might be a sort of granny flat."

"Brilliant. Go on!" Jim had called Helena to his side and held the phone so that she could hear. He was busy writing the details down. "That's sufficient evidence of how clever you are but I know how you work. Jane Martin is still alive and you have her address, don't you?"

"It'll cost you!"

"Just for some office gossip?"

"It won't be just gossip. Ask yourself why Jane Clayton was the keeper of the suitcase."

Helena was nodding furiously and went to snatch the phone from his hands. He held on to it.

"Helena says the drinks are on her. So you can tell me."

He wrote down the address he was given in bold capitals so that Helena could read it. Bill went on.

"I think at least one of her children lives near her. Best of luck! Here's the phone number."

Early on in the research into Esme Marsh, Helena had started one of her own note-books. These were of her own design. They were divided into two sections. The first section was lined paper. She wrote a fine hand so she used narrow lines. Entries here were entered in the chronological order of when the information was received and they were headed with the date when they were written. The pages were numbered. The second section was organised like a telephone book and was, in fact, an index of the entries in the first section. If there was a name associated with a piece of information, that name earned an entry in the index; as did any key word in the information.

Now she wrote down the details culled from the phone call and in the index made entries under 'Suitcase' 'Clayton, Jane' and 'Martin, Jane, Mrs.' and, for good measure, one under 'Jane'.

"My phone call, I think." she said.

Jane Martin's phone rang several times and there was no answering machine. Esme was about to put it down when the receiver at the other end was picked up.

"Hello." was a single word response and, immediately,

Helena was certain that this was Jane Martin herself. It was the voice of an elderly lady and it gave nothing away. It was how all her family answered the phone and she was sure it derived from her great-grandfather. It was incumbent on the caller to state their name and purpose first. Helena did so succinctly. She had prepared what she would say. It was not going to be entirely truthful but would make more sense.

"Mrs Martin, my name is Helena Mason. I am researching my ancestors. Esme Marsh was my great-aunt and I understand that you worked with her."

There was a short pause and then a non-committal reply.

"I'm sorry I took so long to get to the phone, I was watching the television. Can I call you back?"

This elderly lady sounded as bright as a button. For a second, Helena thought to apologise for interrupting her program and then it occurred to her that the training that Jane Clayton had received in her work had stayed with her. Jane Martin was checking the identity of her caller.

"Of course." she replied and gave her own phone number.

Within minutes, the phone rang. Helena's supposition had been right. It was not a television program that had been the cause of Mrs Martin asking to return the call.

"Hello!" she said and was greeted with a laugh from the other end of the line.

"Hello, yourself!" said Jane. "You are indeed Helena Mason and would have been Helena Burroughs and you are in pursuit of the elusive Esme. How do you do? I'm told that I may answer your questions freely. You must realise, however, that I might not be able to. After all, I didn't know her for very long. I'm sure you appreciate that. Can you tell me how you got to me?"

"Yes, I can. We bought, by chance, a suitcase from the clearance sale of your old house. It was labelled 'E. Marsh'."

"The suitcase! Gosh, I had completely forgotten about it. How extraordinary."

"Mrs Martin, can we come and see you."

The lady at the other end of the line chuckled. "You bet you can; and you'll be more than welcome. You will have gathered that I am in a 'granny flat'. It is an ideal situation for all sorts of reasons but I've moved away from my neighbours so, apart from the family and visitors, I don't get too much chance for an old-fashioned natter. I would love to hear about that strange business. You will know a lot more than I do but what I can tell you I will."

Helena arranged to visit her in a couple of days, checking with Edgar that he was free.

"I don't think she'll be able to tell us much but it's worth a try and we do need some help."

She made an entry in the diary and turned back to her husband. Edgar had sorted out a couple of phone numbers and was ready to phone them

"I think we ought to hire the full use of the balloon. Do you think they would let us do that?" he asked.

"Sounds great. It might be expensive!"

In the event, they decided that they could afford it and made the booking.

CHAPTER 30

17th December 1945

Jim Bygrave had rescued his civvy suit from the back of the wardrobe, breathed a sigh of relief that it did not smell of mothballs. It was a good suit that he acquired recently but he only wore it when he did not want to display his rank. He found a crisp white shirt ("Where did that come from?" he asked himself) and a tie that he was proud of. His shoes were O.K. – they even had the army shine. He put the clothes aside, shaved for the second time that day, cursing when he nicked his cheekbone, and took a shower. He blessed the army for having the sense to provide showers; even forgiving them for those occasions when they ran cold.

Greatly daring, he splashed a few drops of his after-shave onto his face. He contemplated the bottle of hair-oil that he had bought some time before and never used. He remembered, as he decided against the idea, that his father used it to lubricate the mantelpiece clock. He climbed into the clothes he had set out and tucked a handkerchief pressed into a triangle into the breast pocket of his jacket.

"I'm more nervous now than I was last night." he thought. "Then I was facing the Government's most powerful security system. Now I'm facing a slip of a girl." and he added the rider. "But what a girl."

The image he saw in the mirror was, he thought, the best he could manage. Would it be good enough?

He raided the wardrobe again and took out an overcoat. This was a garment he seldom wore. He had bought it, on a whim, in a church jumble sale. It was a Crombie, a name to conjure with, and had been made for its previous owner in black woollen serge and lined with silk. The loop used to hang it from a cloakroom hook was a thin chain of steel. No other garment he possessed gave him such confidence. He shrugged himself into it, leaving the coat unbuttoned and stuffed first one and then a second scarf into a pocket and, for good measure, a woollen hat.

His own quarters were in walking distance of Esme's office and he set off too early. It was twenty to five when he arrived there. He walked around the block and he was still too early so he back-tracked. He had passed a florist near there many a time. It would still be open to get the trade of those wanting bouquets to take home to their wives or, like James Bygrave, to their dates.

'What sort of flowers do you buy for a girl on your first date?" After asking himself the question, he asked the woman in the shop. He just stopped himself from calling her Eliza and recognised that he was back in the babbling phase.

She was a smart woman, middle-aged but still attractive. Jim noticed how well she had laid out her shop but was thrown by the choice available. The florist, however, was ready with her answer. It was not the first time that she had been asked that question but never by someone as off-balance as this young man. "Lucky girl!" she thought as she summed him up. She reached forward to take the handkerchief from his breast pocket and handed it to him. "Put that away; it's dated." she said and only then answered him. "You need one rose and, with that tie, a yellow one. We'll put it in your button hole. It is good that your jacket has one." she suited her actions to her words. "When you decide it is the right moment, you take it and you say, 'This is for you!'"

Jim beamed at the florist. "You're a fairy god-mother, aren't you." he said and she waved an imaginary wand.

This had taken up time and Jim had become anxious that he would be late. He looked at his watch and the florist agreed. "You'll have to hurry. The rose is on me. Just come back when you need a dozen red ones." and she reached up and kissed him on the cheek. Her eyes were alight with laughter. "Good luck!" she said and ushered him from the shop.

He still reached the rendezvous with a few minutes to spare and saw the first of the office workers emerging from the building. One or two looked at him as if in recognition and others waved. Most of them had gone and he was still waiting when one of them approached him.

"You'll be Jim Bygrave." she said, frowning, "I'm Jane Clayton and I work with Esme Marsh." Suddenly his joy since the phone call, even the mood of optimism engendered by the florist dissolved. Esme had sent this woman to tell him she had changed her mind.

Jane saw his stricken look and hurried to explain.

"No." she said. "I am not a bringer of bad tidings. Esme asked me to tell you she'd be a little late. It's your fault. She's only wearing her work clothes. She's got to do something to smarten them up. Why couldn't you let her go home and change?"

She took a tissue from her handbag and reached up to

wipe Jim's cheek and then showed him the lipstick that came off. Jim threw his hands up in mock horror.

"I can explain everything!" he said and was about to indulge in histrionics but realised that the relief of Jane's explanation of her presence had thrown him off balance again and he stopped.

"I do seem to making a muddle of all this." he said quietly. "I only realised that particular gaff as I came here. In my defence, I can only say that I'd taken so many risks already that I didn't want to take any more. If I were outside her office, she couldn't escape."

Jane's frown had disappeared but her voice was still serious when she said. "Jim Bygrave, Esme has only been with us a short while but we are very fond of her; she creates an atmosphere of friendship. You treat her with care, or else! Here she comes."

"I promise." he said and turned to face the doors of the office. Moving forward, he took Esme's hands in his and Jane Clayton, watching with approval this affectionate greeting, sighed quietly and left them to themselves.

"Jane has told me off for not letting you go home to change and I apologise. On the other hand, you look —" and he stopped. She was wearing a black, belted overcoat with large buttons that shone almost silver under the street light. She had allowed the white blouse which was her standard office wear to show at her throat and with the collar standing up; a wisp of a white scarf was tucked into it. All this framed her curls and a face alight with fun. What he was about to say may have been what he thought but would it be the right thing to say on a first date?

"I look?…" Esme still letting him hold her hands, looked up into his face with a twinkle in her blue eyes, and he said it in any case.

"Stunning! As in 'I am stunned'. I have carried an image of you in my mind since last night and I must have modified it, toned it down because now you put it to shame. Esme Marsh, you are stunning."

Esme had been much impressed by the self-composed soldier who had 'picked her up' – that surely was an accurate description – the night before but his babbling over the telephone had shown her an even more attractive man. Now she was almost embarrassed at what he was saying. She studied the lines of his face. Did he really mean this or was it just part of a come-on? When would she tell him what Gerald had identified him?

He wasn't conventionally handsome; perhaps his cheekbones were too prominent, but it was as though every thought he had was reflected in his face. She didn't think he could dissimulate. His eyes, she noted once again, were almost green rather than hazel and had an intensity as he looked at her that was beyond flattery. She made no attempt to stop his remarks about how she looked but, suddenly, he stopped himself.

"Jane also had occasion to wipe some lip-stick off my cheek. I confess that now and can and will explain it at 'the right moment'. She also warned me 'to treat you with care' and I promised to do so."

He had pulled himself together and was now putting into action his plan for the evening. He needed to explain it first to Esme.

"First of all we need a place to sit down. I've chosen such a place where it will be quiet." and, holding one of her hands, he led her along the street and then through the doors of a hotel. The sign outside had said 'Cocktail Bar' and that was where he took her. No one else was there except the bar-man polishing glasses that already shone crystal clear. He perked up when he saw he had some early customers.

Jim pulled back a comfortable arm-chair at one of the tables and asked Esme if she would like something to drink. She would have preferred not to, thinking that she might need to have her wits about her, but she decided it was incumbent on her to ask for a sherry. Jim turned towards the bar to place the order and then turned back.

"Or a soft drink?" he asked but he did not know why. Something in her voice made him do so and he was rewarded by her response.

"Is that all right?"

"Well, I was planning on getting you drunk so that I could have my wicked way with you. Now, I'll just have to use my charm to sweep you off your feet. This barman does fresh squeezed lemon juice with crushed ice in a glass frosted with sugar. Taste it, if you don't like it we'll get you something else." he said. "I need a stiff drink though, it will stop me going on like this."

He brought the drinks and sat opposite her.

"This part of the evening's plan is so that we can examine the rest of the evening." he said. "The plan depends on your approval. If you don't approve, we can look at alternatives here in peace and quiet."

Esme didn't say anything but sipped her drink. It was very sharp but she was enjoying it.

"When I said we needed to meet, I meant a little more than that. I think we need to get to know each other. I hope you feel the same. Am I being portentous?"

"I think you need that drink. Yes, I do think we should get to know each other. That just makes sense." Esme was trying to be cautious. So far Jim Bygrave was meeting her expectations but he might have some awful habits. He might be philanderer, or, and she shocked herself with the thought, even be married. Jim, unaware of such thoughts, was carrying on with explaining his plan.

"When we've had this drink, we are going to a restaurant. I hope you like Indian food. If you don't, I have an alternative."

"We go Dutch!" she said.

Jim was stopped in full flow. He had included the possibility that she might make such a suggestion in his plan and he had also included a way to deal with it; but he had not expected it to be put forward which such force or so early. He regrouped.

"Can I come back to that?" he asked. "Would you like an Indian meal?"

Esme had always wanted to try an Indian restaurant and for some reason had not done so even at Oxford. This would be a fine opportunity to do so. She was going to enjoy this evening. Who was going to pay for the meal and the possibility of Jim being married could wait. Long ago, Salty had said that she should not pretend. She was not going to do so now.

"A first for me." she said. "It's been a long time coming. Keep going Jim Bygrave, I'm with you so far."

"I have asked for a table in a quiet corner and we can talk there. After the meal, since I have ordered a mild night, we will walk along the river bank and if there is anything left to say we can say it then."

He waited for her comments. Somehow, Esme felt that this man could be trusted but he did seem to be very familiar with a restaurant where they would give him a table for two in a quiet corner. Feeling very silly, she asked herself how many other girls had sat, perhaps where she sat now, and listened to this plan.

"Tell me about the restaurant!"

"Well it's called the 'Taj Mahal', many of them are. We call it Ben Ali's after the chap who owns it."

"We?"

"Sorry. The 'we' are the rugby crowd. Those of us who haven't found something better to do after a game phone Ben. He will stay open late on Saturday nights if we do so. Why an evening of dancing and drinking beer makes you so hungry, I don't know. We sober up there before going back to the barracks."

"And, sometimes, you haven't found 'anything better to do'?"

"Usually!" he said and did not expand on the brief answer. "I haven't finished with the restaurant. You should know that it serves only vegetarian food and this is why it doesn't cost much. Which is another reason why I've chosen it. There is no financial reason why we should 'go Dutch'."

"First date should be Dutch." Esme was quoting an idea

that the girls in the office had discussed at length in their breaks. At Oxford she had always paid her way. It made it easier to keep any relationship on an even keel.

Jim wanted to say that this was not the first date he had had with the girl of his dreams. He wanted tell her that he had fallen in love with the school-girl he had seen at St. Ermengild's. That a hundred times he had imagined taking out that girl. What a poseur he would seem if he said so.

"Is that a law of the Medes and the Persians? My 'Little Book of Etiquette' says the Gentlemen look after the Ladies. I promised Jane I would 'take care of you.'"

"And you promised me that I had to approve the plans for the evening."

"Esme Marsh. We are having our first quarrel."

This made her laugh. Now she knew that she should not have insisted but it was too late to back down.

"We could toss a coin." said Jim. "But I have a better idea. We go Dutch tonight, for the meal, as long as it does not create a precedent. I have powerful arguments that I will use on our second and subsequent dates."

Esme reached out for his hand. "Thank you." she said. It was the speed and understanding with which he responded to her wishes that was so impressive. How did he know that she did not really want the sherry? This man was caring for her. Meanwhile she could savour the words 'second and subsequent.'.

CHAPTER 31

15th August 1986

Edgar was acting as Helena's assistant as she spoke into her microphone. He took out what looked like a small jewel case. Glanced at Helena to get the go ahead to open it. Before he did so, her comment was "dark green, much scuffed jewel box some five inches by two with a secure clasp' and when Jim opened it, "No, it is not a jewel box. It holds a medal with its ribbon. I'm pretty sure it is the 'War Medal'"

Without asking, Edgar crossed to the shelf of reference books, pulled out the relevant text, and turned to the illustration of the 1939-1945 medal. He showed it to Helena. "Yes!" she went on. "That is it; red, white and blue ribbon, the crowned head of George VI on one side and a lion standing on a rather horrid eagle-like creature on the other."

"And, the ribbon has a tiny metal oak-leaf attached to it. Looks as though it is bronze." She went on.

Edgar looked up from the reference book. He was astonished by the plethora of possible awards and the variations that occurred as the years passed. These badges of honour had, he hoped because of the respect in which they were held, become collectors' items. In the text he was looking at their market value seemed to be the most important thing about them. Though he did note that the provenance could enhance that value, especially of the name of the original owner could be attached. He looked up because he heard the triumph in his wife's voice. Helena was frequently called upon to consult war records in her job. She had come across the bronze oak-leaf before.

"What's that about, then?"

"The person who earned this medal was 'mentioned in a despatch'. That's what the oak-leaf means. I've never seen one before but I'm pretty sure that's what it is."

Edgar found a picture of the same and showed it to her. It was a 'bronze oak-leaf' all right.

"And you'll be able to find the despatch?"

"If it was Jim, it will be easy. There should be the despatch itself and there will also be a copy of the certificate which will record 'His Majesty's high appreciation of our soldier's actions'. On the other hand, the medal may belong to someone else and it would be well nigh impossible to trace it."

It took just one phone call. Searching the military records was one of the day-to-day tools of Helena's work. She gave her name and asked if a specific clerk was available. He was and was pleased to hear from her. Her requests for information were much more interesting than his normal work. Moreover, she was wont to buy the office an occasional box of biscuits.

Within the hour, he was back on the phone. He apologised for the delay. He claimed that some work had got in the way and then he gave them the news they were hoping for. Jim Bygrave had been 'mentioned in a Despatch on May the twenty-fifth of 1940'. This information was extracted from a copy of a letter written to Jim expressing the King's thanks. No details were recorded of the gallant action that the corporal had actually carried out.

"That's just before Dunkirk, isn't it?" asked Helena.

"Spot on! Dunkirk was May the twenty-seventh to June the fourth. On the twenty-fifth, the army would have been heading for the beaches. Your lad must have been caught up in that action. Was it a posthumous award?"

"No, he was still alive years later. Thanks again. Sometime I'll tell you about it."

The evidence was building up in support of James Bygrave rating high in Esme's life. He had been awarded the oak leaf to decorate his war medal. Esme's suitcase held such a war medal. Not the sort of thing that you gave to a casual acquaintance.

Helena introduced a note of caution first and then a bombshell.

"Earlier, you said you wanted our unknown lover to be her future husband! You were always were an old softy yourself. But seriously, what are the chances of that? She must have had other boyfriends and the relationship she had with Jim may have just been a casual affair."

This led to a protest from Edgar. "No!" he said in emphatic terms. "I don't care if it is an assumption. My construct, as you put it, of Esme Marsh does not have casual affairs. If you can prove that she did, I shall have to start all over."

Helena lived with this dichotomy in her husband's character and delighted in it. At the same time as being an incurable romantic, he was, in the day-to-day business of the real world, both far-sighted and extremely pragmatic. She did not want to bring him down to earth but they had to move forward from a sound base.

"There is a family rumour that Esme was not married at all. There is no evidence of a ceremony in any of the family archives. I suppose that's why they called it a hole-in-the-corner wedding. If you think about it and we accept your wish that these were soul-mates, then, if something happened to prevent them getting married, all the more reason for Esme to treasure mementos of the affair. Perhaps we had better do Somerset House tomorrow. We've put that off too long."

"Are they open on a Saturday?"

CHAPTER 32

17th December 1945

Esme had thought hard about whether she should ask Jim why he had said nothing about driving Gerald to St. Ermengild's. She had decided that sometime she would have to but that she could put it off for the time being. So far, she thought that she had been justified and now she was ready to ask more general questions.

"Can I start the 'getting to know you' bit?

"Go ahead! The rest of the plan can wait."

"O.K.! Why the civvies?"

"Well, first of all —" he started but Esme Marsh had enough of his careful and disciplined responses. He was not the only one that was nervous. "Jim." she interrupted. "Drink your whisky and relax. I can see now why you need it. I don't want a report, just a response."

Jim Bygrave took no offence at this. If anything he seemed to approve of Esme's direct approach. He did take a substantial mouthful of his drink and then responded without preamble. "It seemed a truer image." he said. "I'm not a soldier; merely a conscript, just another civilian called up to serve his country in its hour of need. I'll 'fight them on beaches' all right, in fact, I did, but only if there is somebody to fight. In any case, I've only got one more job to do. It shouldn't take long and then I get my discharge. I thought I'd better practise."

Esme heard the echo of Salty's advice about not pretending in his 'truer image'.

"That's better, but before we go further, tell me about the 'flaming A'. You're not supposed to wear that I understand."

Jim raised his eyebrows, another gesture that Esme liked. "You've been doing some homework. I suppose I've got a file in the Secret Service Records."

"Well, if you didn't have before, you'll have one after gate-crashing the party last night. Was it only last night? No deep research was needed. It took just one phone-call to an old friend; but you haven't answered the question."

"I wear it because I earned it. Nine months of the dullest book-work you could imagine. Four hours of lectures every day. Thirty young men under the threat of total war, sitting in cold huts on folding chairs at disintegrating tables without even a decent blackboard and learning about colour-coding and time-and-motion study. The living accommodation was nothing to write home about either – though I did. Even the playing at soldiers bit was a relief from the boredom. After the nine months and a practical exam, I qualified. I am a qualified Ammunition Examiner as are those who studied with me. The 'flaming A' is the badge that says I am and I am proud to wear it."

"So why shouldn't you wear it?"

"It is meant for the Other Ranks. I'm a Commissioned Officer. The army is hierarchal."

"And is it a dangerous job?"

"No! Most of it is just checking ammunition. Dull but essential. As for danger, you're thinking of the Royal Engineers. They deal with unexploded bombs. The only things we deal with that are comparable are unexploded missiles – something fired from a gun or, in the case of grenades, thrown by hand. Bombs come from the enemy and are dangerous by their nature and can also be booby-trapped. The R.E.'s job is not a nice one. Missiles, on the other hand, are ours and the ones we are called out to are usually just chucked in the back of the wagon to be dealt with later."

"Usually?"

"The odd hand-grenade might look dangerous. If it does, we tape a detonator to it, lead a wire from it to a safe place and blow it up. It is against regulations to take risks. I suspect because it costs so much to train us."

Now Esme was learning fast; not just about his army career but also about how he felt. She detected an angry edge against the system and she felt the loyalty that he had towards his companions. His respect for his colleagues in the Engineers was touching. Would he have liked the more dangerous trade?

"In any case. I've had a desk job for the last couple of years."

"One more question then. Major is a bit of an elevated rank for a conscript."

"How do you know that? They made me a major so that I can give instructions – 'orders' they would call them – to subalterns. As a sergeant or even as a corporal, I could tell a colonel or a brigadier what to do and they would do it. They would have enough confidence to credit an expert opinion. Junior officers, on the other hand, might stand upon their dignity because they out-ranked me."

He paused.

"The army decided that I had something they wanted and they offered me the rank – with the salary and all the privileges of being an officer to do a job for them."

"Gerald said you were a bright boy."

"Gerald?"

"The 'old friend.'" This time, he raised one eyebrow and she giggled. Why should she tell him? But she resolved to grasp the nettle and did so. "Not that sort of friend! In fact, you know him. It is Gerald Knight and you have been rather naughty. You were his driver when he came to St. Ermengild's. Why have you not said so?"

The question was out and Esme waited his reply nervously. Could she accept that he had forgotten what had happened? Was there some ulterior motive in concealing this previous meeting? Actually they had not met. She had seen him carrying Gerald's son and sitting in his vehicle. Had he seen her at all?

"Damn!" was his first response. "I'd hoped you had not realised. Why should you? You had other things to think about. Now we have a complication. Just when I thought I hadn't made a complete mess of it."

"Answer the question!"

"I don't know what to say. If I tell you the truth, you won't believe me. If I make something up, I will have lied to you and I don't want to do that. Indeed I must not. Can't we just carry on?"

He looked lost. Jim Bygrave, she noticed with surprise, was showing a measure of weakness. She almost weakened herself in sympathy.

"It has to be the truth." she said and she meant it. She

knew there could be no half measures in this relationship.

"O.K. But you won't believe me. I didn't tell you because I wanted to start as though we had no history. For me, this was not so but I thought that need not impinge on us now."

He stopped and drank the rest of his whisky before going on.

"You need to put the visit to your school in context. Gerald and I were both shattered by the Dunkirk business. He was wounded and I had to drive all the way from Dover. We had stopped overnight, which helped, but not very much. We reached your school in the afternoon. I'd done my job and was entitled to relax. If I couldn't do so in the grounds of a girls' boarding school, where could I?"

"I glanced across the soft green of your lawns to the solid grey masonry of your buildings and I saw three school-girls standing on the terrace. This, I thought, was the England we were fighting for and then you moved across to join Gerald. I knew that he was visiting his sister and, at first, I thought that that was who you were. Your reaction to him said otherwise. The very way you stood said that you were in distress. I wanted to comfort you!"

He was looking intensely at her and he moved as though to take her hand but he did not.

"It didn't make sense then and it doesn't make sense now. I'd never met you and you were forty or fifty paces away. What had this school-girl to do with me? I made some excuse, I think I was giving Charlie a carry, to get out of the car and get closer to you. I heard your voice with its soft West Country but not what you said. I had half hoped that you would have that ghastly public school nasal twang and that

244

would break the spell and return me to a sane world but it seemed that everything about you was charming. You and Gerald walked away from the others and I watched the two of you. I could see that Gerald was saying something that cheered you up. I told myself that I wasn't needed. You were surrounded by friends who were comforting you. I could relax and, in any case, it was none of my business. Then Gerald's sister brought me a tea tray and I could not prevent myself from asking her questions about you. She must have thought me very odd. "

Esme reached over herself and took the hand he had nearly offered her. Nothing could have been more gratifying than his revelations but he was increasingly embarrassed by what he was saying. It was time to help.

"She did – think you odd." she said. "Why should this 'war-hero', we were calling you that by then, be interested in a school-girl? I'm afraid that to me you were just another soldier. But that was five years ago." It was almost an accusation. Why had he not done anything about it?

Jim asked the question for her.

"And why didn't I ask Gerald about you? Well, I actually asked about his sister. 'How kind it was of her to bring me tea! What a pleasant girl she was.' The mad drive from Dover through the countryside to Scotland must have been about you and I had seen you walking with him. Remember that Gerald and I had served together under conditions where men show their real selves. He is an old-fashioned gentleman. The four of you were together. I had been excluded. He did not want to appear snobbish; so I learned why he was there."

245

"He told you about Brotherton, didn't he?"

"Yes, he did. Gerald Knight had asked me to drive him several hundred miles so that he could do something important. Now he was excluding me from what he was doing and from the rest of you. His code said that he had to tell me why this was the case. I had half determined on crossing and saying 'hello', or even 'good-bye' to the three of you to make some sort of contact with you but knowing why he was there, I could not. Indeed, the more I knew about you, the less I was able to do what I wanted. This was not the time to approach you. In any case, the whole idea was irrational and intangible and I prided myself on the application of reason. I asked myself what could I have done to help and I could think of nothing. That did not stop me thinking about this dream of a girl and I've dreamed of you ever since."

Esme was enjoying these compliments; who would not enjoy being called a dream of a girl. On the other hand, she could feel sympathy for the dilemma that Jim suffered at the time and it explained why he had not said anything about St Ermengild's. The trouble was that it just created more questions. What had happened in the last five years? He must have met somebody else. He answered that particular question prosaically and almost before she had phrased it in her mind.

"I was on the Continent and you were at Oxford. Yes, I knew where you were. Gerald had dropped a remark about his sister working towards a university career and the three of you wanting to go up at the same time. The student lists at Universities are in the public domain and, although I resolved not to research them, I could not stop myself from doing so. Nothing prevented me from trying to meet you. Nothing, that is, except common sense. When you are not there, I am a rational human being; I behave with common sense. Only when you are around do I behave like an idiot. You were hundreds of miles away from me and I resolved to live in the real world."

He paused. "I could have taken time off and visited Oxford. How proud I was that I resisted that temptation. What a numskull! The resolution didn't even prevent me from fantasising about you."

Jim had started to ramble and Esme brought him up short.

"Well I've been fed some lines in my time." she said, "But that beats them all." and only the laughter in her eyes rescued Jim from despair. Instead, he grinned himself until she asked the dreaded question.

"Were there any girls in this 'real world?"

Jim ducked his head as though to ride a blow. "Yes, there were girls. I was pretty desperate. First of all I wanted to put an end to the enchantment. I thought that would be easy. All it would need would be an affair, however brief, with someone who was seeking the same thing. I found that I really wasn't interested. I didn't find it easy to say so. I couldn't use you as an excuse. Usually, I said that there was 'someone else'. Only one of these experiments, there's no better word for them, lasted longer than the first date. She looked a bit like you but wasn't like you. That was inane and I knew then that it was. Since I didn't know what you were like, how could I decide how she compared? After a while, I got very selective and then I stopped hoping. There was never the chemistry. I did wonder if there ever would be."

Somehow, the two of them had stood up and Esme had moved close to him. She put her hands on his chest and looked up into his face. Then she reached up and touched the scar under his eye. There were more memories of Jim Bygrave buried in her mind than she had thought. At St. Ermengild's he had had a plaster on his face. Did she remember that herself or was it from one of the other girls asking about it? Everything of that occasion was covered in the mist of Gerald's re-assurance about Brotherton.

"That was what Gerald described as a bullet graze. I remember now, he said that you were luckiest man alive and all you had done was stick a plaster on it."

"What else would you expect me to do? Some of the blood was getting in my eye." he said. He was fond of that old joke.

Esme reached up on tip-toe to kiss the scar. She had begun to realise how he understated some of his heroics. How much had he understated his response about other girls? She would leave that; for the moment certainly. Perhaps they would never mention it again. His casual remark about where he had been in the last five years, or at least some of it, needed challenging.

"'On the Continent' is a bit vague. Sounds like a guided holiday. Tell me what was happening 'on the Continent' while you were there. Wasn't there a war going on? Any more medals? No important injuries from enemy fire, I hope?"

Esme had asked the question and he should answer. That was what they were doing but it was so easy to dramatise and he did not want to.

"I had some work to do where the action was at first. Just technical stuff. The R.E.s dealt with all the work with explosives in the front line. That was their job. Mine was danger-free. I knew what I was doing and, I can assure you, I took no more risks. I'd had enough of risks. In a way, my caution led to the job I'm just finishing. There was a great deal of ammunition issued to the troops and not fired. Something has to be done with it. It was 'on the Continent' that I started to do so. In answer to your other question. During that time, 'I jested at scars'"

There it was again. Another quotation from Shakespeare; again from 'Romeo and Juliet' and again slightly misquoted. "Pedant!" she said to herself; it was unfair for her, with the benefit of three years study, to criticise. Then she remembered the context. Romeo had fallen in love with Juliet and was dismissive of his friends who did not understand his passion. They 'jested at scars' because they had 'never felt a wound'. Jim knew his text and had used it to answer the actual question about any girls in his real world. There may have been girls but he had not been wounded by love. He had escaped what she had referred to as 'enemy-fire'.

She reached up once more to kiss his cheek.

"Let's finish this first." he said, "You have more questions?"

"Just one. Did you know I was at the office party?"

"No, I did not. That was pure chance and it was not a chance I was going to miss. I'd spent five years regretting the last missed opportunity. I was scarcely into the room when I saw you and the magic had returned. It was just as illogical as it had been the first time but this was the second time and now I knew exactly what I had to do. You wouldn't remember me from St Ermengild's so I could start from scratch. I had to be calm. I had to strike up a conversation, make a casual and unthreatening advance but not monopolise you. I could come back to you later and ask if you would like to meet again, perhaps for coffee. Then I could get to know you properly. I started all right but dancing with you in my arms threw me off balance – and you're doing the same now."

"Do you want me to stop?" she asked and was disconcerted when he said, "Yes, please. We need to sort a few things out" and then he pulled her to him gently, looked into her eyes as though asking permission and kissed her. It was a soft kiss and unexpected. Esme was unable to give it the credit it deserved. "And that's the first thing sorted. There would be no point in going any further if I didn't enjoy kissing you."

Esme burst out laughing. "Have you got a check list?" she asked. "I met a man at Oxford who had something similar. I liked him very much but he decided I wasn't worth kissing. Everything else about me was all right."

"Well, I suppose I have. I know it's daft but I've had five years to compile it. That kiss was a bit like pinching myself to make sure that I was awake. You see, I have kissed you a thousand times but our lips have never met. Don't worry about the check-list, there aren't many points left to tick; even the way you laugh fits what was my fantasy and is now becoming my life. Hang on, I forgot to ask. Did you enjoy it?"

"Yes I did." she said and then, with mischief in her eyes;

"I usually do." but she went on more seriously, "Well, we can't start from scratch but I think I'm a long way towards understanding the 'war-hero'. Do you want to leave that for now?"

"We can't forget that nincompoop fast enough. How many men have the luck to fall in love and then talk themselves out of doing something about it for five years? I disown him!"

Esme was beginning to think that she liked the 'daft' Jim Bygrave perhaps even more than the smooth, competent one. Even as she thought it, the smooth, competent one presented himself.

"Enough about me. It's my turn next." he said. "But it's time to eat. The restaurant is just round the corner."

The more the evening progressed, the more Esme relaxed. Jim Bygrave did not have a wife tucked away somewhere or even a dozen girl-friends. Some of the time, he was composed, almost smooth, as though he had vast experience of taking girls out. Every now and then, however, he was off-balance and started to babble.

Ben Ali, the owner of the restaurant, dressed in the full Indian gear, greeted him as an old friend and then turned to Esme with a smile.

"We are pleased to welcome Memsahib." he said and Jim told her to take no notice, he was just showing off; that he had been born in Hackney and gone to an English public school. Ben Ali just got more aloof and Jim introduced him to Esme. She, however, was re-assured. Ben Ali was clearly curious that Jim had brought a girl to his restaurant which meant that it was not something he did as a rule. He guided them into a sheltered alcove with a table set for two and then disappeared.

"Don't, I repeat, don't, look now but Ben's wife is giving you the once over." said Jim so that only she could hear. "I hope they approve."

He shifted his chair so they could both look at the menu at the same time. Esme, although she had not been taught the Indian languages, delighted in the names; Dahl and Biryani, Pilaus and Poppadums; Murgi Mosalla and Bhajis. The menu told you how spicy the dishes were. They ranged from 'mild' to 'very very hot'. What it largely failed to do was translate the Indian name into English. Esme tried possible translations and pronunciations in her head and decided that this would be her next project.

But that could wait. Jim was telling her how the menu worked. "The idea is that we order a number of different dishes between us, then we can share any or all of them. Some of the dishes, as it says, are highly spiced. Tonight we'll only have the mild ones. It is usual to have some form of rice and or bread. There are different types of both. If it is all right with you, I'll order for the both of us. It doesn't matter if we order too much. Ben will pack the left-overs so we can take them away. Would you like a beer? It is normal to drink beer with curries – they sell a sort of bottled lager."

Esme nodded her agreement both to his ordering and to the beer. Exotic, mouth-watering cooking smells came from the kitchen. The air was full of hints of spices and the lighting and the furniture added to this atmosphere. She was not sure about the wall-paper, dark red and, apparently, furry. Overall, even without the food, this was an experience for her.

The food itself was an eye-opener. Tastes she had not come across before blended with some carefully prepared vegetables – some familiar, some exotic. Jim used the pliant unleavened-bread to scoop the food into his mouth. Esme tore pieces of it off and ate it separately as she would have done with ordinary bread or a French baguette. It had a texture of its own and a mild, savoury taste.

They tried to tell each other about themselves but it was difficult, not only because of the food but because they kept being diverted. Jim would tell a funny story and Esme would cap it. They had a brief argument about the importance of Jane Austen in English Literature and whether Georgette Heyer was a worthy successor. Esme was oddly pleased that he had read any of the latter's work and astonished at the width of his reading and the acuity of his down-to-earth criticism. He could have held his own with any of her fellow students and he would have delighted her lecturers.

However, Esme had managed to give him some idea of her upbringing and learned from him that his parents had been killed early in the war in an air-raid. He had joined a commercial firm as an office-boy when he was fifteen. The firm had promised to teach him the trade. He learned rapidly and was equally rapidly promoted to keep a set of books. When he was conscripted, the army decided that he could learn a military trade as well. Which was how he became an Ammunition Examiner. He said nothing about his present position. Esme recognised the silence about prohibited subjects from her upbringing and her own work.

She investigated another of the dishes and made noises of enjoyment. Then she changed the subject.

"Now tell me why we were calling you a 'war-hero'. Gerald said you saved his life."

"In a sense, we saved each other's lives. That's what happens when people are killing each other. I'm sure Gerald made too much of it."

Esme made a sound that said that he was talking nonsense and he shrugged but still said nothing.

"O.K. I'll accept that you are modest, but modesty will get you nowhere. You wore a uniform that you claimed was yours yesterday – with your medal ribbons. Your medals included a D.S.O. and you had that pretty little bronze oak-leaf that says you were 'Mentioned in a Despatch'. You are not the only one who can do research. I need to know about both incidents. I can ask elsewhere but we are supposed to be finding out about each other."

Jim took a good look at her and assessed her resolution on this point. He tried to tell the story without embroidery or false modesty.

"The D.S.O. is down to the report that Gerald made. We had fallen back to delay the enemy's advance and were slow in escaping and we realised this when an enemy tank appeared and was manoeuvring to fire at us. I was sitting in my jeep which held a fair amount of explosives. One shot would have blown it and me and anybody in a twenty yard radius to smithereens. Fortunately the explosives included a rather clever anti-tank device. I picked it up and fired it and it worked – Germany had one less tank. All this was driven by fear."

Esme's thoughts were that the fear itself made it a braver action. The modest way in which he told the story gave Esme an extra thrill of pride.

This was her first Indian meal and she found that she kept eating just a little bit more of each dish. Fortunately Jim did not suggest any thing to follow for, even without a pudding, she felt a trifle distended by the time the coffee was served.

In the saucers of the demitasse cups were small greenish-white seed pods. Esme asked what they were.

"Cardomen. You can chew them and they are supposed to sweeten the breath and clear the palette – they function a bit like after-dinner mints. I find that chewing them means that bits get stuck between my teeth."

"And the despatch?" Esme returned to his 'war-hero' role. She was not going to let him get away with his self-effacing report on one action.

"That was some General. I suspect he didn't have much to write about except that he was retreating again. Something to keep up the morale of the troops. All I did was press a button."

"On a lift?"

Jim, realised he wasn't going to get off that easily, and became serious.

"One of the Royal Engineers had mined a bridge to prevent Jerry from advancing their vehicles. He was about to detonate it when he was hit by a sniper. I wouldn't call him a friend, except that we were all friends, but we'd had a few drinks together. I remember he was called Clark, 'Nobby' for short. It would have been a great waste if the bridge was not destroyed after all the work he had put into the explosives. I think I was probably the only one there who knew what had to be done. He had a device that was not in general service. I wired the connection and pressed the button. He was good at his job. Nobody was going to cross that bridge any more. A couple of the medics pulled him clear. I caught up with him later and told him he owed me a pint. He pretended that he had lost any memory of the incident but he must have reported to his superior officer. He did buy me a pint."

Esme did not press him any further. If the Engineer was hit by a sniper, what happened to the sniper? This 'pressing a button' had been an act of courage under fire. She was glad she had asked but decided she had had enough of the risks Jim Bygrave had taken even before she had a chance to meet him.

He called for the bill and it was brought, not by Ben, but by his wife. Jim introduced Esme to her.

"I hope you enjoyed your meal." she said and Esme recognised this as more than a conventional line from 'The Restaurateur's Guide to Good Relationships with Customers'.

"Thank you. It was a delightful evening. I found the food exciting. Do I call you Mrs. Ali?"

Jim, carefully studying the bill to allow the two women to speak to each other was pleased with the friendliness offered by 'his girl'.

"Miss Marsh, I hope you will call me Judith – for that is my given name."

"Only if you forget the Miss Marsh and call me Esme. I've already persuaded your husband to do so."

In response, she said that she and her husband were fond of Jim and then she turned to him and said. "You take care of this girl!" and, almost embarrassed, went back to the kitchen.

Jim beamed at her retreating back. "I'm afraid your fate is sealed, Esme Marsh. Everybody tells me I've got to look after you." but he saw a touch of apprehension in her eyes and continued smoothly, "I've never seen myself as a father figure before. I'll just have to do my best."

Then they returned to the problem of paying for the meal. It was with surprise that Esme saw how small the bill was and, once more, was cross with herself for insisting that they went Dutch. Jim added a tip to round up the total so that it was easily divisible by two.

"Next time, we renegotiate." he said and that was enough for Esme. At that moment she thought that 'next time' could be on any terms he chose.

"Would you like to go for a walk now." he asked. "I did put in an order for fine weather."

"Is a walk part of the plan?"

"Yes it is. We'll walk along the river bank and across a couple of bridges. We can continue talking or just walk."

Ben Ali helped them into their coats and, before they went out into the cold, Jim fished out one of his scarves and wrapped it carefully around Esme's neck. She already had a scarf but it was more for decoration than warmth. Jim tucked the ends of his into her coat. Before she could protest, he pulled the woollen hat he'd brought for that purpose over her curls.

In the event, they said very little on this walk. London was emerging from the restraints of war and the lights reflecting from the Thames made magic its flowing dark.

They crossed on the footpath of Hungerford Bridge and then back over Waterloo Bridge and along the river-side to Cleopatra's Needle.

Esme had put her arm through his and leant on him gently. It was a togetherness walk that needed no conversation. The river with its history enfolded them. When they reached the Needle he stopped and turned to her.

"My plan ends here, I'm afraid. "I have to go to Scotland for a few days. I will phone your office the moment I return."

She had prepared for this moment but had expected it to be at her flat. Nor had she expected such a drastic finish. She could not stop the disappointment in her voice as she exclaimed. "A few days?" and then, more composed, "If it is after work, use this number. Make sure it is the very moment that you return." She gave him the card on which, before she had left the office, she had written her own address and home phone number. She had told herself then that she could decide whether or not to give it to him. Now there was no decision to make.

A cab drew up to the curb, as though summoned, and he guided her into it with the remembered skill he had used to lead her onto the dance floor. She realised that it had indeed been ordered when she heard him say to the driver. "You have your instructions. The lady will give you the address. Could you see her to her door, please?"

To her, he said. "Hang on to the hat and scarf. You'll feel the cold when you get out of the cab otherwise. The cab's paid for." and he closed the door

"This is a bit of a let down." thought Esme but the thought was arrested when he opened the door again, half stepped into the cab and bent to kiss her. This time it was a committed kiss, full on the lips. More than that, it was a kiss that gave her time to respond in kind; time that she did not waste.

As he stepped out of the cab, he held her hand briefly and said, "That, I did not plan."

She saw that another car had drawn up behind them. It was an army staff-car clearly intended for Major Bygrave.

CHAPTER 33

Summer 1986

Edgar was somewhat taken aback by Helena's revelation. As far as he had been told, his wife's great aunt had married a man called James Bygrave. It was a solid fact in a morass of rumours. Now his own reconstruction of Esme and her lover was shot to pieces.

"That's a bit of a bummer." he said, trying to sort out his ideas. "Yes, we had better get to the records as soon as possible. They needn't, of course, have gone through a ceremony but I hope we haven't got a real life Romeo and Juliet."

Helena pretended not to hear him and took another look in the suitcase and brought out a rather tatty booklet.

"Why would she keep a copy of the 'Office Regulations'?" she said opening it carefully; but not carefully enough to stop something falling out of it. She picked it up off the floor and handed it to Edgar and he said. "She's not keeping the book, she's keeping the flower. It's a rose; not a red one – which is a shame. It's either white or yellow. But no provenance – we won't learn anything from this."

"There is provenance." said Helena. "By association with the booklet, it comes from an office. This office is the one she worked in as a translator. A present from a boyfriend and much treasured."

Edgar smiled and Helena looked cross and said, "A boyfriend. We can't go further than that." Then she held up a hand in submission. "All right. Let us accept as a working hypothesis – but that's all – that Esme met and fell in love with James Bygrave. I'll assume that he is the subscriber to the phone number. We have to stop now, I think and get some concrete facts."

So they took a break from the material while Helena set in motion the search for the person who had that phone number in 1945. It would be easy enough to discover what exchange the three letters referred to but she had not been sure whether she could trace the actual number itself. Now she was going to assume that Bygrave was the subscriber and that should make it easier.

Whatever Helena said about caution, they both knew that they did not really need anything in the package of letters that would help them with the identity of the man who wrote that appeal. Esme would scarcely have kept it and then married someone else. It had meant something to her. James Bygrave was a near certainty even if they had not gone through a ceremony. Nonetheless, the ground rules said they could make no assumptions

Edgar was muttering to himself. "I can't adjust to the 'not married' idea." he said. "Is everything about this girl mysterious? So what do you know from the family about the romantic James Bygrave? We know he quoted Shakespeare to his girl-friend? I don't see much chance that we are going to get him from the suitcase. Tell us again about the 'not married' bit."

"Let's leave that until we have looked at Somerset House.

If we assume a James Bygrave, we can get something of his relationship from the suitcase but, for the moment, only speculatively. I'm trying to remember the family stories. Mum was very fond of my grandmother, her mother-in-law, and when the old lady was dying last year she sat at her bedside for hours at a time. Grandma was in great pain and full of drugs but she insisted on telling her what she knew about Esme. She was her sister, after all, but Mum said that a lot of it was rambling."

Helena changed the subject.

"Shall we get something to eat? We are in a right mess at the moment. I need to think about this. I would like to separate the facts from the speculation. We might even get something from Mrs Martin."

"Good idea. I need to stretch my legs. I'll get a take-away. Indian suit you?"

"Yes please. Don't forget the spinach this time, what's it called, sag aloo?"

★★★ ★★★ ★★★

Helena phoned to confirm their appointment with Mrs. Martin and they drove down to visit her. Esme Marsh was taking up a great deal of their time but they did not allow her to interfere with their work. Both of them had established a reputation for reliability and it was important that these were maintained. Esme did, however, interfere with their social life. For the past two evenings they had worked solidly through until bedtime. They relied upon take-aways for their food. This was not a healthy regimen.

They had arranged that their meeting with Mrs Martin be a morning one and Edgar suggested they take a break for the rest of the day. A pub lunch and a walk seemed to fit the bill and they put their walking gear in the boot of the car.

Mrs. Martin's 'granny flat' turned out to be a bungalow in the grounds of her daughter's house. Her children had done her proud. It was a charming little house with pretty pink roses growing around the front door and bright geraniums in terracotta pots lighting up the patio in front of it.

Mrs Martin's daughter was there to greet the visitors. She was a neat, well-set up, dark-haired woman in country tweeds. If she was suspicious, she concealed it behind her welcome. Helena assumed that she was 'just checking' for her mother seemed more than capable of acting as hostess. Jane Martin, who appeared at that moment, seemed like a mature version of her daughter but more lively. She could not really be described as an old lady. She was far too full of life and although her hair was an iron grey, it shone with health. Her skin was smooth and without blemish and there was a youthful sparkle in her eyes. She may have just qualified as being 'elderly'. A quick calculation told Helena that she was in her late sixties. She certainly did not look it. She had been in the garden and she came around the corner of the house and was carrying a single yellow rose.

"It's O.K., Karen." she said to her daughter. "This lady is the spit and image of Esme Marsh." She turned to Helena, handing her the rose, "And just as pretty. This, my dear, is for you. Major James Bygrave was wearing one such in his lapel when he was waiting outside the office for their first date. Esme had it on her desk in a tiny vase for days afterwards."

Helena and Edgar greeted this information with triumph. It was Helena who delved into what she now called her 'evidence bag' and produced the rose that Esme, so many years ago, had attempted to press. She had found a flat box to carry it in and padded it with tissues paper. The yellow in the petals had faded to cream and the leaves were dark with only just enough colour in to suggest that they had once been green. This was a pale shadow of Jane Martin's vibrant flower; it was the ghost of Jim Bygrave's offering.

Jane was suitably impressed. "That came from the suitcase, did it? Typical of Esme to keep it."

"I think that's the sort of thing that we are here for." said Helena. "We are constructing a picture of Esme and, increasingly, we get these delightful messages from the past.

"That flower's marvellous." said Jane "And in keeping with Esme Marsh. Sometimes, it was as though she belonged in a fairy story."

Once more there was this allusion to a fairy story. Helena thought that this was going to be a really worthwhile interview and she wanted to get as much as possible out of it. So far she had been diverted by the delightful welcome and the charm of Jane Martin. She interrupted Jane to ask if she could record the interview.

"Only if you will send me what you find out about Esme. There is a romance there that should be written up."

"Can we start with Jim Bygrave?" asked Helena. "Tell us what you know about him!"

"Sure. It isn't much and I'll give you it all. He first

appeared when he gate-crashed an office party. One of the staff was retiring. I actually saw him walk into the room. I was talking to Esme at the time and looking in that direction; which she was not. You couldn't miss him. Apart from anything else he was in uniform and we were all wearing our party gear. He came in with an air of complete unconcern, looking around the room as though searching for a particular person. He was not what we called handsome in those days. We based our criteria on the Hollywood film stars like Errol Flynn or the subtler Cary Grant. His face was alert and interested. He looked in our direction and stopped. If I'd been conceited, I might have thought he was looking at me. But I don't think I had the power to stop a man at twenty paces. Esme was different, she shone most times but she had made a special effort for the party. I thought she felt out of place. She had only been with us for a short time and didn't know anybody very well. Even so, she was the prettiest girl in the room and it would not have been long before the young men would overcome their shyness and approached her."

She stopped and turned to her daughter, said. "Could you make us some tea, please, Karen. We'll take it out here. I think there's some cake in the tin, if you look. You should join us. I have a feeling that this is going to be interesting. I'm sure Helena and Edgar would like you to hear." and she turned back to her visitors.

"By golly, that man could move fast. Ten seconds, he stood looking at her and then moved through the crowd as though they were not there, never taking his eyes off her. Before she had time to realise what was happening, he had guided her onto the dance floor. If you had been there you would understand what I mean by her being something out of a fairy story. Here, on cue, was her Prince Charming. At the end of the dance, they stood talking. I saw that one of the security guards was moving towards them. It was too far away for me to stop him but something Esme said meant that he lost interest. Then, within minutes, Jim had gone. I knew that we would see him again. Even across the room there was an intensity about what he did that was impressive, not to say, startling."

Karen had brought the tea out and, without interrupting her mother, poured cups for everybody. There was cake, a sort of Victoria sponge with crystallised ginger added to the cream filling. They took a mini-break to consume it.

"Esme was told off the following day because someone had sent her a note. No private correspondence was allowed but I think the supervisor picked up the vibes because she did not pursue the matter. Esme phoned Jim and they arranged to meet after work outside the office.

I had the job of taking a message to Jim that she would be delayed. That was the second time that I had seen him. I was there to present her apologies for being late on what was their first date – actually she was only late by a couple of minutes but she was frightened that he wouldn't wait. He was just as bad. He thought I'd come to make her excuses for crying off. I thought he was going to faint. Then, when she came through the door, he was a different man. It was as though he had been switched on. For a second, I was jealous that someone could feel so strongly. Only for a second; David, my husband, was already the rock of my life. I never learned how he would react in a crisis, he never let a crisis happen. If he had been that mercurial, he would not have been David."

"This," said Edgar, devouring the Victoria sponge, "is the cake on the icing."

"Hush." said Helena.

"What happened then, Mrs Carter?"

"It is 'Jane' not Mrs Carter. I feel I know you already – you share Esme's gift for friendship. She seemed to enchant most people that she met. Remember that I did not know her for very long. This was her first job after university and she was remarkably good at it. Then, having captivated us all and, apparently falling in love with Major James Bygrave, she disappeared over the Christmas break. That is all I know about him"

"Bygrave is a bit of mystery." Edgar said. "We've got his military record but that doesn't tell us much about the man except that in the field he was a brave and resourceful soldier. He proved later to be a fine administrator. He finished his term of office in the army and we can't find any record of him after his discharge."

"What happened then in the office?" Helena was trying desperately to find out more about this critical period.

Jane sipped her tea and there was a far away look in her eye but she attempted to respond to the question.

"I only met that young man on three occasions. Each time, he impressed me with his competence and also with a fixity of purpose with respect to Esme. Perhaps I'd better tell you what I know about her and then you can ask questions."

"All right. You tell us what you can of her history from your point of view – every little helps."

In her mind, Jane had told this story many times but her training and, indeed, the Official Secrets Act had prevented her from making it public. It was more than time that she got it off her chest.

"To start with, it consisted mainly of hearsay. By the very nature of the work that we did in the department, rumours abounded and nobody official could or would confirm or deny them."

"Reginald Marsh, he wasn't 'Sir' then, had arranged that his daughter's talent for languages be realised to its full. He was particularly interested in Russian and Polish because he wanted someone he could trust completely in his department to translate sensitive documents. Regulations insisted that Esme have security clearance and that had been done some time ago but then she had not left school and, obviously, not yet been employed for that purpose."

"She went to university from school and her father arranged that she have access to specific documents. He seemed to be trying for her to have a normal life and, at the same time, work for the department. All clever stuff and what one would expect of him. She wouldn't be the only student with a part-time job. When she got her degree, she came into the Department."

"The office staff were forbidden to talk about their work so they indulged in a fair amount of social gossiping"

"The rumours she brought with her referred to when she was still at school. These were only rumours remember. It goes like this. Somehow, the Russian Secret Service had found out about the research into Esme's background. In the story I heard, the person who actually carried out the research was a Russian agent. Reginald Marsh, at the time, was setting up a cooperative policy with the Americans; liaising with their secret service wing. They were hoping to be able to pool their discoveries; especially any information they had about the Russians. Although the Russians were officially allies, it was thought by some, including Esme's father, that the real enemy in the post-war years would be Russia. The Russians set out to drive a wedge between the British and the American Secret Services. If they could discredit Reginald Marsh, that would be of great help to the Russians. They tried to do so by claiming that he was using his daughter as a secret agent in a honey-trap; that she was sleeping with a spy. Esme's father had moved mountains to squash the story and, at the time, had succeeded. The Russians and, indeed, the frustrated newspapers, had filed the story for future use.

Jane paused to add hot water to the tea-pot.

"In 1945, with Reginald due for retirement, the Russians hoped they could resurrect the story. This was after they had shown their true colours and we were at the start of the Cold War. We had reports from our agents and we also received enquiries asking for interviews from the press. They expressed interest not so much in Reginald as in Esme. You know the sort of thing:- 'I am writing a feature on father-daughter relationships at work.' The interesting thing was that the press tried it on. They knew that nobody in the department was allowed to speak to the media. They were just preparing for the line. "Whitehall – or whatever other term they intended to use – offered no comment."

"Then I met Major Bygrave for the third time. The Department held a dinner-dance as a Christmas party just a few days after the previous one. This was a time for parties. We could bring a guest if we wanted to and Esme brought Major James Bygrave. She was proud and shy at the same time. The Major wore his uniform. If it had been a film, he would have been the handsome hero. I suspect, he was not happy in that role but I'm certain that, by then, he would have done anything for her. A little embarrassment was not to be regarded. I was able to speak to him privately and warned him that she may be at risk from newspaper reporters. He promised me that he would look after her. If it were possible for one man to do so, James Bygrave was that man,"

"Tell us about the suitcase! How did you get it?"

"That was the only message that I got from Esme. When I read of her disappearance after the Christmas break, I was not all that worried. We learned in the office that Jim had disappeared as well and I was confident that he would look after her. I did think it might be something to do with the media interest.

Then she stopped. Edgar, fascinated with the account of Helena's relatives, was absent-mindedly picking at the cake-crumbs on his plate. Jane looked at her daughter, who, involved in the story, had missed the signal from Edgar. She returned to her role as cake-dispenser and cut him another slice of the cake.

"You realise that means he has to walk another couple of miles today." was Helena's comment. Edgar said nothing. Helena knew that, if they had been on their own, he would have had something to say about exercise.

"Back to the suitcase." Jane took up the story again.

"What you must understand is that, even at the best of times, we were a secretive bunch in the Department and there was, at that time, an unpleasant atmosphere. There was a suspicion that somebody was leaking secrets. When I returned from the Christmas break, I had a pile of letters to deal with, mostly routine. There was one envelope addressed to me by name. It had been sent through the post and was marked 'private and confidential'. Which in itself was odd – such missives were normally labelled 'Top Secret' whether they were or not. The address was typed. The envelope contained a left-luggage ticket and a brief note, also typed. It read something like: 'Look after it, someone will call to collect it from you, tell no one, burn this, I rely upon you.'. How dramatic can you get? She didn't even sign the note. Cryptic as it was, it was reassuring. Esme had known in advance that she was going to disappear."

"How did you know it was from Esme?" asked Edgar.

"No one else I knew would have written such a note and, by then, we knew of her disappearance."

"And?" it was again Edgar who asked; Helena was more patient.

"Well, I waited a couple of days before going the left-luggage office. Whatever it was, it was as safe there as anywhere else and, as I say, we were all watching our backs. I didn't want to rush out on receipt of this note; probably an unnecessary precaution but it cost nothing. Esme, from her note, was not going to need it in the short term. I can tell you that I did not expect that whacking great suitcase but I kept a straight face when I collected it and borrowed a trolley to get it to the taxi stand. I was amused that she had left her name on it – not exactly covering her tracks there."

"I took the thing home. What else could I do? For a while, it was left in a handy place for collection, then it was moved into places more convenient for us and, finally, it went up into the loft. Other things cropped up, including Karen and her brother, Richard, and I'm afraid to say, that I forgot completely about it."

"Did you have any idea what had happened to Esme?"

The short answer to that is 'no'. I made what I thought were discrete enquiries but met with a brick wall. I was even warned off. Her father retired shortly afterwards and shortly after that, he died. There were accounts of that in the newspapers. It was clear that I was not the only one asking after her. She had said, 'tell no one!'. I hope that she didn't mean 'for ever'."

There was a short pause. Jane was looking particularly at Helena, dying to ask the question but it was Edgar who addressed it.

"No." he said baldly. "We do not know what happened to her either. We have traced her up to Christmas 1945 when, as you put it, she disappeared. Nor have we been able to trace Major James Bygrave. He was discharged from 'Whole-Time Military Service' as an Acting Sergeant, Ammunition Examiner. Theoretically, he was, at the same time enrolled into 'Part-Time Service' but the army has no further records. The reduction in his rank was standard procedure but may have been part of the smoke-screen. The date on the forms was the twenty-second of December."

"Yes, when we heard at the office that Jim had also

disappeared, the more romantically-minded of the girls had a coach-and-four heading for Gretna Green but we all took comfort in the assumption that he would be with her wherever she was. The suitcase doesn't help?"

"No." said Helena, "It includes no plans for the future. A lot of it is school stuff. It does have some things that you might be interested in. I've brought them with me. You didn't try and open it?"

"No. David, my husband, said that it was probably full of drugs or Government secrets. It might even be full of money. He was joking, of course. He had met Esme, even danced with her and, in any case, he knew what I thought of her. He was curious but never suggested that we break into it. What have you got?"

"Two items – apart from the rose – a sort of invitation for a party at your office with a phone number on it. We are pretty sure it Jim's number but it has not proved easy to trace it. Not only have some of the records gone astray but, if he was in army accommodation, it wouldn't be listed under his name in any case. We haven't yet trawled through the old telephone directories, that would take a great deal of work. The second item is a note. Edgar has called it 'a love letter distilled to its essence'. We need to confirm that it came from Jim."

Jane picked up the second item and paused before answering. The other three waited patiently. Jane Martin was, briefly, in a remembered world of her own.

"This was from Jim, all right. I remember it arriving and Esme's despair that she couldn't phone him. It was only when she went back to the invitation that she had stuffed in her bag that she found a phone number. Your Edgar has got it right. That's a fine way to describe it, but a bit slap-dash."

Her own David would have written the phone number in words and numerals.

CHAPTER 34

18th – 20th December 1945

Jim had said 'a few days'. So she did not rush to the phone when it rang on Sunday since it was only two days later. It was a curious call from a newspaper asking for an interview. Workers in her office did not give interviews, write articles, nor, in any other way, feature in the media. That was in their contract and, since much of the work they did was sensitive, they had all signed the Official Secrets Act. So that was easy enough; the answer was 'No!'. The other girls in the office had mentioned such requests. To Esme, however, it reminded her of similar requests before she had officially joined the department. She did not want a repeat of that. Her father had to do a great deal of work to squash the rumours then. She did not think that he would be able to do the same now.

Then she got one from her father. He was asking her to confirm that she would be joining the family at Christmas in Somerset. It happened that, being a newcomer to the office, she was not scheduled to work over the holiday but she hesitated. Jim would be back by then.

In the short pause while she considered, her father cleared his throat and then said. "I'd like you to bring your new boyfriend." Esme was used to her father knowing all about her movements. He knew about her work and even about her social life but this was unexpected. Whenever she taxed him about this surveillance, he fell back on his promise to her mother. He could not fulfil that promise unless he knew what she was doing. Esme was old enough now not to protest. She told herself that he felt guilty about leaving her to be brought up by her grandmother and tried out sophisticated words like 'overcompensation'.

This, however was different. He had never asked to meet any of the boys she had gone out with in the past. Not that any of them were in any way significant, certainly not serious. How did he know that Jim was special? In any case, was he special? A meeting, one date, two kisses, only one of them serious and the promise of a phone call. However special that made him to Esme, to an outsider, he could not even be given the status of a 'boyfriend'.

Esme decided to treat this calmly.

"I suppose you mean Jim Bygrave." she said. "'New boyfriend' is coming it a bit strong. I've only known him for a couple of days and, in any case, he's in Scotland."

Her father cleared his throat again. "He should be back in time." he said. "Tell him I would very much like him to join us."

'A royal summons' thought Esme. She wasn't sure how Jim would react to such a command. It occurred to her that he might feel that he was being coerced. Then she asked herself why her father wanted to meet him. He had said that Jim would be back 'in time'. She had some experience of her father's power to get things done. She only hoped that he was not messing up Jim's work. There had been satisfaction in the way he had spoken about the completion of his task. She would not be pleased with her father if he prevented that completion.

It was late in the afternoon when the phone rang again. She answered it as she always did by just saying "Hello". Something that she had learned from her Grandmother but had difficulty in remaining calm when Jim replied, "Hello to you too!" and then announced that he was in the telephone booth not a hundred yards away from her front door and that he would be knocking on it within minutes.

"As quick as you can." was all she said and when she opened the door, she pulled him into the hall and closed the door behind him. He was wearing his uniform and carrying an overnight bag. There were lines of weariness on his face. Esme reached up on tip toe so that she could put her arms around his neck, lifting her face to his. Nothing loath, the tall young man wrapped her in his own arms and kissed her – he noted that it was only the third time he had done so – until, breathless, she pulled away. All he said was, "That wasn't part of my plan either and I wasn't consulted but I do approve."

Jim must have been travelling all day so, in the few minutes warning that he had given, she had made some coffee. Now she sat him down in a deep arm-chair and offered him a mug. Before he took it he presented her with a small flat box.

"A present!" he said. "Since you asked about it."

Esme's eyes danced – now he was showering her with presents – and she took the lid off the box to find the 'flaming A' insignia that had adorned his sleeve. At once Esme understood. From what he had said, James Bygrave valued this badge more than the decorations he had won for bravery. He wanted her to have this precious thing and he had added a warm glow to the complex feeling that she had for him.

She touched his hand but she was close to tears and could say nothing.

Jim took her hand firmly but, just for that moment, had glanced away. He looked around the living room of her flat with approval. It was a civilised space with books and pictures and a couple of striking bronze ornaments. It was only a brief assessment for it was Esme that he wanted to look at. He drank from the mug and then holding it in both hands for the warmth said, "You don't seem surprised that I'm back so soon."

She had thought to pretend surprise when he came back early. She was going to ask him how he had managed but had discarded that as a stupid idea. This was her 'new boyfriend' and she had to tell him about her father and the royal summons. She was glad now that she had decided to do so. She took the mug from his hands and put it safely on a table. Then she sat in his lap, enjoying his arms around her and half buried her head on his shoulder before she said, "It's Daddy. He feels he should help."

Jim held her a little away from him so that he could see her face. While she was in his arms, she was stopping him from getting cross about her father but he was not going to complain. It did pass through his mind that referring to her father as 'Daddy' was an indicator of her social class but, at the moment, he wasn't going to complain about that either.

"Are you telling me that your father, Reginald Marsh, a shadowy figure in the upper hierarchy of the Foreign Office,

278

probably of the Secret Service, flew me to Scotland and back as a present to his daughter? How did he know what I was doing? No that's a silly question. If he can't find out something as simple as that then there is something wrong with our Secret Service and we are all in trouble. But why should he?"

"He wants you to join the family for Christmas. He called you my 'new boyfriend'"

"That's quick. Do all your boyfriends get an immediate inspection?" There was no anger yet in Jim's voice just astonishment.

"Jim, please!" It was just two words but they stopped any resentment developing. Whatever her father did or thought, this girl was all that concerned him.

"Sorry!" he said, "I'm shattered. I'll be all right when the coffee starts working."

Esme turned to kiss him on the cheek and wriggled into a more comfortable position.

"Thank you again. One day we'll have a proper quarrel but for now, just 'thank you'"

"Sitting on my knee was a stroke of genius. How could I quarrel with you in my arms?" he said. "Tell me about 'the family'. Do they gather every Christmas?"

"It is a long tradition. They certainly did so before the war; the whole clan – as far as the cousins-twice-removed. They tried to continue but it was only a token event throughout most of the war years. This one is supposed to re-launch the idea."

"Do you know many of them?"

"There are very few actually in the nuclear family. There

is my sister, Stella; she'll be on our side, I've already told her about you, and there is her husband Edward Burroughs – Ted for short – they have a young son, called Mark. Oh, Ted has only one arm. He was injured at Arnhem. I'd almost forgotten. I think that's because he ignores it himself. We have had one funeral recently and a wedding and most of them turned up. They won't approve of you! It has just occurred to me that your invitation may have been to pre-empt my not going but spending Christmas with you. I had suggested this to Stella."

*** *** ***

Jim discussed with Esme whether he should accept the invitation or not. He was not happy at the thought of being inspected. He certainly did not want to be seen as someone at the beck and call of Esme's father. He would be at a complete disadvantage in the man's own home. On the other hand, Reginald was Esme's father and was due respect. If he had not been so imperious, Jim would have welcomed such a meeting. It was a close call but they decided that it was the only way forward.

"I should say that only your rank makes you in any was acceptable to 'the family'" said Esme. "Will you wear your uniform?"

She asked the question without any emphasis but was sure how he would respond.

"Use the King's uniform for the benefit of your antediluvian relatives?" he started indignantly and then, once more, he saw the mischief in her eyes.

"That was naughty!" he said. "I'm certainly not wearing my demob suit. That will do for gardening. I think I would like a garden. We are going to have a garden aren't we? I've got some gear that should be ready at the tailor's. I was not sure whether I needed clothing coupons but he said they weren't necessary."

"The others will be wearing black-tie for dinner" she said and then registered what he was saying. "You've finished your work, haven't you? I should have asked. I was worried that you might not be given enough time."

"Yes, thank you. I'm not sure whether it is a comfort to have you worrying about me. I should say something like 'Don't worry your pretty little head!' but I could get used to knowing that you were. It went very smoothly. The system is in place. There is a trained force to employ the system. They don't need me anymore and I just need my last pay packet and a bit of paper saying that I'm now in the Reserve. There's some gear at my billet. I'm not sure what to do with that."

For him, events were moving so fast that the army life might have finished last year rather than yesterday. He could clear up the loose ends later. Right now it was the trip to Somerset that he had to deal with.

"How do we get there?" he asked.

When they had sorted those details, Esme said she had another request. There was a Christmas party for the office staff that evening. Not in the office this time but in a local hotel with a dining-room and a ball-room. The staff were expected to bring guests. Would Jim like to come?

"I want to show you off." she said. "You could sleep here

281

and take a shower. There will be food at the party. This time you should wear your uniform. The girls would expect it. What do you say?"

"Well, apart from a change of linen, I've only got my uniform here so it will have to do. If I used your sofa, what would you do with yourself?"

"Jim, you can take this perfect gentleman thing too far. You will sleep in my bed. If you insist, I'll change the sheets."

"I'm glad I'm your new boyfriend." he said, "And don't change the sheets. I might even dream."

Jim used Esme's bed and it carried the subtle smell of her body as well as the more insistent scent of her perfume. He buried his head in her pillow and fell asleep smiling.

When he awoke, he sensed that the flat was empty and took a shower. The shower curtain was still wet so he assumed that Esme had done the same. He had his overnight bag and was able to shave and generally smarten himself up for the party. He had done all he could and went into the kitchen to put the kettle on when he heard Esme at the front door calling, "Are you decent?" before she came into the flat.

"Good, you're up." she said. "Did you dream?"

Jim hedged; he had certainly dreamed but he was keeping that dream to himself.

"Can't remember!" he said.

"You are a fibber, James Bygrave. I can tell you that when I emerged from my shower, clad only in a towel, you were stirring in your sleep with a silly grin on your face. I did think I might join you but you were murmuring this girl's name."

Jim remembered his dream and it did involve a girl.

"What girl's name?" he asked.

"Have we got a choice?"

"Not since I met you." he replied and took her in his arms. "What girl's name?"

"Well it was an Esme something. Now what was it? That's right, it was 'Esme Darling'.

"And so you are." he said. "What stopped you from joining me?"

"I didn't want to compete with your dream girl." she answered and avoided looking at him.

"Esme, you are my dream girl. I've dreamed of you since I was a teen-ager even before seeing you at St Ermengild's." Then, more seriously, he asked. "Aren't you ready for the next step yet? You assume that I am. You may be wrong."

"Jim, you give off sparks. You almost glow in the dark. If you are not ready for that next step, you are giving the wrong signals."

"So, you are not?"

"I had to go for a walk to stop myself." she said and this time she blushed and turned away. "Now go into the kitchen and make some tea so that I can get ready

★★★ ★★★ ★★★

Esme wore a dress in air-force blue that added grace to her slim figure and emphasised her colouring. Jim felt privileged to be the escort of such a girl. They certainly had the attention of her workmates, who were already enjoying themselves. Some of the attention was because they were interested in the 'gate-crasher'.

This party was organised as a dinner-dance. The tables

were set and name-plates arranged. Esme and Jim were placed next to each other and he was flanked, he was pleased to see, by Jane Clayton. The girl who had brought the message that Esme would be few minutes late. The girl who had told him to take care of Esme 'or else!'

"You told me to look after her; how am I doing so far?" he asked so that only she could hear.

She did not answer his question but introduced him to her husband, David. "The place-cards are my job." she said. "Dance with me. David will look after Esme." The dance was a waltz. It was clear that Jane wanted to speak to him privately so Jim made only the smoothest of turns. The girl was skilled in following and was able to speak quietly, without concern for the steps.

"As for looking after her, you would get a medal from me." she said. "But you don't have to look at her all the time, you are supposed to be dancing with me. That girl of yours is a shining star."

Jim acknowledged that it was Esme who had his attention and he said nothing about the description of Esme as being 'that girl of yours' but he added it to the 'new boyfriend' title and was content. Jane continued in the same even tone as though they were engaged in social chit-chat but softly so that only he could hear.

"Something is going on concerning her that I do not like. You know that she is one of our translators. Perhaps you don't know how good she is at her job. She can handle papers in half a dozen languages as though they were in English and she has top-level security clearance. Not many of us have. The powers-that-be don't like us underlings reading the sensitive stuff but they have to put up with it because they can't read much of it themselves. Esme is therefore at risk and, at the same time, is a risk to the Department. To come to the point, we have had requests from other agencies and the newspapers for interviews with her. You must keep her out of the newspapers if you can."

She stopped and looked into Jim's eyes. "I should not be telling you this and I don't know why I am."

"You are telling me this so that I know there may be some danger to 'my girl'. There is no need for you to worry about security. It will go no further – and I will take care of her. Thank you!"

Esme and Jim left the dance early. They had a train to catch the following day. They took a cab to her apartment and Jim asked the driver to wait while he escorted her to her door. She had complained about his 'perfect gentleman' behaviour but enjoyed it nonetheless. It was a brief good-night kiss for not only was the cab waiting but Esme had things to do.

CHAPTER 35

19th August 1986

August, up to then, had been more like April. The last couple of days had been foul and they had been warned that the balloon flight could only take place if the winds were not too strong. Arising early, Edgar checked the barometer in the hall, turned on the television to check the weather forecast and finally went to the window and peered out at the morning sky. All three sources promised him decent weather. He felt like spitting into the wind for luck but decided it wasn't worth leaving the house to do so.

By the time he was ready, Helena was up and about. The two of them felt anxious about the weather and about the arrangements they had made. If everything went smoothly Marilyn and Bill would have, instead of a drinking session that neither of them wanted, an enjoyable and romantic experience to start their conventional relationship. Both Helena and Edgar were doing everything they could to make the balloon trip work.

Edgar walked around to Bill's place first to get him up and to borrow his car. He would use this to drive both of them. His excuse was that Bill would be drinking and that he would have to drive him home so he might as well get used to the car. This meant that Helena could take Marilyn in her own.

It was quite a drive to the launching site which was, sensibly, some way from any habitation. The people who managed the balloon trips used the parkland of a stately home and this parkland had the added advantage that there were no beasts grazing.

It was a smooth run through gentle countryside. Bill, at first, was busy telling Edgar about the files that he had brought with him that concerned the Esme Marsh investigation. He had been hard at work on the case and tried to get as much done as possible because his contributions would stop now for some time. Then he noticed the rural nature of the trip. He had been imagining that they would be heading for somewhere that provided some lunch-time entertainment before they went on to the night-clubs or similar and began to ask questions.

"What have you got laid on for me?"

"One of the rules is that you are not supposed to know what is going to happen."

"You're going to kidnap me?"

"You put me in charge. Now you've got to put up with it. All I can promise you is that I tried to fix you up with a stripper."

"Marilyn will crucify me!"

Edgar turned the car though a field gate, offering thanks for the fine weather. The broad acres of neat meadow-land that presented themselves had been washed clean by the overnight rain and the welcome sun seemed to sparkle on every blade of grass.

The parkland, held, incongruously, a minibus with a trailer and a bright red inflated hot-air balloon whose basket was anchored firmly to four stakes. It dwarfed everything else around it. The parkland also held a car, Helena's car. Bill took in the scene and exclaimed.

"What a super idea." he said. "Where are the rest of the lads?" Then he recognised Helena's car and the two women, Marilyn and Helena, talking to the man who was in charge of the balloon. "What are they doing here?" he asked before he realised what was going on. When he did, he was enthusiastic.

"It's still a super idea." he said. "Or it will be if Marilyn approves. She said I was to have a last night of freedom."

"Well, I know she approves of the balloon. Whether she approves of sharing it with you, I don't know." Edgar took the files that Bill had left on his seat and tucked them under his arm

Helena also had succeeded in bringing her charge to the site in ignorance of the plan and the two women now moved towards their respective partners. Marilyn started by walking and then broke into a run. Bill, for a second, looked worried but it was with delight that Marilyn ran into his arms.

"I hope you think its a good idea." she said.

Bill, much pleased with her reaction, said. "He promised me a stripper."

"No. I said I'd tried to fix you up with one. I thought it was a good try."

"What does a stripper do?" asked Marilyn innocently. "Perhaps we can make some arrangement."

The balloon, brilliant red and enormous was tugging at its basket, almost animal in its eagerness to set off. The pilot was already in the basket and his assistant was impatient to get the passengers aboard.

Only then did Bill realise that Helena and Edgar were not going with them. Edgar confirmed this by handing him the keys to his own car.

"They'll bring you back here." he said. "In the glove compartment, you'll find the details of the hotel we've booked you into. It's not far and it's just for one night. The hotel bill is down to Marilyn's father – he said it was instead of paying for the photographs – I've taken a few already. I'll call on you, at home, on the great day. Which, by the way, is the day after tomorrow. Remember that you mustn't see the bride before the ceremony! I'll be early."

He took some more photographs as the two climbed into the basket and as the balloon was released and shot upwards. Then, he put his arm around Helena and she reciprocated as they watched their friends climb into a cloudless sky.

"So what do we do now?" asked Edgar. "Did your brilliant scheme have any further role for us? I'm not letting you get at the stuff Bill gave me until at least this evening."

"It wasn't part of the scheme but, at the moment, going home feels pretty attractive."

"Great minds think alike." he replied and they strolled back to their car. When they reached it, Helena opened the boot and took out a plastic bag which held a cardboard box. "I put some gear in the car earlier and I found this. What is it all about?" she asked taking the box out of the bag. The box held a set of bathroom scales.

"Great!" said Edgar. "I thought I'd left that in the shop and we'd have to go back for it. That would really have been a Freudian error. I'd put it in 'safe place.'"

Helena made an impatient noise and he responded.

"You'll remember the cake at Jane's place and your unkind remark about my girth."

"I didn't mention your girth – lovely word 'girth.'"

"Not directly perhaps but by implication. Whether you did or not, I resolved to do something about it. So I bought a set of bathroom scales. That was step one. Step two is that I have resolved to weigh myself daily. Step three will be to lose weight."

Helena smiled to herself. She had noticed his girth. It was typical of Edgar that he only needed the gentlest of hints to respond. She knew that he would devise a regimen that impinged very little on their daily lives, that would be barely perceptual to their friends and would work. Once again his pragmatism was made to serve his romantic ends.

She also had the feeling that, shortly, she might welcome such a set of scales for herself.

Much as they enjoyed the day, especially the return home, neither of them could leave their pursuit of Esme Marsh for very long and that evening, they were back at the problem of Esme's boyfriend and was he her husband?

Helena cudgelled her brains to try and remember what her mother had said about James Bygrave. At the time she had not been all that interested and, in any case, her mother had not given the information very much credence.

Her great-aunt Esme had been the subject of much rumour and Helena was still struggling with what was rumour and what was fact. Less still was known about Esme's supposed husband. He did not stay around for very long. She attempted to tell Edgar what the facts were.

"As I remember it, the family did not think much of

Esme's choice. Those who wished to make the point referred to him as 'that book-keeper'. Definitely working class. He was an officer in the army but not of a regiment. 'Something to do with ammunition.' they said scornfully. There was also talk of a 'hole-in-the-corner' wedding. All this comes through word-of-mouth, you understand."

"Sounds as though you had some very snooty relatives." Edgar said. "What did 'hole-in-the-corner' mean? A pregnancy, perhaps?"

"My grandmother was a few years older than Esme and mostly she travelled with her father on his overseas postings. Mum said she was pro-Esme." Then she stopped. "I remember the story now. How extra-ordinary; it has been sitting waiting for this moment for years. I may leave bits out but here it goes."

"One Christmas, Great Grandfather Reginald. The big cheese in the Foreign Office, Esme's father, summoned the two of them, James Bygrave and Esme, to the family home in Somerset for Christmas. Mum used the word 'summoned' quoting from Grandma. This was an annual meeting of the whole tribe – a very big event. This was the first Christmas after the war, so it was bigger than usual. Esme and James had only just met but they must have been close for him to receive such a summons. Mum was pretty firm that it was not a normal invitation."

"Reginald and James were closeted for the best part of an hour in his study and Esme's father had looked pretty grim when he asked James to go with him. The assumption was that he was coming the heavy father. A bit much in 1945. 'Are your intentions honourable?' The rest of the clan saw nothing wrong with that, James Bygrave, to them, was not suitable to be associated with the Marsh family."

"Then, apparently, there was some coming and going with Jim and Esme and her father. Finally, when they emerged, the two men had obviously come to some sort of agreement. Reginald spoke to the butler and, instead of the usual cocktails, he brought in champagne. On the other hand, no toasts were drunk."

"Four days later, on Boxing Day, the young couple disappeared. Grandma claimed that they had not been seen for three days before Reginald raised the alarm."

CHAPTER 36

21st December 1945

They travelled First Class by an early train. The tickets were returns to Frome in Somerset and had been delivered by special messenger. The crowds of people travelling to their families for Christmas made them thankful for their reserved seats. They breakfasted on the train and were made to feel that the rationing of food was a thing of the past. The presence of their fellow travellers in the carriage meant that they were unable to talk freely.

So they did a cross-word puzzle together. A process that gave rise to a certain amount of mirth. Both of them were pleased that it was a common interest and that the other had the skills and that they were able to display their own. Then Jim fell asleep. Just before he nodded off he told Esme, in a quiet voice so that the others could not hear him, to wake him if he started to talk in his sleep.

At the station they were met by a chauffeur-driven Rolls. Esme regarded it with affection. It might have been the same one that had taken her to St. Ermengild's each term. She greeted the driver with more than affection for it was Treadwell himself. "I am glad it's you, Arthur" she said. His presence meant that her father was already at the house. Treadwell was now his personal driver and accompanied him wherever he went.

"It is a great pleasure to see you, Miss Esme."

"If you don't get rid of the 'Miss' bit, I will start calling you Mister Treadwell, or even, God forbid, 'Treadwell'. There no need to show off in front of Jim he's privy to all our secrets."

Then she introduced him to Jim. This was a new world to Jim Bygrave and it was only the warmth of the friendliness that Esme and Treadwell clearly shared that saved him from regretting accepting the invitation. Old family retainers belonged in books written before the war but this giant of a man, who beamed at him with such friendliness and shook his hand so firmly, was part of Esme's life and Jim was glad that this was so. Treadwell, he felt was an ally.

"Pleased to meet you… " he started and Jim interrupted the formal greeting.

"Not 'sir'!" he said. "My name to those who stand in the relationship you do to Esme, is 'Jim'" and the big man nodded.

"I'm Arthur!" he said 'Thank you for what you said about my relationship to this young lady." Jim Bygrave was pleased to note that this was not just a chauffeur being polite to a guest of his master but part of the establishment which amongst other things provided a shield to protect Esme.

When they reached the front door of Bridge House, the family home. Esme asked Arthur Treadwell to look after the cases

"I want to take Jim on the 'walk' before the light goes." she said. They had entered the porch that guarded the front door of the house; a porch cluttered with waterproofs, boots, shoes, umbrellas and walking sticks. Esme lost no time in changing into a pair of her walking shoes that lived in the porch, she looked at the shoes that Jim was wearing and decided that they would do.

"There is a thin skim of ice in places'" was Arthur Treadwell's contribution. He had dropped the formal address but had yet to call her just 'Esme'. "A stick might help."

Jim selected a stout ash-plant which met with the chauffer's approval. Was the stick just for walking?

Esme was pleased to be at what for her was the closest thing she had ever had to a home. She wanted to show it off to Jim.

"The 'walk' was designed by my father when my mother was ill." she said. "It is wheel-chair friendly. Daddy bought her one that she could move herself. For a time, she was able to do so; later someone had to push her. She would wear a brightly coloured shawl so he could keep an eye on her. You will see, as we walk it, that she was never out of sight of his study; that room up there."

They set off together. Esme's hand was tucked under his left arm and she leant slightly upon him. The stick was useful. The cloudless weather had meant that the temperature was a couple of degrees below freezing and there were slippery areas on the walk. Most of it, however, was covered thickly with the long-fallen leaves of autumn.

"I used to walk here as a child." said Esme. "Sometimes with my sister but mostly alone. I used to imagine that my mother was walking with me. I did not think of her as sitting in a wheel chair." There was a catch in her voice and Jim, desperately wanting to comfort her, knew that it was best if he said nothing, just applied a little more pressure on the hand under his arm.

He was rewarded by her saying in a much more cheerful tone. "You are the bee's knees." when what she really meant was that he always seemed to know how to respond to her.

It was Mrs Treadwell who took him to his room when they got back to the house. He heard her say to Esme that she had put him in the best guest-room and the thought passed through his head of the traditional preparation of sacrifices. Nothing was too good for the lamb before the slaughter and the calf had to be fattened. He also reflected on how the rest of the family would feel about this newcomer in the 'best' guest-room?

"There you are Mr. Bygrave." she said, "If there is anything – anything – that you need just ask me. I'm usually in the kitchen."

"Your husband now calls me Jim." he said. "I would feel at home if you did the same."

"He said! I would be happy to if you call me Margaret. Arthur says he is relying on you."

Here was another ally and he appreciated it. There was also yet another friend of Esme's implying a deep relationship between Esme and him. He hoped that their wishes that he would look after her would be granted. He wanted to show his appreciation. "Esme tells me that you would provision her with tuck to share with her schoolmates and how grateful they were. She mentioned some home-made biscuits."

Friendly before, Mrs Treadwell could not control her smile. She nodded and pointed to an old-fashioned biscuit barrel at the side of his bed. She was about to speak but he interrupted her.

"Yes, I will take care of Esme. That I can promise you."

"You'd better!" she said standing up to him. "But now you must come with me. The master wants to meet you in his study. I'll show you the way."

"So soon!" he thought, and then, "The sooner the better."

Mrs Treadwell knocked on the study door and then announced him formally and closed the door as she left.

Two walls of the study, as the house-keeper had called it, were lined with books. A third was hung with maps. There was a solid bench for display of open books that was big enough to spread the maps on. It was lit by bright lamps, placed to throw pools of light on the working surfaces. This was indeed a place for study.

Reginald Marsh was seated behind his desk, a huge mahogany structure dating from some past century. This was apt for Reginald himself gave such an impression. He was a powerful looking man dressed in formal office wear and entrenched in his seat. He made no attempt to rise and did not offer his hand in greeting.

Jim Bygrave froze. The hackles on the back of his neck rose. This man was being deliberately rude. That he was doing so in his own house to a guest was as broad an insult as anyone could offer. Jim's first reaction was that he should walk out of the door and out of the house. He heard his father's homespun credo. 'Let no man insult you without retribution' but it was followed by 'to be rude to someone who is rude to you, brings you down to their level.' He was tempted to say nothing until the other man spoke but he was not going to stand, like a naughty schoolboy in front of his host.

"May I sit down?" he asked and did so, without waiting

for a response, in a chair so placed that it that meant that Sir Reginald had to turn to address him. Address him he did and without preamble.

"I understand that you are courting my daughter. Since I knew nothing about you, I have asked you to come here to Bridge House to see if you are a suitable match. I have since learned that you lack the education that any husband of hers will need and that you have virtually no family of your own to help you. What family you have has nothing to recommend it. You have no money of your own and you work only as a book-keeper and could not support her. I will tell her this evening that such a marriage is impossible. You should know that I have complete control of her finances until she is twenty-five and if she continues to see you I will not release a penny of her estate."

Jim Bygrave bridled at the very tone which Reginald Marsh employed and, as he went on, had difficulty in believing that he was hearing this archaic pronouncement. There was something wrong with it. He tried hard not to interrupt but the idea that Esme could be told something like that in the form of an order made him speak.

"Sir. I have known your daughter for only a few days. You do not know her at all. Be sure of one thing, if Esme wants to marry me she will do so. You have a daughter you should be proud of. She is her own woman and will make her own decisions. Not you, nor your medieval ideas about suitable matches and parental permission would move her."

"Have you already proposed to her? Do you really wish to marry her?"

"'No' to the first – you may be 'fleeing the boar before

the boar pursues'. I know that I will but only when she knows enough about me to make a reasoned answer. When that time comes, her reasoned answer may be 'no'. 'Yes' to the second. As soon as we met, I felt that it was my role in life to look after this girl. Every hour that passes reinforces that feeling."

Esme's father had risen from his desk and walked to the window and while Jim was answering his questions. He looked out at the darkening skies.

Jim felt, once more, that there was something wrong in the way this interview was going, something wildly off-beat. Then his host asked a question that seemed much more rational.

"What will you do when you leave the army?"

"I will get a job in an office. There, I can earn a living and a good one. I was doing so before I was conscripted and the army also seemed to think I was worthy of reward."

There was a pause and Jim decided to take the initiative.

"Sir, it should be clear to you by now that I intend to marry your daughter. We will have to devise a framework which allows for that and for your opposition. For the moment, that can wait. Right now I do not wish to create trouble between Esme and yourself so I think I should leave your house as soon as possible. I'm sure you could receive a phone call that meant I had to leave urgently."

Esme's father did not reply, instead he said, still looking out of the window, "'flee the boar'; that's Richard the Third isn't it?" Jim nearly answered this, impressed that Sir Reginald had not only placed but had corrected the quotation. This, however, was not a literary discussion.

His host turned from the window. "Can I offer you a drink." he said, crossing to the drinks table. "I think I'll need one for the next bit."

Jim declined. He needed a clear head.

"What does that mean?" he asked "'The next bit? '"

"First of all, my apologies. You will have gathered that I have made enquiries about you – and I apologise for doing so. When I have explained everything, I hope you will realise that such enquiries were justified. They discovered a universal approval of your work, integrity and character. Every professional source I consulted gave me a glowing account of your work. The same can be said of the portrayals of your character, though these were all from friends of yours. Have you no enemies?"

He took a substantial mouthful of his drink before he continued whilst Jim wondered at the contrast between this obviously embarrassed man and the strange domestic tyrant that had greeted him.

"More and humbler apologies are due for the interview you have been just subjected to. But I needed to know."

Jim began to realise what this was all about. He was both incredulous and angry.

"This is a test, isn't it? You're like something out of the Ark or a Shakespeare play. You'll be setting me seven labours next."

"Only one." he replied and, for the first time he smiled and it lit up his face. There was, in the smile, something that checked Jim's anger. It was an echo of Esme's. "And it is a labour you have asked for. I want you to look after my daughter. You have claimed that that is your role in life. I trust that you will fulfil it well. She is in the library next door. If I may, I will speak with her briefly and then she will tell you what this is all about. You should know that I am not and never was concerned about your family or indeed about your financial expectations. I know them to be an irrelevance but I was concerned about your education. I need not have been. She deserves an informed and intelligent partner. It is clear that she has found one."

Only the fact that he had referred to Esme as in need of his care prevented Jim from exploding. Yes, he did want to look after, cherish and protect Esme. He had to listen to the justification that this man was offering for his behaviour.

CHAPTER 37

Morning 20th August 1986

What with Esme Marsh and, now, Jim Bygrave and with the hot-air balloon and the imminent wedding, the work in the studio was piling up. Edgar woke and rose even earlier than usual. He was anxious to clear the decks in preparation for the album he had promised Marilyn's dad. The hotel bill for the pre-nuptials had, in a roundabout way, been payment for that.

They had spent some more time on the suitcase but there was not much left in it that they could use. They had found an envelope with rail tickets, unused first class return tickets from Frome to Waterloo. Esme and Jim had not used those for their departure from Bridge House. Why were they there in the first place?

He was going to try some panoramic shots of the gathered families of the bride and groom if the weather was half good and he had already tried out the technique on some of the shots of the balloon. These he developed now and was much pleased with them. The photogenic balloon itself was a major success but he had captured some of the pleasure of Marilyn and Bill as they understood what had been laid on for them. The work was, he thought, already worth what Marilyn's father had paid for it.

There were a couple of other minor jobs which he dealt

with and he wrote a couple of letters. As best-man, he had to appear in a number of the wedding-photographs. He had arranged for his assistant to press the shutter for those shots. The assistant was a young man called Barry Spenser who worked with talent and an enthusiasm that Edgar enjoyed. Edgar thought he could do something about his untidy mass of hair; either a haircut or tie it back in a pig-tail. He called him affectionately, 'the last of the hair-bear bunch'. Edgar wondered if this fashion made him more attractive to girls but it certainly did not interfere with his work. Most important, he was completely reliable. He was Edgar's first choice whenever he needed someone to help. Critically, he had a driving licence. Judging that the young man should be out of bed by now, he phoned him to give him some further instructions.

"Barry?"

A sleepy voice at the other end of the line answered him. "Barry here, if only just."

"Barry, this is Edgar. I want some more lighting for tomorrow. If it's dull we'll need some spotlights in the marquee – stand alone jobs, we don't want any wires lying about – and we are running short of film. Could you sort that for me? Also, I've just realised that I will be in the church when Marilyn steps out of her car. Get shots of her doing so and of her father."

"Sure, boss. More lighting for the marquee, more film and me to be at the church early to photograph the arrival of the bride and her father. What about Bill and you arriving?"

"Good idea! Make sure you set your alarm, and allow for traffic on the way to the church." The two of them had worked together for some time and by now, Barry knew that Edgar was not treating him as a simpleton, he was simply enumerating the precautions that he took himself.

Only when he had sorted everything he could, did Edgar take a pot of tea on a tray with two cups through to his wife. She was just stirring and sat up to drink hers.

"What do you call a pre-empted honeymoon? A prequel?" she asked

"Marilyn and Bill pre-empted any honeymoon years ago. Nonetheless, I think they would have enjoyed yesterday – and this morning."

"I enjoyed yesterday."

"Your idea!. Brilliant, that balloon."

"I wasn't talking about the balloon." she said, putting her cup down.

Later, Edgar suggested that he make a fresh pot of tea but Helena vetoed it. "'I'm meeting someone at Somerset House. I've got a train to catch." she said and glanced at the bedside clock. She was out of bed in a flash and searching for her clothes.

Without being asked, Edgar phoned for a cab. Helena hated being late for an appointment. This did not stop him from delaying her departure with a kiss and a murmured,

"And I enjoyed this morning too."

Whilst she was away, Edgar cleared his outstanding work. It took him most of the day. By the time he had finished and prepared the workshop for the wedding project, Helena was back. She looked tired from the journey and her face was bleak.

"Esme Marsh did not marry James Bygrave in this

country. Esme Marsh did not marry anybody in this country. James Bygrave didn't marry anybody in this country."

"Country being the United Kingdom?" asked Edgar.

"That's it." was the terse response and then, "And neither of them died here either."

"That doesn't mean they didn't get married. We are sure that they 'disappeared'. That could just mean that they emigrated. There was a lot of it going on at that time. They could have got married overseas, perhaps even in Ireland. A strong possibility is the States."

"It does mean that that trail has gone cold." said Helena.

CHAPTER 38

21st December 1945

Jim stood up as Sir Reginald left the room and paced up and down, frustrated by his ignorance of what was going on. Then Esme came in. Her father was not with her. He wanted to hold her and then told himself that that was now a condition of his life. He wanted to hold her always. She was clearly as embarrassed as he was but there was humour in the way she greeted him.

"Just as well I didn't succumb yesterday." she said. "That would have made it a proper shot-gun wedding." and in that light-hearted quip demonstrated her ability to make him accept the oddness of any situation. She added, laughing at him, "Daddy claims you said he was like something out of a Shakespeare play. I think he was actually pleased with the comparison with Prospero. Where did you pick up all these literary references? They've certainly helped you with Daddy."

For a second, Jim resented the question. It smacked of snobbery. Why should he not have knowledge of Shakespeare? Then he told himself that he would have to grow a thicker skin. Most people did not go around quoting things. He already knew that he was odd in that way. In any case, this was scarcely the time to debate English Literature. Then he realised that this was exactly what the two of them needed – to talk, it did not matter what they talked about.

"I'll take that on its face value." he said. "Some of it is from my father. He used to declaim Tennyson, particularly at Christmas. I remember now the fresh splendour of the sound as he quoted from the *Morte d'Arthur*. I suppose that contributed also to what you called my 'perfect gentleman' act."

"You said your father was a bank-clerk, didn't you?

"Yes. Do not underestimate the lowly clerks. H.G.Wells worked in a haberdashers. Dickens worked in a blacking factory. The Old Man did serve in the army however. We thought that his love of words found a source in the barrack-room ballads, the ones that Kipling exploited. He also did Music Hall songs and the 'Lays of Ancient Rome'. "

With dramatic gestures and resonant tones, Jim quoted:-

" 'And how can man die better

Than facing fearful odds

For the ashes of his fathers

And the temples of his Gods?'"

Somehow, his voice gained a timbre that he did not use in ordinary speech. It was as though the words took on a life of their own.

"You would be amazed how many bridges I kept at the right hand of Horatius when I was a boy."

This was another Jim Bygrave. Not babbling through anxiety but carried away with the sound of the poetry.

"Then there was a poem about the Battle of Naseby." and he declaimed again:-

"'And the Man of Blood was there, with his long and hennad hair.'

What boy could not be moved by such melodrama? I

never understood what 'hennad' meant until I was sixteen and then I found a version that read 'long essenced hair', nothing like the same punch. Did the Old Man make up the 'hennad'?"

"Was Macaulay part of the syllabus at Oxford? He should have been. Apart from his appeal to courage and tradition and his own entrapment in the concept of Empire, he preached an ideal state when 'lands were fairly portioned.'"

"Yes he was. We had to read a biography. It included a claim that when he was four he had hot coffee spilt over his legs and responded to concern by saying 'Thank you, Madam, the agony has abated.'"

Jim was enjoying this. He felt he could speak to Esme as he had never spoken to anybody else. He did note that he had referred to his father as 'the Old Man'. Esme called hers 'Daddy'.

Esme was enjoying it too. It had much more impact than an Oxford seminar and she felt that her old professor would have delighted in Jim's enjoyment of the language. His rendering of the quotations added to her pleasure. There was the trace of the London accent and an impressive modulation.

"No Wordsworth or Keats?"

"Not from him. Remember there would have been little room for the Romantics in his life. Later, I had a schoolteacher who helped. He would read Rider-Haggard and Buchan to us. The sort of books, I note from his shelves, that your father has kept from his childhood. I think that they will have contributed to his unquestioning patriotism. Then this teacher made us read Shakespeare in class but in allocated roles – not whole plays but extracts. Just nudging us into understanding what Shakespeare was saying. I remember we did 'The Merchant of Venice'. He showed us, without us even realising it, both the poetry and the insight into human beings. He had the whole class laughing, demonstrating the way Portia would have walked when she pretended to be a man."

Jim tried to show how and was rewarded with a laugh from Esme.

"Go on!" she said. "I'm glad I asked. I bet he gave you some good parts."

"Well, I did a pretty good Shylock. At least I think I did. I remember I started off exaggerating his Jewishness until I came to the speech when he asks if a Jew is any different from anyone else. I think the teacher's skill was in letting authors speak for themselves. He selected the bits that we were ready for."

Esme almost hugged herself. She was already certain about this man but everything he said and did reinforced that certainty. His face, as he emphasised what he was saying, changed to fit the way he felt. She had seen his first reaction to her question and realised that she had not thought how it would sound to him. She saw then how he had checked his own thoughts.

"Daddy claimed that you said he was like something out of the Ark. You are one brave boyfriend. He was quite impressed"

Jim shrugged. "Well he is." he said. "As far as I can gather, I'm to marry you to fit into his agenda."

"That's a bit over the top, as you well know. You might

just as well say that you were going to propose to fit into Judith Ali's agenda. Be honest, you nearly asked me then; when she said you had to look after me."

Jim remembered the moment well and was still wondering why she had shied away so quickly. He asked now. "And you were frightened that I would, why?

"I knew that if you did, I would say 'yes'. We had known each other for less than twenty-four hours. A dance one day, a phone call and just the beginning of a date the next. It would have made no sense to agree. Then I regretted that you had not, simply because you had been so tactful. It told me that you cared for me and could sense my feelings; that you were willing to disregard your own."

By now that were sitting together on Sir Reginald's sofa but facing each other and Esme was more her normal resilient self. In a much more serious mood, she turned fully to him and said, "Do give Daddy a chance. He says he promised my mother that he would do everything he could for Stella and me. The worst of it is that there were many things he could not do because of his job. So whenever he could do anything he did so, whether it made sense or not. Once he brought in an expert to teach us self-defence. Actually that did come in handy. You see what I mean, I hope. This is his last chance to do anything out of the ordinary. He retires after Christmas."

"Less about your father and more about us."

"O.K. I'll ask the question and you had better give the right answer. Are you going to ask me to marry you?"

"Yes, I am. Is that the right answer? I think I decided that I was going to when you lied to the security guard – and with such panache, too."

Esme, however, was still being serious. "Jim, I don't want to pressure you and the sooner you know what this is about the better but just one more question before I tell you. Would you marry me tomorrow if I asked you?"

Jim looked at her closely and saw the concern in her eyes. Something other than any proposal was troubling her.

"Hang on!" he said. "You know I'm going to ask you – which is one of the silliest things I've ever heard – but I don't know whether you will say 'yes'. Which, if anything, is even sillier. Nor do I know if the answer is going to be conditional. 'Yes, if I've got enough money. Yes, if I'll adopt your illegitimate child?"

This last brought a gurgle of laughter. "How did you know?" she said and then, "Forget the last question Jim, ask and I will tell you."

"This was supposed to be under a full moon with the distant sound of violins and perhaps even a bottle of bubbly; but, if you insist, at least I can make the traditional gesture."

Jim, in one smooth movement from his seat on the sofa, and holding one of Esme's hands in his, knelt down on one knee. "Esme Marsh, will you marry me?" he said and it was a sincere question.

"Yes." she replied, with the same measure of sincerity. "I will" and she reached down to touch his cheek. She spoke formally as though going through a ceremony or making an oath. "Nothing, after what you have gone through, could have been more romantic. What resolution? I think, even though it is only days ago that we met that I know you well enough now to understand that you have thought about the practical consequences as well as the romance. Nothing has deterred you; not my relatives, not this different world that I have been brought up in and least of all my father. I would like to match that resolution with my own. Be sure my answer is unconditional; I am going to marry you come hell or high water. Nothing and nobody will stop me."

It may have been an unusual way of proposing marriage but Jim judged that it was incumbent upon him to return to the conventions. He stood up still holding her hand, lifted her from her seat to kiss her and the resulting embrace left her breathless. He knew that he had yet to be told what her father had in mind and that she would tell him shortly. For the moment, he did not care.

Esme disengaged herself and sat back on the sofa but moved into the corner; indicating that he should sit beside her. He did so but realised that he would have to move if he wanted to hold her. She wanted to make what followed as impersonal as possible and when she started speaking it was as though she were delivering a lecture.

"A few years ago, the Russians attempted to discredit my father. He was negotiating with the Americans to share intelligence. The Russians decided that the easiest way to get at him was through me. They suggested that Daddy was using me as a honey-trap. Their story was that I was sleeping with a spy to incriminate him or get information from him. I was seventeen and still a schoolgirl. There were circumstances that made the suggestion more plausible – including Brotherton. If such a rumour had reached the American press that would have been the end of the negotiations. There were plenty of people in the States who were anti-British and the popular press would have enjoyed savaging him. Daddy succeeded in preventing publication of the rumour then but it is tucked away in both the newspaper files and those of the journalists that sell such stories for their living."

Jim could hear the tension in her voice. Esme was near to tears but he dared neither move nor speak. She needed to focus completely to complete the story.

"There are signs that they are interested in pursuing that theme today. A couple of phone calls asking me if I want to give interviews and Daddy has learned of enquiries being made in the Department."

Now she looked directly at him and her voice faltered.

"You haven't said anything."

"I have questions but you haven't done yet and you'll probably answer them."

"O.K. Let's think of your questions. Was I sleeping with a German spy?"

"Don't be daft! My Esme Marsh as a Mata Hari? Wrong genes, wrong upbringing, wrong person. Moreover, the idea casts aspersions on me. Would I fall in love with someone who could do that?"

Esme was impatient. "It may be daft to you but Daddy had already decided to use me in the Department as a translator and he had me investigated to ensure that I would be cleared for access to sensitive documents or even to be present at high level meetings. He was already sending me, by special courier, low level documents to translate With that sort of information – and it had been leaked – all the papers would need would be a photograph of me in a swimming costume or in a night club standing next to a blurred figure and their job would be done. The American press would have made a meal of it."

"The next question you should ask is: 'Is it important now? Yes it is, because Daddy is retiring. That itself will be news but not what the press would call newsworthy. Throw in a daughter working as a secret agent and some sex and it might even be worth the front page. And the Russians are still trying to drive a wedge between us and the Yanks. It is also important now because when he does retire, in a few days, he won't be able to do anything about such publicity – and this is what drives him – he won't be able to help me."

"O.K. So far that makes sense. Do you care?"

"Now it is you who are being daft. You want to marry me. You, as well as I, will care. You'll care when our wedding is reported with a photograph of me as a pin-up and a cartoon on page two about you making an honest woman of me. You'll care when our children are born with suggestions about their parentage."

"Enough! I know you are exaggerating deliberately but you've made your point. Especially about our children. How do you know I want any children? We haven't discussed that yet, have we?"

Esme saw he was in his called his babbling phase and asked for a question from him.

"The next question follows logically. What do we do about it? Not about the children." but this time he did not pause but pressed on. "Perhaps I should ask what your father is going to do about it?"

"That's the question that counts. Daddy was proposing that I should disappear. If the press could not get at me there

314

would be no story and, in my new identity, I could live a normal life. Since I would need someone to look after me, he'd have to disappear too. With me this would be no problem; the mechanism for changing the identity of individuals has worked well for some years. With him it would be more difficult if not impossible. There is another reason why he could not."

She stopped and looked at him to see how he was taking it. As she had noticed before and enjoyed, his face changed with his thoughts in a remarkable way. Now she could see that he had worked out why he was at Bridge House.

"Yes." she said and did so with apprehension. "You arrived on the scene as though you had been written in for the part." His face changed again and she threw up a hand to stop him speaking. Almost laughing, she said, "No, I knew nothing of his scheme until this evening. How could you think otherwise?"

"It was only for an instant." he said. "You've thrown me in at the deep end and I've yet to find out if I can swim. The Esme that could not agree to trap an enemy spy could not be so devious as to trap a poor book-keeper."

"Let me get this straight. Your father has a plan to protect you from the press and, I suppose, to protect his relations with the Americans. That's important and the Russians don't want it. He will arrange for you to disappear. I am a suitable candidate to disappear with you so that I can look after you."

"You've got it in a nut-shell. Now you can swim! Daddy said you thought that that was your role in life. He would not have suggested it otherwise."

She took a breath. "Do you want to?"

315

He took her hand and pulled her gently towards him. When he was holding her firmly, he replied.

"Well I don't want to disappear but if that is the price I have to pay to be with you, the answer is 'Yes! Yes, I do and yes, I will!"

Esme, who had found how comfortable it was to be held in this firm embrace, put her arms around him and held herself even closer. She did, however, speak, as far as she could, in a matter-of-fact fashion. It was a though she was trying to give some normality to this bizarre situation.

"Well, we have to tell Daddy, but I have a condition. As far as I can gather, this disappearing trick means that we can take nothing with us. Well, I have some stuff that I want to keep. It will mean going up to my flat and packing it and then making sure it ends up in a safe place."

"Will your father wear that?"

"We can make it secure if we move fast enough. If he wants his scheme to work, he'll have to agree."

It was a tough interview; with Esme facing her father down and Jim astonished at yet another facet of her character. Reginald Marsh finally agreed in principle to what she was asking but pointed some difficulties. It was here that Jim stepped in.

"Get me a fast car. We can leave before dawn and be back by the evening." was his claim. "You could pretend we had done some touring; that I wanted to see Stonehenge." Esme's father looked sceptical but, by then, he had no alternative.

"There's a Morgan in the garage." he said. "Treadwell will get it ready for you. Fortunately the roads are clear of snow. Have you driven a Morgan before?"

"I have indeed." he said but did not expand on his experience. He turned to Esme. "You'll need to wear plenty of clothing. Start with woolly underwear.

CHAPTER 39

Afternoon 20th August 1986

"We can't go any further chronologically with the suitcase." said Helena. "It can only take us as far as the family house-party at Christmas of that year."

Helena had reached the stage where she was creating a narrative. Meticulous as ever, she was trying to block in actual dates for the courtship between Esme and Jim. The two of them had fully accepted that Esme and Jim had fallen in love. Edgar was sustained by this as an idea, worried that it might lead to tragedy but was intent on finding out as much as possible of their story. His wife was less emotional about it. He listened closely to her outline of the courtship.

"By golly, that must be one of the fastest romances imaginable. It's like a speeded up film. They meet one evening, have their first date on the following day. Then they are parted. All true lovers have to be parted at some time or another. Their parting is only a short one. They go on a journey. The boy is introduced to the girl's family and then the couple disappear."

"'You will go on a long journey!' Edgar joined in. "That sounds like a reading from the stars. Actually they went on two journeys and a third one when they disappeared." Since they had no further evidence to examine, he was indulging in some deductions.

"One journey to Bridge House. What was the second one?" Helena was curious.

"The suitcase has to get to the railway station's 'left-luggage' office."

"Do they have to take it there?" Helena was fulfilling her usual role and emphasised the 'they'.

"Where does it come from?" Edgar was building his argument. "Esme was living in London. The suitcase would be in her flat. She'd had it since she was at St Ermengild's. I suspect she used it also at Oxford. It certainly didn't get that much wear being transported to and from school by a private chauffer in a Rolls Royce. In a London flat it would be used as a trunk. There would not be much room or storage space in a London flat. She wouldn't be the first young woman to store her secrets under the bed."

"Some of these things weren't 'stored'. They came from the whirlwind romance." Helena was tidying up his hypothesis.

"Which is my point. The case had to be filled with special things before it can be delivered to the left-luggage office. Mementoes of childhood, passionate quotes from her current lover all in the same case. It had to be packed by Esme and she had to get to it to pack it. Hence the second of the journeys."

Helena was looking increasingly impressed.

"Sounds right." she said. "When? You haven't got much time to fit it in."

"Couldn't she do it after they were supposed to have disappeared?"

"Possibly. That would depend on why they disappeared. We have no certain answer to that question."

"They are unlikely to risk going to a main-line station after their disappearance was reported in the press. I think we have a pretty tight schedule and the journey has to be around the Christmas period. Not the best time to travel especially by public transport, and, if it is then, they have to get back to Bridge House for the celebrations. A fast car? Do they borrow the Rolls?" Edgar was in his element.

"Somerset to London and back. Could they do it in a day?" was the sceptical contribution by Helena.

"Oh yes! They could even just about do it in daylight – they'd have about eight hours." Edgar had had an early passion for motor cars and he had sacrificed it for photography. His father had indulged him from the age of ten when he became interested in old motor cars. "It kept him off the streets." was his excuse and he admitted that it was an excuse because he too enjoyed the process of buying an old banger that was falling apart and restoring it. He even got access to an old aerodrome where his son could drive any road-worthy results. The father and son toured Southern England every Sunday morning.

Edgar spoke with authority. "Even with only arterial roads – no motorways then – they would need no more than four hours each way. In a fast car, less."

Helena was still sceptical. "Why would she do that?"

Edgar shrugged. He was at a loss. His reply was a frustrated, "Well, you said earlier that she put into it those things that she wanted to save. You could liken it to rescuing your treasures from a burning house; that's a very good analogy. Her life was about to change and she wanted to take her most precious things into her new life. Her new life is marriage to Bygrave and her father has cast her into the snow crying 'Never darken my door again!'"

It was a brave attempt but they both had known that there would be questions without answers. Unless they learned more about the actual disappearance, there would be many such questions.

CHAPTER 40

Dec 22nd 1945

It was a beautiful car, bright scarlet with chrome side-lights and enormous tyres on wire wheels. The soft hood was black and the fittings shone silver. Treadwell handed the keys to Jim. He looked a trifle doubtful but reported that he had serviced it. He had filled the tank with petrol and there were spare cans in the boot and a spare wheel. He pointed out where the tool kit was and was reassured that Jim already knew. He had checked the oil and tyres personally. He did not say so but he had also washed and polished the car itself. "It pulls to the left a shade, Jim." he said.

"Thank you, Arthur. You look concerned but, rest assured; I can drive the car." The chauffer accepted this and he held out his hand and enveloped Jim's within it.

It was as well that the two travellers were well wrapped up. Treadwell had found sheepskin jackets for the pair of them from somewhere. Esme's was somewhat large for her but she had added, underneath it, an Arran jumper and was now almost spherical. Pilots' helmets, together with goggles and gauntlets, completed their ensembles. It was cold enough when they left the house. It was a lot colder once Jim had settled into the driving seat and got the measure of the car's personality. He eased his foot down on the pedal as though giving it permission to accelerate and created a freezing wind that whistled though every crack and fissure between the hood and the car itself. Everything about the interior of the car was as small as possible. The steering wheel seemed just to have enough room for his hands and the instruments were tiny on a tiny dash-board. The rear-view mirror was the same. Even the windscreen wipers were in miniature. Jim had long desired to own such a car. More than once he had borrowed one and he was enjoying himself immensely.

The bonnet extended so far in front of them that it concealed the dips in the road if the car was climbing and it waggled and vibrated at speed. At times, it even resonated dramatically.

Esme was going to ask him exactly how much experience he had had in such a car but the sound of the wind on the hood, flapping and cracking, prevented them from hearing each other speak. She was soon satisfied that his smile had been justified and settled down to try and enjoy the drive. The suspension left a great deal to be desired especially as Jim drove the car as hard as he could whenever he could do so safely. He had said, as they got into the car, that they provided their own suspension with their vertebral columns.

There was snow on the surrounding hills and icicles suspended in profusion from overhanging grassy ledges. The rising sun glistened on them so that they shone like crystal in the morning air. The hedgerows were stark and bare of leaves. The sky, as the light grew, was a clear blue and Jim would have liked to have told Esme that it was the colour of her eyes. Compliments like that were not designed for shouting into the wind and he saved up the idea for another time.

She was watching his face and thought she could detect

a sadness as he took in the scenery. Was he thinking that he had to say good-bye to a landscape that was friendly even in this weather?

In the early hours of the morning there was little traffic on the winding lanes but they had the satisfaction of their first act of overtaking. It was an easy one; by-passing a farmer's tractor. Jim only needed the bare minimum of clear road to put his foot down and the car responded with a throaty roar.

A tender memory of her father reading 'The Wind in the Willows' to her came to Esme remembering Mr. Toad in his goggles and gauntlets and she quoted to herself "O bliss! O poop-poop! O my!". She looked across at Jim, intent on his driving, muttered one more "O bliss!" and snuggled down.

Jim drove for the best part of three hours with total concentration, pushing the car as hard as he dared. They were driving on a long stretch of arterial road and he pulled over onto a lay-by. Esme had actually been able to grab a cat-nap but both of them needed to stretch their legs and take advantage of the way-side bushes. By chance, the lay-by overlooked a reach of a slowly moving river. The last wisps of the early mist were swirling on its surface, driven away by the wintry sun.

Esme took his arm and put it around her shoulders. She rested her head on his chest and said. "You're thinking of how you'll miss it, aren't you? You can still change your mind!" She owed him that offer. He was giving his whole life for her.

He said nothing, just put his other arm around her and enveloped her in his now familiar bear-hug.

They opened the picnic basket prepared by Mrs

Treadwell and drank some of the coffee from the thermos flask. They devoured sandwiches and returned to the car. Jim retained a large bar of chocolate which he took into the passenger seat. For a short run on that road, Esme drove. She did so cautiously but with, for Jim, satisfactory competence. It allowed him to relax the muscles of his hands and feet that had begun to tire. The clutch was not well placed for him and his left ankle was beginning to feel the strain. He broke off bite-sized pieces from the chocolate bar and fed them into her mouth one at a time.

More important, he no longer had to concentrate on the road. Only a few minutes were needed to tell him that Esme was a good driver so he had no need to worry about that. His thoughts turned to what she had said. Not to her offer to let him change his mind but to an earlier statement. Esme would marry him 'Come hell or high water' she had added later 'if he wished it so' and he did so wish! Then, he thought instead about what he would be missing. Not just the countryside and the history and the feeling of belonging but the resurgence of the nation from the tribulations of war to the great promise of peace. On this front, he had been encouraged that the nation was ready to take a new look at itself and not discard the lower classes, was perhaps ready even to discard the concept of class. They had elected a Socialist Prime Minister who was bold enough to shed the trappings of Empire. Esme and he had not touched on politics and he was worried that perhaps they would disagree. After all, she did call her father 'Daddy'. Now he asked himself how he would take it if Esme turned out to be traditional Tory.

"On the chin!" he said to himself. He took over the driving to get through London with Esme reading the road map and giving directions with clarity and precision. She gave him exactly the right amount of time to prepare for any turns that he needed. "Take the second left!" she would say in ringing tones and just when the first left became visible. "You'll need the right hand lane at those traffic lights ahead". Perhaps, just as important, she said nothing other than her instructions. Jim could not have asked for a more competent navigator.

As their relationship progressed, they learned more about the character of each other. It seemed there was a pleasant surprise with each new characteristic. "There must be something about this girl that is not perfect" thought Jim. "Apart from the fact that she calls her father 'Daddy'. Perhaps she *is* a Tory." If he did but know it, this thought passed through his mind at the same time that Esme was asking herself, "Is there anything this man cannot do?"

They parked two streets away from Esme's flat. If the Morgan had a disadvantage for their purpose, it was because it was so beautiful a car. People would stop to look at it. It was best if they did not park the car outside the flat.

She went directly home and told Jim to get some fish and chips, and when he brought them, to make more coffee. Some to recharge the thermos and some for drinking then. There were still plenty of sandwiches from Mrs Treadwell.

She, herself, started straight away to gather the things she wanted to save. Most of them were already in the suitcase that she had used at school and university. She took the contents out of the suitcase and repacked it, discarding some things and replacing them with others. Since she could take nothing herself from the past, she had to send some things into the future. There were just a few items that were to do with Jim and those things were so precious that they had to go in into the suitcase. She could not contemplate losing them for ever. She had more choice with her own memorabilia and had to make a couple of decisions. She used her party frock from school as packing. This carried the memory with it of Brotherton but also that of George and, by now, George with his local yokel act meant more that the nasty taste of Brotherton. She spent a couple of minutes writing to Jane Clayton.

All this did not take her long. They ate the fish and chips whilst they were still hot. Jim had dealt with the coffee problem and had been watching Esme making her decisions. He could do nothing to help so he just enjoyed the neatness of her movements and her mutterings as she made her choices. Now there was a quiet moment as they got ready to go and he asked her why she had been so adamant about securing her mementos. She had replied by telling him how she had thought of the quote from 'The Wind in the Willows' as he overtook the tractor. "There were nice things in my life." she said, "Even before you came along." she added smiling. "But there were long periods of bewilderment and unhappiness. I want to keep the good things. Don't you feel the same?"

"Up to now, Esme darling – I'm reluctant to give up the 'Esme' – our lives have been very different. Mine was always on an even keel. If I was unhappy it would short lived and about little things. There was certainly no bewilderment and

I am, at least I was, a steady, almost a stolid, person. I have no need for a material record of my past. At least, I had not until St Ermengild's. After that, there was an emptiness. Nonsensical and nebulous but always there. Now I don't know. I lost my balance completely when I saw you at your office party and I still have not recovered it. Later I might question what is good for us. Right now, you say jump and I'll jump."

"Good!" she said. "Because it's time to jump. I'm glad you said 'good for us'" They made sure that the flat was secure. Esme took a farewell look at what had been her home and they left, carrying the suitcase.

They drove to the railway station. Jim took the suitcase to the left-luggage office while Esme drove the car round the block so that they did not have to park. Jim returned with the left-luggage ticket and Esme moved to the passenger seat. They were on their way back to Bridge House almost without taking a breath. Esme navigated them as far as Richmond where they stopped to post the ticket to Jane Clayton.

They had done what wanted do. They needed to be back in time to suggest that they had just been for a spin in the Morgan for the pleasure of the drive. Esme slept again and Jim drove on without waking her. The roads were clear and once he had driven out of the outskirts of London, the traffic was light. By now he was in a groove and the suspension of the car had become almost part of himself. They stopped for coffee once and the light was dying as they drove through the gates of Bridge House.

CHAPTER 41

Morning 20th August 1986

Edgar had done some work on the cuttings that Bill had given them the previous day. With his usual industry, Bill had trawled through the war years before concentrating on the Christmas of 1945. The earliest item that he had chosen was of the meeting between Churchill and Roosevelt and their talks with the Russians in 1941. Edgar, if not Helena, was now sure that Reginald Marsh had, by that time, seen the importance of the Russian threat in the post-war world. Bill had included this item to emphasise that point. Reginald, Edgar thought, had planned for Esme to use her language skills to provide him with a secure source of information from the original material, rather than relying upon the official bulletins. This was confirmation of what they already thought. He and Bill were thinking on the same lines.

He could not remember the details of the meeting of the 'Big Three' but he did remember that the Russians had later reneged on one of the items of the agreed treaty. He had the impression that the Americans were more concerned about the Pacific and the threat from the Japanese. Later, they were outwitted by Stalin.

He had sorted out a pile that he was unable to connect with their investigation. There was one about Soviet spies in Canada and several about food rationing and the threat that it might be brought back because of a world shortage of food. There was one about how slowly the demobilisation of the troops was progressing. Why had Bill included these? He left that question and turned to those that were obviously pertinent.

When Helena had showered and started her breakfast, she asked about the files and he was ready to summarise them for her.

"They are mainly about the disappearance of Esme and Jim. They are mostly cuttings from newspapers. Here's a typical one:- "Diplomat's Daughter Disappears!" That has a paragraph with just the fact that Esme and Jim have been reported missing. Reginald called in the police on Boxing Day. Good timing in many ways. No policeman was going to do anything about a young couple disappearing in the middle of the festivities. Even after the holidays, they took some time before treating it under the heading of 'missing persons'. Any trail that might have existed had gone cold by then."

Helena picked up that cutting and read it through. When she finished it, she commented.

"No suggestion here that they were not seen after the twenty-second of the month. Remember that the family story is that Reginald interviewed the two of them and whatever took place then caused them to up sticks and elope. You can take your pick of the suggestions that have come down through the family as to why. One story is that he declared that they couldn't marry at all; another that they had to wait three years. There is even one that says he threatened Jim with a prosecution on criminal charges but that just stands on its own, just more unlikely than the rest."

"So how could he stop them?

"Esme had some money left to her by her mother, it was held in trust and he was the trustee. So for a start, he could impose financial restraint. More than that; in practice, he was her employer. As far as Jim was concerned, he could certainly arrange for a poor reference from the army for him. That these factors might not weigh with Esme and Jim would not occur to the people who would be spreading such rumours."

Then she stopped and said nothing for about ten seconds. Edgar claimed that she had a 'professional look'. If she did, he thought, she was wearing it now and she asked the question she was so often asked in her work. "What happened to that money?"

Edgar did not think that there was much future in pursuing that theme but such pursuits were what his wife did for a living. If Esme had money held in trust and she had disappeared, who did the money belong to? Someone might have tried to trace Esme to get the money to her. It was a line that Helena knew how to follow.

Edgar offered her more coffee but she refused. He poured himself a cup and shook his head, almost mournfully.

"None of this helps us find out what happened to Esme and Jim." he said in frustration. "Is it possible that this is what it is all about? We may have a smoke screen here? There is a possible delay in reporting their disappearance. It is reported exactly when any investigation is likely to be non-existent. There are several rumours broadcast about what is happening. It could be a put up job."

CHAPTER 42

December 22nd 1945

Esme and Jim were greeted in the driveway by Treadwell who offered to put the car away and congratulated them on their timing. "The guests are dressing for dinner." he said tactfully.

"Can you jig the mileometer" Jim asked. "Stonehenge and back and a little sight-seeing is the story."

The chauffer nodded assent and they hurried into the house.

"You know my room." said Esme. "Knock on the door and take me down."

Jim raised a hand in acknowledgement. The officers' mess was a formal place and he had had to learn the conventions there. To escort Esme into the company of her family was part and parcel of a social world that had the advantage of rules that could be followed with certainty. In this setting, he needed the assurance provided by convention that his behaviour was correct. For instance, when Esme had said 'black-tie', he was only too thankful that he understood what she meant.

Some weeks before, in preparation for his demob, he had gone to the local branch of a national chain of tailors. He could afford for one of his suits to be hand-made. What he called his 'interview suit'. There, in the cutting room of the shop, was one of the men who had been with him in his squad from the army. Nine months they had shared the tedium of the ammunition course. They arranged to meet that night and they had relived the experience in one glorious pub-crawl. Jim's suit when he went to collect it, did them both proud.

The tailor seemed to think that he owed Jim a big favour – something about a problem with the military police; 'red-caps' as he called them. He remembered that Jim had sorted it for him. Jim had not thought it that important but when he mentioned that he had no dinner-jacket, his friend had found him one off-the-peg but certain to fit since he had Jim's measurements.

"That makes us square!" he said refusing to take any payment. The suit, with its coat-hanger, was provided with a protective cover and when Jim extracted it, he found that it included a black bow-tie, already made up and requiring only the fastening to be adjusted, a dress-shirt – no frills – and a set of shiny cuff-links. There was also a white silk scarf which he did not need. Jim offered silent thanks.

It did not take him long before he was ready to knock on Esme's door but he stood outside it to give her a minute or two. Any girl needed time to smarten herself up, especially after the sort of day that they had had. Then a gong rang from below, so he risked it. Sure enough, she was ready.

Jim said nothing. For once he could not find a quote or words of his own. She was wearing a black 'cocktail dress'. Off-the-shoulder with some silver work at the neck-line with matching work on the hem of the skirt and on her shoes.

He was struggling to articulate the wonder he felt

whenever he saw her afresh when her face lit up as she took in his appearance and it was she who spoke.

"I suspect you call that a 'monkey-suit' she said. "But not tonight, because it suits you." He marvelled again at her ability to produce the phrase and the smile that would make him feel part of her. After that comfortable greeting he had no need for words.

Bridge House could easily have been described as a mansion. It certainly had a fine staircase that led, centrally, down into the extensive entrance hall. It was in this hall that the guests were assembled and down into which James Bygrave, a Major of the Royal Army Ordnance Corps, took Esme Marsh, daughter of his host.

Jim, proud as Punch to have her on his arm and, walking tall, paused at the head of the stairs. He decided that she deserved a dramatic entrance. Reginald, himself, moved to the foot of the stairs to look up at them and every eye followed his. Esme was just short of blushing and Jim had great difficulty in hiding his grin. It was only for a moment or two as he 'took her down' but what a moment!

Esme's family may not have approved of James Bygrave but more than one second cousin, once-removed, would have changed places with Esme if only for the look on Jim's face.

There was time for Jim to be introduced to Esme's sister and her husband, Edward Burroughs. Stella was taller than her sister and she took after her father but there was enough in her appearance of Esme, especially in her colouring and in her slender frame, for Jim to warm towards her even before she spoke. Edward Burroughs was several years older than his wife and showing the early stages of thinning hair. He had been injured in the war and had smashed his left arm just above the elbow. The military medics had done a decent job in amputation and the sleeve of his jacket was pinned up. Edward Burroughs, himself, ignored this handicap. The couple behaved with the easy togetherness of long companionship but, every now and again, Jim detected Edward looking at her as though they had just met and he was still bewitched. Jim knew how he felt; he had learned that feeling in the last few days. He began to think that the visit to Bridge House was a much better idea than he had imagined.

Then there was the almost solemn announcement that 'Dinner Was Served'. It meant that Reginald Marsh had to lead his younger daughter through into the dining room. He seemed nearly as proud as Jim had been. The long table of oak, cared for through the centuries so that its polish had almost a visible depth, was laid out immaculately. Jim noticed immediately that each place had a name-card. Reginald's staff were well-trained and he found that he had been guided, without noticing it, to his own seat.

He was not, of course, seated next to Esme. Husbands could not sit next to their wives and this convention extended, it seemed, to 'boyfriends'. He found himself placed between one of the grand dames of the family and a young girl clearly on her first venture into adult society. He did glance down the table to catch Esme's eye and was rewarded with a big smile.

"Right you are, Jim Bygrave, let's show this lot your metal." he said to himself and turned first to the young girl.

"Eloisa." he said reading her place-card. "What a charming name." and he took a chance. She did look as though she would understand. "But such a sad story."

He was right. At first she turned to him, surprised that he knew her name until he pointed to her place-card and then, as she took in what he was saying, she nodded.

"Did you know that the entry for 'Heloise' in the Oxford Companion to English Literature simply says 'See Abelard'? Was it sadder for him or for her?" she asked and, distant cousin she might have been, but there was something of Esme in her face.

"You are James Bygrave. I don't need your card to tell me that. You are Esme's new boy-friend. What an entrance you made. Isn't she beautiful? Everybody is talking about you and there are those who would give you the same treatment as Abelard received." All this came out in a rush; this young girl had been quiet for too long.

Jim winced at what she had said. He was amused by the reference but, if he had got it right, the unfortunate Abelard had been castrated by his father-in-law.

"'Jim' to you, not 'James.'" he said. "You looked very solemn sitting there. Are you on your 'best behaviour'? "

"It's the first time I've been allowed to dine with the grown-ups." she replied, glancing round." The same people that don't approve of you, will also be watching me carefully. Is it true you've known each other for less than a week?"

"In answer to your question, it is about a week but I've stopped counting. But let me tell you that your *best* behaviour is when you smile. The ogres may disapprove but their disapproval will have its roots in envy."

At this, she almost giggled and then did so as he went on. "And I can see that Esme is already jealous. Have you got a boyfriend, yourself?"

"I'm far too young." she said indignantly and it was Jim's turn to smile. "Lucky fellow!" he said.

He could see that she was beginning to enjoy herself and turned to his other neighbour.

"I've been neglecting you." he said, "And I apologise. I judged that Eloisa had the greater need. One should enjoy, not fear, the steps forward in life."

The place-card for this woman said that she was Lady Elizabeth Forster. None of which meant anything to Jim. She was a tall lady and her evening gown was simple and adorned only with a single brooch. Her iron-grey hair was severely disciplined and her long slim fingers were without any rings. It passed through his mind that she really needed a lorgnette to complete the picture but he reserved judgement when she turned to look at him for her eyes had that mischievous look that said she was related to Esme. It was almost as though she was teasing him in the way that Esme did.

"You are someone then, James Bygrave, who relies on your own judgement?" she said and the question was sharp enough.

"If that is all I have to go on, yes. I think I would like you to call me Jim."

"All right, Jim. But we do not have time for the charm. Reginald said he was satisfied that you had intelligence enough to deserve Esme and, whatever the appearance may have been, that was his only real concern. Intelligence alone won't be enough. I suspect from what you just said that you are not sure why you are sitting next to me. You are asking yourself if Esme's father is throwing you to the wolves. Relax! He is convinced that you have been sent by fate."

Jim had already worked out that Esme's smile when she saw how he was seated had been more mischievous than rueful and he said so.

"You and Eloisa are Esme's greatest fans, aren't you?" and in response to her nod, he went on. "She seems to enchant all the people I like. I feel that a crowd of friends and well-wishers are gathering around us; a protective wall of people. They all tell me to look after her."

He paused. The servants were removing the soup bowls and replacing them with dinner plates. They loaded the table with plates of roast meat already carved and numerous dishes of vegetables. Jim realised, for the first time, that the Bridge House estate also included a farm and a productive kitchen-garden. He had not seen such a range of vegetables since he had spent a week-end with the family of a fellow rugby-player who also grew their own vegetables. They did so on an allotment.

He offered one of the dishes to Eloisa. "You need to eat your greens. They'll make your hair curl."

"All right, then." she said and took some. "I sometimes wonder if I'm an odd person because I do like cabbage."

Jim had rolled up his sleeves to tackle what he thought would be an awful experience but, here he was, enjoying himself thoroughly. That he should be acceptable to some of Esme's relatives was not high on his priorities but he was happy that this was so for her sake. Once more their eyes met and he could feel her approval.

There was another ordeal for Jim to go through. The

ladies withdrew from the dining room leaving the gentlemen behind with the port and they moved their seats so that conversation could be general. Jim knew nothing about port and he sensed that Reginald had broached something special for his guests. He tasted it out of curiosity but he did not refill his glass as the decanter was passed around the table. He had the feeling that he would need his wits about him as the evening progressed. It was clear that the men of the family were not completely opposed to this incomer but after the eager charm of Eloisa and the intelligence of Lady Elizabeth Forster, he found them somewhat dull and was only too pleased when Reginald stood up. Jim thought that he did so with a little difficulty. Had his host drunk too much?

"Shall we join the ladies?" was the formulaic suggestion and they did.

Bridge House even had a ball-room; a small one it was true and after the ladies had withdrawn, Stella marshalled the staff to make the final touches to allow space for a half dozen couples to take the floor. It was Treadwell who was in charge of the gramophone.

Reginald danced with Esme. Jim watched them briefly and was suspicious that Esme was supporting her father. He, himself, crossed to where Eloisa was seated on the far side of the room and gave her the full treatment.

"Will you do me the honour, Miss Eloisa, of dancing with me?" and he bowed and took her hand. The girl responded with her half-giggle.

"You are too kind, sir, the honour is mine." and when they were on the floor, "This is to make Esme jealous, I suppose. You are just playing with my affections."

Jim was pleased. The apparently timid young girl, worried about her first adult social occasion, was now thoroughly enjoying the evening and if the young men of her family did not queue up to dance with her, they were a poor lot.

True enough, as he left her in her place after the dance and walked across to Esme, one young man, more alert than the others, was already at Eloisa's side.

Now Jim could dance with his own girl and she relaxed into his gentle hold.

"That was kind." she said. "You've helped Eloisa no end."

"It wasn't kind." Jim replied. "It was purely selfish. I enjoyed it beyond measure. What a heart-breaker she is going to be."

"Never mind what it was. Your job now is to be my dance partner and pretend you are passionately in love with me."

"Well I can manage the dancing. What was the second bit? But you're being serious aren't you. Explain!"

"It is part of the plan. Shortly, Daddy will tell us everything."

"O.K. Now I want to be serious too. Your father is either under the influence of drink or some other drug or there is something seriously wrong with him. Tell me!"

"You don't miss much do you? Have patience, that also will be explained."

The number of guests in the room thinned out as some of those who had travelled a long way that day went to bed. Treadwell closed the gramophone and announced that there was tea or coffee in the drawing room. Esme's father made the rounds of those who were there, making sure that he spoke to every body and wished them good-night. When everybody was settled, he did so formally. He apologised for abandoning them and said that he had some business to conduct with, as he put it 'Young Bygrave and my daughter, Esme.'

CHAPTER 43

Early morning 21st August 1986

It was the morning of the wedding and Edgar woke early. He had to get his own gear ready for his photo shoot and get dressed. It was also up to him, as 'Best Man' to ensure that Bill was on time. He left the bed-room quietly in his dressing gown; he wanted to do a little more work on the files that Bill had provided. Even though he had a full day to look forward to, there was still an urge to do something to move forward with the Esme Marsh saga. His eye fell on a cutting which reported the New Year Honours and he read this again.

Reginald Marsh, who they described as a diplomat had been given a knighthood, was now Sir Reginald Marsh, but the report featured him especially because he had been taken to hospital suffering from cancer. He was in a private ward and was being treated by the leading doctors in the field. The newspaper wrote that, typically, he had continued to work until and after Christmas. If Helena's Great Grandfather had organised the disappearance, he had left it until the last minute.

Edgar, in following this up, had left himself short of time. To catch up, he showered and, for a change, went into breakfast still wearing his dressing gown.

This was still an early breakfast. The post had not yet

arrived but the paper had, so he tackled the cross-word puzzle in a half-hearted fashion. He was worried about the clothes that Helena had laid out on the bed for him. What would it be like to have a valet? Marilyn and Bill had gone in for the full kit. The morning-dress that he had hired had looked all right in the shop but the lighting there had been flattering. Although the tailor had instructed him in the archaic fastenings of the suit and the mysteries of attaching the cravat – fortunately it was a made-up one and only required fixing – he was not entirely happy. He had the flowers and the ring to worry about as well. Most worrying was the speech he had to make but had yet to compose.

Helena joined him for breakfast. He drew her attention to the articles he had spotted. They had known that Reginald had become Sir Reginald. It was a matter of family pride but Helena had not realised how soon afterwards that he had had to go into hospital. She remarked on his fortitude in entertaining the whole family when he was so ill. It made sense of his asking Jim Bygrave to visit. It would be his only opportunity to meet Esme's boyfriend. Edgar was worried that something was not right about the sequence of events as they saw it but it was forty years ago so it could wait for a couple of days.

Helena was relaxed about the wedding. All she had to do was to get there. She seemed otherwise pre-occupied and in a chatty mood. She was certainly not her usual self; certainly not as interested as he thought she would be about the wedding. Edgar was just a little worried.

"How long do you think this is going to last?" she asked and her question seemed to have nothing to do with either

Esme's history or the Wedding. It was a question that Edgar, intent on his own worries, did not understand. Nor had she signalled it by asking him if he wanted more toast.

"'This'? 'This' being?" he replied, puzzled.

"'This' being us!"

Something was going on here. Helena was not given to cryptic utterances, especially first thing in the morning. Edgar paused for thought.

"If you mean by 'us' – us together in legal if not holy wedlock, I trust you are not looking for a divorce on grounds of 'it has lasted long enough'. I tell you it lasts until one of us dies. On this point, I'm with Piglet. Piglet tells Pooh that he would wish to die the day before him because he could not live without him."

"That's a sobering thought but I wasn't going as far as that."

"You mean 'us in transports of delight'? Well, regrettably, even though 'custom will not stale your infinite variety', there will be a gradual depletion in my testosterone levels. We may be talking sixties, seventies – no more than that, I'm afraid."

"Won't other things distract us?"

"What other things?" thought Edgar, but not saying it, Helena answered the unspoken thought.

"Children might prove an inhibition, for a start. You never ask me if I'm pregnant."

"You know why I've stopped asking that question. I'm ready but I'm happy to wait until you are and I don't want to nag. The real reason why I don't ask is because I know you will tell me the instant you know."

He stopped and turned to her; a huge grin spread across

his face. "That's what this is about, isn't it? You're telling me now!"

Her face alight in response to his, she nodded. Edgar rose, walked around the table and pulled her up into his arms. After a little while, he asked if she was sure.

"I'm four days late." she said. "Being a selfish male, you didn't notice. That doesn't happen with me, I'm never late. There hasn't been any shocks or illness; so, yes, I'm pretty sure. I've an appointment with the doctor tomorrow."

"Would it have made any difference if I had noticed? I don't have to be gentle with you just yet, do I?"

"No, you don't. You may have to put up with wild mood-changes and I may even go into a corner and knit. If I demand pickled gherkins you have to scour the country for them only to find that I don't want them after all. Do you think you can handle an irrational wife?"

"I thought a pregnant woman was supposed to be more attractive to her husband because that made him more protective. I've always looked forward to that. I couldn't imagine you being more attractive and wondered what form this would take."

"You'll probably have to settle for cantankerous. I wonder if Esme had any children. Now there's a random question to start with. Where did that come from?"

Edgar prevented himself from suggesting that the disappearance of Esme and Jim might have been the result of a fatal accident. One of Bill's cuttings was of a rail crash in which a number of bodies had not been identified. It was not anywhere near Bridge House or even on any of the routes out of the West but Bill had put it in. He, at least, was sticking to the rule and assuming nothing. Edgar could have complained that Helena had broken her own rule. He did not; no sad thoughts should spoil the pleasure that her announcement had generated.

Not surprisingly, Edgar was no longer focussing on Esme Marsh. His most immediate attention was on Marilyn and Bill, his most important attention on Helena.

"And Co." he said to himself.

Then, like every expectant father, he started to worry. There was always a health risk to a woman carrying a child. She was seeing a doctor tomorrow. What if he discovered something wrong? Then there was the change in their life style. No more late nights and, certainly, less booze. Edgar thought to himself that he would give up drinking – or most of it – to support Helena. They would have to avoid places where people were smoking. Fortunately both of them had given up years ago.

Then there were the finances. At the moment they had two fairly good incomes and their only outgoings were on themselves. Helena would want to stop work; at least to start with. They were better off in that respect than most couples. Helena worked mainly from home though she did have to visit libraries, churches, and local authority archives. Then there was the expense of bringing up the children. They had always, in discussion, discarded the idea of having only one child. 'All very well in theory' thought Edgar. 'All very well putting money aside for the future, what about the present?'

His mind went racing into the future, would they need a bigger house? They had not decided how many children they would have but agreed that it would have to more than one.

What were the schools like around here? Was Helena all right? Suddenly, his world was changed, the ground was shifting under his feet.

"He'll probably have two heads!" Helena spoke the words in a sombre voice but they brought him up short and seeing her laughing at him, he laughed with her. She knew that he was trying to allow for all eventualities.

"He?"

"I wouldn't wish two heads on a baby girl."

"Stop it. There are things to think about. You look after the baby, I'll think about them. Tomorrow I'll make a list." he said.

"Today, as in now, you'll get into your glad rags. You have work to do."

"You're right. I need to make some phone calls."

CHAPTER 44

22nd December 1945

"So this is what Esme meant by 'Daddy will tell you everything' and 'All will be explained'" thought Jim as he watched Reginald Marsh take Esme out of the room. As he followed, he heard one of the ogres say, "That will be the marriage settlements. That is one lucky young man." and, to his surprise he also heard the reply from another of the old ladies. "And one lucky young lady." Perhaps even the establishment wing of Esme's family were not as universally repellent as he had expected.

Reginald Marsh had arranged to have this interview in his study. By the time Jim, who had stopped to say good-night to Eloisa, had caught up with them, his host was seated behind the massive desk and Esme in a deep leather arm-chair. There was another chair clearly arranged for Jim. He ignored it, crossed to Esme and held out his hand. Without thinking, she responded and he pulled her gently from the chair and took her to the matching sofa. The two of them then sat down together, hand in hand, to face her father.

"Esme tells me that you are prepared for this, Major Bygrave. Is that the case?"

"No longer 'Major', sir. I have my discharge papers – somehow they seemed to have come through more quickly than I expected. Plain 'Mister', unless you can bring yourself to call me 'Jim'"

He made this a friendly suggestion but he knew that he still resented the treatment that this man had handed out and was, even now, manoeuvring for position. If he did not meet Esme's father now on equal terms, he would always be at a disadvantage. Nor was he answering the question.

Reginald Marsh had already had experience of his future son-in-law and the way he stood up for himself and, once more, was thankful for his daughter's choice. It was not crucial that he made friends with Jim but it would help and it would make Esme happier.

"All right, 'Jim', since you regard it as being important. Are you prepared to give up everything and take on a new identity?"

"Yes, I am. Esme has explained that and to be part of her life I would sacrifice everything, even my pride." he said and was rewarded by pressure from her hand. "Anything you ask me to do, I will do. On the other hand, I think that the more I know about what is happening, the greater use I will be."

"Fair enough. That is what this session is about."

With that, Esme's father got down to business.

"The process of changing a person's identity – of making them disappear – has been honed to a fine edge. It is designed with the assumption that those who wish to find the subject have powerful motives and great resources. In principle, there must be nothing about the new person that had anything to do with the old one. You have to be invented anew. It helps, however, if the possessions of the old person disappear with them. That is such possessions that they might want to take with them if they were just going away on holiday."

All this was reasonable, almost essential. Jim knew that a witness protection scheme existed for those people willing to give evidence against professional criminals. Such witnesses must feel safe from revenge or they would not appear in court. With Esme, those interested in her whereabouts would include the press and the full force of the Russian Secret Service; both of whom would have their own motives and, indeed, enormous resources.

"One of the key factors is that none of your friends or relations can have any knowledge of the new identity. There are many other minor considerations and we have learned from mistakes in the past."

Reginald was now speaking about the technical aspects and speaking as a professional. Jim made a mental list of those people who would wonder what had happened to him. It was a short one and none of them would feel too big a gap. He had no family to speak of, perhaps one cousin whom he met but rarely, and few friends. His years in the army had separated him from any school-friends and because he had been constantly on the move he had not had occasion to build up any relationships with fellow officers. He only met with the people he had played rugby with occasionally. His absence from their re-unions would be mentioned and then he would become just a face on the photographs. He gave a passing thought to the colleague who had challenged him to gate-crash Esme's office party. He owed him a great debt but that debt would have to be paid with the two tickets to the Windmill that had not yet been forthcoming.

It was Esme that he felt for. He had to accept that she too would lose her friends. She would lose all contact with her father and her sister. She had spoken so warmly of her two school-friends that he knew that there would be great sadness there and then there was Jane Clayton. Another example of how her own generosity of spirit drew people to her. She relied upon Jane's loyalty but could offer her no hope of a future to their friendship. Abruptly, he realised that it was only himself that she could carry into her future. Would that be enough? As he asked himself this question he realised fully why her father had acted as he had. Esme needed him.

Reginald had passed on from the strategy of the making two people disappear to the tactics.

"Esme, you are to pack suitcases as though you were going away for, say, a fortnight. Jim had best take everything he brought with him. The suitcases are not important in themselves, it is the gaps in your wardrobes that are significant. The cases and their contents will be disposed of. Your movements will be a bit complicated. Early tomorrow morning you will drive the Morgan to Weymouth. The exact location is a car park and you have a map. Leave the map in the car. It is useful that you have already used that car. You will leave the car there and you will be picked up and taken to a safe-house and, believe me, our houses are safe. You will take the packed suitcases with you. Our people will supply you with new outfits and the suitcases of your new identities. They will dispose of your old ones completely. Then they will fly you to Dover. The story at this end is that you have gone for another spin in the car as Jim and Esme and have not returned. Either the car has broken down or you have had an accident. There is a rumour that you eloped to escape from the disapproval of Esme's family – and I'm included in that rumour. We don't report you missing until Boxing Day."

Jim heard, in these instructions, the echo of the way the army delivered its orders. 'B Company' will take the machine-gun emplacement on the right flank!' Reginald was dealing with the details concisely and without emphasis. His plan allowed for no errors so they were not to 'try to take the gun emplacement' they would do so. Jim and Esme, who exchanged glances of mutual sympathy, were beginning to take on board the finality of each of the procedures that he outlined.

Now Esme's father unlocked one of the drawers of his desk and drew from it a brief-case, which he also unlocked.

"Here is the paperwork." he said. "Birth certificate or, rather, a copy of the same, of one Thomas Ralph Morrison. That's you, Tom. You can call yourself Ralph if you prefer."

"Ralph is better." said Jim.

"Stick to it then! Don't switch at all! Second birth certificate; this time of one Marjorie Gillingham. That's you, my dear."

Esme who had been quiet throughout all this was moved to protest. "Marjorie!" she exclaimed. "For the rest of my life, I'm to be called Marge?"

Jim saw her father's ironic smile before she did and smiled himself; not so much at the humour as at the evidence of the bond between father and daughter. Esme's answering smile as she realised what was going on was the mirror image of her father's

"Marjorie is authentic. It is the sort of expertise that I

expect from my staff. Who would choose to call themselves Marjorie today? You too have a choice. It is actually the birth certificate of Marjorie Susan Gillingham. I thought of Rachel or Deborah but decided against them. Each of you has a somewhat battered Identity Card. Susan's is still in her maiden name."

He was piling the documents neatly on the table and chuckled as he dealt with the next one.

"Here's a certificate of a marriage solemnised at the Register Office in Exeter between the said Thomas Ralph Morrison and the said Marjorie Susan Gillingham. This was five days ago. Belated congratulations!"

"Separate passports." he went on without pausing. Jim had leaned over and kissed Esme's ear. She had pretended not to notice and Reginald ignored it. "Susan's has no previous entries and is in her married name. Ralph has done some travelling. They have both got some useful visas. Ralph and Susan have both been vaccinated against small-pox, just as well, since both of you have."

With the same measured tone, he proceeded. "My people have put together accounts of the lives of Ralph and Susan. Read them, absorb them and burn the notes. All the points that are included are authenticated. Don't elaborate. You don't need to. In the first instance, you are newly-weds and nobody will ask any questions other than to have a touch of your joy."

"Tickets. Now that will be something you will be interested in. You cross the Channel by the ferry. There will be a hired car in Calais, a nondescript Citroen; you will drive to Toulouse. You have plenty of time to get there. Both Ralph and Susan have driving licences valid for the Continent. You are visiting a pen-friend, believe it or not. You have tickets from Toulouse that will fly you eventually to Christchurch, New Zealand."

Neither Esme nor Jim had anything to say. This was outside their experience. How could they comment? Reginald stopped to see their expressions and, this time, burst out laughing. His laughter came to an end in a fit of coughing and a curse. "God damn it! I haven't got time for that." He pulled himself together and went on with his briefing.

"It's a honeymoon." he said in explanation of his laughter. "Some of your stopovers are exotic and you'll get the best hotels."

Jim had been following all this and his much maligned 'book-keeper' persona was adding up the cost. He asked the obvious question as simply as he could.

"Money?" It was almost a challenge. It was characteristic that Reginald, with the increasing respect that he had for his son-in-law and his concerns, answered directly.

"The money itself, and there is, as you recognise, need for plenty of it, comes in the first instance from a slush fund. These are moneys that the Department has accumulated over the years which we use when we don't want anybody to know where the finance of an operation comes from."

Jim raised an eyebrow and Esme knew exactly why. For a second she was cross with him; he had said he would sacrifice his pride. Let him do so now. Then his face changed and she knew that he would do just that and she was sorry for wishing it. Her father had not seen his expression and was continuing his explanation.

"I have already arranged to transfer enough of my own money to the fund to cover all the costs and you will have a substantial bank account. In fact, three bank accounts. One each for day-to-day expenses and a joint capital investment account."

Again, Jim raised an eye-brow. This time, a simple query. Reginald responded to it, "I will be unable to assist you any further after we have got you safely on your way." he said. "Any communications with my daughter would jeopardise the whole operation. The moneys transferred in this way will have to compensate from any legacy she might have received. They will be untraceable."

"And in Christchurch?"

"Then you are on your own. Amongst the papers you will find recommendations from Ralph's former employers which should get you interviews for suitable jobs. None of them overstate your abilities. You need not worry if your new employers take up the references. That's covered. Susan has an honours degree in Modern Languages from Oxford. That took some swinging. She has no work experience."

It seemed that Reginald had finished his briefing but it was Esme who prompted him further.

"Daddy, Jim deserves to know!" she said in a small voice.

"Deserves to know what? Is there more?" Jim asked this question of Reginald directly.

"Yes, there is. I have not told you before because I judged it would put unfair pressure upon you."

Esme rose from her seat beside Jim and joined her father behind his desk. She stood behind him with a hand on his shoulder. He looked up at her and went on. "I am suffering from cancer of the pancreas." he said. So stark was this statement that all three of them froze. For the count of ten, not a sound was made by any of them.

It was Reginald who broke the silence and he spoke steadily. He had lived with this for some time. Esme knew something of it but although Jim had seen that there was something wrong with him, he had no idea how serious it was.

"The cancer cells have invaded other vital organs and their proliferation is accelerating. The doctor says that I have days rather than weeks to live. I have held on this long hoping to protect the deal we have with the Americans and to give Esme a chance of a normal life." He attempted to lighten the atmosphere. "Thomas Ralph Morrison if you don't take care of my daughter, I will haunt you."

Jim, whose original resentment of Esme's father had been slowly turning into a reluctant respect, was overwhelmed. This man, unable to avoid the inundation of his relatives, pressured by the media and the country's enemies and staring an unpleasant death in the face, had laboured mightily to protect his daughter. At the same time he had held on to his own integrity, refusing to use perhaps his most powerful tool to persuade Jim to co-operate with his scheme. What was astonishing and a measure of the man's quality was the way he had concentrated on what Jim was beginning to think of as the escape plan. Jim saw now that the dying man had spiritual support from the faithful Treadwells and from his daughters but otherwise he had succeeded in reaching this point by his own self-control. He had also controlled the important aspects of the plan.

Jim had offered to be of help. He had not realised how much that help was needed. He looked now at Esme and saw the pain in her eyes that she had previously hidden and then at her father, who had delivered one last defiance against his fate.

"Sir!" he said, and, for the first time, he spoke to Reginald with real rather than conventional respect. "I promise you that that is one burden that you can lay down. Marjorie Susan Gillingham, as was, will, while her husband lives, be secure as Marjorie Susan Morrison."

"One more thing. The Exeter wedding I'm sure would stand up in a court of law but I would like to add something to that if Susan agrees."

Reginald nodded at the use of Esme's new name. "Go on!"

"I would like what you may call an 'avowal'. This is a version of the ceremony that predates Christianity and certainly predates the Register Office. Marriage to the Romans was valid if the couple acknowledged their relationship to each other before witnesses. The same process was legal in this country until at least the seventeenth century."

"'Measure for Measure', in spite of the nasty Angelo!" Susan chipped in, proud to place the reference. She remembered the plot of the play and, to make sure she had got it right, said, "The hero was due to have his head chopped off because he had got his espoused – that was the word – girlfriend pregnant. In spite of the espousal, the magistrate – the 'nasty Angelo' was going to have him executed for 'fornication'."

Ralph, who felt increasingly at one with his titular wife, raised a hand in a gesture of acknowledgement.

"A hit!" he said. "A palpable hit!" Susan, in spite of the fraught circumstances, was enjoying yet another aspect of their relationship.

"Yes, I agree." she said. "I'd like that. It would make a fine story for our grandchildren and it would stop us from being fornicators."

"Witnesses?" Reginald emphasised the plural and ignored the by-play.

"Treadwell?" was Ralph's response. "Names would not be necessary!"

"Well, I can't see any reason why not. It sounds safe."

So he called in his chauffeur who, when it was explained that the couple wanted the ceremony for sentimental reasons, was more than pleased.

"Tell nobody!" said his employer.

Nothing could have been simpler than what followed but both Jim and Esme felt uplifted by it.

"I take this man for my husband."

"I take this woman for my wife."

They said it three times for good measure and Treadwell left them, beaming to himself. If he continued to beam like that, Ralph thought, it would not be long before he had to tell Mrs. Treadwell.

On Reginald's desk there was a decanter and three glasses. The decanter, a bell-bottomed one in clear crystal held an amber liquid that was touched with glints of gold. The glasses were robust tumblers in cut crystal and a matching jug of water sat beside them.

Reginald lifted the decanter and poured a small measure of the liquid into each of the glasses and then added tiny stream of the water to each from the jug. "Malt." he said, "I can still pull some important strings." and handed each of them one of the glasses. He picked up the third himself. His gesture of raising his own glass induced them to do the same. He offered no pledge, indeed said nothing but all three of them drank at the same time. Each was silently wishing the same thing.

"Now, if you'll excuse me. I have one or two things to do that need doing." Reginald looked exhausted but content. "And so, I imagine, have you." he said.

The young couple left him nursing his glass. They closed the door of his study behind them as Susan and Ralph Morrison and, as they did so, they completed one of those things. When he had finally released her, she said, with a catch in her voice, "We've been married five days and that's the best you can manage?"

"Is now a good time?"

"You heard what he said." Esme's eyes glistened with tears. "He has been telling you what to do for some time. You are to look after me. I know you don't like instructions but, just this once, do as you're told."

"Well, young Ralph is a different person." he replied. "And he rather fancies this new girlfriend. I think I'll call her…", He wasn't allowed to finish the sentence. "You will call her 'Susan' – not 'Sue' – 'Susan'. And you'll get no favours from 'Marjorie'"

'Young Ralph' gallantly escorted his wife to her room, lifted her in his arms and carried her across the threshold.

Meantime, he was trying out various adjectives; 'dear' Susan, 'dearest' Susan, 'beloved' Susan – at which stage he was stopped.

"There was that girl you spoke to in your dream."

"I remember." he said as he closed the door behind him. "At least I can only remember the 'Darling!'"

Neither of them mentioned her father again. In effect, he had instructed them not to. He had examined his daughter's boyfriend and judged him worthy. Now he had delegated the responsibility of his daughter to him. In passing, he had arranged that they be man and wife and, finally, he had given them his blessing.

Young Ralph was still holding her and she said, speaking softly in his ear, "You use the dressing-room while I get ready. You'll need to bring a towel."

"A towel?" he asked bewildered and then he understood what she was saying and a happy smile spread across his face.

"Yes, Ralph." she said burying her head on his shoulder. "I do mean what you think I mean. I trust you are impressed."

"Madame, I can call you 'Madame'? I am honoured to be asked to fulfil this service but I have no specific experience."

She lifted her head and he could see the twinkle in her eye. "I don't expect too much." she said. "I have read the books."

He carried her to the bed and, finally, put her down. "Well I've read the books too but I don't trust them. I will do my best!"

"What sort of lover have I got? 'I'll do my best'. Is that the language of poetry? 'I'll do my best'?"

Jim had nothing to say except, "I'll get the towel!"

Some half an hour later, she lay beside him, her head nestled into his shoulder and with one arm stretched across his body.

"You found much better books than I did!" she said

CHAPTER 45

Mid-morning 21st August 1986.

Edgar started to feel that he was earning his keep as 'Best Man'. He had arranged for the ushers to be fitted for their morning-dress and organised the return of these garments after the wedding.

He had confirmed that Bill had the marriage licence and had put both suit-cases ready for the right car.

Marilyn's father, with the enthusiastic support of his wife and daughter; in fact, of all three of his daughters – bride and bridesmaids – had gone to town on this wedding. He had taken advantage of the modest beginnings of his own marriage when the family had lived in a small village and where, in the village church, Marilyn had been christened. Her father had arranged that she be married there also.

The grounds of the church abutted on an old-fashioned village green and on this there now stood a marquee. A magnificent structure, its walls as white as the sails of a tall-ship and with banners and flags bedecking its masts and corner posts. They stirred gently in the scarcely detectable breeze.

Edgar looked round for his assistant. The marquee deserved to feature. He need not have bothered. The young lad, Barry, was already on the job and he had clearly packed plenty of rolls of film

Edgar had completed yet another job. He had got Bill dressed. Neither of them were familiar with the way in which the waist-coat worked but at least he had already gone through the process of dressing himself. Then, more importantly, he had got Bill to 'the Church on Time'. He had had to put up with Bill singing the song all the way there. This was an ordeal that he considered he should not have suffered. Of less import, he had delegated the distribution of the button-holes to the relevant people and now he and the groom stood side-by-side in the front row of the pews. He thought to check that he had the ring. The waistcoat had watch-pockets which helped and, sure enough, there it was. Bill was still singing to himself.

The place was crammed with guests and the robust pews of this small church, which claimed a history of several hundred years, were garlanded with a variety of white flowers and the air was heavy with their scent. Edgar gave a thought to the hundreds, perhaps thousands of couples who had taken their vows here, to the children christened here and to the services offering solace to those of the parish who had come here to say goodbye to their loved ones. Marilyn and Bill were adding to the procession that had passed through time here. Others would do so in future and perhaps give a thought to them.

The church itself was much cherished. Every piece of brass-work gleamed golden, the linen draperies on the pulpit and the alter shone white and were decorated with gold embroidery. Edgar suspected that the coloured glass in the windows had been washed the day before and it shone in the sun portraying obscure biblical stories. This was a church adorned with gargoyles and decorated with pagan monsters. He felt himself involved in a 'Mystery Play'.

Not the organ, but a quartet of musicians, each sporting a different instrument, all of which had a medieval appearance, struck up the wedding march. Edgar looked round to see Marilyn, on the arm of her proud father, walking down the aisle. She was wearing a gown of dove-grey and carrying a bouquet of red roses. With her dark colouring, she presented a heart-stopping picture. Bill turned to look down the aisle and stopped singing almost as though he had no breath to do so. Edgar looked for Helena. She had been concealed behind a substantial matron but now was also looking at the bride. She was wearing matching grey, and presented a different image altogether. She turned to exchange smiles with her husband and there was mischief and triumph in hers. Some of Edgar's own smile was for the bride. As a friend he was delighted that she looked so beautiful; as a photographer he was thrilled with the picture she presented. Most of the smile, however, was for his wife, her image, to him, was dazzling, especially with the hat. He vowed to preserve that hat for ever.

The bridesmaids, Marilyn's two sisters, were in white. Their roses were also white. Edgar, who wanted to reach for a camera; prayed that Barry had seized his opportunities and then realised that he would be in charge of the photographs himself shortly.

It was a straight-forward ceremony. There was no variation of the vows and the clergyman who joined them 'in holy matrimony' spoke with sincerity and without intonation.

Edgar did not fumble with the ring but he did wonder briefly if Helena might not have preferred such a ceremony to the one they had gone through in a Register Office. Then, as he done before a hundred times, he told himself not to wonder about the past. He knew all about the 'butterfly effect'. Change one thing, however small, in the past and it might lead to different present. He did not want a different present.

Meantime, he had his professional job to do. He offered thanks once again for the way in which his young assistant, Barry, had dealt with the work so far. The next sequence of shots, however, meant the marshalling of the principals and the guests. It was too much to ask the young man to tell the bride and groom, or their parents where to stand.

The proximity of the marquee meant that they did not need any cars to pick up anybody from the church. Nonetheless, Marilyn's father had laid on a Rolls to drive them the thirty yards or so and Edgar wanted a couple of shots of that happening. His idea was that the photographs of this particular wedding would illustrate a narrative rather than just a record of the people present. He liked to think of Marilyn and Bill showing their album to their grandchildren and explaining what was happening. He had started with recording the episode with the hot-air balloon. In fact he had already produced some large prints of that episode and had them pinned up on a board inside the marquee.

Nonetheless, everybody would expect the conventional group photographs, bride, bride and groom, bride and groom and her parents, bride and groom and his parents and then as many additions as he could manage. The back-drop for these was ideal. The soft turf of the village green ran up to a tall beech hedge-row. The recent rains had made the colours fresh. Edgar knew he had to use such a backdrop but he did want one other shot first. He took Marilyn's roses and handed them to Bill Then he took her hand and led her away from everybody else. He stood her in front of an herbaceous border planted by some local authority enthusiast. He moved her so that she was a short distance from one end of this blaze of colour. When she realised what he was trying to do, her puzzled look broke into a smile of delight. He was using the flower border as the train of her dress. Edgar used his wide angled lens and he hoped that the shot would succeed.

Then, with a smoothness that was part of his professional expertise, he persuaded first Marilyn to stand alone in front to the hedge, holding her red roses at her waist. Then he called Bill across to join her. With each set, he asked for them to smile and then to think about their favourite pet and he took several photographs both casual and formal. Edgar was working with a tripod but both he and Barry also used their hand-held cameras.

He built up the groups with speed. He was not too concerned with the time it took but some people might get bored and he did not want to photograph any bored people. The procedure was understood by everybody, it was part of the celebration and it also gave people a chance to mingle, chat with old friends or make new ones. Certainly the two bridesmaids had attracted a number of young men. He saw also that Helena had her own cluster of admirers. He did not blame them. As soon as he had finished his work, she would have another one.

For his final group, he fitted the special lens that he had tried out on the balloon flight. He lined the whole congregation up backed by the dark green of the beech hedgerow, caring not what order they stood and knowing that this would sort them in a natural way. Barry stood beside him as he did so and, when he was satisfied, he headed off himself to stand beside Helena – where he belonged. The instructions had had given Barry were simple, "Shoot as many as you can – make as though you have finished, count slowly to twenty and then shoot some more. They'll start to head for the marquee, try not to let them know you are still photographing.

When he reached Helena, she held out her hand to bring him to her side, looked up at him proudly. "Can you relax now?" she asked.

"Well I'm going to." he said and bent to kiss her, hoping that Barry would get that unconventional shot. It would be one for their own album.

Then, the wedding breakfast in the marquee and he had two more jobs to do. The first was reading the telegrams and that was easy. Then he had to toast the bride and groom and that too was easy but involved the speech that had worried him so much. In the event, he had managed to write a few notes and he did relax to deliver it. He said that Marilyn had introduced Bill to Helena and himself early in their relationship and that they had recognised their deep compatibility almost at once. He spoke of their continuing love. He told anecdotes about Bill, which raised a laugh and he related the story of the balloon trip. He told also of Bill's singing on the way to the church and how seeing Marilyn had stopped him mid-verse. Finally he made remarks about the shining eyes of Marilyn's sisters. He was rewarded by the look of relief on Bill's face and the clear appreciation from the bride and from his own wife.

Marilyn's father had organised a dance in the village's tithe barn to follow the wedding breakfast. He danced with his daughter and, before Bill could do the same, Edgar managed to sweep her away. He had always enjoyed dancing with Marilyn, it was relaxing. On this occasion she was a bit on edge but she soon settled down to enjoy it herself. Then, as the sky lost some of its brightness, they took a break for a fire-work display.

At one stage, Edgar found himself standing next door to 'the founder of the feast' as he called him and was thanked for the way he had juggled his two jobs. He was amused that Marilyn's dad muttered something about he hadn't realised how much this was going to cost him and that he was bribing his other two daughters to elope.

Edgar had also organised the car that would come in good time to take away Bill and Marilyn. He had not been told where they were going for their honeymoon. His instructions had only been the time it was needed and they wanted it for the rest of the day. The driver would take orders from Bill.

Bride and groom had disappeared from the dance floor and Edgar had reluctantly surrendered his wife to one of her relatives. He was thinking that it was incumbent upon him to dance with the bridesmaids. He saw, without surprise, that his services were not required. Both of Marilyn's sisters had more potential partners than there were dances. Edgar went to the bar for a glass of water. It had been long day and he still had to drive home.

He glanced at his watch and was surprised how late it was. The hired car should have arrived. He put his glass down and crossed to rescue Helena from her dancing partner. She would want to say good-bye to the couple. As he tapped her partner on his shoulder, he thought of the times he had occasion to do so in the past – "Excuse me!" was the formula effectively claiming his own. Usually at dances, he only did so when Helena signalled that she wanted rescuing. Helena claimed that when he did so, he loomed. This was not true. Only once, early on in their relationship, had he found it necessary to loom. Helena had enjoyed that occasion. This time, he simply showed Helena his watch and she understood immediately and excused herself from her partner. Edgar hurried away to check that the car was waiting.

It was and he tried to extract from the driver some indication of where he was to take the couple. He claimed that he did not have any idea where they were going. Edgar was joined by Helena, who thanked him for the rescue.

"A nice young man but he had two left feet. I had the feeling that, until you appeared, he was thinking of making a pass. You do a good loom."

Edgar grinned, accepting her interpretation. He certainly had not noticed that her partner was not behaving himself. Perhaps he did loom. "Just as well with that hat." he said "It is woven with magic spells."

Bill appeared but no Marilyn. He was holding a large brown envelope. "Mrs. Thomas will join us within seconds." he said with a certain amount of smugness in the use of his wife's new name. This you have to have. You can thank me when next we meet. All my cleverness is here enclosed. I have assumed that none of it is for publication, which is a shame. I've told Marilyn, of course, but I have sworn her to silence. Restraining myself will make us square after the balloon trip."

Within seconds, Marilyn, elegant in a trouser suit, almost ran up to them. Before Helena and Edgar could ask any questions, they had delivered their farewell hugs and were driving away.

Edgar was left holding the envelope. "A plane to catch with that luggage? I don't think so." he said. "I didn't see any labels."

"I thought Bill looked pretty triumphant." said Helena.

"So he ought. He's just married the love of his life and escaped the confetti."

"Not about that. It was when he gave you the envelope. There is something in there that he thinks we would be pleased to see. We will now say good-bye to people and depart without further ceremony. You need a drink and I've pinched a bottle of the champagne. I've also got a doggy-bag so we don't have to cook."

"There was me thinking that you were intent on casting spells on every man here under the age of sixty. O.K. I certainly feel like an old married man after that lot. Do you know that Marilyn's dad is going to bribe his other two daughters to elope?"

So a brief farewell and still clad, she in her posh frock and enchanting hat and he in his morning-dress, they headed for home and the brown envelope.

CHAPTER 46

24th December 1945

The newly created couple, Susan and Ralph Morrison drove to Weymouth as instructed. They had walked together to the garages behind the house in the still air of the first light. There had been a frost in the night and random drops of water fell from the coated branches of the trees crisp with ice. The last of the leaves, now yellow more than autumnal, reluctantly let go their hold and fell, scarcely fluttering, as if exhausted, to join the bronze carpet of those already coating the paths.

Susan and Ralph greeted the Morgan as an old friend and strapped their cases onto its luggage rack. Susan cosy in the sheepskin jacket, curled herself up into her seat thinking that she would be sad to part with that garment and the helmet and goggles. Ralph had opened her door for her and tucked her in with a blanket left there by Treadwell. He might now be Ralph Morrison but it was Jim Bygrave's courtesy with which he treated his wife and it was Jim Bygrave's skill he used to drive the car.

It was Susan, she told herself – a different person – who watched her new husband as though he were a theatrical performance. There was the smile that stayed regardless of his concentration on the positioning of the mirrors and the adjustment of his seat. Every now and then he would look at her and his smile became a grin, almost a grin of triumph. As she watched him, she practised her new identity especially in the relationship with him. Most of this practice was repeating to herself his new name in sentences that meant something. "Ralph is wearing a sheepskin jacket like the Spitfire pilots did. Ralph would have loved to fly Spitfires. Ralph is thinking about last night, I can tell from his face, he has that soft smile of contentment. Ralph's eyebrows have gone up, he's thinking of something that he had not expected. That certainly gave him a surprise but how well he responded; even more gentle, tender and considerate than usual. How right was Marjorie Susan Gillingham to wait for him; to wait for the man who would take care of her. Now Ralph is almost laughing, he has remembered that he knocked over his glass of water."

There was a tricky bit of winding country lanes and, for a little while, Ralph had to concentrate on his driving. Susan could see that his thoughts had returned to the journey. She started her rehearsal of her new identity again. "Is Ralph wondering if anybody has put a flask of coffee in the car?" she thought and tried the practice aloud.

"Ralph." she said quietly and got the immediate response.

"Darling Susan!" which made her burst out laughing.

There was one secure aspect of the masquerade. No one could doubt that this was a recently married couple. Susan's regard for him was palpable and his care for her beyond chivalry.

Although he possessed the same skill, it was with a different approach that Ralph Morrison, not Jim Bygrave, drove the car. He drove it with care, getting pleasure not from speed but from the way it responded to his gear changes, from the way he could change down into the bends in the road to accelerate out of them. Above all, he got pleasure because the speed he was driving at allowed him to look at his wife. They may not have gone through an official ceremony but this was an 'until death us do part' relationship. Perhaps they could have a big ceremony somewhere. He did not think Esme – no, Susan needed to; he certainly did not but it might be fun. What form of words could he use that meant anything to match the way he felt about her. He had made a pledge to her father, to a dying man, but even that was a mere token of his commitment to this woman.

Reginald Marsh, clinging to his life and senses at home, might no longer be in full control of his department but his staff had been the model of efficiency. Ralph and Susan had no sooner parked the Morgan where they had been instructed, than a nondescript saloon car drew up next door to them and they transferred their gear into it.

"What about the keys?" Jim asked, hoping that they were not going to total the car. No, they would not do that. The car had to be discovered apparently abandoned by the eloping couple. Reginald's staff had laid a trail that suggested that they had hired a boat.

"Bring those with you, sir, please!"

Within seconds they were driving away and within minutes, they were escorted into a detached house that stood in about an acre and a half of its own grounds and was hidden from the road by bushes and trees.

Susan had a number of concerns. These people were going to provide her with not only a complete change of clothing but also washing gear and make-up. She was not, she told herself, vain but she was particular about the clothes she bought and about her toiletries. She need not have worried. This 'safe house' was more like a department store than a house and, for the first time that morning, she had something to smile about other than Ralph – she hoped she would always be able to smile about him – and her own internal device for fitting into her new identity.

It was the Housekeeper of the safe-house who showed her the available wardrobe.

"We knew your size, Madam, and your colouring but I persuaded them that we should have a wide choice. You need to take off all your clothes and jewellery. Would you like to do that now? I'm supposed to check. Some of our clients – we call them that – don't fully understand the importance of the procedures. They try and keep something precious to themselves – not a good idea. I am sure that you understand so I won't bother with that. There is an assortment of brooches, ear-rings for you to choose from and engagement and wedding rings. Perhaps your husband should choose those."

The housekeeper had made Susan smile so, in return, she insisted that she do her job as though she were dealing with a normal client.

It was the 'Madam' that had made Susan smile.

She wondered how Ralph would react to a full body search. He had said that he would sacrifice his pride to be part of her life. He would not have expected to do so in these circumstances.

CHAPTER 47

Evening 21st August 1986

Edgar had opened the champagne and they had toasted the bride and groom yet again but they had not yet got to the doggy-bag. Instead, they had taken off their wedding togs and hung them up with great care. They donned their dressing gowns and returned to the kitchen to toast each other. Edgar had then carried his wife across the thresh-hold of their bedroom.

Now Helena was still snoozing but Edgar, enlivened by his full and very successful day, had put the brown envelope from Bill to one side and started on the albums. Business came first and, in any case, he owed it to Bill to get the work done before he investigated his contribution to the Esme saga. Bill had put himself out when he was preparing for his own wedding. It was the least that Edgar could do to repay him. Strictly speaking there was no rush since they had no idea where Marilyn and Bill were going for their honeymoon so they could not get the product to them in any case. It would be nice, however, to get a complete album to Marilyn's parents.

He was also restrained by the fact that he dared not open the brown envelope before Helena was awake. Since he felt energetic, he would get on with something he was allowed to do. Now he was choosing which of the photographs to include in the albums. They were not just of the wedding itself. There were shots of the two of them in the years before the wedding, carefully composed to allow any interpretation of their pre-marital relationship. There were photographs of the balloon ascent. Some dominated by the balloon with its vibrant red canvas but others that emphasised only the reaction on the faces of Marilyn and Bill as they realised what was in store for them. Edgar had approached these shots technically as studio portraits but he had captured some fine pictures in which the faces of the subjects were animate. Their great grandchildren would look at these and think what nice people their ancestors were

Then there was the narrative to be composed using Barry's shots as well as his own. In this he was interrupted. Helena stood in the doorway of his studio looking at him. She was wearing what he called her 'come-on' dressing gown but it was not that sort of look.

"You are a human dynamo." she said. "Where do you get your energy from?"

"Well to start with, you looked so adorable at the wedding that I had to do something about it. These I think are the result of the release of tension." he said and he was indicating the album work. "I was more worried about the best-man business than I realised and the adrenalin is still flowing."

Helena crossed the room and kissed the top of his head. "Well it can stop flowing right now. I'm hungry. While I'm having my shower, you can see what is in the doggy-bag. It's in the fridge."

Helena had selected from the sea-food. There were prawns and smoked salmon and there was dressed crab – a compilation of the foods that the both of them enjoyed. The remains of the champagne was also in the fridge. There was a tea-spoon in the neck of the bottle. Edgar wondered if this did make any difference but the wine was chilled and still sparkling and just right for the sea-food. He laid this out artistically on two flat plates and cut wedges of lemon for garnish. There was some wholemeal bread in the bin and he toasted a couple of slices, cut them into triangles and spread them with butter. He was pouring the wine when Helena joined him.

"What a marvellous day!" She had showered and dressed in a denim skirt and a jumper. A garb that said she was ready to relax. Had she forgotten the brown envelope?

Edgar sat back in his chair and took a long look at his wife.

"It's true!" he said. "I did not think it possible but you are more beautiful. No wonder you attracted that host of admirers"

"You keep up that patter Edgar Mason. It makes me go weak at the knees. I had thought about the brown envelope but I think perhaps a video and early bed."

"I'm with you there. But then, my knees are always weak."

They dispensed with the video but their embrace ended only with sleep in each other's arms.

The brown paper envelope had been postponed until the morning. It had been judged to have no relevance to their mood that night. It was just as well that they had set it aside, for its contents were astonishing and would have destroyed all hope of relaxation and they would have had a very different sort of an evening.

CHAPTER 48

24th December 1945, and after.

The newlyweds kept to their cabin, Reginald's staff had booked them the best one on the ship for the crossing, giving out that they suffered from sea-sickness. The rest of the passengers, mostly French and hoping to get home for Christmas, assumed that they this was just an excuse. Some of them used it as excuse for themselves to drink a toast as they wished the couple well.

They were wrapped up warm when they disembarked and their faces were hidden beneath the layers of scarves. Before most of the rest of the passengers had got ashore, Mr. and Mrs. Morrison were in the hired car and heading south.

The smooth efficiency of Reginald's organisation continued throughout the journey. They did not really enjoy the flights necessary to get them from Toulouse to their destination. What Reginald described as the 'paperwork' included hotel bookings and a courier service. It also included large sums of money in different currencies. The bank accounts were in a New Zealand bank which they could access if necessary. It was not necessary. Reginald had provided enough money so that at no point did they have to leave a paper trail of their transactions.

By the time they reached Australia, it really was turning into a honeymoon for Mr. and Mrs. Morrison. The learned more and more about each other's history and their present needs. Susan had exchanged Esme's memories of a dream presence with the reality of Ralph Morrison. He fulfilled all her fantasies including the erotic ones and there was indeed a great deal of Shakespeare about him. He seemed to have a quote for every occasion. She had never felt so complete, certainly never so secure.

On his part, Ralph had even stopped regretting the 'five lost years' as he called them. Whenever he started to think that the life they were living was abnormal, she would say something that made it all acceptable and exciting.

Sydney provided them with perhaps their most luxurious hotel. Reginald's staff had excelled themselves and booked them into the bridal suite. This had the biggest bed either of them had ever seen, a shower big enough for two and a bathtub they could almost swim lengths in. A porter had brought their bags up and beamed at them. He beamed even more when Ralph tipped him and ushered him out of the door. The two of them were then able to burst into the laughter they had suppressed. Susan threw herself on the bed and, after bouncing about, assumed a seductive pose but couldn't stop giggling.

It was when they were in the departure hall of Sydney Airport, waiting for their flight that they picked up an English newspaper, a copy of the Times.

"We'll do the crossword puzzle as we fly over the Tasman Sea." said Susan as they were shown to their seats on the plane. These were a pair of seats on one side of the aisle and Ralph ushered Susan into the inner one which had part of a port-hole for her to look out of. Then he sat down beside her. This arrangement was fortuitous. Susan was sorting the newspaper out so that they could get at the puzzle when she saw and read of Reginald's knighthood in the New Year's lists. There was a bland account of his career. The report also said that he had been admitted to hospital.

She drew Ralph's attention to the newspaper and held out her hand. He knew instinctively that she was asking for a handkerchief. He supplied one and he put his arm around her, turning her head onto his shoulder. To the air-hostess who passed just then to enquire after their needs, this was the newlyweds in yet another embrace.

Ralph made a mental apology to Reginald. In spite of his absences, his daughter had loved him dearly and the love was returned. If his responsibilities had prevented him from fulfilling the sort of role that Ralph's own father had, he had tried to make up for that by using all the many powers that his job gave him. Ralph hoped that he had accepted the pledge that he, himself, had made. By now, he was probably dead – he had said 'days rather than weeks' and the paper was several days old.

He became aware that Susan had stopped crying and had fallen asleep, nestling up to him.

"At least I can provide a shoulder for her to cry on." he said to himself and hoped that this was more than just physical.

Following these thoughts came the more pragmatic ones of how he was going to put that pledge into practice. He knew how much Reginald had deposited in the accounts in the bank in Christchurch but he had very little idea of the cost of living in New Zealand. Nor did he have any idea of how much money he could earn with his skills in administration. He did have one idea which he thought might work. It would use Susan's talents as well as his own. They both needed to commit themselves to their new lives and try to forget their old ones.

CHAPTER 49

Breakfast 22nd August 1986

Helena and Edgar had cleared the morning for the brown envelope. They had showered and sat down to their breakfast coffee. Edgar was dealing with the post.

"Here's one that could lead somewhere." he said. "The travel firm that picked up the option on the Orkney photographs have expressed their delight at my work. That's good for the ego if nothing else. Here's their brochure. They've made my stuff look even better than I thought possible. Will I come in and discuss the possibility of my using my talents in other localities. They're a big firm and they paid well."

"What other localities? If their interest is in selling holidays, the one thing you can guarantee is that they'll be nice places."

"I'm not so sure about that. Some people want to see the Northern Lights or the battlefields of the Civil War – ours, not the Americans. Any rate they want me to come in on Monday morning. Have we got anything on then?"

"No, Monday's clear!"

"I'll give them a ring. Their head office is in London and they are offering expenses. That must mean a hotel. Do you want to come? We could go down on Sunday, perhaps do a show and come back on Monday afternoon or extend our visit."

He made the phone call. Not surprisingly, the travel firm offered him accommodation. That was their business after all and they invited him to bring his wife. The friendly girl on the other end of the line even asked what show they would like to see. They were getting the sort of package deal that the firm sold to its customers. Helena and Edgar had no objection to being looked after.

"I'll put a portfolio together." said Edgar. He knew he had some outstanding shots of scenery but he had little experience of photographing interiors.

He dealt with the rest of the post. Helena was just finishing her coffee and looked at him over the rim of her cup.

"O.K." he said. "Let's see what Bill was looking so smug about." and they sat together so that both could read it at the same time.

Bill had used his dramatic skills. The contents of the envelope were loosely bound and clearly organised to be read in sequence. He had typed the pages in appropriate fonts. The cover was titled

PROBLEM SOLVED!

with a short paragraph beneath it:-

A young couple vanish without trace from an English country home.
What is the mystery that shrouds their apparent elopement?

The next page of this page-turner read:-

> Major James Bygrave, D.S.O., who served
> throughout most of the war in Europe, disappeared
> at Christmas 1945 when he was visiting the country
> home of Sir Reginald Marsh, one of England's most
> distinguished diplomats. Twenty-two-year-old Esme
> Marsh, younger daughter of Sir Reginald, was also
> reported missing. Family suspicions were that the
> couple had eloped following a quarrel between Sir
> Reginald and the young Major.
>
> Despite rigorous searches by all interested
> parties, nothing was ever heard of either Esme or
> James again.

This text was laid out to fill the page and there was a clear
need to turn to the next. On this page Bill had waxed more
intimate. He had written:-

> That is until your reporter, William Thomas, was
> asked to examine the fusty records of the affair.
> Applying his brilliant analytical mind he was, at first,
> frustrated. He believed that the diplomat had arranged
> for the young couple to assume new identities. He
> found that all the resources of the press and of foreign
> governments did not suffice to defeat the expertise of
> Sir Reginald Marsh. Then, instead of pursuing the long
> dead trail; one that had run cold forty years before, he
> asked himself a simple question. 'If those two people
> had assumed new identities, what would they then do?'

Esme Marsh was a language polymath, James Bygrave a genius administrator. Why would they not use the skills of the latter to exploit the abilities of the former?

A trawl through companies that might involve those talents, especially the translation aspect, threw up some thirty odd possibilities. One of them, an international company had the official foundation date of 1947 but research showed that it had existed in embryonic form in 1946. It had branches in Japan, America and New Zealand. The Managing Director of the American branch was one Deborah Wilson. She was English, had married an American called Peter Whinstanly and was the mother of three. I did not bother to get in touch with her. She must be the girl you told me about at that boarding school.

The parent company was called 'Morrison and Co.' and it offered a service to manufacturers that brought devices on to the market that required instructions for their use.

If you made a vacuum cleaner or a radio or even an electric screwdriver and wanted to sell it in more than one country it was necessary to tell the purchasers how to use it in their own language. Morrison and Co., for a fee, would do just that. They were, and still are, the best on the market and their contracts involve royalties. Go to the instructions for operating your latest gadget. If, for example, it was made in Vietnam and the English version was written by the makers, you will find the text risible. If they got Morrison and Co. to do it for them, it will be a model of clarity. The same is true of most other languages.

Bill had finished the page there except at the bottom he had written, by hand:-
NEXT PAGE!
Helena and Edgar looked at each other.
"He's a real showman, isn't he?" was Helena's comment.
"Are you ready for it." was Edgar's and they turned the page together.

The last page was also hand-written. Its message was simple. It gave the address and telephone number of a Mr. Ralph Morrison and his wife, Marjorie Susan, in South Island, New Zealand and that was all.

"And a confident one!" said Helena. "Is this all he's got? Does he want us to pursue this couple by air-mail and get the response, 'Esme. Esme who?' or fly out there on the off-chance?"

"Did he have time to follow this up, do you think? Or did he decide the honeymoon was more important? We don't know where he is so we'll have to wait until he returns. Is it a fortnight they've taken?"

"Hang on. There's a little arrow at the bottom of this page."

He turned it over and there was Bill's final piece of advice.

'Try Somerset House! Do you want me to do all the work?'

CHAPTER 50

25th August 1986

Helena and Edgar had used the week-end to catch up on those things that they had neglected because of the wedding and the pursuit of Esme Marsh. Was she now Marjorie Susan Morrison? It sounded an authentic name but then, James Bygrave had sounded sufficiently establishment for the Marshes.

On the Saturday, they had cleared the decks in the house; study, workshop and the living spaces that had been sadly neglected and Edgar prepared the portfolio for the travel firm. He sorted some prints of scenery of the same ambience as the successful Orkney work but he added, for good measure, some more rugged stuff from a holiday in the Rockies and some restful work from rural Devon.

They took Sunday off. A country walk in the morning to a pub for lunch before returning home. In the afternoon, they packed and travelled by train to London and by cab, to their hotel. The travel firm had done them proud. Edgar surmised that the hotel suite allocated to them would have been one that they used for paying customers. They were probably lucky that it was free for their use. That did not stop them enjoying it.

On the Monday morning they parted company. Edgar headed for his interview and Helena for the shops in the West

End. They had arranged to meet for lunch in the cafeteria overlooking the food-hall at Harrods.

Edgar sat looking over the balcony. He saw his wife heading across the food-hall, carefully avoiding stopping to look at the display but festooned with bags of purchases. He waved and she, with difficulty, waved back. When she reached him she put the packages down and pushed them under the table as though that would remove them from sight and mind.

"Well?" she asked, averting any comment on how she had spent the morning.

"Well indeed! I think we've struck gold. It is almost unbelievable. It will depend on a one-off trial assignment. That will be just a couple of days in Cumberland. They've just acquired hotel there and have refurbished it – on the edge of one of the Lakes but miles from any tourist spot and needing advertising. It sounds a bit like our honeymoon hotel. Then, if they are happy, they want a contract for several locations. There are three problems with that. We've seen something of one of the already on the Orkney trip. They control the dates. That seems reasonable because they want, in some places, seasonal photographs. New England, for example, has a short season in the fall when the trees are at their best. The second problem is related. They have deadlines. Both of these mean that I will be tied up when I might want to be at a wedding or similar."

"Something similar might be a christening." put in Helena. "And we don't want you to be an absentee Dad."

"That's the third problem. They offer to pay your expenses as well mine. They are a travel firm and the cost to them will be small but they want me to sign a contract. No, I'm not going to be an absentee Dad or even an absentee Dad-to-be. It will have to be a short term contract. How long do you reckon that you should continue to travel?"

Helena treasured Edgar's unassuming concern for her. Sometimes, without even thinking about it, he went over the top. Now he was not even considering the financial advantages of a contract with the travel firm if it interfered with their domestic life. He was also, she realised, extending his chivalry to include their child. She stretched out her hand to him but answered his question immediately.

"Six months." she said. "Unless there are complications."

"Right! We now have a bargaining position, they may accept single assignments. Then we have to think about the shop. I think Barry is ready to take on that full time for short periods and he is totally reliable. He can certainly keep the flag flying. We'll employ a shop-assistant as well – perhaps part-time."

He was holding something back. There was something he had not dealt with and Helena wondered what it was.

"Now tell me what the unbelievable bit is? The money?" she asked

"The unbelievable bit is that one of the locations is New Zealand. It is at a specific time and it would fit."

The work that Edgar had done in Orkney had really impressed the high-ups in the travel firm and they were most amenable in drawing up a potential contract over a period of just under five months. The timing depended on the seasons that the localities were most attractive. In each case, the product would appear in the brochure for the following year.

Any contract would be very specific. Edgar would be given a brief for each location and would be advised about the scenery by one of the firm's employees. He would take his photographs and send the firm the negatives. They then owned the product, selected what they thought best for their brochures and published them. They would have the right to use Edgar's name on the brochures and on all their publicity. If they sold any of the photographs themselves, Edgar was entitled to fifty percent of the profit. All expenses for Edgar and Helena would be covered by the firm. As far as their travel arrangements were concerned, they were to be treated as if they were customers. Quite apart from any royalties, the money was good. They even proposed a clause that would allow Edgar to cut the contract short if there were any complications with Helena's pregnancy.

They recognised Edgar as an outstanding photographer of scenery. He had an eye for the light which showed a waterfall or a mountain ridge at its best advantage and he had shown this in his portfolio. More importantly, he had shown it on Orkney and already the response to that brochure was outstanding. In addition to the scenery, the firm also wanted shots of the accommodation offered.

Edgar was not so confident about this part of the work. They got out of the van at the Cumberland hotel and he was all for settling into their room. It was Helena who suggested that his employers would certainly want shots of the hotel, especially if they included the attendant staff. That was all he needed. Within minutes, he was taking advantage of the welcoming faces of the manager and his house-keeper and then Helena took him into the entrance hall of the hotel, indicated the column of flowers in the vase on the black marble top of the receptionists counter and then the way a lamp on the wall directed a beam of light on a second vase; this one almost spherical with its flowers interspersed with decorative twigs.

When they were shown to their room. Helena took his hand and pointed to the bed. Its size alone welcomed them. Edgar ushered the bell-boy out before speaking.

"You didn't tell me you had this talent." he said and pulled her into his arms.

"There's no tasteful nude to encourage you." she replied. "I did think you needed a nudge with this king-size bed. When they see your photos, the honeymooners will be queuing up to stay here."

She chose those aspects of the hotel that appealed to her. Edgar photographed them and the images went back to the travel firm. They said nice things about them and they helped to clinch the deal with congratulatory messages from the firm on the choice of interiors. Helena felt she was earning her keep.

CHAPTER 51

October 1986

The extended contract was confirmed. So they travelled south. It was some trip.

They had stayed, for example, in a twenty storey hotel in Hong Kong and Edgar had taken photographs from the viewing balcony. It gave hillside scenery with its young trees opening up to the tranquil waters of the harbour. Helena drew his attention once more to the size of the bed and the soft interior lighting of their suite. She did so with a simple wave of her hand. It needed no more than that.

Her cry from the bathroom was less elegant. "Edgar! Come and look at this. It would do in a high class brothel!"

"What do you know of brothels, woman?" was his reply but when he took in the huge shower and the even bigger bath and, especially, the deep pile of the carpet that covered the floor, he knew what she meant.

They did the tourist spots that they were paid for. Edgar put together a couple of hundred shots of the romantic, picturesque and affluent city for submission. In addition, he took a different camera for what he called his 'reality' images. They included the tenement blocks where the washing hung drying on flagpoles standing out from the windows. Occasionally, he would stop and use this camera apparently at random. Helena knew that he had seen something that most people would not. These images were what he really rejoiced in and indeed where his growing reputation came from. Someone in the travel firm knew that they were not only getting quality tourist shots but also a name that they would be able to conjure with.

Then the flew in to Sydney in the dark with its lights painting the ground a sparkling lace-work. It offered gardens and impressive architectural statements and yet another harbour of delights. Their employers – Edgar had acknowledged to them that Helena was his advisor on interiors – would have difficulty in selecting from the surfeit of scenery and other photographs that Edgar sent each day by air-mail back to England.

The final assignment was the scenery of New Zealand and the last leg of their journey had been the most dramatic of all. The flight from Sydney gave them a good view, in daylight, of that gleaming city and of the Pacific Ocean with its snow-white, multi-textured clouds. More exciting was the Western seaboard of New Zealand's South Island and some of its alps. Mount Cook, regrettably, was in cloud and so was the plane for a while until they reached the checker-board fields and the estuarine network of the Canterbury Plain.

They were late because of a late take-off and there was a deal of turbulence. Moreover it was raining at Christchurch's airport. Their own cases appeared rapidly but it took them some time to recover Esme's suitcase. Then the Customs people had questions to ask about the photography gear. They loaded all this gear onto a trolley and it proved recalcitrant, swerving resolutely to the left. All of which tempered their excitement a little.

Then, to lift their spirits, a man in a chauffer's uniform

was standing at the gate that was the last of the customs and excise barriers. He was holding up a placard which read simply. 'Mason'. This travel firm had all sorts of perks thrown in for its people and the New Zealand branch had heard good things about Edgar's work and were giving their new photographer and his wife the treatment.

The man with the placard drove them to their hotel. He explained that the car he was driving was the one that the firm had made available for them to drive while they were in New Zealand. He was driving it now so that he could explain any idiosyncrasies. He and Edgar agreed how much better it was to drive on the left hand side of the road.

Christchurch might have been a market town from pre-war England, except that its lawns were much lusher and more carefully tended. It was certainly more affluent. It had a faint resemblance to Oxford or Cambridge with its meandering River Avon. Indeed the river was flanked by roads named Oxford Terrace and Cambridge Terrace.

They arrived at their hotel and received their usual service. Their driver wished them well and handed the car keys to one of the attendants who had emerged from the hotel to carry their bags. He recommended a restaurant if they wanted to venture out into the town.

The rain had stopped, however, and they resolved to get settled in, order dinner and then take an exploratory walk in the evening sunlight. They felt that the hectic part of their journey was over and now they needed to relax. Indeed, the town and the hotel were relaxing. Their hotel suite had nothing of the opulence of some they had recently shared but it did have a decent shower and a big bed.

Their employers had specified the sites that they wanted pictures of and they had to work out an itinerary to cover them. One of the localities was fairly close to the address that Bill had found for the Morrisons. Planning over breakfast, Edgar and Helena decided that the time had come for a phone call to them. They would drive to the firm's site. If the weather was suitable, they would take their photographs and then phone. If it was not, they would call first and, they hoped, finish their search for Helena's relative and take the photographs for the firm afterwards

They had a cover story for the phone-call that Helena would make. It was that she was visiting New Zealand on a holiday but she had brought with her a photo-copy of a fourteenth century Polish document that needed translating. This was from a colleague of hers who had heard of Mrs. Morrison's expertise. It wasn't a very good cover story but the Morrisons they could hardly refuse to see them. If they were indeed the couple that had disappeared from Somerset forty years ago, the story would not matter. If they were not, Helena had got such a document. One of her fellow archivists was only too pleased to provide one. She would have liked to know what it was all about but was prepared to remain in ignorance. Helena had been a help to her in the past.

Edgar had raised the possibility that even if the Morrisons had been Esme Marsh and James Bygrave, they might not want to be reminded of the fact.

"It is possible that after forty years in their current identities, they would be simply embarrassed, perhaps horrified, by the consequences of having to deal with their original selves." was his argument.

"I can see what you mean." Helena replied. She had been so keen to uncover the Esme of the past that she had not considered the Susan of the present. It was clear that Edgar's suggestion would not be the ending that she hoped for but she took his point. "In which case, we stick to the Polish manuscript story and take the suitcase home."

CHAPTER 52

January 1987

The weather had been just right for capturing the magic of a group of three waterfalls. Edgar had done the shoot in the late evening to get the light the way he wanted it. He knew he had done a good job. Their plan now was to phone the Morrisons. The time had come to take the plunge.

The phone rang some six or seven times before it was picked up and a woman's voice said, "Hello!" Helena sharing the earpiece of the receiver, gave it the thumbs up. This was her family's way of answering the phone.

Helena told her story. She was most apologetic but she had not wanted to refuse an old friend. Could they call?

Whoever had answered the phone had covered the mouth-piece. Some consultation was going on.

"Can you get here the day after tomorrow?" was the response from the woman at the other end of the line. Had they bought the story?

"That would be fine." said Helena and took details down of how to get there.

Helena and Edgar had studied the map beforehand and phoned from the centre of a small town about half a day's drive from the address which Bill had written down. They discussed the response to the phone call and decided to find a bed and breakfast, or, as they had learned to call it, a 'home-stay', for two nights and relax. Since they were not being looked after by their employers, they now experienced the hospitality more characteristic of their host country. At the first of these they tried, they thought they had got no response but, before they could go away disappointed, a cheerful woman came round the end of the house and hailed them.

"We are having a cup of tea in the garden, come and join us!"

They did so and the cheerful woman introduced herself and said she was sorry she hadn't answered the door. Most guests would have come looking. Since they were from England, they were forgiven.

It was, indeed, like a stay in a friend's home. It started with a pot of tea and home-made cakes in the shade of a delightful garden and it never looked back. The en-suite room went one better than most of the hotels they had stayed. It had Jacuzzi instead of a bath. Their hosts, for the cheerful woman was joined by her cheerful husband, recommended a restaurant in town, showed them how to use the shower which was housed in a little room of its own, and insisted that Helena and Edgar join them for a drink before they ventured forth.

Two nights they stayed there and basked in the welcome. Edgar shot a roll of film as a present for the couple. They were impressed when Helena told them who they were working for and the interesting thing to her was that they did not see the travel firm as a rival for their trade. They argued that a variety of accommodation styles could only increase the number of tourists.

Helena and Edgar were sorry to leave but they had come a long way since the that day when the suitcase first made its presence felt and they could feel the end of their journey a couple of hours drive away.

The house where the Morrisons lived was, they found out, some half a mile up a steep and winding road above a small town. They had decided that they would leave the car in the town and walk up. It was not very far and they had travelled far enough in the car to enjoy stretching their legs. The road zigzagged up the slope of the hill but most of the early climb they could see the house itself. It was a single story building with a wide veranda. In the clear air, they could just make out that someone was sitting on the veranda. Every now and then, there was a flash of light from there. Someone was watching them through binoculars. As they got closer the rise of the ground hid the building behind a tall hedge.

This meant that their final few yards brought them slap up against the man who had been watching them. He was a tall, slender man. His hair, almost white and very thick, declared that he was elderly and the lines on his face said the same. He rose from his chair with great care, favouring his left hand side.

He was about to offer a greeting but he caught sight of Helena and said in astonishment "Well as I live and breathe!"

Something in the way he said this suggested that the Polish document would have no place it what was to follow.

He suddenly became more active. "Young man, could you press that button there. Press it twice, pause and then press it a third time."

Edgar did as he was asked. Pressing the button produced

a very loud noise like an old-fashioned car horn. When he had done so he turned to the elderly man who was now pointing across the parkland which surrounded the house. They could see a splash of colour moving rapidly towards them. At the same time, a middle-aged couple and a youth of about seventeen came hurriedly out of the house itself.

"That's the signal for everybody to come running." said the elderly man. "We'll wait for Susan." The three who had come from the house stopped in their tracks and stared, open-mouthed, at Helena. The splash of colour was now the figure of a woman running as fast as she could and then they could see the anxiety on her face. Her sprint had not even made her breathe heavily. She too, when she reached the veranda, stared at Helena but, instead of just staring, she burst into laughter. She walked across to her and wrapped her in a big but gentle hug. Helena had just time herself before the hug to realise why these people were so astonished. Susan Morrison, one time Esme Marsh, for surely it was she, may have been sixty odd years old but the likeness between her and Helena was uncanny. If anything, Susan was slimmer than Helena; who was just beginning to show her pregnancy, something that the older woman acknowledged with another gentle hug.

"And you are not here to seek for a translation of an archaic Polish text." she said holding both Helena's hands in hers. "Let me see. You'll be Stella's grand-daughter? You actually look more like me than Stella. We took some photographs when we got here. People expect such things. You could be me in those photos."

"You'll need to sit down. Jimmy will get some more chairs."

Jimmy, it became clear was the young lad. He hurried away to do so and hurried back. These were strange happenings and he did not want to miss any of them.

"Ralph and I still read the London Times. You would be surprised how much one can gleam from it. I do know, for example that Stella died last year. I was sorry hear that. I had not seen her for forty years but, even so, it was a bit of my past now gone forever."

"Introductions are in order. This is my daughter Patricia. I think a pot of tea is in order, Pat." Her daughter was reluctant to leave. She did not want to miss what was going on. "And her husband, Christopher Ranken. The young man there with his tongue hanging out is their son, Jimmy. You'll gather that this cripple here is Thomas Ralph Morrison." and she emphasised each of his names. "Our cover is blown, Ralph. Time to tell the kids."

"He raised a hand in acknowledgement and Susan turned to the others. "This is my great niece, Helena. Why have you not heard of her before? All will be revealed!"

Edgar and Helena observed this domestic scene into which they had introduced such a dramatic note. They, especially Helena, were deeply impressed by the composed way Susan and Ralph had taken their intrusion. It was as though nothing could shake the intimacy of this family. Edgar helped Helena into a chair and, as he did so, managed to say into her ear. "This is how long it is going to last!" and she could not stop herself smiling up into his face.

Ralph kept looking from his wife to Helena but mostly at his wife. "Less of the 'cripple'!" he said. "They said two more weeks – then you watch out!"

It was their daughter who explained. She was used to her parents ignoring the world around them. "Dad has had an operation to give him a new hip. They say that it will be better than the old one! That's one of the reasons why we are here. We are part of the firm but we usually operate from Christchurch. Dad has just called a conference here. Jane and her tribe will be here tomorrow. Jane is my sister. She has branched out on her own. Her husband runs an import-export business and she does his books and brings up three children. I suspect now that, in addition to some sort of reorganisation because of the hip, this family gathering was called because of you two. I hope we don't have to wait for the others before 'all is revealed'."

"Spot on, Pat." Ralph had eased his hip into a comfortable position and began to explain. "Your mother got a phone call. She said there was something suspicious about it. The caller claimed to have a document in medieval Polish. Could Susan translate it? She was right to be suspicious, the call was from this lady here. Susan thinks, and I'm sure she's right, that we now have to tell you about our murky past. In any case, it was only a matter of time before this young sprog would find some funny answers to the questions he's asking."

He turned to Edgar. "Jimmy here has developed an interest in genealogy. He wants to know who his ancestors are and what they did and – stop your ears, Jimmy – he is both clever and tenacious."

"You are Helena's husband I assume. How did you find us?"

"Yes, I am. My name is Edgar Mason. We didn't find you. To cut a long story short, a friend did some lateral thinking.

402

He looked for successful commercial translators. Helena's great aunt – I gather we are to continue calling her Susan and you Ralph – would do the translation; you would ensure the commercial success. Your names go with your firm. Your marriage is recorded in Somerset House. It says that Thomas Ralph Morrison married Marjorie Susan Gillingham at the Exeter Register Office just before the Christmas of 1945. Which you couldn't have done because at the time Esme and Jim were elsewhere. There were other clues."

The tea-pot appeared. It was a big pot and it needed to be. Patricia poured, trying at the same time to listen to all that was going on. Her father struck the side of his cup with a spoon to get everybody's attention. When he had done so, he spoke seriously.

"If it is not too late, I think we need some ground rules." He turned to Helena and Edgar. "We have other family. They will be here tomorrow and we must tell them. First of all does anybody else know?"

Helena reassured him that nobody except Marilyn and Bill knew of their identity and that they had given their word to keep the matter to themselves.

"In which case, ground rule one is that Edgar's assumption is correct. I will continue to be Thomas Ralph Morrison and Susan will continue to be just that, unless you want to annoy her and call her Marjorie. We've been that for forty years. It would be far too complicated to change back again."

"Ground rule two is that these forty-year-old, now family, secrets remain so until we can all discuss the matter and make a decision about them."

He turned specifically to his daughter and her husband and son.

"For your benefit, Susan and I changed our identities before we came to New Zealand. Our names from our former life are not important but they were Esme Marsh and James Bygrave.

Ralph told the story of Esme and James with great restraint. He avoided any over dramatisation and produced a skeletal but factual framework that had great clarity. His listeners were spell-bound. Helena reached for her tape-recorder and thought better of it. It was the teen-ager, listening closely, who made the first comment. He addressed his grandparents with awe.

"You two had only known each other for a fortnight when you got married!"

It must have been forty years since they had considered this as odd. Ralph was amused. "Well I did have a sort of preview." he said. "I'll tell you about that sometime and it was hard work persuading your grandmother that I was a suitable match. She'd known me less than a day and she had spurned my advances."

Ralph and Susan had deliberately chosen to sit some way apart. Which was just as well, since Susan protested loudly at this and her husband countered, when she denied it. "Have you forgotten Judith Ali?" and she burst out laughing. Their minds went back to their first date and the Indian Restaurant where he had nearly proposed to her, having known her for less that twenty-four hours,

Their humour was infectious and everybody was smiling even though they did not know what they were smiling about.

Susan stopped Ralph from teasing their grandson.

"Yes, Jimmy. Those are the facts and you are right to be astonished. It does happen sometimes that two people are instantly attracted to each other. Your Grandfather and I have been blessed in that the attraction has lasted."

Nobody had yet asked why Susan and Ralph had changed their identity and Edgar felt that they would come to that part of the story later.

"Can we bring the car up here?" he asked. "We have something to show you."

"Please do, you can put it in front of the house if you need to off-load. You'll be staying here for a while, of course. There's plenty of room. We used to run the place as a 'Home-Stay' – 'Bed and Breakfast' to you Brits – so we are geared for large numbers."

Edgar walked down the hill. There was no rush. The Morrison family had a lot to discuss. He did not take Helena with him. He had observed Susan's responses to her relative's appearance and thought that the two of them should enjoy their meeting.

He drove the car to the front of the house and parked. He left Helena's case and his own in the car together with the bulk of his camera gear. He selected one small camera and fastened its case to his belt. He hoisted out the leather suit-case that had inspired their search and carried it into the house.

There was still a great deal of questioning and some answering going on as he returned to the family. He saw that Susan recognised the suitcase but he said nothing as he took it to the table at one side of the room. He took the key from his pocket and placed it on the case.

Helena spoke quietly to Susan. "Jane kept it for many years, waiting for someone to collect it. A short time ago she moved to be closer to her children. Only when they were clearing her old house did the suitcase come to light. It was pure chance that Jim spotted it. We've been through it and the Customs people were a bit rough with it but we tried to repack it as it was. We had photographs to help us."

She then turned to the others and, simply with a movement of her head, suggested to Patricia that they needed to leave Ralph and Susan alone.

"Edgar and I would like to see the view from that look-out up there on the hill. Perhaps you could take us up there." she asked.

Patricia gathered her men folk together before they noticed and escorted them and the visitors from the room.

"Bring your camera!" she said as though their walk was the most important thing on the agenda.

As they walked up the hill, leaving Susan and Ralph together with their suitcase, the young sprog, as his grandfather had called him, could no longer contain himself. He had realised that his mother had effectively chased him out of the house and decided it was time to ask a few questions.

"What was all that about? What's with that suitcase?"

His mother put her arm around his shoulders and gave him a hug. It was Helena who answered his questions.

"In that suitcase are the memories of your grandmother's schooldays and early adulthood. When she knew that she and Ralph had to change their identities, she packed it and arranged that a friend would look after it. There are also just a few scraps of paper that are even more important to her and to your grandfather."

Helena paused for a minute, thinking that Edgar had said. "This is how long it lasts." and realised that they too had been fortunate. When Helena had first visited his shop, festooned with photographs, some of herself, Edgar had asked if she was talking 'love at first sight'. She had dismissed the idea. As their relationship developed, she wondered if she had been wrong to do so. There was an initial mutual attraction and that had never wavered but grew stronger and stronger. The chemistry between Esme and Jim that had brought them together so long ago was still there.

"Your grandmother said some couples were lucky enough to experience an immediate mutual attraction. In the suitcase is the evidence that she and your grandfather were so attracted. Susan deliberately stored it there, planning to recover the items when the two of them were no longer threatened by exposure. They are just scraps of paper, though there is a long-faded rose. Edgar and I, with the help of some good friends researched particularly Susan's reactions to Ralph. Those scraps of paper tell a love story that we found almost unbelievable. You know that, in their case, that attraction has lasted a life-time. Your grandparents do not need those mementos but they have not seen them for over forty years. I think that now they will need an hour or so alone together."